DREAMFIELD

A Novel

ETHAN D. BRYAN

September Sky Press

An Imprint of 50/50 Press, LLC

Dreamfield

© 2017 by Ethan D. Bryan

For permission requests, write to the publisher, addressed "Attention: Permissions Coordinator," at the address below.

50/50 Press, LLC

PO Box 197

1590 Route 146

Rexford, NY 12148

http://www.5050press.com

Editor: Megan Cassidy

ISBN-13: 9781947048065

ISBN-10: 1-947048-06-6

Library of Congress Control Number

LCCN: 2017945535

For more information on the author and this work, visit

www. americaattheseams.com

Printed in the U.S.A.

First Edition, June 2017

To Jamie—

I'd find a way to travel through time to be with you.

To Kaylea and Sophie—

May you always have the courage to chase your dreams.

To the real Losers Club—

You guys are the best.

To Springfield, Missouri—

Thanks for Andy's, cashew chicken, rolling hills full of green, four distinct seasons, great coffee shops to write in, Askinosie chocolate, and being a wonderful place to call home.

To those who read this—

* High five! *

What do we want?

Time Travel!

When do we want it?

It's irrelevant!

— As seen on a protest sign

1

Time travel is a fascinating concept. Storytellers have loved toying with our imaginations by employing it.

Doc Brown's DeLorean magic at 88 miles per hour using 1.21 gigawatts.

The mystical wardrobe entrance to Narnia.

Al and Sam in Quantum Leap.

Whatever really happened in *LOST*.

Hermione Granger's time-turner.

I used to love reading books and watching movies where alternate time lines created multiple storylines to follow...

Until I experienced it personally.

2

September 18, 2015

Another successful trip around the sun. Awesome.

Despite several attempts, my eyes refused to open. I slowly sat up and swung my feet off the side of the bed while replaying last night's dreams of being hunted by Native Americans. I wondered what it meant.

For as long as I can remember, I've been fascinated by my dreams. When I was in seventh grade, my science teacher challenged my class to set an alarm clock for the middle of the night, waking up long enough to remember what we were dreaming and write it down, then go back to sleep. The month-long science experiment stuck; for the last two-and-a-half decades, first thing every morning, I've tried to remember my dreams.

After a few moments, I remembered the Royals played Cleveland last night. Now that dream made sense.

I remembered only one other dream, one that has been replayed thousands of times over the past two decades, flashing across the screen of my subconscious or wherever it is that dreams hang out until they decide to burst forth into your awareness. In this dream, I am a senior in high school and I've just been approached by the varsity baseball coach. Standing outside the school gym, he hands me a workout program for the fall semester and encourages me to tryout for the varsity team in the spring. "See you on the field," says Coach, and then the dream fades. Every time I have that dream, I wake up filled with regret.

As I processed the dreams and visions, I gently massaged my right knee, paying particular attention to either side of the three-inch scar adjacent to my kneecap. The scar was a constant ache. A storm of significant size and power must be approaching.

It's been a decade since my knee surgery — repairing a torn ACL-meniscus-cartilage from a pickup basketball game in East St. Louis. The day after surgery the doctor told me it was one of the worst tears he'd ever seen. I know there's a snappy comeback I should have said, but I still haven't been able to think of it. Instead, I just nodded and replied, "Thank you." My meteorological skills, however, have radically improved.

Reaching behind me, I nudged my wife as I heard my daughters' footsteps pound across the old, creaky wooden floor, rushing to get ready for school.

"Wake up. We gotta leave in twenty."

"Turn on the teapot?" she asked.

"What's a good-looking teapot like you doing in a place like this?"

She sat up and kissed me. "Would you please make me a cup of tea?"

I resisted the urge for more early morning obnoxiousness. "You got it, babe."

"Oh, and happy birthday." She kissed me again.

As soon as I stood up, I heard the clickity-click of toenails against the floor. Bella, my massive black lab, sat at the threshold to the bedroom door, waiting not-so-patiently for me to come and play.

"Get your ball, pup."

She whined and raced back down the hall. Clickity-clickity-click.

I sighed and grunted and pulled on a Royals t-shirt and the same jeans as yesterday. My knee was throbbing; hopefully walking around would force it to loosen up, at least a little bit.

I unplugged my phone and quickly checked in with Royals Twitter as I walked to the kitchen. There were several celebratory mentions from friends rejoicing in Omar Infante's career game, and one particularly salty mention from a ticked-off Indians' fan, "Go to hell."

"As a Royals fan, already been there for two decades. This is too much fun!" I replied.

"Kill 'em with kindness," I thought. Closing Twitter, I scrolled through the notes, to-do lists, and inspirational quotes for the day.

"There's some good in the world, Mr. Frodo, and it's worth fighting for."

"Dare to dream audacious dreams daily."

"Seek first God's Great Story, and God will take care of everything else."

"Happy birthday, dad!"

"Yeah, happy birthday."

Both of my daughters greeted me with high fives and hugs.

"Got any big plans today to celebrate?" Elisabeth, my oldest, asked.

"Last day of the conference. A few stories, a few songs, and sign a few books for some new friends."

"Which story are you gonna close with?"

"How God made us dreamers in His image."

"Ooh, good choice. They'll like that one."

"I thought so, too."

"And the big party's tonight, right?" asked, Sarah, the youngest.

"The big party's tonight."

"And how old are you? Forty?"

"Forty-one, thank you very much. Though I'm pretty sure I could pass for half that age."

"Whoa," exclaimed Sarah.

"Of course you could! Bald never ages," Elisabeth laughed.

Bella started running in circles, growling impatient while she held her favorite orange and blue ball in her mouth.

"I think it's her happy birthday dance," Sarah said.

I laughed and nodded. Ten minutes later, after making tea for Annie and a cup of coffee for myself, all four of us were out the door, off to discover the good stories of the day.

3

September 19, 2015...
...and 1992

I was having the high school baseball dream again.

Leaning against one of the flat-white painted concrete-block halls inside Kickapoo High School, I waited for Coach Engel to step out of the gym and hand me a workout schedule. The shoulder straps of my backpack dug into my right shoulder and I was already dreading the thought of having to sit through Calculus.

I saw Coach open the door and nod in my direction and I slowly started walking down the hall toward him.

The moment I took my first step, the concrete walls started collapsing on top of me and the dream world darkened; I was knocked to the ground face first, the backpack landing hard on the back of my head, my vision darkened.

I tried to jerk myself awake, but a massive force pressed down on my chest pinning me to the bed and I couldn't open my eyes. I felt trapped.

I couldn't inhale.

I couldn't exhale.

I couldn't breathe.

I tried to move my arms, my legs, move my anything, but my body was completely unresponsive. I swear I could hear my ribs cracking. Sweat beaded up on my bald head and streamed onto my pillow.

The very moment I thought my heart might actually burst, I snapped awake and was staring at the Bo Jackson posters on my ceiling.

I gently squeezed my eyes shut, trying to catch my breath. Panting, gagging, heaving, I used the cool sheet to wipe the sweat off of my head.

Opening my eyes once again, I reached for my glasses and found them on top of the AM/FM tape deck and alarm clock sitting on the night stand next to the bed. I quickly glanced around the room.

To my left, a four-shelf bookshelf leaned against the wall. On one of the shelves sat a small TV with rabbit ears and two manual knobs for UHF and VHF stations. Attached to the TV was a simple gray box with two remote controllers, an original Nintendo Entertainment System.

The remaining shelves were full of baseball cards and autographed baseballs, an abundance of Kansas City Royals memorabilia, and well-loved books: Shoeless Joe, The Baseball Encyclopedia, Pete Rose's Winning Baseball, and Ball Four.

A five-drawer wooden dresser stood next to the bookshelf and a Nerf basketball hoop was loosely draped above the single closet door directly opposite my bed. Baseball posters and pennants covered almost every square inch of the light blue walls. The room had a distinct odor that can best be described as "locker room-ish."

My parents have lived in the same house my entire life. Once I was finally able to focus — to breathe and think — I knew exactly where I was.

I just had no clue when I was.

After I caught my breath, my heart still pounding furiously within, I slowly sat up and turned to set my feet on the floor. Immediately, I noticed:

There was no scar on my knee.

4

On countless occasions I have been asked, "If you could go back to high school, knowing what you know now, would you?"

Every single time I answered, "Never. High school almost killed me the first time. I couldn't survive it again."

Initially, I was convinced I was just dreaming. Maybe this was that dream where I forgot to study for a test, or finish homework, or some other lingering high school nightmare.

I tried to stir myself awake by pinching the fat around my stomach, but the familiar layer of middle-aged girth was gone. I pinched hard enough on what I could grab to break skin and tears formed in my eyes. Questions flooded my mind faster than I could process them. With each question, my pulse increased and breathing shallowed.

What happened last night?

How did I get here?

What do I do now?

I tried to pray, but struggled even knowing what to say. "Have mercy, Jesus, have mercy. I could really use your help, God."

Out of instinct, I reached for my cell phone and immediately felt a sense of loss.

No cell phone. My anxiety went through the roof. I had to do something.

I turned on the TV to learn the day or date or *anything*, but there wasn't any reception. I remembered that the clock-radio had stopped working as a radio at some point when I was in junior high. I tried anyway and turned it on only to hear the expected and annoying buzz of static.

I got dressed quietly then slowly walked down the hall and into the living room, soaking in as much information as possible. Mom was sitting on the couch in a blue fuzzy robe, humming an old hymn as she read the front page of the newspaper and sipped her hot tea, served in a china glass, never a mug. Her hair was far more black than gray and a black lab puppy sat at her feet, wagging its tail.

Bella?

By the sound and smell of things, Dad was in the kitchen making breakfast.

I quietly walked past Mom, kneeling to pet the dog for a few moments. I grabbed the dog collar; it read "Dodger." The rabies tag said, "1992. Home Vet Service."

The palms of my hands were dripping. We got Dodger my senior year in high school! I wondered if Mom could tell that something was different just by looking at me.

"Help me, God. Help me, please," I murmured to myself.

Mom didn't even look up from the paper, but just gave me a standard, relatively pleasant first-thing-in-the-morning greeting, "You're up early for a Saturday."

"Trying to find a worm." I softly cleared my throat. "Got the sports section over there?"

"It's on the table."

I walked into the kitchen and there was Dad — all 6'6" of him — lean, strong, moving quickly, almost dancing as he scrambled eggs and fried bacon and stirred up pancake batter. He had let his stubble grow out in preparation for his winter beard.

Another five years down the road, the very day I graduated from college, Dad would get in a horrible car wreck that would leave him walking with a permanent limp with scars up and down his body. He flipped a couple of pancakes with flair, obviously showing off, and greeted me with a smile, "Morning, Chief. Hungry?"

I was so completely mesmerized watching him move — so full of joy and ease, so free of any signs of pain — that I didn't actually respond to his question.

"Working at the range tonight?"

The driving range I worked at in high school is no longer in existence. It has been replaced by a Wal-Mart Neighborhood Market, an Academy Sporting Goods, and a fast food burger joint. One of my favorite memories of working at the driving range is turning off the lights after all the customers had left and hitting golf ball after golf ball into the dark night sky. All that free practice sharpened my game considerably.

"I haven't the foggiest," I mumbled.

"What's that?"

"I'll give them a call in a little bit and check."

I grabbed the sports page and quickly scanned the headlines.

Saturday, September 19, 1992

Royals Edge Yanks, 3 – 2

Holy…!?!

The paper confirmed my instincts. My heart responded by hammering inside of my chest. Adrenaline flooded my system and I wanted nothing more than to get away and get alone.

I hid my face in the paper, took a deep breath, and tried to think.

What in the world is going on, God?

September 1992. Beginning of my senior year. I have to get Dad's permission to drive his car. I won't get my own car until after I graduate high school.

 I groaned inside before humbling myself to ask, "Hey Dad? Can I borrow the car for a little bit? There are some errands I need to run this morning."

"Errands?"

"Gonna swing by Starbucks and then…"

"What's Starbucks?"

I swallowed hard. "It's this new coffee place near the college. Some of my friends were telling me about it and we were talking about trying to meet there this morning."

"The car needs gas. Keys are on my dresser. Be back by noon."

Walking down the hall to my parents' bedroom, I bumped into my younger sister as she left her bedroom. Two years my junior, she was roughly my size as her growth spurt occurred long before mine. Her untamed mane of brown curls was going in every direction and make up wasn't yet concealing all of her freckles.

"Did you get some new clothes?" Katy asked.

"No?"

"Since when do you dress like this?"

I had thrown on a pair of jeans and a solid blue t-shirt in my haste to get dressed.

When I was in high school the first time, I was a full-blown nerd. I tucked in my polo shirts, buttoned them up to the neck, and wore the same hat every day, a sweat-stained Royals hat, protecting my bald head from any sun burns.

I studied and stayed at home most weekday and weekend nights. I did have a couple of friends, but none of us were the partying-going-out-cruising type. I was never part of the "cool" crowd, although being completely bald as a teenager did place me in a category by myself.

"Um, you know, senior year, time for a change."

"Looks good. I like it."

I grabbed the keys to Dad's car, pilfered $20 from his wallet, picked up my backpack from my room, gave Dodger a pat on the head, and headed to the garage.

No freaking way.

Parked on "Dad's side" was a tan 1988 Ford Taurus, a car I had totaled in an unexpected, freak ice storm mid-November of my senior year.

Unbelievable.

I hopped into the driver's seat, scooted it forward a considerable distance, and adjusted all the mirrors. I started the car and M. C. Hammer's "2 Legit 2 Quit" was on the radio.

I cruised the main streets for a few minutes while I tried to think, but my mind felt like a jumbled mess. When I passed St. George's Donuts, I stopped for a couple of chocolate-iced chocolate cake donuts and a large coffee before heading to Git-N-Go to put gas in the car.

And I noticed everything that had changed, and everything that had stayed the same about Springfield, Missouri.

Springfield, Missouri — the third largest city in the state and home of Bass Pro Shops, Cashew Chicken, and Brad Pitt. It is not the Springfield of *The Simpsons* or Lincoln fame, but, even when I lived elsewhere, Springfield has always been home.

5

The coffee greatly aided the synapses in my brain. I decided to drive to the library at Missouri State University, the local state college and my future-past alma mater, to try and remember everything I could about my life in the previous millennium.

I found a metered parking spot and filled it with some change from the ashtray in Dad's car. I walked into the library on the campus of *Southwest* Missouri State University — the name wouldn't change until 2005 — in search of a pay phone to call my employer. Once again, I was reminded of the privilege and convenience of my cell phone. Having no cell phone felt like someone had died, an irreplaceable hole.

I decided to call in sick to the range, if I was, in fact, scheduled to work. I couldn't risk ruining my past — present? future? — life, especially if I was only going to be here for a few days. Hopefully, just a few days.

"Please, only a few days. Ok, God?"

I knew I couldn't afford to be fired and didn't want to imagine the ripple effects that would set off in my life.

My first impulse was to find the computer stations and Google the phone number of the driving range. Again, I was reminded of *when* I was, and had to ask for a phone book at the information desk, thumbing through the yellow pages trying to remember the actual name of the range and the owner.

"Swing Right Golf, this is Ken."

Success.

"Hey, uh, Ken? Yeah, this is Ethan. I'm not really feeling like myself today and don't think I can make it out tonight to pick the range."

"You sick?"

"Some kind of virus, I think."

"Rest up. You're still good for next weekend, though, right? I'm gonna be out of town."

"Sure."

"Friday and Saturday?"

"You got it."

I took the stairs to the basement, instinctively wondering if the wi-fi worked well down there. I found an empty desk in the back corner with no one else around and pulled a notebook and number two lead pencil out of my backpack figuring that writing would help jog my memory and give me some idea of what to do next.

1992. Senior year.

Best friend—Nathan

Schedule – Choir, Calculus, English? Teachers… ?

As I started writing, thinking, trying to remember anything about life in high school, I remembered the baseball playing dream, the dream that had, somehow, sucked me back into this world. I wrote "BASEBALL" in all caps at the top of the page, underlining and circling it a half dozen times.

As soon as I wrote the word, I knew that baseball was a key to this reality. My biggest, lifelong regret is not playing baseball my senior year of high school.

I remembered trying out for the team and playing baseball my freshman and sophomore years, but then switched to the golf team for the final two years of high school. At only 5'7" and 110-pounds, I could hit the ball a long way and had a pretty decent game overall.

Both years, I made the varsity team and played in the state championship. My senior year, I had quite the solid season, placing in the top-five in multiple tournaments and winning the conference championship with an even-par round.

I quit baseball because I was small for my age and was afraid to do the hard work necessary to keep playing my favorite game competitively. This regret, I know beyond the shadow of a doubt, is the source of the dream that refuses to leave me alone.

I stared at the scripted word and knew beyond the shadow of a doubt — I was here to play baseball.

"Baseball, God? Really?"

6

After two hours in the library, my "things remembered" list was pathetically short. I spent most of my time scavenging the shelves for anything and everything on theories of time travel, but nothing was particularly helpful.

Some of Einstein's writings seemed relevant as did some of Carl Sagan's. I made copies of a few pages and tucked them in my backpack.

Most of the time travel stuff was ridiculous fiction mumbo-jumbo. More than anything, I wanted to talk to someone, but wasn't sure who I could turn to, who would begin to believe me.

I didn't even know if I really believed me.

University Heights Baptist Church, the church my family attended, the church I would get married in just five years later, sat catty-corner from the southern side of the SMSU campus. The pastor's son, Drew, and I had been best friends for years, and through him I had formed a good relationship with my pastor.

I thought that talking to Pastor Gibson might be as good a place as any to start. I left the library and drove to the church before I remembered that it was Saturday; no cars were in the parking lot.

I slowly drove back home, paying close attention to all of the stores not yet built. On the way, I remembered that Elisabeth, my oldest daughter, was supposed to play a cello solo at a concert with the Springfield Junior Youth Symphony that night...

Or that night 23 years later.

In my *other* life.

I could feel the beginnings of a headache and whispered a prayer as I drove. "God, please help me. Please help. Please."

"Hey Chief, glad you're home. How was that new coffee place?" Dad's words broke through my prayer.

"Couldn't find it. I just went to the library and studied."

"You know, the lawn could really use a good mowing and trimming."

"If I mow the lawn, do you wanna play catch?"

"You bet, Chief," Dad smiled.

Mowing the lawn gave me more time to try and figure out what in the world was happening and what I should do next. I decided not to tell my family anything, but to try and "act normal." Maybe I'd say something to Pastor Gibson after worship tomorrow if there was no one else around.

Surely this is just a dream.

But what if...?

My prayer had been reduced to a simple, one-word question, "God...?"

I thought about what all this would mean come Monday morning— Surviving the halls and ways of high school life. Remembering the names of people I hadn't seen for decades. All the stupid, meaningless tests that would have no real bearing on my life.

I had to have someone on the inside help me survive.

I decided to call Nathan.

I had forgotten about the awkwardness of calling a friend before cell phones. After finding and dialing Nathan's number, I stammered, "Um, hi Mr. Walls. This is Ethan; is Nathan there?"

"Hey Ethan! Sure thing, hold on just a second."

Nathan Walls was one of the best backstroke swimmers in the state and the editor of Kickapoo High School's *Prairie News,* the bi-weekly newspaper. Although somewhat skeptical when it came to faith and church, Nathan was my best friend. He was also my ride to school.

"Whassup, Slick?" Nathan greeted me with a booming bass voice I hadn't heard for years.

"Got any plans tonight? Wanna grab something to eat?"

"Lifeguarding. Covering a shift. But I'm free all day tomorrow."

"Cool. Can you pick me up after church for lunch?"

"Make a run for the border?"

"Perfect."

"Hey, have you decided who you are going to ask to homecoming?"

"I, uh, well…"

"I finally asked Rachel last night and she said yes! Figured we'd double date again this year, right?"

"Sure, yeah, right."

Nathan told me his ideas about homecoming and my mind went straight to Annie. I honestly couldn't remember if I even went to homecoming my senior year.

"So what do you think? Ethan?"

"Sorry. My Dad's yelling at me. I promised him a game of catch after I mowed the lawn. I gotta go. See you tomorrow."

I hung up the phone abruptly. It felt like someone had just sucker punched me. What in the world was actually going on?

7

The aroma of a freshly mown lawn is the perfect setting for playing catch. For the body in which my consciousness currently resides, it had only been a few weeks since the last time Dad and I tossed a ball back and forth.

Dad paced off sixty feet and we started warming up.

We tossed in silence for a couple of minutes and then I blurted out awkwardly, "I'm thinking about trying out for the baseball team next spring."

"Really?"

"Yeah, just got a gut feeling about it."

"Didn't you shoot under par a couple weeks ago? And weren't you just telling me about trying to get a golf scholarship at SMSU last weekend?"

I had no recollection whatsoever of that conversation. Last weekend, I was in 2015 and Dad and I were talking about his retirement plan and the possibility of the Royals going deep in the postseason.

"It's your call, Chief. If you don't make the baseball team, they'd probably still let you play on the golf team."

"I'd really like to give baseball one more shot. You know, give it everything I've got."

"So, let's see what everything you've got looks like."

Dad crouched low and flexed open his catcher's mitt.

I went into my windup, reared back, and let it fly — six feet over Dad's head, over the wooden fence, and into the neighbor's yard.

"Well, that's a start."

8

September 20, 1992

Sleep did not come easy; my mind simply refused to slow down. I had no idea what to say to Nathan to make him believe me or if he'd just think I was pulling some elaborate ruse. Pranks were a daily part of our high school life. Like the time he TP'd my bedroom. Or the time he ate my lunch while I was talking to a teacher. Or the time he hid my shoes after PE and I had to walk around in my socks all day.

I knew Nathan's first instinct would be to assume I was setting him up for something. I kept rehearsing lines and running through possible conversations, trying to imagine just how they'd sound.

Mom knocked on my bedroom door and startled me awake. "Leaving for church in thirty minutes. You coming?"

I grunted in the affirmative, rolled out of bed, and threw on my jeans and a nice t-shirt.

As I shuffled toward the kitchen, Mom passed me on the way, "That's what you're wearing to church? What happened to that new pair of slacks I bought you and one of your new ties?"

It was too early for my brain to fully engage; I had not yet had my morning cup of coffee. My forty-plus-year old brain seemed to need the caffeine, even if my eighteen-year-old body did not. I yawned and stuttered an answer, mostly out of sleep-deprived stupidity, "Mom, you and I both know I wear clothes like this to church all the time."

In my *other* life, after I got my graduated seminary with a Master's of Divinity degree, Annie and I moved to Kansas City, Missouri where I helped plant Hope Church, serving as a co-pastor and worship leader for more than ten years.

Hope Church was a fun community of faith-filled people who intentionally worked on making new friends. Hope was also only twenty minutes from Kauffman Stadium. Countless times I'd come to the office and find free Royals' tickets for my whole family lying on my desk.

My mother's annoyance brought me back to the present. "Excuse me?" she said, giving me the look only mothers can give.

I rubbed my eyes and faked a yawn, "Nothing, Mom. Sorry. Must still be dreaming."

"You and your obsession with dreams. Are you hungry?"

"Not really. Just want a cup of coffee and I'll be good."

Mom stared at me and frowned, then shook her head and walked off.

9

University Heights Baptist Church was, and still is, a stunningly beautiful, three-story building, completely constructed in a special limestone brick from southern Indiana. Dozens of incredible stained glass windows told stories on every side of the building. The sanctuary s is truly breathtaking.

My daughters call this church "Hogwarts Church" after the gothic architecture of the school in the Harry Potter series. Large, gothic arch doorways, a wooden ceiling with crosses for supports, several massive stained glass windows on the walls, and a stained glass rose window of Jesus as the Good Shepherd sits centered high above the blue-robed choir and baptistery.

While I'm still in college, a student at then-SMSU, I'll preach my first sermon here. Not too long after that, Annie and I will get married here.

The high school Sunday school class meets on the third floor, mainly because our legs and knees are strong enough to carry us up three steep flights of stairs. A public elevator won't be installed in the church until 2007.

I trudged up the stairs and slowly peeked into the classroom. About fifteen teens sat scattered on "the pit" — a U-shaped, carpet-covered plywood construction. No iPods plugged in to sound systems to break up the awkward morning silence or screens for DVD-based teaching series or even PowerPoint games. No one texting or tweeting or checking in on Foursquare or updating Facebook statuses. No one staring at the phones in their hands at all; the students gathered were just quietly talking to one another.

Paula and Darrell, a married couple in their mid-40s, taught the high school Sunday school class for as long as I could remember. Darrell, a red-headed engineer by trade, and Paula, an always smiling blonde and stay-at-home mom, did a wonderful job of extending hospitality and creating a safe and sacred space for teens to explore what it meant to follow Jesus.

Every week, they made certain to have donuts and orange juice available. I walked into the room and headed straight for the donuts. I grabbed a couple of chocolate covered glazed donuts and asked Darrell if I could have a cup of coffee instead of orange juice.

"You must be maturing in your tastes."

"I like to think so."

"How do you take it?"

"Just a little creamer."

"Here you go, sir."

"Obliged."

Darrell handed me the coffee in a white Styrofoam cup and I slowly walked to the pit, looking for a place to sit. Even at church, there were teenage social stratifications — pecking orders of popularity and acceptance.

I forgot how much I hated that aspect of teenage life. Drew nodded his head at me so I sat next to him. Drew was a fantastic athlete with flawless skin and every blonde hair perfectly in place. He wore the latest styles and was always in a serious dating relationship. A senior at Glendale High School, Kickapoo's main rival school, Drew was one of the stars on their varsity baseball team, a soon-to-be four-year letterman in centerfield. He was only one month older than me, but looked at least three or four years my senior.

"Sup?" he asked, extending his right hand.

I set my coffee down as we did the hand-clasp-bro-hug of high school athletes everywhere. "Not much. You?"

Old speech habits die hard.

"Off-season baseball workouts start this week. Looking forward to another good season. Gotta try and impress some colleges and hope for a scholarship."

Paula and Darrell quieted the buzz of conversation and started the class session with a prayer. Paula then pulled over a white board from the corner of the room. On it, written in black dry-erase marker, was one simple question, "What is the Gospel?"

"Who can answer this question?" Paula asked. Typical for a group of teenagers on a Sunday morning, no one volunteered to speak.

Fulfilling all expectations as pastor's son, Drew finally spoke up, "Well, 'Gospel' literally means 'good news.' So the Gospel is the good news that, thanks to Jesus' death and resurrection, we can be saved from our sins and live forever with him in heaven when we die."

A lot of heads nodded in silent agreement. I didn't mean to, but I rolled my eyes.

"Ethan? You disagree?" Paula asked.

Before going to seminary, I never talked in group settings. If you asked any of my high school or collegiate teachers, they would tell you that they never heard me say a word. Ever. Even as an adult, I am extremely introverted and take a long time processing and wrestling with new information, figuring out exactly how to say what it is that I want to say. I still get nervous just thinking about the possibility of talking in groups. And when I started as a worship leader, I got nervous and nauseated. Every. Single. Sunday.

I cleared my throat and spoke softly, "It's not that I disagree, but there's so much more to it. The good news is that, through Jesus, the kingdom of heaven, God's reign over all things, is breaking into earth. Jesus didn't divide his life into a 'spiritual' life and a 'physical' life like we always talk about. He lived wholly in God's presence, worshiping God by being human."

Once I started talking, I couldn't stop.

"And just like God sent Jesus into the world, Jesus now sends us out to all the world, in the power of the same Spirit that raised him from the dead. Our job, whatever we find ourselves doing, is to live as fully and freely in the center of God's grace and love as Jesus did, inviting new friends along the way to join us. We are truly ambassadors, representing the reigning King of all creation, wherever we go.

"Jesus never said it would be easy. Feeding the hungry and clothing the naked or visiting those in prison and caring for widows and orphans, I mean, that's not the kind of stuff that makes headlines, you know? He said that following him meant carrying a cross and Peter wrote that following Jesus would lead down the path of suffering.

"Of course, following Jesus isn't easy, but no good story worth living and telling is, right? The best stories are where the character tries and fails and tries and fails and simply refuses to give up. The good news, really, is that Jesus has promised never to give up on us, no matter how much of a mess we make out of life. He is always with us and for us. And I've messed up enough to know how amazing that really is. The good news, is that God's kingdom is as near and real as our next breath."

As soon as I took my next breath, my head turned beet red as I felt the weight of everyone staring at me. I hadn't talked that much during one lesson in my youth group ever. Immediately, I wanted to leave the room. I wanted some space to breathe and not be noticed, to crawl in a hole and hide.

Darrell broke the awkward silence, "That's a fascinating perspective, Ethan. Thanks for trusting us enough to share your thoughts. So, how can we learn more about God's kingdom in the here and now?"

Seeing as I had no real choice, I answered, "Well, Frederick Buechner said that all theology is just autobiography. So, if we learn to tell our stories as truly and honestly as possible, facing our fears and sharing our vulnerabilities, we'll catch glimpses of God's good news along the way."

Darrell responded, "I love that idea! Ok, then, who wants to tell us a story about their week and we'll listen closely and see if we can catch a glimpse of God's good news."

My friends shared their stories about family and struggles at school and bizarre part-time job co-workers. For the rest of the Sunday school hour, I was completely silent as I ate my donuts and finally drank my coffee.

Sitting next to me on the wood-backed, maroon-cushion padded pew, Drew nudged me and passed me a note written on the bulletin.

"Where did that come from?"

"Books."

"What books?"

I furrowed my eyebrows, trying to think. I wanted nothing more than to text my friend Byron who owns a bookstore, or at least looked up some publication dates on Google to see which of my now favorite authors and theologians were old enough to be writing in 1992.

"Calvin and Hobbes," I answered.

Drew grinned and shook his head as the minister of music invited everyone to stand, open their hymnals, and lift up their voices in song together.

We sang one of my favorite hymns, "Be Thou My Vision." Without realizing it, I found myself singing words I had substituted in one of my arrangements I did while working at Hope Church.

Thankfully, not even Drew heard me.

10

I drove my family home after church in our big brown conversion van. Nothing says "cool" like a big brown van. It even had a CB radio we used to talk with truckers on long family vacations.

While I waited for Nathan, I sat in Dad's recliner staring at ESPN, but not really watching. Pastor Gibson's sermon was stirring in my gut, and I wondered if there was some deeper meaning behind being sent back.

Surely there's more to it than just baseball?

Maybe this is some kind of test?

I didn't get a chance to say anything to Pastor Gibson which was fine. I have no idea what I would have said anyway.

Nathan honked as he pulled into the driveway and I jumped to my feet.

In hopes that they were listening, I yelled to Mom and Dad, "I'm going to get lunch with Nathan. Be back later."

Mom called out, "When will you be back?"

"By five?"

"Ok. Tell Nathan to drive safe! And love you!"

I hopped into the shotgun seat of Nathan's blue Suzuki Samurai. "Shiny Happy People" by R.E.M. was blaring on the sound system. Nathan's braces-filled smile greeted me.

"How was church?"

"Thought provoking."

"I bet. I just picked up this single yesterday! Do you like this song?"

"Sure. How about cashew chicken and Dr Pepper?"

"Dr Pepper? Thought you were a Coke guy."

"Yeah, Coke or Dr Pepper, just a generic term. Like some people say soda or pop."

"Well, which do you say? Soda or pop?"

"I say 'Dr Pepper.' Or 'Coke.' And I'm really hungry. Let's go eat."

"Shiny Happy People" had just finished. Nathan pushed the rewind button on the tape deck and sped off.

We settled on Taco Bell since Nathan really didn't want to burn extra gas driving to the north side of town where all the good Chinese food places were. We ordered off the dollar menu — which was really only .59 or .79 cents! — and snagged a small booth next to the window by the soda machine, making refills incredibly easy.

Nathan started talking about lifeguarding and this crush he had on the new girl who worked there and about going to see the new Robert Redford movie *Sneakers* with his mom and I had to wait for him to take a breath and take a bite before I could get a word in.

"Hey. I need your help."

"Yeah, sure, no problem. What's up, Slick?"

"Two days ago, I was in 2015."

Nathan laughed loudly, almost snorting Mountain Dew out his nose. He looked out the window and nodded his head to the mutual friend who just drove by having ordered in the drive-thru. "Right. Sure. Ok. What did you *really* need to tell me?"

I looked him straight in the eyes and said it slowly, quietly, and as sincerely as possible, "I am from the future. I do not know how I got here. I do not know how to get back to my real life. I woke up yesterday morning and was *here*, in 1992. And every time I open my mouth I say something completely out of line for 18-year-old Ethan."

"Prove it," Nathan said, wearing a Cheshire-cat-like grin.

"How? How can I prove it? I've been thinking about it all night, all morning. What would convince you that I'm really from the future? Ask whatever you want and I'll tell you the truth."

"Flying cars?"

"No."

"Are you rich?"

"No."

"What do you do?"

I hate this question.

"I'm a storyteller and a musician."

"A storyteller?"

"Used to work in a church, now a freelance writer."

"*You* are a *writer*?"

I nodded my head in the affirmative while taking a bite of a burrito.

"Famous?"

"Nope."

"Married? Got any kids?"

"You were one of the groomsmen at my wedding! Yes, I'm married and have two daughters."

"Names?"

"My wife's name is Annie. My daughters are Elisabeth and Sarah."

"When are your daughters' birthdays?"

"Elisabeth was born in Waco, Texas on November 2 and Sarah was born in Kansas City on March 23."

"What years?"

"'02 and '06."

"Are we friends in 2015?"

As soon as he asked the question, I felt a pang of guilt and a deep sadness settle in my soul. After my wedding, Nathan and I completely lost touch. No phone calls. No letters. No real attempts at correspondence whatsoever. For someone who had been my constant companion during some of the hardest years of my life, we had completely grown apart.

"We stay in touch online. You own a chain of fast-food joints somewhere on the west coast."

"'Online?'"

"Online is everything. It's email and cell phones and texting and Facebook and Twitter and laptops and streaming videos and you can listen to any song you want to at any time of day. Online is how computers are connected to one another. You know I'm probably completely screwing up the space-time continuum telling you this stuff, don't you?"

"Like in *Back to the Future*?"

"Exactly."

"Do you have any fading pictures?"

"No. That's stupid."

"What else can you tell me about the future?"

"On September 11, 2001, there's a terrorist attack in America. The twin towers in New York City are completely destroyed. Three thousand people die. In 2015, the President of the United States is an African American, racial tension is still everywhere, speaking politically correct is incredibly important, and Vanilla Ice has a TV show renovating houses. Oh, and one of the funniest shows on TV is about nerds."

"Vanilla Ice fixes houses?"

"Yup."

"Does he rap while he does it?"

"Nope."

"And a show about nerds like you?"

"Yup. Nerds are actually pretty cool in 2015."

"Almost believed you until you threw in the nerd bit."

We sat in Taco Bell for two hours as Nathan grilled me with question after question. Multiple bathroom breaks were necessary after refilling our 32-ounce cups with Coke or Mountain Dew or Dr Pepper.

Finally, Nathan gave in a little bit. "Ok, let's say I believe you. What do you want me to do?"

"Nathan, I am 41 years old. My brain space is consumed with paying bills each month and trying to figure out ridiculous health care stuff and car maintenance issues and being a father and husband. I really don't remember much of anything about my senior year in high school. I remember I sang in the choir and hated Calculus and played golf. I don't know my schedule. I don't know where my locker is. I don't know my locker combination. I don't even remember most of my teacher's names."

"You said you're a musician?"

"I play guitar and sing at churches every now and then."

"You play guitar?"

"Yup."

"When did you start playing guitar?"

"I started playing shortly after my wife Annie and I moved to Texas."

"Let's go find a guitar. I wanna hear you play."

Since it was a Sunday afternoon in Springfield, all of the music stores which sold guitars were closed.

When I was in eighth grade, my family moved from one side of Springfield to the other. I went from living in the Parkview High School district to Kickapoo's. In my old neighborhood, some dear friends of my family were part of an award-winning bluegrass band, *Radio Flyer*. Dudley and Deanie Murphy and their kids played and sang at Silver Dollar City and bluegrass festivals all over the Midwest. I knew Dudley would have a guitar I could play. More importantly, I also knew how to get to his house.

I gave Nathan directions and told him all about GPS devices and smart phones.

"So, it's like a bag phone, right?"

"Yes and no. Same basic concept, but mine easily fits in my pocket."

"And you can do online with it? And all of your music?"

"Yep. Mine could hold a few thousand songs, and I can listen to or read books on it too."

"A thousand songs? I'm starting to think you're pulling my leg again," Nathan shook his head.

We pulled into the driveway at the Murphy's house and I agreed to do all the talking.

After a couple of knocks Dudley answered the door, wearing John Lennon glasses, a handlebar mustache, and a well-loved straw cowboy hat.

"Ethan! I haven't seen you in months! How are you doing?"

"Just fine, Mr. Murphy. Good to see you too! This is Nathan, he's one of my best friends at Kickapoo and tries to keep me in line. I'm sorry for bothering you on a Sunday afternoon unexpectedly, and I don't know how well you've kept in touch with Mom and Dad, but I started playing guitar a while back. I've been working on writing my own songs and I'm stuck. We were just out driving around and I just had an impulse to drop by as we passed your house. You see, it's like I can hear a chord in my head but I can't find it on the frets. I was hoping I could play a little for you and get your help."

"How about that? Come on in! Can I get you guys something to drink?"

"No thanks, I'm good."

Nathan just smiled and shook his head no.

"So, what kind of guitar are you playing?" Dudley asked.

Shortly after Annie and I moved to Texas, Mom and Dad made a trip to celebrate my birthday. Dad actually bought one of Dudley's old guitars for me as a surprise.

"Usually a Sigma."

"I think I've got one you might like, then."

Dudley handed me a Sigma six-string and the guitar felt incredibly familiar in my hands.

"Got a pick?"

"Check the case and strut your stuff!"

Whenever someone asks me to play something, my mind almost immediately goes blank. The only song that came to mind wouldn't be written for another decade, but I decided to take a chance that Nathan and Dudley would forget they had heard it.

Dudley grabbed his Martin guitar and noodled along behind me.

Ten minutes later, Dudley had helped me smooth through the "rough patch" in the chorus. I shook his hand and thanked him multiple times for his help and generous hospitality.

"Don't be a stranger. I really enjoyed that," he said as he waved from his front door.

As we buckled up our seatbelts, Nathan turned to me, "I'm impressed. You can play guitar and write songs."

"Well…I couldn't actually think of any of my songs. John Mayer wrote that one, it's called *Daughters*. Pretty big hit, too, but sounds nothing like what we did in there."

"Who's John Mayer?"

I didn't feel like explaining. Instead I said, "So I haven't told you the weirdest part yet."

Nathan raised his eyebrows in moderate interest.

"One of my biggest regrets is not playing baseball my senior year — *our* senior year — in high school. I know this will sound ridiculous, but I think God sent me here to play baseball."

"Why would *God* send you here to play baseball?" Nathan emphasized the word "God," underscoring his religious skepticism.

"Dude, I don't know. Maybe if I play baseball now, I'll be a better husband. Or I'll have a better job. Or I'll go pro and donate hundreds of millions to charities around the world."

"You really think *God* cares about baseball?"

"I think God cares immensely about all parts of our lives."

"You sound completely crazy with all this *God* talk. Besides, I've never been very good at baseball."

I shook my head, smiling, "You don't have to help me with the baseball stuff, but I need a ton of help with school stuff."

"Like what?"

"What's my first hour class and where is it?"

"French."

"French? You have got to be kidding me."

I have spent years studying Biblical Greek and Hebrew, picked up a few German and Latin terms along the way, and as an adult, I learned enough Spanish to help me locate a bathroom or order a burrito without onions. The only thing I remember from French class is the phrase *baleine échoué,* or translated, "beached whale."

Nathan said, "You've been in French for two years!"

"I guess I never paid enough attention," I shrugged.

He shook his head again, "I usually pick you up around 7:30 and we head to school together, walk the halls for a little bit until the bell rings, and then the next time I see you is in last hour, A. P. English."

"So, any ideas on how I figure out the rest of my schedule?"

"You could go to the office and ask for a copy of your transcript. Say it's for a college application or something and that you're trying to get it in the mail for a scholarship deadline. I bet they can help you."

"Brilliant."

With 5:00 nearing, Nathan dropped me off back at my parents' house and agreed to pick me up at 7:30 the next morning.

As he backed out of the driveway, Nathan rolled down his window and motioned for me to come over, "You really think you're good enough to go pro?"

"Crazier things have happened."

"I'm still not sure I believe you."

"I don't blame you. I wouldn't believe me either."

11

September 21, 1992

At some point between 3:00 and 4:00 AM, I finally figured out a way to convince Nathan that I was from the future. Nathan's mom, Randi, is an insurance agent with American Family Insurance.

Shortly after Annie and I got married, we needed a new car and, for some reason, as we sat in the office at the dealership signing papers, I memorized the VIN. And the best part, we bought an old car, which means that, in 1992, it is currently in existence. I could tell Nathan all the details about the car, and we could ask his mom to look up the VIN and confirm them.

I woke up early Monday morning, again unable to sleep well, threw on some clothes and walked to the kitchen. Dad handed me a cup of coffee and raised his to me in a silent gesture of good morning.

"Thanks."

I was sipping the coffee, sitting on the couch watching *SportsCenter* on ESPN when I heard Nathan honk as he pulled in the driveway. I gave Dodger a quick pat on the head and grabbed my backpack on the way out the door. Katy yelled down the hall, "Hey, wait for me!"

"Shotgun!" I yelled instinctively.

"I know. Underclass in back."

I had written the VIN on a small piece of paper and tucked it inside my pocket. I tried to wait patiently for a good time to give it to Nathan.

Nathan drove us the half-mile to school and parked next to the football field. Katy rushed on inside ahead of us so I started talking, "I've got another idea how I can prove to you I'm from the future," I said, handing him the crumpled-up piece of paper.

Nathan read it out loud, "JHMBB7238GC022144. What's that?"

"That, my friend, is the VIN to the first car Annie and I purchased after we got married. It's a red 1986 Honda Prelude 2-door with a moon roof and awesome stereo and tape deck. I thought that your mom could look it up when you get home and prove to you that I'm not completely crazy."

"Sure. Why not?"

The closer we got to the two-story brick building with goldenrod painted doors, the harder my heart thumped. I was nowhere near prepared to go back to high school.

In my other life, I had even worked as a substitute teacher at Kickapoo, but all the pointless rules and red-tape paperwork to try and control kids instead of engage them in the learning process drove me crazy. Standardized tests and busywork are the death of creativity and initiative.

"Schedule time."

"Good luck."

We walked in the main entrance off the parking lot and entered the commons area, then proceeded through the band hall on the way to the office. The band hall formed one side of the courtyard, an outdoor, walled-in space where students could hangout during lunch or free periods. The office was located in a hallway perpendicular to the band hall where it was easy to monitor the students in the courtyard.

Nathan followed me to the office and waited in the hall. I walked in and immediately spotted and recognized Mrs. Freeman, the red sweater vest wearing secretary, assistant to the principal, and behind the scenes manager of the entire student body. I told her about my need for a transcript and she was able to print a copy off on the spot. I quickly read through my schedule:

French V

Choir

Calculus

Literature of the Bible

Earth Science Honors

A.P. English Literature

"Bring back good memories?" Nathan asked quietly.

"Something like that," I muttered.

We left the office and were about to head to our locker when I heard a familiar voice call out my name, "Hey Ethan, come here a second please."

It was Coach Engel. The buzz-cut, muscle-bound, always chewing-gum-and-blowing-bubbles varsity baseball coach. He was standing in the hallway between the gym and the choir room.

In an instant I knew: I was re-living the dream. I could see the offseason workout schedule in his hand. I tried to act as normal as I could.

"Heard you had a pretty good season last year with the golf team. We should hit the links sometime, but you'd have to give me some strokes and promise to take it easy on me," Coach said, then blew a series of small bubbles, inhaled them, and smashed them.

Pop. Pop. Pop.

"State was fun, but I couldn't hit it straight. Shot under par with Dad a couple weeks ago though."

"I'm not surprised. Baseball offseason workouts start next week. Any interest in playing ball again in the spring?"

Pop. Pop. Pop.

Coach handed me the workout schedule, just like I'd dreamed for more than twenty years.

"Is this both weights and throwing schedules?"

"Weights three days a week, throwing on your own on the in-between days."

"Count me in. Thanks, Coach!"

He nodded and popped a large bubble that echoed down the hall.

As we turned to walk toward our locker, Nathan whispered to me, "Guess dreams do come true, huh?"

"Remember how to open one of these?" Nathan asked as we stood in front of our locker.

"Yeah, I go to the Y daily."

"You have a membership to the Y? You really are an old man!" Nathan laughed heartily at his joke. I ignored his response.

"The girls love to swim while I do yoga."

"You do yoga?!?" Nathan said it so loudly that several heads turned our direction.

I punched him hard on the shoulder. "Hardest workout I've ever done. What's the combo?"

"13-28-7."

It took me two tries to open the locker and then the bell rang.

"French class. Here goes nothing. See you in English, right?"

"Bonne chance, Slick."

I slowly headed toward French class, hoping that I'd remember where I sat and recognize some familiar faces. Stepping into the room, a girl with rosy cheeks and a long, braided ponytail was waving at me, motioning me in her direction.

"Are you ready? We're first!"

Becca. I remember her!

"First?"

The tardy bell rang.

"Ah! Bonjour, classe! Comment était votre week-end? Bien, bien. Jacques et Becca, voulez-vous commencer notre classe aujourd'hui?"

Something about my expression must have clued Becca in to the fact that I had no idea what the teacher — Mrs. Johnson! — was saying.

"Ethan! That's us! Seriously, are you all right?"

"I didn't hear her say my name."

"You've been Jacques for the last four years!"

"It was quite the rough weekend."

I stood up and walked to the front of the class and whispered a lie about being violently sick all weekend to Mrs. Johnson. She graciously gave me and Becca a two-day extension on our "project."

Choir was by far the best part of the day. Mrs. Mullins spent the majority of the class time working with just the Madrigal Singers, a small group of singers with only six vocalists representing each part. The time spent with Mrs. Mullins and the Madrigal Singers years later gave me the confidence I needed to try and lead worship for Hope Church. We practiced songs in preparation for our winter concert, spending a significant amount of time on a Christmas carol medley. Making good music with friends is an incredible, life-giving gift. Even more so as one prepares for Calculus.

Calculus was the inverse of choir. Other than balancing a checkbook, the most recent math experience I had was helping Elisabeth with junior high algebra.

The expressions and phrases from Mr. Freeman were as foreign to me as first hour French. I sat with a blank expression on my face for the majority of the period watching the student in front of me create digital masterpieces on his graphing calculator. On two occasions, I had to audibly answer, "I don't know" when I was called on. It was humiliating.

Lunch followed Calculus. I followed the queue into the cafeteria and tried to learn by observation just what I needed to do. I got in the hot food line and grabbed a couple of slices of pizza, some fries, and a couple of cartons of chocolate milk. As I was walking to the cashier, I accidentally ran into another student. He dropped his tray and shattered the plate.

"Way to go, shiffer brains," he yelled at me.

I handed him my tray and a couple of bucks and just walked out to the courtyard. I could wait until after school to eat.

I slowly walked to the Literature of the Bible class, thankful for a subject that should be a breeze. I didn't recognize any faces and couldn't remember the teacher's name. We were given an in-class writing assignment — a two-page response essay noting the similarities and differences between the first two chapters in Genesis. I finished in fifteen minutes and took a nap for the remainder of class.

At the beginning of Earth Science, another teacher whose name I couldn't remember called me to the front of the class. She told me that it was my turn to go to the counselors' office to work on collegiate applications and scholarships.

The counselors' office is adjacent to the main office. I opened the door and was immediately greeted by Mr. O'Neal, "Been looking forward to working with you, Ethan. Let's get started! Do you know where you wanna go to school next year?"

Mr. O'Neal was a large, kind, generous man with an infectious laugh and a genuine passion for helping teenagers make sense of their lives. He always dressed to the nines and maintained a perfectly manicured, completely white-gray beard. Mr. O'Neal didn't know just how cool he was.

"Yessir, Mr. O'Neal. I'm heading to SMSU."

"No Ivy League schools? Or at least out of state? You've got a lot of potential, young man. Go, explore all the world has to offer."

For a moment, I actually considered Mr. O'Neal's words. Did I choose the wrong college? Did I pursue the wrong vocation, the wrong calling? Was this a real second chance? In mere seconds my palms started to sweat as I reconsidered my future and all the ramifications. But if I went to another college, how would I meet Annie? Briefly, I felt like a real eighteen-year-old. It was tempting, but as soon as I thought of Annie, though, I knew my answer.

"Thanks, but SMSU is my choice. So, what's next?"

We spent the rest of the hour filling out applications for possible scholarships. Mr. O'Neal continued to try to get me to broaden my interest in colleges on either coast, but I was stubborn and politely refused.

"I'll submit these," he sighed. "Let's touch base again next week and see if there are any new scholarship avenues we can pursue."

"Sounds good to me."

The bell rang and it was finally time for the last class of the day — A.P. English Literature. The teacher was the same as the Bible class in fourth hour. I spotted Nathan in a back corner and he gave me a nod in the direction of where I was supposed to sit.

"Nathan, what's this teacher's name?" I mouthed quietly.

"It's Mr. Clarke. Welcome back to the Losers Club!" he said with a smile.

The Losers Club!

There were six of us in the Losers Club. By chance, we sat together in the back corner of English. Not by chance, Mr. Clarke never acknowledged us during class. Some of the other students liked to joke that we shouldn't even bother coming. The Losers Club spent the majority of English class composing horrible poetry and passing notes back and forth. We were never caught. A quick glance at the faces surrounding me and I remembered names and things I had forgotten for decades.

Junior was tall and skinny, wore tortoise shell glasses, and was by far the best tenor in the school, possibly the city. I sat next to Junior in my very first class our freshman year, Old Lady McGrady's English I Honors. It was rather fitting that we sit next to each other in the last class of our senior year.

Henry, Junior's folder partner in choir and Madrigal, was also an excellent singer. He was the only person in the Losers Club taller than Junior and was incredibly quick-witted. Henry once raised his hand for the entire period just to see if Mr. Clarke would say anything. Mr. Clarke never once looked in his direction.

Stacie, the shortest person in the Losers Club, sat right behind me as her last name came after mine alphabetically. Stacie always smiled and was nigh impossible to stump when it came to rhyming or finding the perfect ending to one of our ridiculous poems. She was skilled with a video camera and wanted to be a preschool teacher. I lost touch with her too, and wondered for a moment if she ever achieved that dream.

Amelia was already getting things ready for her medical career. She'd been accepted to UMKC and hoped to be a pediatrician before 25. She was almost always seen carrying a camera and worked with Nathan on the newspaper as well as the yearbook staff. I knew how Amelia turned out. She'd been our children's pediatrician for years. Elisabeth and Sarah loved her.

"How's your day been?" Nathan asked.

"Hellish. And I'm starving."

"Border run after school?"

"Awesome."

When the final bell rang, Nathan and I walked to our locker. I tried to stuff every textbook into my backpack only to rip a seam in the bottom of the backpack in the process, allowing all of its contents to spill onto the floor in the hallway.

A perfect ending to my first day back in high school.

After a mid-afternoon meal at Taco Bell, Nathan took me home. I spent the remainder of the night sitting at the kitchen table studying French vocabulary and Calculus nonsense. At midnight, completely exhausted trying to re-memorize tenses in translation and useless formulas, I turned off the lights and went to bed.

The joy of being a teenager.

I thought I had outgrown this.

12

September 22, 1992

Nathan picked up me at the same time on Tuesday morning; Katy got a ride with one of her friends.

"Bad news, Slick. Mom couldn't look up that car by the VIN. She said her computer doesn't work that way."

"Really? In my *other* life, my aunt and uncle are my insurance agents and they can do that with no problem."

"Internet?"

"Yep. I've got another idea. Free after school?"

"What'cha thinking?"

"Let's head to Fun Acre."

"You wanna play mini-golf?"

Fun Acre is one of the tucked away treasures in Springfield, Missouri. The price for a round of mini golf in 2015 at Fun Acre is *exactly the same* as it was in 1992. My favorite part of Fun Acre isn't the mini golf, however, but the batting cages. Five pitches for a quarter and I can vent pent-up frustration for much cheaper than talking to a counselor. I can also work on hitting gap-shot doubles or opposite field line drives. In 2015, I go to Fun Acre every Saturday to work out the stresses of the week in the fast cages.

"Fun Acre?"

"Yup."

"And this is going to somehow prove to me that you're from the future?"

I smiled and nodded.

After surviving my second day wandering the halls of Kickapoo, the majority of which felt incredibly irrelevant to the rest of my life, Nathan drove us a few miles south to the mini-golf facility with the alligator, windmill, and bowling pins.

Nathan pulled into the Fun Acre parking lot and I jogged across the street.

"Hey! Where are you going?"

Directly across the street from Fun Acre was All-Pro Honda, a small automotive repair shop where Dad takes his cars for oil changes and tune-ups. Rick, the owner, was always good for a laugh and was personally willing to loan you his car should yours require multiple hours of repair work.

And, just like all good Springfield establishments, next to the cash register hangs an autographed picture of Brad Pitt, "To All Pro, Drive safe, BP."

Rick knew my family well and greeted me by name as Nathan and I stood at the counter, "Afternoon, Ethan. Who's your friend?"

"Hey Rick. This is Nathan, my best friend. I've gotta quick question for you."

"Fire away. What's going on?"

"If I give you a VIN, can you identify a car for me?"

"Well, there's a good chance I can help you. You've got it written down somewhere?"

I rattled off the number and Rick typed it into his computer.

"Mrs. Thompson's car! We've seen that car in here several times."

"Can you tell me what it is?"

"A 1986 Prelude, 2-door with a moon roof. If I remember correctly, it's a nice shade of red. How did you get this VIN?"

"Oh, Mrs. Thompson's a friend of the family and I told her that if she ever wanted to sell her car to give me a call," I lied.

"And she gave you the VIN?"

"Yessir," I lied again. "She said to come talk to you to see how much you thought it was worth."

"Gotcha. Only six years old and she only drives it around the city. How much are you willing to spend?"

"I've saved up $2000." Another lie.

"This car's way outta your price range."

"Maybe somewhere down the road then."

"Maybe."

I sprinted back across the street ahead of Nathan, excited for the chance to hop in the batting cages and see what I could do.

I picked up one of the dented aluminum bats leaning against the chain link fence and popped a quarter into the red painted box. The red light at the base of the mechanical arm blinked on as the arm clicked into motion. After I took my swings, I turned to Nathan, who was shaking his head.

"Fine, I give. I believe you. Happy?"

I flashed him a Cheshire cat-like grin, dropped another quarter in, wiggled the bat, and took my stance.

Frodo had Samwise Gamgee.

Calvin had Hobbes.

I had Nathan.

"Yeah, I am."

And that was the truth.

"Now what?" Nathan asked as I dropped another quarter in the machine.

"What do you mean?"

"So, I believe you're from the future, and you think it's so you can try and play baseball again, but that doesn't start until the middle of the spring semester. That's, like, five months away. So, what are you going to do in the meantime?"

"What do we usually do?" I took a swing and hit a bullet of a line drive.

"We play video games and go to football or basketball games and watch movies and talk about girls... and we dream about college what the future looks like."

I nodded. Another swing, another line drive.

"You gonna start going to offseason?"

I nodded again. Another line drive.

"Have you thought any about how you're gonna get back to 2015?"

Another nod, another line drive.

"What if you're stuck here?"

I shrugged my shoulders and swung hard, completely missing the ball.

What *if*...?

Another pitch, another swing and miss.

What if I screw up my whole life? What if this isn't a God thing?

Another swing and miss.

I could feel doubt filling my body with each successive breath. I tried to smile and laugh it off, but my heart wasn't in it.

What if?

Late that night, long after everyone else in my house was snoring, including the dog, I was still wrestling with the fears and doubts that came with trying to figure out what was going on in my life.

Kneeling beside my bed, I tried to pray, but the words just wouldn't come. I crawled into bed and remembered all the times Mom had knelt down next to me, whispering bedtime prayers followed by her favorite verse.

"Trust in the Lord with all your heart and lean not on your own understanding; in all your ways acknowledge him, and he will make straight your paths," she'd say, followed by a kiss on top of my bald head.

A part of me wished she would wake up, walk down the hall, and once again whisper those words of comfort.

"Trust in the Lord with all your heart…"

Baseball season is so many months away, what am I supposed to do until then?

How can I trust when I'm living out a lie?

"Lean not on your own understanding…in all your ways…"

"Nothing makes any sense, God. I trust that you know what's going on."

Eventually, I fell asleep with the verse running through my head on repeat as I dreamed about sky diving.

13

September 25, 1992

I managed to pull a B on the French project with Becca and was elated to get a C- on the weekly quiz in Calculus.

Friday afternoon had finally arrived and I had a weekend of relative freedom in front of me. Nathan had to go straight to work after school, so I either had to bum another ride or just walk home. Since it was a picture-perfect fall day, I decided the walk could do me some good. I took a shortcut and cut across the field on the south side of Primrose Street.

In 2015, Jefferson Avenue, the street that runs on the west side of Kickapoo, extends south of Primrose Street. The natural grass is gone, now completely covered in concrete. Brick duplexes for retired citizens, a few small businesses and banks, and a massive credit card call center now stand where Dad and I used to hit golf balls when we were too lazy to go to the driving range.

On multiple occasions, just for the sport of it, Dad took us on "cross-country" drives in the big brown van, cutting through the field to head to McDonalds or Burger Station.

I crossed the street and enjoyed listening to the rhythmic crunch of the yellowed grass beneath my feet. I took a deep breath and chuckled to myself.

Forty-one-year old me survived a week in high school.

Old dog, new trick.

Working at the driving range on the weekends provided more than sufficient income to sustain my fast food, frozen custard, and movie-consuming habits. I worked diligently, driving the golf-ball-picking-up tractor back and forth, while a steady stream of customers pounded more golf balls down the hill.

I delighted in taunting the teenagers who kept trying to hit the protective cage surrounding me on the tractor as I picked the range clean. The chugging drone of the diesel engine was the perfect background music as I processed this first week.

So, what *do* I do now?

What am I missing?

I drove the tractor up the hill and unloaded the baskets full of beat-up golf balls. A couple of the teenagers nodded and pointed at me, making sure they still had chances to try and hit a moving target. After taking about ten minutes to wash and clean the mud off the golf balls, I loaded them into the dispensing machine and headed back out on the tractor.

I wasn't paying particularly close attention to where I was driving and got a little too close to those who were hitting the golf balls. One of the teens crushed a drive straight into my protective cage; the plastic cover on the ball shattered, splitting into pieces. One of the pieces caught me square on the cheek and snapped me out of my reflective state.

I slapped my hand to my cheek and ducked my head instinctively, then looked at my fingers to see if it had drawn any blood. Even over the din of the engine, I heard a roar of laughter from the teens who were thrilled at their success. I glanced their direction as they exchanged congratulatory high fives; I noticed one of them wearing a maroon sweatshirt with a large white "S" on the chest.

Strafford?

And in that moment, I knew what I wanted to do next.

14

September 28, 1992

Nathan pulled into the driveway promptly at 7:30 Monday morning. Katy and I were both ready, grateful for the chance to get a ride to school in the pouring rain.

"Rain sucks. Thanks for the ride."

"That's what friends are for. Good weekend?"

Katy spoke up, "Death by dance! We're getting ready for the Christmas shows in Branson. Between that and school, I barely have time to eat and sleep."

If you were ever in the same room with me and my sister, you would have a hard time figuring out that we're related. We look nothing alike — me and my bald head; she with a veritable lion's mane of brown curly hair. We share none of the same interests, vocational aspirations, or hobbies.

Growing up, when we both lived at home, we were always going our separate ways, me to one sporting event or another and she was off to the dance studio. One summer I did date one of her dancing friends, but she was never happy about it. I looked at her and listened to her and was immediately overwhelmed with powerful and conflicting emotions. Seeing her from an older vantage point, I wished I had been a better big brother. And she was roughly the age of Elisabeth, who had always wished she had a protective and proud big brother. I swallowed hard and took a few deep breaths to center myself.

"You dance in Branson?" Nathan asked, sounding shocked.

"I've danced all across this country with my troupe. This year, one of the shows in Branson asked us to perform in their Christmas show."

"Which show?"

"The violinist, Shoji Tabuchi. Just background dancers for a few numbers."

"Are you going to see any of her shows, Ethan?"

"Absolutely. She's fun to watch. I've got no dancing genes whatsoever."

"Can you get me a ticket too?"

"Yep. You staying for off-season workouts today?"

"Gotta get ready to make waves. Chasing dreams, you know," Nathan said with a small smile and a wink. "Besides, if I place at state this year, I'm going to get a tattoo."

"Really?" Katy asked.

"Yeah. 'Eat my wake.'"

I rolled my eyes at him. "Hey, Katy, we'll be working out after school, so you're on your own to find a ride, ok?"

"Or I'll be dancing in the rain..." she laughed.

No one really wants to be at school on a Monday. The majority of students are sleepy or grumpy or a fun combination of both. Teachers facing the audacious task of inviting hormone-laced zombie-like beings into the world of education often find themselves wishing they had chosen another career path. There is but one goal on Mondays for all people within the halls of a school: survive until Tuesday.

I spent the majority of Monday wondering what the off-season workout would be like. When the final bell rang, I headed to the locker room and looked for a place to change quickly, spending as little time as possible in the cold concrete-floored room. There is not enough deodorant or bleach in the world to mask the smells of a high school boys' locker room.

I crossed paths with Nathan on the way to the workout room, "See you in an hour." He nodded in affirmation.

The "workout room" was just a large, unused classroom full of weight benches, dumbbells, bars, and racks of plates. I noticed a list of suggested workouts written on the white board and took a deep breath.

I was the smallest person in the room by far; my growth spurt would continue through my senior year in college. I spotted an open corner in the back of the room and slowly walked toward it, squeezing by those already bench pressing, those squatting, and those building biceps with dumbbells. Instinctively, I started with a few yoga poses to help stretch my shoulders, hips, legs, and back.

"What the hell're you doing there, E?" I looked up and saw a couple of the football players staring at me. The varsity football team also lifted on Mondays.

"Just stretching. You guys don't stretch?"

"Not like that."

"These are special stretches to help increase the velocity on my fastball. Just wait until baseball season; I'll be throwing so hard you wouldn't have a chance getting a hit off of me." It was a bold-faced lie, but they didn't know it.

"Whatever you say."

After fifteen minutes of stretching, I read through the suggested workouts and opted for my 2015 workout routine instead — twelve exercises using only my body weight, a chair, and a wall. I found the routine one morning when reading the *New York Times* online and have been more than challenged by it ever since.

Also in 2015, almost everyone has an iPod or a phone or something else to play MP3s that help power and motivate them through their workouts.

When everyone else was tuned into their own worlds, distracted by the melodies and artists of their choosing, I could do my own thing and be practically invisible. Kinda like Batman.

Not so among the high school athletes of 1992.

A boom-box blasted the tunes of one of the local radio stations.

As I moved from jumping jacks to wall sitting to push-ups and crunches, I could feel the stares of the entire offensive line.

"Hey E, fastball workout stuff?"

"It's a scientifically-based, specially designed workout for smaller athletes to help them get the most out of their muscles. I don't think you guys could do it because, well, you're the size of small mountains already."

They laughed and left me alone. I worked through the circuit twice, ran a mile, and then finished with a couple more yoga poses without any comment from the football team.

Day one of offseason was a success.

There were only 154 days until baseball season started. If I was going to do this, I was going to do it right — with all the passion and power this 110 pound body can muster.

15

September 29, 1992

I woke up Tuesday morning feeling a little stiff, but also excited to get into a throwing routine. Dad greeted me with a cup of coffee when I entered the kitchen.

"Wanna play catch tonight? I want to get into a throwing routine as quickly as possible."

"You're serious about trying out for the baseball team, aren't you?"

"Some dreams never leave you alone."

Dad pulled into the driveway less than an hour after I got home from school. Setting your own schedule is just one of the benefits of working for yourself.

Mom and Dad moved to Springfield long before I was born and Dad started his own veterinary practice. After a few years in a traditional clinic, he transitioned to making house calls. "The animals are more comfortable in their home environment and I can decide how many surgeries and routine visits to schedule in a day," Dad would tell new clients.

I had already finished all of my homework and greeted him at his car with gloves in tow. In the backyard, I set up a place to practice pitching, complete with a plate and five gallon bucket for Dad to sit on. Dad took a few minutes to unload his car and get something to drink then met me in the backyard.

"Good day?" Dad asked, knowing that throwing a baseball has always been the best way to get me to step out of my introverted-ness and just talk.

"I guess," I answered in between the pops of the leather mitts.

"What's on your mind?"

"Just thinking about future stuff," I said, carefully choosing my words.

"Senioritis?"

"Something like that."

Part of me really wanted to tell Dad everything, to tell him about the dream and his horrible wreck and his granddaughters but I could feel in my gut that, at least for now, the timing wasn't right. Dad pounded his catcher's mitt and took a seat behind home plate on the orange and black bucket. "Let's see what you've got."

Rolling the ball in my fingertips, I settled on a two-seam fastball and went into my windup. The ball caught the corner of the plate and popped loudly in Dad's mitt. I knew from Dad's nod that it was a strike.

I threw for about ten minutes without saying anything, just listening to Dad's calls of balls and strikes, settling into a good rhythm of throwing and mixing up pitches. After bouncing a curveball in the dirt and hearing a call of "ball four," I stepped off the homemade grass mound and stretched for a couple moments.

"Dad, do you ever feel like everything is just kinda happening to you and you're just standing by, watching your life as it happens?"

"Like a movie?"

"Yeah, kinda like a movie."

"Remember *Dead Poets Society?*"

"Yep."

"Remember his speech in the hall?"

"Nope."

"*Carpe diem.*"

"What?"

"Seize the day. *Carpe diem* means not giving into your fear or feeling trapped by everything that's happening around you, but doing what you can in that moment to truly make life extraordinary. You are responsible for writing your life's story. It's living in the present tense, here and now, not in some distant, unknowable future. Make sense?"

I nodded as I processed his words. It struck me as odd that, in this moment, Dad was only a couple of years older than the 2015 me. Dad stood up from his seated position and continued.

"You only get one senior year. So instead of wasting it worrying about the future, try to make the most of every single day. Isn't that why we're out here?"

How do I not worry about the future?

"*Carpe diem,*" I whispered.

I toed the grass mound and kicked at the ground, smoothing out the spot where my foot would land.

Seize the day.

Dad pounded his mitt, "Fire away, Chief."

I stared at the mitt and was in awe. His daily running regimen has him in better shape than the majority of Kickapoo's football team. But the next two decades are going to be so hard on his body, through no fault of his own. Is it possible I'm here to change his future?

16

October 1, 1992

I quickly glanced at the sports page while eating a banana and waiting for Nathan.

Royalty!

Brett's #3000th hit secures Hall of Fame

In a game against the California Angels, one in which his brother, Ken, was working in the broadcast booth, George Brett went 4-for-5, becoming only the 17ᵗʰ player to reach the 3,000-hit plateau. This impressive achievement guarantees George Brett a plaque in Cooperstown, making him the first Kansas City Royals player in the Hall of Fame.

I read the entire article slowly until I heard Nathan honk. On the way out the door, I tossed the sports page on my bed. I wanted that page framed.

17

October 2, 1992

For every two seconds that the clock clicked forward, I swear it clicked back one second as well. Time slithered as I waited for Friday night.

After the Wednesday afternoon workout, Katy and I went to church to spend time with youth group friends. Four square was played. Songs sang to a strummed guitar. Prayers prayed for tests and quizzes of all kinds.

The highlight of Thursday was another throwing session with Dad. One of my fastballs significantly missed the target and went *through* our old wooden fence. Dad just laughed and had me pose for a picture standing next to the perfectly round hole.

"Someday, this will make for a really funny story."

Friday afternoon's Earth Science class found me spending more time staring at the wall clock than anything else. I had finished the chapter test quickly and was bored waiting for everyone else to complete the test. Fully engaged in the midst of a Mitty-esque daydream, Mrs. Foster finally got my attention and waved a green hall pass in my direction.

"Counselors' office, Ethan."

I smiled sheepishly and thanked her on my way out the door.

"Ethan, I'd like you to enter this essay scholarship contest sponsored by the Kiwanis Club. Winner gets $2,000 to help with costs of school. You've got as good a chance as anyone here."

I quickly scanned the details and found the theme of the essay, "Write 1,000 words about the connection between leadership and service."

"Deadline?" I asked without looking up from the paper.

"I'll need a typed-copy by October 14. Are you going to do it?"

"Absolutely. Thanks Mr. O'Neal!"

That Friday afternoon, while the Losers Club created poetry in honor of Dante's *Divine Comedy*, I started working on my thoughts about leadership and service. The bell rang; I scribbled down a few more thoughts before rushing to meet with Nathan at the locker.

"Still in for tonight?" I asked.

"Yes. Anything else you're gonna tell me?"

"I'll fill in the details while we eat."

18

Nathan picked me up a few minutes early and we grabbed a dozen tacos in the drive thru at Taco Bell.

"Where to?"

"Strafford."

"Where's that?"

"About ten minutes east on I-44."

"Why Strafford?"

"So I can watch my wife perform at halftime."

Toto's *Africa* came on the radio. Nathan and I heard the drums and blessed the rains as best we could, then continued to lift our voices in relative harmony as we professed our faith in a silver Thunderbird driving God. As we neared the Strafford water tower, I pointed out the house where my future-current mother-in-law lived.

"So, what's this girl's name again?"

"Annie."

"And how did you two meet?"

"At SMSU."

"And you're sure she'll be here tonight?"

"Yep. She plays in the marching band."

"Are you gonna say anything to her?"

"We'll see."

We pulled into the parking lot, walked up to the stadium gate, and paid the $2 admissions fee. Nathan wore a University of Kansas sweatshirt and I had on a Royals hoodie; both shades of blue stuck out boldly in the maroon and white colored student section.

Shortly before kickoff, the band started playing from somewhere behind the stands and marched into the stadium, much to the delight of the entire Strafford High School student body.

"There she is! Second trumpet from the left," then quickly looked around to see if I spotted Annie's parents.

Marching in formation in her wool maroon and white uniform, Annie's dark chocolate hair draped down to the middle of her back; what skin was showing was quite tan from the hours of practice before and after school.

My heart skipped a beat.

Is there any conceivable way I could invite her to homecoming? What could I say? How could I talk to her?

Nathan nodded his approval and gave me a high five, "Nice!"

"She'll be the homecoming queen next year."

"Next year?"

"Yeah, she's a year behind us."

The game began and no one in the student section sat down.

I glanced at Nathan, "When in Rome…"

Throughout the first half, I caught myself staring more at the band than the game on the field. I made one trip to the concessions stands and didn't buy anything, just so I could walk in front of the band. With only two minutes left in the first half, the band slowly filed down toward the field in preparation for the halftime show.

My pulse quickened; I was getting nervous on Annie's behalf, a quirky trait of my personality that still manifests itself anytime my daughters do anything in public. As soon as the music started, I recognized it — *Robin Hood: Prince of Thieves.* That soundtrack would be one of the first CD's I would own, getting it as a Christmas gift my freshman year in college.

I watched the formations and hummed along to myself as the melodies stirred something deep inside me, touching those raw inner places like only music can do. As soon as the band finished, I elbowed Nathan and nodded toward the parking lot.

"Don't you want to try and say something to her?"

I wanted to, but then had the horrifying thought that I might screw everything up. I shook my head, desperately trying to fight back tears until we got in the car. I ran on ahead and climbed into the passenger's seat. Thankfully, Nathan never locked his car. Like any normal teenage boy, the tears made Nathan incredibly uncomfortable.

After a couple of more than awkward moments of silence, Nathan spoke in an earnest attempt to lift the mood, "There's no crying in football."

The stupid almost quote caught me off-guard. I dried my tears and wiped my nose on my hoodie sleeve.

Nathan continued, "Wanna grab an Andy's? My treat."

Andy's Frozen Custard was another Springfield treasure and one of the best desserts anywhere in the world. In my 2015 body, I simply cannot eat ice cream as it ties my stomach up in knots. "Lactose intolerant" is what the doctors said. The joys of growing older — weird adult-onset allergies. On rare occasions, I'd take a small bite from one of my daughters' cones just to remember the creamy goodness, but I hadn't had my own cone in over 15 years. As soon as Nathan said it, I almost started drooling.

"Your treat? That sounds great!"

I ordered a large chocolate concrete with hot fudge, Reese's peanut butter cups, and marshmallow cream.

"Geez, Ethan. When I said it was my treat, I figured we were just getting cones."

We both sat down on the concrete ledge and watched the cars pass by on Campbell Avenue.

"So good. I can't remember the last time I had this stuff. I'll pay you back, promise," I said, cramming another large spoonful in my mouth.

"There's no Andy's in 2015?"

"Oh, there are Andy's locations all over the place in 2015. I just can't eat it anymore. Doesn't agree with me. I'm old."

Nathan laughed and we watched a cop pull someone over.

"So, what happened back there at the game?"

I nodded my head for a few moments and hoped to avoid any brain freeze.

"I miss her so much. In those moments between asleep and awake, I expect to find her in bed next to me and when I open my eyes and she's not there…I don't know how to explain it. When I saw her tonight and knew that she had no idea who I was…I don't know if there's any truth to that 'space-time continuum' stuff, but I didn't want to risk our future together and couldn't be that close to her without wanting to be with her."

"Do you mind if I ask you a personal question?"

"Ask away," I said, taking another huge bite of custard.

"What's sex really like?"

Even with a mouth full of custard, I started laughing.

Typical teenage boy.

"Better than you can imagine," I answered, after I had swallowed enough custard to be able to talk.

"That's all you're gonna say?"

"You want a longer answer?"

"There's no way I'm asking my parents about it."

"Yeah, I get where you're coming from. Nothing embarrasses my daughters more than when I try and talk about sex."

I thought I saw Nathan flinch a bit at that comment. I ignored it, and took another bite of custard as I organized my thoughts.

"In 2015, sex is everywhere. It's used to sell stuff and it's in movies and on sit-coms and in almost every song on the radio. It's in discussions about breastfeeding and what clothes kids can wear to school and some court somewhere is debating gay and lesbian rights and what legally defines rape.

"There are more STDs than I can possibly begin to list and the only time you ever hear sex talked about at church is from a fearful perspective, the accessibility of online pornography or scandals in one denomination or another. And every woman's magazine proclaims new ways to have 'the best sex of your life' or 'mind-blowing sex secrets' every single month. Sex is everywhere.

"But sex really is more than just a physical act between two beings; there is definitely a deeper spiritual-emotional-psychological connection and to ignore what it means to be human.

"Both Annie and I waited until we were married to have sex, and that made all the difference. We don't have to worry about the diseases and all the scary stuff. But we also didn't have any regrets or old emotionally complicated connections to anyone else. Sex is one way we celebrate one another — and a pretty fantastic way at that! It's really all about communication and acceptance and the longer we're together, the better it gets. And," shoving a large spoonful of custard into my mouth, "that's all I'm gonna say about that."

Nathan nodded his head and furrowed his brow, apparently mulling over my thoughts.

"Not the answer you were looking for?" I asked.

"No. I mean, I'd just never really thought about it like that."

"Trust me, you can't believe anything you hear in the locker room or see in the movies."

Nathan smirked. After a couple more moments of silence, Nathan asked, "Wanna go see a movie?"

"Marvelous idea. I could use a good distraction. What's playing?"

"*School Ties* just opened."

"Great movie. Haven't seen it in years."

We finished our custard and climbed into the car just as "I Still Haven't Found What I'm Looking For" started on the radio.

"Turn it up to 11."

Nathan rolled down the windows and maxed out the stereo as Bono encouraged us to keep running.

19

October 3, 1992

I slept in until noon.

It felt terrific.

I cannot remember the last time I slept in past 7 AM.

I finally woke up when Dad pounded on the door, "Hey, we're headed to Steak 'N Shake for lunch. Wanna join us?"

I grunted in the affirmative and got dressed in a hurry.

"So, what'd you and Nathan do last night? We didn't hear you come in," Mom asked as I climbed in the middle seats of the van.

I always get carsick sitting here.

"Went to a friend's football game and then saw School Ties. Good movie."

"You guys doing anything this afternoon?"

"Nah, he has to work and I've got the weekend off. Hoping that Dad will be up for another game of catch at some point this afternoon."

Dad was lost in his own thoughts until he heard his name mentioned.

"What was that?" he asked.

"I just said I hoped that you'd be willing to play catch sometime today."

"We can play catch after you rake the leaves."

Sitting around a table full of steakburgers, shakes, and fries, Mom started the conversation, "Imagine yourselves ten years down the road. Where will you be and what will you be doing?"

Katy spoke up almost immediately, "I'm back in Florida studying marine biology."

Her answer caught me completely off guard. I knew that teenage boys were self-centered. I had no idea just how self-centered I had been. "Really?"

"Ever since we saw the ocean after our Disney World trip, I've wanted nothing more than to get back and learn everything I can about it."

"That's pretty cool," I replied.

"In ten years, if I don't hit the lottery first, I would like to be a collegiate professor," Dad said.

Again, I was completely surprised.

"What subject?" Katy asked.

"Something in the sciences."

"I'd like to go back to school, too," Mom added. "After staying home with you guys for so long, I'd like to get back in the classroom and teach again. What about you, son?"

I answered in the safest way possible, "In ten years, I'd like to be playing baseball for the Kansas City Royals."

"What's your backup plan?" Mom asked.

Backup plan? How do I answer this true to 18-year old me?

"Live off the interest earned from Dad's lottery winnings."

It was truly a lazy Saturday afternoon. I really didn't mind raking the leaves, there weren't all that many, and Dad and I had fun playing catch. Mom cooked homemade pizza for dinner, which made my decision to stay at home that night all the better.

The first time I lived in 1992, I loved Saturday nights because there was nothing better on TV than Saturday Night Live. The cast was truly incredible and hilarious: Chris Rock, Chris Farley, Dana Carvey, Mike Myers, Kevin Nealon, Rob Schneider, Adam Sandler, Al Franken, and Julia Sweeney. Everyone watched SNL; it was usually the first topic of discussion on Monday morning.

Dad sat in his recliner and Mom was reading a book when the special guests were announced: Tim Robbins as the host and Sinead O'Connor was the musical guest. Overall, the show was great. I'm pretty sure I even heard Mom laugh at a couple of the jokes.

Sinead O'Connor was introduced for her second performance and she stood alone, wearing a white lace shirt in front of a table full of lit candles. She sang a haunting, a cappella version of Bob Marley's "War."

I remembered seeing this performance live the first time; I was moved even more in this second live viewing. This time I caught that she had altered the lyrics. Instead of singing "racism," she sang "child abuse."

At the end of her performance she declared, "Fight the real enemy," and tore a picture of Pope John Paul II into pieces. The television went completely silent. Mom and Dad both raised their eyebrows and exchanged glances.

"Wow," I whispered.

By 2015, stories would abound, proving the heart behind Sinead's actions. She still doesn't mince words or worry about hurting feelings when it comes to challenging the church and the truth about child abuse scandals.

I remembered reading an interview in which Sinead explained her SNL performance. She was convinced that the world didn't need a pope, that Jesus truly was enough for everyone. She knew far too many stories of child abuse perpetrated by priests and was completely disgusted with their hypocrisy. She wanted the beauty and power of faith to be displayed in her songs, in bringing the truth to light.

I tried to read the expressions on my parents' faces, but couldn't tell their thoughts.

"What'd you guys think of that?"

And with that question, for the next thirty minutes, we talked about faith and life and the scrutiny and responsibility that comes with fame. Life felt normal. It felt like a typical conversation we would be having after dinner on a weeknight while the Royals game played in the background. All that was missing was the other three-fourths of my family. For a brief period, I forgot when I was.

"I'd be curious to hear what your friends thought of it," Mom said. "Do you think they'll talk about it in Sunday school?"

And just like that, I was brought back to this version of reality.

I shrugged my shoulders, said goodnight, and walked toward my bedroom.

My mind was firing on all cylinders. I knew that sleep was not going to come quickly. I sat propped up on my bed and remembered some of the joys and several of the frustrations I experienced working at Hope Church.

For a people who were supposed to be defined by love, forgiveness, and grace, I experienced a lot of judgment, finger-pointing, and fear-based name-calling. I didn't regret my time on staff, but sure wished the church could quit thinking of itself like a business and recapture the simple joy of joining in the Spirit's adventures.

20

October 4, 1992

I didn't say anything in Sunday school last week and wasn't really planning on saying anything this week until I saw the question on the white board, "Who saw *Saturday Night Live* last night?"

Did Mom contact Paula and Darrell?

Everyone saw the performance. Instead of talking about Jack Handey's "Deep Thoughts" or Kevin Nealon's "Weekend Update" or any of Stuart Smalley's "Daily Affirmations," the conversation centered on the torn picture of the pope.

I grabbed a couple of doughnuts and a cup of coffee and sat down next to Drew.

"Did you see it?" he asked.

"Yep."

"Stupid publicity stunt. She's just hoping to sell more records."

"Pretty risky for a publicity stunt."

Paula and Darrell got everyone's attention and started the class with a time of prayer.

"So," Darrell said clapping his hands together, "who wants to go first?"

"Music is just entertainment," Samantha, a bright sophomore at Hillcrest, commented. "She was just trying to do something so people wouldn't forget her. And today everyone's going to be talking about her. Who cares about some singer's opinion on religion in the first place?"

Melissa, another senior from Glendale and one of my close friends, also weighed in, "There was a lot of passion in that action. I don't think she was doing it just to get attention. She's got a story to tell and she took advantage of the opportunity to tell it on SNL."

For the next fifteen minutes, almost everyone said something about the performance; with each statement the emotional tension increased. My heart, my uber-sensitive-compassionate-bleeding heart, started hammering and sweat beaded up on my head.

I really, really didn't want to talk. After a couple more minutes of increasingly intense conversation, I finally summoned up the courage to slowly raise my hand. Paula noticed almost immediately.

"Ethan? Is there something you'd like to say?"

I nodded as I took a small drink of coffee. I'd been working on my answer ever since my conversation with my parents. "I think she's like the prophets. She's speaking a truth that no one wants to hear."

"And what truth is that?"

"For starters, the Catholic church in Ireland has been covering over child abuse for years. It's almost like abuse is part of the system instead of the exception. And she's not anti-Catholic at all. It's because she does love the Catholic Church that she did and said something. Just like the prophets did ridiculous things to try and get people's attention to the truth of God's love."

"I don't know, Ethan. That's an awfully big stretch. Where are you getting this information?" Darrell asked.

"Well…"

Thankfully, Paula redirected the question, "Hold on, just a minute. What kind of stuff did the prophets do?"

"Isaiah ripped off all of his clothes and streaked for three years. Jeremiah wore the yoke of cattle and Hosea married a prostitute and gave his kids terrible names. Ezekiel took a nap on one side of his body for an entire year, then rolled over and did it again on the other side. He also used poop to cook his food. Elisha made an ax head float on water and Daniel became a vegetarian."

I couldn't believe I was talking so much *again*, but I couldn't stop myself, "The prophets weren't concerned with being cool. Their calling was to proclaim the truth of God's kingdom in the midst of systems that thrived on abuse and neglect, even if everyone thought them completely crazy. And I think that's exactly what Sinead O'Connor did last night. The only way to know if a prophet is telling the truth is to wait and see."

Paula, again, shifted the focus of the conversation, "Can you guys think of any prophets living today? People whose lives look crazy but they are just trying to passionately and completely obey and serve God?"

"Mother Teresa," Melissa and Samantha said at the same time.

Thomas, the best man in my wedding who wore his Naval Academy dress uniform and looked better than I did in my tux, raised his hand, "Well, there's this kid at Parkview, he's really odd. It's not like he wears religious t-shirts all the time or carries his Bible in his backpack, but, like the other day, there were these two guys fighting after school, and he just ran into the fight screaming and yelling like a madman and the fight stopped. I mean, who does something like that? I've seen him pay for other kids' lunches and picking up trash on the lawn after school while he waits for his ride. He's on the cross-country team with me and there was this one time we were just running at practice and he was kinda dragging behind, so I slowed down to make sure he was ok. But as I got closer to him, I heard him mumbling prayers and stuff while he was running. It was like he was in a whole other world."

"That's a great story," Darrell replied. "Maybe that's what we need to be thinking about this week. Are we doing things just to get others to notice us or are we truly living out our faith, regardless of what others think?"

21

October 5, 1992

I thought everyone would still be talking about Sinead O'Connor's performance on Monday morning. Nathan and I definitely noticed a buzz in the hallways as we headed to our locker; it only took a few minutes before Henry, one of our friends in the Losers Club, found us and filled us in.

"Heard the news yet?" We both shook our heads no as Henry continued, "Chris Henderson died."

"What happened?" Nathan asked.

"Alcohol poisoning."

"I didn't even know that was possible," Nathan replied.

"The story going around is that he was out camping with some friends and they got to drinking and, well, you can imagine that there was some bragging going on about who could drink the most the fastest. So after a couple hours, he passed out and the other guys there thought they'd just let him sleep it off and laugh at his hangover the next day. They moved him into his tent and, when they woke up, he wasn't breathing. One of them drove to a gas station and called 911 and he was pronounced dead on the scene."

The news came as a complete shock. I had known Chris for a long time. We played together on YMCA soccer and Little League baseball teams. We even had a couple of classes together our freshman and sophomore years.

Almost instinctively, I wondered if there was something I could have done to help him, to prevent this horrible tragedy. Before we could ask any more questions, the bell rang and the three of us parted ways.

At the request of Chris's parents, the principal made an announcement on the all-school intercom system as soon as the tardy bell rang.

"Students and friends, as many of you are already aware, one of our own passed away this weekend. Chris Henderson died as the result of a poor choice, from consuming too much alcohol in a short time. His parents want us to remember the good things we loved about Chris and to let his death be a warning to us as well. We will start this morning by observing a moment of silence in Chris's honor."

For sixty seconds, not a single sound was heard.

"Thank you for your cooperation. For those interested, there will be a student-led memorial service held in the gym on Thursday night. For more details on the service, there is a flyer available in the office."

I raised my hand and asked Mrs. Johnson if I could go get one of the flyers. She said yes, and asked that I get enough for the entire class. I jogged down the stairs and ran into Heather along the way. Heather is an incredibly sharp-witted, bright-green-eyed-and-freckled debate champion who is also the president of my graduating class.

In 2015, Heather and I had remained friends. Her nephew is diagnosed with the same auto-immune system disorder I have — alopecia areata — which means that we both save considerable money on haircuts and conditioner. On occasion he and I have gotten together to play catch and discuss important things, like, which baseball team really is better: the St. Louis Cardinals or the Kansas City Royals.

I started talking to Heather before I fully realized what I was saying, "Hey Heather, are you doing anything with the service for Chris on Thursday night?"

"I'm helping plan the evening, mainly giving students a chance to share some stories about Chris and create space for us to mourn together."

"Will there be music?"

"Hadn't got that far, really. Do you have any ideas?"

"I can play guitar as background music, just to break up the silence. We could close by singing Amazing Grace as a prayer, or something like that."

"Could you be there about thirty minutes early, too, just so there's music playing while everyone is coming in?"

"Absolutely. I'd love to be a part of the night."

We reached the office and I grabbed a small stack of the flyers and slowly walked back to French class when I had another idea. My friend Erica is one of the best high school cellists in the state of Missouri.

In 2015, I've played countless pieces as a duet with Elisabeth on the cello. I knew I'd see Erica in English and tried to think of the best way to approach asking her to play with me on Thursday night.

Sometimes, the right song can begin to place the broken pieces back together.

In English class, after Heather confirmed that I was the plan for Thursday night music, I convinced Erica to play with me.

"Guitar and cello will sound terrific together, I promise. I'll skip Wednesday offseason workouts. We can practice after school. My mom's got some old hymnals from church and we could just play through those."

Erica hesitantly agreed on one condition, "Don't ask me to sing."

22

October 8, 1992

Erica wore a simple yet beautiful floor-length black dress to the service Thursday night. At her suggestion, I wore black slacks and a long-sleeve white button-up dress shirt. Mom convinced me to wear a tie.

There were a couple of tables with pictures of Chris on the sideline where the teams sat during basketball games; each table also had a notebook for those who wanted to write something to Chris. In between the tables stood a single microphone on a stand for anyone who wanted to share a story with those gathered.

Erica and I started playing music at 6:30, slowly working through songs from an old Baptist hymnal; students and faculty filled the gymnasium to maximum capacity. Heather started the evening with a general word of welcome, and then sat down near me and Erica.

For almost two hours, students shared stories and memories of Chris. They talked about elementary school and the occasion when he accidentally went into the wrong restroom. Some stories were serious, the majority were humorous, and when the line at the microphone was gone, Heather pulled it close to me.

"We're gonna close tonight by singing an old hymn as a prayer. For those of you who know Amazing Grace, please sing along."

Everyone sang.

Erica and I quit playing our respective instruments and the last verse was sung a cappella. When the song finished, students slowly and solemnly filed out of the gymnasium, stopping frequently to exchange hugs with friends and strangers alike.

As I carefully packed up the borrowed guitar, I heard a familiar voice call me by name — Mrs. Mullins, the choir director, was walking my way.

"Ethan, I'd like to visit with you for a few moments tomorrow morning before school."

"Yes, ma'am." I answered as my pulse sped up.

"Good!" she said with a smile and turned and walked away.

I looked at Erica, "Wonder what that's all about?"

23

October 9, 1992

"Did you know that *Silent Night* was written to be played on the guitar?" Mrs. Mullins didn't waste any time getting to the point, "I'd like you to play it with the Madrigal Singers as an introduction to the carol medley we've been working on."

Mrs. Mullins dressed in goth fashion long before it was *en vogue* making it easy to intimidate her students. As a teacher with perfect pitch, Mrs. Mullins expected perfection from her choirs and knew how to teach in such a way as to achieve it every single time. It was impossible to tell Mrs. Mullins, "No." So I didn't.

"Yes ma'am, what key would you like me to play it in?"

She handed me the music before I could finish asking the question. "I'd like to practice it with the class next week, so please bring your guitar to school."

Like I said, it was impossible to tell Mrs. Mullins no, but I wondered if there would be any future repercussions. And then I wondered if, maybe, I misinterpreted my dream. With the baseball season still several months away, was it possible I was sent back to focus on music instead? If I really poured my passion into perfecting my scales and skills…or maybe I was just overthinking everything.

"Will do."

Later, I thought about my quick reply. Again, I forgot I was a kid in high school with a part-time minimum wage job.

How am I going to get my own guitar?

I stared out the window in English and wrestled with the question when I remembered my Dad's old love for making bizarre bets.

My freshman year Dad took me to Bass Pro Shops, the granddaddy of all sporting goods stores, and bet me I couldn't carry a set of weights to the front of the store.

"You get them to the register and I'll buy them."

"You're on."

The box was incredibly bulky, and I couldn't get a grip or any kind of leverage on it. After a few minutes of struggling, Dad gave me a pat on the back, "One of these days, Chief."

The very first time I won a dollar off Dad was on the golf course. I had just made a thirty-foot double-breaking putt to save par and Dad said, "Bet you a buck you can't do that again."

I walked to the cup, retrieved the ball, placed it back at the original spot, and sank the putt for a second time. Dad immediately started laughing, paid up, and shared the story with multiple friends when we reached the clubhouse.

At the same golf course, we also had a standing bet. The seventh hole is a short, nondescript par three tucked into the corner, surrounded by fences denoting the out of bounds. On this hole, less than one month after Annie and I got married, Dad and I took in a quick nine holes on a beautiful Sunday afternoon and I got to witness Dad's first hole-in-one. The standing bet was simple: if I get a hole in one, Dad would buy me a car. I have yet to ace that hole… or any other one, for that matter.

I finally had an idea for acquiring my own guitar.

Meanwhile, the Losers Club composed at least a dozen solid poems in iambic pentameter during class mocking Shakespearian literature while waiting for the bell. As soon as the bell rang I rushed to the locker, threw all my books inside, and waited for Nathan.

"What's your hurry, Slick?"

"Gotta make a bet with Dad."

"Weekend plans?"

"Not much. You?"

"Visiting the University of Kansas with my parents, pretty sure that's where I'm headed next year. We're driving to Lawrence tonight and touring the campus tomorrow."

"Cool," I said, and started laughing. Then continued in a quieter voice, "Was gonna tell you to text me some pics, but that's not gonna happen. Catch you Monday."

I already knew Nathan's trip would change his life. He would completely fall in love with the school and degree program. One weekend in Lawrence and he'd be inspired to finish out his senior year strong, earning fantastic scholarships. I kept my mouth shut and decided to let him live his life.

24

Dad pulled into the driveway, as I was backing out the big brown van.

"Hey Chief! Have a good day?"

"Just trying to take over the world."

Dad laughed. "No gloves?"

"Headed to the guitar store. Wanna come with me?"

"The guitar store?"

"I'm a man of many talents."

"A man?"

"Ouch."

Dad made me laugh all the way to the store as he shared stories of the nice and not-so-nice animals he'd treated on his house calls. As I listened, I went over the bet in my head, trying to get the words just right.

Hundreds of guitars were on display at Springfield Music, hanging on the walls, sitting in stands, ranging from super cheap to thousands upon thousands of dollars.

I walked around the store, intentionally avoiding the guitars I knew were out of my price range, trying to find a Sigma like the one Dad bought me. I found a couple different models and sat down, pulling a pick out of my pocket to strum some simple chords. Dad, too, picked up a guitar and sat down next to me.

He ripped off multiple riffs of various 1960s songs.

And I echoed them back.

"Impressive. Where'd you learn?" Dad asked.

I couldn't say YouTube videos, so I dodged the question and answered with my own question, "Wanna make a bet?" I continued to noodle softly.

"What kind of bet?"

"I bet you that I can play the next song that comes on the radio. If I can, you buy me this guitar."

"How much is it?"

"Almost three hundred, with a travel case."

"And if you can't?"

"I'll wash and detail your car tomorrow."

Dad laughed, which I initially understood to mean, "You're crazy."

And then he surprised me, "Ok, Chief. You're on."

I closed my eyes to better tune into the radio station softly playing in the background. Good news: it was the oldies station. The DJ came on the air, "And here's one for you baseball fans, to get you in the mood for tonight's play-off game."

The rhythmic claps of John Fogerty's *Centerfield* started and a smile crossed my face.

Who says God doesn't have a sense of humor?

I played loud and sang louder, "Put me in coach, I'm ready to play, today. Put me in coach, I'm ready to play, today, look at me, I can be centerfield."

The store worker looked my direction and raised his eyebrows, then smiled at my squeaky voice.

Dad shook his head, "I guess this is an early merry Christmas to you."

I was grateful, but still, I woke up early Saturday morning feeling incredibly guilty about how I acquired my new guitar.

Was it fair to use skills that had taken years to perfect and pretending they were coming to me naturally? Then again, was it fair taking away my family and life and sending me back through the tortures of my senior year in high school? Is there a manual for morality in time travel?

Either way, by lunch time, I had washed, vacuumed, and Armor-All-ed Dad's car. As I finished cleaning, Dad greeted me by tossing me my glove.

25

October 12, 1992

I had completely forgotten how much of high school life is driven by inane routine. Classes, homework, cramming for tests and quizzes, surviving the Monday through Friday grind, staying up until all hours on the weekend.

After only three weeks back in school, I had become fully accustomed to the numbing schedule and was craving a break from the norm. I was still processing the death of Chris and just needed some space from the ridiculous tedium of school.

Senior skip day.

Nathan picked up me and Katy on Monday morning and told us all about his trip to KU; he was completely in love with the campus and had filled out all the paperwork necessary to go there next year.

"What a life changing experience! I can't wait to start college, man," he said.

"College was a blast," I commented off-hand, before I realized what I'd said.

"How do you know what college is like?" Katy chimed in from the back.

"I meant to say, 'I bet college is a blast.' Sure looks cool in the movies, you know."

It seemed to be a sufficient excuse as I saw Katy nodding along out of the corner of my eye.

"Wanna skip school tomorrow? I just want a break from all of this," I said, nodding toward the school.

"I'm in."

26

October 13, 1992

I woke up early and excited about the thought of no school. I told Mom and Dad and Katy ahead of time that I'd be skipping, figuring the attendance counselor would be calling at some point to check on me. I really didn't care.

To quote skip-day hero Ferris Bueller, "Life moves pretty fast. If you don't stop and look around once in a while, you could miss it."

Nathan picked me up; Henry and Junior were already in the car.

"Hope you don't mind, I extended the invitation."

"To my cohorts in crime," I said, tipping my hat.

The day began with breakfast at Aunt Martha's Pancake House followed by a game of team hide-and-seek at Bass Pro Shops. We voluntarily left after the third round, aware that we were being closely monitored by a couple of the in-house security staff.

We each took a couple rounds in the batting cages, played a game of tag-team-hockey-mini golf at Fun Acre, then went to Casper's for some chili and hot dogs.

As soon as we sat down, Nathan started talking about his trip to KU. Junior and Henry asked several questions about the experience, both in the middle of the "Where in the world am I going to go to college and what in the world am I going to do with my life?" senior year crises. Even years later, I well-remembered those sleepless nights worrying about my future, anxious about all the transitions and responsibilities that come with being an adult.

"What about you, Ethan? Do you feel ready for collegiate life?" Henry asked.

"Oh yeah, it's no big deal," I answered through a mouthful of chili.

Apparently, that was the wrong answer.

"Where you go to college determines your future," Henry replied. "Make the wrong choice and you'll pay for it for years."

"You don't really believe that, do you? I mean, life is so much bigger than just which college we go to."

Another wrong answer. And it was in that moment I realized that I was talking more like a parent than a friend.

"I just think our attitudes play a bigger role. I'm looking forward to the new experiences and people I'll meet. I think college is gonna be really cool wherever I go. Seriously, though. I skipped today so I wouldn't have to think about school. What do we want to do next?"

"We could go see a movie," Nathan said, following my lead.

"Or we could go roller skating," Junior commented with a smirk.

"I haven't been roller skating since I was in…," I said.

"Pretty sure Skateport's not open until after school lets out, though," Nathan added.

"The arcade?" Junior asked.

"Game on!"

We walked into the arcade and immediately I spotted some of my all-time favorite video games — Star Wars and Galaga and Gauntlet and Dragon's Lair. When Henry and Junior raced off to end the debate about who really was better at air hockey, I whispered to Nathan, "In 2015, there's this place downtown called '1984' and all these games are in it and you can play all day long for only five bucks."

"That sounds so cool."

"One time, they had a Gauntlet marathon and discovered that the game, literally, has no end."

After spending considerably more than five dollars on video games, we went to Andy's for frozen custard, then stopped at Blockbuster to pick up a movie which we all agreed would be best to watch in the basement at Nathan's house with Domino's pizza.

The entire ride to Nathan's house, Junior freestyle rapped making fun of the "Be kind, please rewind" sticker on the VHS box. I thought it was hilarious. When we got to Nathan's, I called home, as was expected of me in the years before cell phones, and let Mom know that I would be home a little after dinner.

"Mr. O'Neal called to remind you that your scholarship essay is due tomorrow."

I completely forgot.

Immediately, I felt sick to my stomach.

"No worries, Mom. It's practically finished; I just need to type it out."

27

The connection between leadership and service…

I turned on Dad's "new" Smith Corona word-processor and massaged the not-yet-existent wrinkles on my forehead.

One thousand words.

I took a deep breath, popped my neck, and slowly exhaled the air out of my lungs, focusing all my attention on the blinking cursor.

I can do this. I started to type…

```
           The Servant-Leader

We live in a culture that is obsessed with
leadership.

Some are obsessed with the privilege of power
and prestige that come from positions of
leadership. Some proclaim that everyone is a
leader and, in so doing, lose any hope for a
true vision and direction to be established.
Some believe that leadership is only for the
called, the select, the few, causing fights
among those who anoint themselves as one of the
fortunate few.
Conferences, books, and consultants carefully
construct highly-nuanced definitions of
leadership to better suit the ears of the
gathered crowd. Is it conceivable that those
who are fanatical about and infatuated with the
newest and latest in leadership styles and fads
are desperately seeking a modicum of power,
control, or that intangible "something" to
stroke their pride?
```

Leadership is not about amassing hordes of lemming-like followers whether one is the CEO of a Fortune 500 company or the president of one's senior class. Leadership is not a skill that can be taught like changing a tire or riding a bicycle.

And leadership is not sitting at the top of whatever pyramid or ladder one might desire to climb. Too often, the imaginations of those who sit at the heads of boards and call meetings and rearrange budgets have been held hostage by the pursuit of the mighty dollar, instead of the common good of all people.

True leadership is an audacious and courageous way of life that only begins through wholehearted acts of service.

Mother Teresa displays this kind of leadership. If you get a chance to look at Mother Teresa's feet, you will notice that her toes are deformed, that they are full of knots and bumps and more than oddly shaped. Mother Teresa's toes are thusly shaped because of her servant style of leadership.

On regular occasions, Mother Teresa's mission receives shipments of shoes to be freely distributed among the broken and needy of Calcutta, India. And Mother Teresa chooses her pair first, digging through the boxes and piles of shoes to intentionally find the worst pair. Regardless of how poor the fit or horrible the condition of the shoe, Mother Teresa claims the ones no one else would have chosen so that those she serves, those she leads, would not have to wear them.

Over the course of years and years, this practice of leadership literally deformed her feet. There are those who live in constant pain and cannot afford to make such a sacrifice on their bodies; Mother Teresa chooses to lead in this manner, and in so doing, challenges all people to ask the hard question, "Where can my comfort be sacrificed for the good of another?"

Jack Roosevelt "Jackie" Robinson also exemplified this style of leadership. Immediately following World War II, America was sharply divided by race. Even though African-Americans fought for freedoms on foreign soil, they were largely seen as second-class citizens at home.

On April 15, 1947, Jackie became the first African-American to play Major League Baseball, forever eliminating a racial barrier that had been in existence since 1876 and paving the way for the civil rights movement that would take place throughout the 1960s.

Simply by playing excellent baseball, Jackie and his family received death threats, experiencing the worst of humanity, even from his teammates. But, by playing the game he loved the right way and not choosing to quit when it seemed that the whole world had turned against him, Jackie paved the way for other African-Americans to rise to prominence and be seen for who they truly are: brothers and sisters in the human race.

Jackie was not flamboyant or demanding of the spotlight; he simply played to win every time he stepped on the field.

"A life is not important except in the impact it has on other lives," Jackie once said, and he demonstrated it both on and off the field. He not only won the Rookie of the Year award in 1947, but he also won the World Series with the Brooklyn Dodgers in 1955. Equally important, although awarded posthumously, Jackie won the Congressional Medal of Honor as well as the Presidential Medal of Freedom.

For any person living within the United States, there is no shortage of opportunities to serve others. From soup kitchens and homeless shelters to helping students learn how to read and tutoring struggling Calculus students, we truly exert influence on others — the most basic definition of leadership — when we are willing to give of ourselves for their good.

The media loves to portray teenagers as self-obsessed, living in a shadow world, or performing on a center stage of their own making. But come walk with me through the sacred halls of Kickapoo High School and you'll find a different story.

There's Randy who volunteers to spend time with special needs students on weekends and Jay who helps out at nursing homes multiple times a month. There's Becky and Tomas who coordinate the adopt-a-street cleaning along Jefferson Street. Josh and John are the unofficial hospitality committee, helping every student to find their place, their own clique and community among the masses. Courtney and Erin and countless others ring bells for the Salvation Army every Christmas.

These students and friends are leaders not because they have titles or are recognized by the majority of their peers as being extra-talented or extraordinary people. These students are leaders because they have discovered the truth of Jackie's statement, that a life of significance comes from using one's talents, gifts, and time for the good of all people.

I challenge those who sit on boards and comfortably behind desks making six-figure salaries from the profit of other's labor: come to Kickapoo. Watch and learn as those the world thinks are "tomorrow's leaders" truly give a class in practical, servant leadership, embodying hope wherever they go.

First thing Wednesday morning, I walked straight into Mr. O'Neal's office and handed him the typed essay.

"Here you go, sir."

"Thank you very much, Ethan. I trust you're feeling better," he said with a wink. "The good news about this scholarship is that it's local. They are supposed to announce the winner the week before Thanksgiving break."

"Good. I hate waiting."

28

October 14, 1992

In 2015, I don't miss the daily drama of high school life.

Having 1600 hormone-charged people who are all trying to figure out their futures while navigating the stresses of individuation with parents, whose pre-frontal cortexes sometimes go off-duty for extended periods of time allowing for the worst of ridiculous decisions to be made, who aren't allowed any down time to nap or play catch or just simply breathe, and then packing them into a single building for eight hours beginning way too early in the morning, providing only fifteen minutes to eat a barely sufficient lunch, and expecting them to remain mentally sharp for tests and quizzes and engaging them in the learning process is truly insane.

I did not pursue teaching as a vocation for a reason.

When Chris Henderson died, I saw this school, this group of people brought together through life's varied serendipitous journeys, experience the beauty and necessity of community in the grieving and mourning processes. We caught a glimpse of the in-breaking of heaven into earth, where we were able to focus on those things that matter most of all — each other. But it didn't take long at all for this community to revert back to "normal," social stratification based on superficial notions of popularity, physical attractiveness, and athletic prowess. I wondered if I could do anything to change that.

In 2015, I drive my oldest daughter to school every day. If I'm lucky, some song from the 1980s is played on the radio and she gets to witness my pathetic driver's seat dancing.

Sometimes, when we're at stoplights, we catch other people pointing and laughing at my truly awful dance moves (Katy really did get all the dancing genes in the family). All that to say that, like most people, by the age of 41, I have truly learned the wisdom and incredible freedom of not caring what other people think about me.

That's a quality that most teenagers don't have. After careful consideration, I decided to ask the Losers Club to help me make the remainder of our senior year truly unforgettable. If I was going to be stuck here, then I wanted to find a way to make a difference in this community. I whispered a short but wholehearted prayer, "I don't have a clue where this road leads, God, but I know you're with me and won't leave me to face these trials alone. I will not be afraid."

As soon as the last period tardy bell rang, I ripped out a piece of notebook paper and started scribbling.

"To the beloved and highly esteemed members of the Losers Club:

"Who else here as a full-blown case of senioritis? This daily routine of homework and grades and just trying to survive is slowly sucking all the life out of my marrow. Twenty years from now, I'd like to look back on my senior year and know that I made the most of the opportunities I'd been given."

I quietly folded up the piece of paper and handed it back to Stacie, who added her thoughts before she handed it to Amelia. Amelia to Junior, Junior to Henry, Henry to Nathan.

Passing notes was so much more fun than texting would ever be.

Quickly scanning the note, the unanimous consensus was the Losers Club was slowly but surely dying from senioritis. Humorous suggested remedies included mandatory skip days every Monday, having Domino's deliver a few hundred pizzas during lunch, and developing a fast forward button for life. I started to quote Adam Sandler's movie *Click* before I remembered that it came out some time in the mid-2000s.

"Instead of wasting time on some pointless senior prank, what if the Losers Club takes the initiative and starts something new that brings everyone together?"

The note was passed around; Amelia and Henry were the only people who commented on it.

"Like what?" wrote Amelia.

"Goonie," scribbled Henry.

I choked back a laugh and replied, "It's our time...Goonies never say die! Losers, on the other hand..."

The rest of the paper was filled with quotes and references from *The Goonies*. In the minutes before the final bell rang, I tore out another sheet of paper and started writing.

"Nathan and I've got offseason workouts for the next hour. Anyone available to come to my house later tonight?"

Stacie and Amelia both had commitments elsewhere; the other Losers agreed to continue the conversation later that night.

In comparison to my easy English class, Wednesday's offseason workout was ridiculously hard — conditioning, conditioning, conditioning.

Jog a mile, then do sprints.

Jog another mile, do more sprints.

Jog a third and final mile, finish with more sprints.

I spent so much of the time just trying to breathe that my brain was freed to daydream and imagine without any internal criticism.

I couldn't wait to share my ideas with the rest of the Losers Club.

Nathan, Junior, Henry, and I took turns playing Super Mario Brothers on the Nintendo while devouring a couple of pizzas and downing a couple of two liters of Dr Pepper.

"While I was running and doing everything, I could not to puke, I thought of some stuff we could do to truly make this year memorable."

"Why do you suddenly care?" Henry asked.

"Fair question," I took a moment to think of a reasonable explanation. All of my initial thoughts sounded far too much like a parent. I took a swallow of Dr Pepper and thought of what eighteen-year-old me would have said.

"When Chris died and it seemed like the whole school gathered at his memorial service, that was truly something special, something that put all of this school stuff into perspective. No one was worried about grades or assignments or tests; we were sharing stories and truly caring for each other. And who knows where we'll be in twenty years, but I don't want to waste time worrying about the things that will pass and miss the chance to make the most of the people I'm sharing life with."

It was the truth. The majority of my adult life has been about making new friends, about embracing the connections that bring us together and taking advantage of the strange and beautiful opportunities presented every single day. Even though I didn't fully understand what was going on, I didn't want to waste this opportunity. I barely kept up with my friends from the Loser's Club. Maybe I could change that too.

"So what ideas did you have, Slick?" Nathan chimed in.

"Instead of just doing one big thing, what if we did something small and intentional every day of the week? For example, we could have 'Live Music Mondays' and before school the Losers Club could meet in the commons and I'll bring my guitar and we could just sing at the top of our lungs. Just for fun, to make people laugh, you know, because no one really wants to be at school on a Monday. 'Tray Duty Tuesdays' where we volunteer to return everyone's lunch room trays and trash and handout breath mints."

"I hate this stupid game," Junior interrupted. "Wanna play RBI Baseball instead?"

"Breath mints?" Nathan asked.

"Junior, go for it. You might have to blow in the cartridge, though, to get it to work. Nathan, absolutely. Something small, quirky, fun," I continued, "On Thursdays, we should do something to thank the teachers and the staff, like putting notes in their mailboxes and have it be from the entire class of 1993, not just the Losers Club, 'Thankful Thursdays.' On Friday mornings, maybe the Losers Club could have some t-shirts printed that say 'High Five Friday' and just give people high fives as they come to school, congratulating them on successfully finishing another week."

"You're crazy," Henry said. "And you forgot Wednesday."

"Couldn't think of anything alliterative."

Nathan laughed, "I bet Stacie could."

"Any thoughts?"

Junior seemed completely focused on trying to run-rule the computer on RBI Baseball. I figured he had simply tuned out the conversation until he spoke, "I'm in. Sounds like fun."

Nathan looked at Henry, "I'm in if you are."

Henry rolled his eyes and shook his head.

"Come on, Henry, what have you got to lose?" I asked.

"I'm just not a big fan of public humiliation and these things sound stupid and embarrassing."

"I get that, trust me, I do. But we're seniors and no one will remember us next year anyway. *Carpe diem*, you know."

"*Carpe diem?* Really?" Another Henry eye roll.

"No regrets, man, you only live once," I said, thinking of all the internet memes and Twitter conversations I'd participated in based on those phrases.

"Ok, I'm in, but on one condition."

"Yes?"

"No t-shirts."

29

October 15, 1992

It took a lot of pieces of paper and note passing to fill in Amelia and Stacie on everything. Toward the end of class, I wrote down all the ideas on a new page and left a blank for Wednesdays. Passing the note to Stacie, I asked if she had any alliterative ideas.

The Losers Club

Live Music Monday

Tray Duty Tuesday (with breath mints)

Thankful Thursday

High Five Friday (no t-shirts or no Henry)

"Walk, write, wave, wish, wander, wonder, welcome, weave, weepy, wacky, whining, whistle, working, wired, withdrawn, worry, worship, wounded, wrestling."

Nothing really jumped out to me; at least Wednesday was still a few days away. I tucked that page in my back pocket and started one more note.

"High Five Friday in the commons before school tomorrow?"

30

October 16, 1992

My daughters remind me all the time that I'm crazy. "Dad," one of them will say, "this world could sure use a few more crazy people like you."

Thankfully, the Losers Club was willing to give my crazy ideas a chance.

The six founding members of the Losers Club gathered just inside the doors on the northeast side of the school in the commons area. Students had to walk through the commons area to enter the cafeteria, and the majority of student drivers and those who bummed rides off of student drivers used this entrance instead of the main entrance on the west side of the building.

I took a deep breath, smiled, and started clapping my hands.

"Woohoo!" I shouted at the top of my lungs. "You survived another week! Congratulations! Gimme five!"

The first few students just stared, intentionally walking out of their way not to be near me. And then someone acknowledged my sticking-straight-into-the-air hand with a, "Yeah, buddy, it's Friday! I won't leave you hangin'!"

"High Five Friday!" Junior yelled as the remaining Losers joined in, whooping and hollering and high-fiving every single person who entered these doors for the next fifteen minutes until Vice Principal Wilton tapped me on the shoulder.

"Mr. Bryan! What precisely is going on here?" he demanded as he cracked his knuckles.

Vice Principal Wilton was too skinny, with dark brown hair buzz cut short, dark squinty eyes, and a thinly-shaved mustache. His suits were oversized and he always seemed angry, ready to drag a student to the office for some obscure reason or another. He also called everyone by their last name, preceded by either mister or missus, whichever was appropriate.

My first experience with Vice Principal Wilton the knuckle-cracker negatively colored every successive encounter. The very first week of my high school career, I was nervously walking through the halls, trying to get to my next class and beat the tardy bell when a fight broke out near me. Vice Principal Wilton happened to be walking through the halls, just around the corner from where the fight started and thought that I had instigated it.

"You, come here! Now!" he yelled, pointing a finger straight at me, and then interlaced his hands and flexed his fingers.

Thankfully, one of my friends stood up for me in that first encounter and I was barely able to get to class on time. Vice Principal Wilton was always stern and intimidating; I never once saw him smile, never heard him say anything positive. I had spent my high school career intentionally avoiding him.

"Hey, Mr. Wilton! It's High Five Friday! We're just celebrating the end of another week and welcoming everyone to school. Gimme five!" I raised my hand.

Though I was shorter than him at this stage in my life, I would still grow a few more inches over the next couple of years, my 41-year old mind wasn't the least bit intimidated. I stood staring him straight into the eyes with an honest and somewhat ornery smirk on my face. "Come on, Mr. Wilton, gimme five."

The bell rang.

"Go to class. All of you," he said forcefully, without blinking.

And then he gave me five!

"Have a great Friday, Mr. Wilton," I yelled walking to class, "Feel free to join us next week!"

"Dude," Nathan said, "You really are crazy. I can't believe Mr. Wilton actually gave you a high five."

"I wasn't gonna move until he did. Can't wait to see what he thinks of Live Music Monday!"

For the rest of the day, people in the halls, in the cafeteria, and in all of my classes were giving me and the other Losers Club members high fives. After lunch, I made the mistake of walking through the hall where the football players' lockers are located; both of my hands were stinging for the remainder of the school day.

In English, Henry started the Losers Club poetry and note-passing session, "Ok, you win. That was actually fun this morning. Can you play oldies on Monday?"

"You name it, I can play it," I wrote back.

The club members started writing furiously, "The Lion Sleeps Tonight," "Brown Eyed Girl," "Be My Baby," "Mr. Bojangles," "Twist and Shout."

"This list rocks!"

31

October 17, 1992

The First International World Series:
Toronto and Atlanta Take Center Stage

The headline on the sports section alerted me to the beginning of one of my favorite annual events — The World Series. This year's iteration pitted the Blue Jays versus the Braves.

In just a couple of days, the first World Series game to be played outside of the United States will happen. I already knew that the Blue Jays would win this year, and then repeat next year on Joe Carter's incredible World Series winning home run, followed by a strike in 1994 that will cause a large number of fans to walk away from the game.

If I was a different type of guy, I might put some money on the Jays. Instead, I was just excited to watch the games with my dad.

The World Series always brings an incredible mix of emotions. The kid-at-heart part of me loves the idea of discovering the champion, the battle of the best of the National League against the best of the American League. Formed in 1876, the National League boasts of being older and better. The American League, founded in 1901, challenged the National League's monopoly on professional baseball. Two years later, the leagues signed a new National Agreement and the first World Series was born. Now, the only real distinction between the two is the American League employs the designated hitters while the NL is known for allowing their rarely-hitting, often-flailing with a bat pitchers to take their three swings and sit down.

I almost always cheer for the American League team, unless the Yankees are playing, in which case I cheer for the National League team. The adult part of me mourns during the World Series, for the end of the baseball season means the end of summer, and I'm just not that big a fan of colder weather and winter. I pray every year that the World Series will go to a seventh game, just for the sake of more baseball.

I spent the majority of the morning in my bedroom practicing the songs that Henry had suggested. I had forgotten how much I truly loved just playing the guitar and completely lost track of time as I wondered what Live Music Monday might really look like.

Mom knocked on my bedroom door, "Sounds good in there!"

"Thanks, Mom. What's for lunch?"

"That depends. What are you making?"

I put the guitar in its case and headed to the kitchen; Dad was busy sharpening knives while humming an old western tune.

"We're watching the Series tonight, right Chief?" he asked without looking up.

"Wouldn't miss it for the world. Hey Dad, isn't Coach Goodwin a client of yours?"

"The baseball coach at SMSU? Yeah, he's got a couple of dogs I take care of. Why?"

"Well, I really want to keep up a regular throwing routine and the weather's gonna be tricky pretty soon. Do you think there's any way he'd let us use the indoor practice facility that his team uses?"

"I suppose I could call him. If I do that for you, would you be willing to clean gutters for me? They're getting pretty full of leaves."

In 2015, I absolutely detest cleaning out gutters. But Dad's offer was fair; he never did like to abuse the trust of his clients who have given him their home phone numbers and addresses.

"Ok, I'll get it done before the game tonight."

Mom cooked my favorite meal, Mexican cornbread, to celebrate the start of the World Series. "Hey Chief," Dad said, "I called Coach Goodwin and told him what you were hoping to do. He remembered meeting you at that summer baseball camp a couple of years ago and said that if we wanted to practice on campus during the week just to let him know and he'd be willing to let us in to their space."

"Awesome!"

We ate together as a family in a room without a television, a habit that I still practice as much as possible with my family. After eating way too much Mexican cornbread, Katy and I cleared the table while Dad started washing the dishes. When the table was empty, I rushed into the living room and turned on the TV in time to be welcomed to postseason baseball by a "young" Tim McCarver.

Tom Glavine was the starting pitcher for the Braves.

"This should be fun," I said, but stopped myself before continuing the rest of my thought, "This guy was just inducted into the Hall of Fame last year."

Dad finished the dishes and kicked back in his recliner just as the Canadian National Anthem was being sung.

"I guess it truly is a World Series, huh?" Dad stated. "Two teams, two countries. Who do you think's gonna win?"

"Toronto, without a doubt."

"The Blue Jays? I don't know. The Braves have an incredible pitching staff. Should be a good series either way."

"Gonna try and learn as much as I can. Last baseball games I'll get to watch before I have a chance to make the varsity team."

"You've put a lot of work in already and I must say I'm been impressed. It's not easy to commit to something so many months away, especially if you don't know if you'll get the results you want."

"I guess it does take a lot of work to turn a dream into reality."

"Ah, the famed entrepreneur's motto."

"What's the motto?"

"Nothing, what's the motto with you?"

Dad laughed heartily at his joke. I rolled my eyes but also smirked. Dad jokes really are the best.

"Seriously though," he continued, "do the hard work building your dreams instead of whittling away building someone else's."

As I considered Dad's response, the first pitch was thrown and the game was officially underway."Time to put in some hard work," I grinned.

32

October 18, 1992

The first time around, Drew and I never got to know each other very well, so it was nice to spend some time with my pastor's son and get to know him as a teenager, who was a clear preview of the man I knew he would become. Drew and I visited a little about the World Series; he's a National League guy and pretty happy that the Braves won the first game.

"There's a reason they play nine innings and there's a reason it's a best of seven series. Toronto's got it in the bag."

Drew shook his head and laughed, "Yeah, right."

Paula started the class with prayer and asked the students to pair off. Drew patted me on the back, "We got this."

"With Halloween approaching," Paula continued, "we're going to spend this morning talking about something that motivates everyone — fear. On the board, I've written some of the top fears and phobias people have. Dying. Public speaking. Loneliness. Failure. Spiders. Snakes. I want you and your partner to honestly answer this question: What are you afraid of and why?"

I immediately tried to remember my 18-year old fears. It had to be related to girls and getting a date. Taking the SAT? Doing Calculus in front of people? Or maybe...

Drew whispered quietly, "I'm afraid of being a disappointment to my parents."

I knew from the fact he wasn't making eye contact that he was serious. This was Drew taking off his mask.

"It's not easy being the pastor's kid. I really love my dad and have learned so much about my faith, but I don't want to work in a church or be a missionary or anything like that."

"What do you want to do?"

"Well, if I don't play ball professionally, I'd kind of like to start my own business. Maybe something with computers. I don't know, really, I just know I don't feel called to work in a church and I'm afraid of hurting my parents' feelings."

"Don't you think following Jesus beyond the church walls is as important as in the church? Aren't we sent out to the ends of the earth? This world could use more faith-filled entrepreneurs and computer geeks, don't you think? And I honestly believe your parents will support wherever God calls you to go, whatever God calls you to do."

Drew smiled. "I like the way you think. What about you? What are you afraid of?"

"Clowns. They creep me out."

Drew laughed. "Clowns? Really?"

I chose my next words carefully.

"I'm afraid of growing apart from my family, of getting so wrapped up in things that don't really matter that I become self-centered and self-absorbed. And yes, clowns. They are spine-chilling."

I found a way to tell the truth and it felt really good. Cathartic. Somehow, this was different from the confessions I'd tried to share with Nathan. Drew and I continued the conversation and spent a time praying for one another at the end of class.

After church and lunch, I spent the rest of Sunday afternoon walking through the house strumming and singing, trying to quickly develop calluses on my fingertips, making up songs off the top of my head and practicing the melodies for Monday. By bedtime, I had played so much the music infiltrated my dreams.

33

I knew I was dreaming. I couldn't figure out the where of the dream, as it was more a series of snapshots and sounds than a scene from a movie, but it still felt familiar.

I recognized Elisabeth's voice. She was running away from me, in front of me, wearing a blue sundress, but I couldn't understand what she was saying. Sarah was a few steps behind, clunking along in pink cowgirl boots.

I saw a glimpse of Annie. She was walking by my side and had turned toward me to smile, but just for a moment. I felt invisible, like she looked right through me without noticing I was there.

I heard music coming from somewhere nearby, a beautifully bright melody, a song I recognized. I tried to sing along, but the words got stuck in my throat. The more I tried to sing, the louder the music grew, the more I felt trapped. By this time, Annie was several steps ahead of me; Elisabeth and Sarah were out of sight.

I tried to run and catch up with her, but couldn't move. I was stuck, frozen in place, slowly sinking into the sidewalk, unable to do anything other than see and hear. The music grew to an ear-splitting volume. I could feel the bass line resonate in my rib cage, the melodies pounded into my brain. As the sidewalk started compressing around my chest, I tried to scream for help.

Snapping awake with a gasp, I pushed myself up against the headboard and reached for the nightlight that wasn't there. Startled, I looked around the room and recognized nothing. I grabbed a red cell phone from the night stand and looked at it.

I pressed the home button.

Saturday, May 4, 8:45 AM.

Behind the time stamp was a picture of me with a boy. The boy had light brown hair and wore glasses on top of his freckled nose. We were standing in front of a brick fireplace, which I immediately recognized as being from my parents' house. Draping from the mantle were Christmas stockings with names sewn into them. And between "Ethan" and "Katy" was "Hogan."

I pressed the home button a second time on the phone, but couldn't guess the passcode to unlock it.

As I strained to focus on the screen, staring at Hogan, I spotted a pair of black-rimmed glasses on the night stand. I shoved them on right as a stringed instrument started tuning, playing scales and arpeggios.

A cello?

I looked for more clues to discern my whereabouts and when-abouts. There were more pictures of me and Hogan on my dresser and in my wallet, but none of them contained another adult. Where was Annie? Where were the girls?

According to my driver's license, we lived in the southeast corner of Springfield. Rifling through mail stacked on the dresser, I deduced that it had to be 2013.

I got dressed — no scar on my knee? — and opened the bedroom door, which I discovered was on the second floor of the house. The cello sounded like it was directly beneath me. A few more pictures of me and Hogan hung on the walls, pictures from various national landscapes. But there were also large paintings, fancy pieces of art I had never seen before. I walked down the staircase, following the music, and spotted Hogan playing in a large back room, right next to a baby grand piano. I guessed at his age. Thirteen, maybe?

"Morning, Sad! Happy Star Wars Day!" he greeted and immediately segued into the famed theme from one of my favorite movie franchises.

"Morning," I whispered. My heart was pounding and my palms were starting to sweat.

At least twenty guitars lined the walls of the room in which Hogan sat — acoustic, electric, all Taylors and Fenders — along with seven different amps and a humidifier.

"Any plans for the day?" I asked quietly, afraid of everything I didn't know.

"Just practice and homework. Music festival's coming quickly. Tour's finished, right? What are you gonna do today?"

Tour? Not knowing what to say, I nodded my head slightly and shrugged my shoulders.

A buzz and electronic blip sounded from near Hogan. He grabbed his phone off the music stand in front of him and read the text. "It's from Gram and Papaw inviting us to lunch. She's making tacos and then Gram wants to practice with me."

"Sounds good to me," I replied.

Hogan resumed playing and I wandered off, locating a study on the opposite side of the house, adjacent to the kitchen with the marble countertops. Centered on the perfectly clean desk was a desktop computer with two screens of significant size. I turned the computer on and whispered a quick prayer, "Please, please, please, please..."

My prayer was answered; the password for the computer was simply hitting the enter key. I googled myself and found my website. I spent the next couple of hours reading stories about my life as a musician, all the places I had toured, all the famous friends I had in the business.

I watched YouTube videos and was amazed at what I apparently could do on a guitar. I learned that Hogan was my only child, now twelve years old, born from my wife, a woman who had died in childbirth. I studied everything I read, trying to memorize who I was supposed to be.

"Dad, let's go! Tacos are calling!" Hogan shouted.

I met him in the kitchen and followed him to the garage. Into the trunk of a silver Land Rover, Hogan loaded his cello, then climbed into the passenger's seat and synced his phone up to the stereo. He blasted classical music and pretended to conduct for the fifteen-minute drive.

We pulled up to the familiar brick house and I was a bundle of nerves.

"You okay, Dad?" Hogan asked.

"Yeah, kiddo. Just didn't sleep that well last night."

"Kiddo?"

My parents greeted us on the porch, all smiles, all healthy, all gray.

"My boys!" my mom exclaimed. "How are my two favorite boys doing today?" she asked beaming from cheek to cheek.

"Hey Chief," my dad said. "Welcome home. What's happening, Big H?"

"It's good to see a familiar face," I said.

"Can't wait for Gram's tacos!" Hogan replied.

We ate and my parents grilled me about life on the road. I faked answers the best I could, sharing highlights I remembered from the tour blog. Hogan entertained them with stories of the end of his first year in middle school, including setting the record for the fastest mile time in his grade.

"People don't understand that being a musician means you need to be in phenomenal shape, right Dad?"

"Couldn't have said it better myself."

I helped Dad clean up the lunch dishes while Hogan practiced playing with my mom.

"I think I'm going to retire after this year," he said.

"Really, why's that?"

"Too much red tape. Government work is getting ridiculous."

I had no idea what Dad was talking about, so I nodded along in ignorance as I dried the dishes.

"I'm sure I could always use another roadie."

He laughed immediately, "I just might take you up on that."

Hogan and mom practiced for forty-five minutes. Dad enjoyed the personal concert.

"He's going to be better than you, you know," Dad said.

"Pretty sure he already is."

After they finished played, Hogan excused himself and retreated to my old bedroom which had been made over into a movie room. And I was left alone with my parents in a time where I knew very little about who

I was and what was real. Mom walked over and sat next to me, rubbing my back.

"Amazing how much he looks like her, isn't it?" she asked.

I nodded, not exactly sure who "she" was.

"It's his smile," Dad said, "and a lot of his mannerisms. Amazing how genetics does that."

I remained silent.

"Are you doing okay? You're awfully quiet," Mom stated.

"Road trips are hard on the body. Looking forward to staying low-key for the next little bit."

"Maybe your dad should take you two to go see a movie? Think Hogan would like that? You get to choose what to see."

"I think that sounds fantastic. What's playing?"

"Rerelease of Jurassic Park in 3D and 42, that movie about Jackie Robinson."

Dad was scrolling through show times on his phone. "If we hurry, we can catch one of them right up the road."

I got up and walked down the hall, "Wanna go see a movie with me and Papaw? There's a baseball flick I think you'd like."

"A baseball movie? Really?"

"Absolutely. Baseball movies are the best. You do know I used to be a pretty decent ballplayer when I was your age, right?"

"You played baseball?" Hogan asked, as if the concept was completely beyond his mental capacity.

Exactly what world was I living in?

"I played at Kickapoo, less than a mile from here."

"I don't believe you. I'm gonna ask Gram."

Mom confirmed that I did play baseball, but that my life changed when I got a guitar my senior year. "You never put that thing down. Both your dad and I were so surprised at how quickly you learned and your wholehearted devotion to it." Mom kept sharing guitar stories. I felt like I didn't know who she was talking about.

"C'mon, Hogan knows all these stories already. Let's go so we can still get a good seat."

After the movie, Dad took me and Hogan to Andy's for a late afternoon treat. We sat on the bench and enjoyed our chocolate concretes.

"I remember reading that if Jackie had failed in baseball, the Civil Rights Movement might have been pushed back a decade or more. Even still baseball was fifteen years ahead of culture," I said to no one in particular.

"Really? Papaw, you were alive back then, weren't you? Do you remember any of that stuff, about Jackie and the Civil Rights Movement?" Hogan asked.

"Just barely, but I do remember it. It was a pretty big deal to see Jackie playing ball, wearing that classy Dodgers uniform. I remember that your great-grandfather, my dad, wasn't very happy about it at all. In fact, we drove to a game in St. Louis and he screamed some pretty hateful stuff from the stands."

"I never knew that," I commented with my mouth full.

"In general, racial issues can be really hard to talk about. For me, growing up under the influence of one of the most racist men in the county. I've spent a lot of my life re-learning the basic truth, 'All men are created equal.'"

Hogan chipped in, "There's a boy in my quartet at school, his mom's black and his dad's white. People make fun of him saying that he doesn't belong anywhere. He sits at my table in the lunch room and we always talk. I really like him."

"I am so proud of you for doing that, for being his friend. I know that's gotta cost you some cool points."

"Yeah, because I get so many lugging that cello around."

"Touché."

Hogan and I drove Dad home. We left my parents' house and drove the long way back to our house, ordering a pizza on the way. I surfed through the channels and learned that the Royals shut out the White Sox, winning 2 – 0 on a complete game effort by Jeremy Guthrie.

"Must have been quite the game," I said.

"You've watched more baseball today than I've seen in my entire life," Hogan commented.

I didn't really know what to say.

"Well, there's more to life than just music," I said flippantly.

"Heretic."

"Them's fightin' words," I chuckled.

"It's just, you're always telling me about the power of music, preaching how it heals invisible hurts and helps make sense of the world and now suddenly you're interested in baseball? What gives? You've not acted like yourself all day."

"Just under a lot of stress and I'm having trouble figuring things out."

"Stress? What stress? I thought you and I were a team and we were gonna make music together until our fingers fell off. Does this have anything to do with my birthday being next week?"

"No, no. Absolutely not." I pulled him in close and gave him a bear hug. I could feel him relax some in my arms. "Just grown-up stuff, son. We'll get through it together."

I tossed him the remote and he landed on a reality TV cooking show.

"I love this Ramsey guy!" he said with a laugh.

We watched the show together, finishing the entire pizza and a 2-liter of Dr Pepper. Hogan put himself to bed and, now that I no longer had to wear a brave face, I felt completely overwhelmed and alone. I walked upstairs to my bedroom, got on my knees, and prayed with all of my heart.

"God, I don't belong here and I don't have a clue what to do. This world is not my home. This time is not my home. Please help me." I repeated the prayer over and over until I fell asleep next to my bed.

34

May 5, 2013

I woke up with most of my body under the bed, my back stiff as a board. As quietly as possible, after getting dressed, I went downstairs and brewed a cup of coffee.

I walked out to the front porch and sipped the coffee, listening to the late spring sounds of the Ozarks — birds I could never identify by call and already a distant hum of multiple lawnmowers.

A mid-80s Honda drove by slowly and tossed the orange plastic-wrapped Sunday edition of the Springfield News-Leader out the window. It landed squarely in one of the bushes in front of me.

"Good effort," I shouted back.

Honk, honk, honk, the car replied.

Only as I held the paper in my hands did it finally connect with my brain that today was actually Sunday. I went back inside and changed into dress clothes, desperate to head to church and see what I could learn.

When I walked back downstairs, Hogan was in the kitchen making himself an egg sandwich.

"I guess today's Revenge of the Fifth?" I asked.

Hogan smirked.

"Wanna go to church with me?"

He tilted his head much like a puppy.

"Don't we always go to Harry Potter church together?"

His answer couldn't have been more perfect.

It started to rain on the drive to church. Loud, heavy, drops pounded the windshield, reducing visibility to mere feet. I dropped Hogan off at the covered circle drive on the east side of the building before finding a place to park.

I sat in the Rover for five minutes hoping the raid would let up. At the sign of the slightest break, I sprinted for the door and got thoroughly soaked. Thankfully, it was a warm rain and didn't feel bad at all.

Unsure where to go or who would be there, I walked to the sanctuary to sit in the back pew and perused the bulletin. The very first thing I noticed was the pastor's name, Rev. Drew Gibson. I chuckled to myself. After a couple more minutes alone, I was greeted by a strangely familiar voice.

"Good morning, Mr. Bryan. I had a feeling I'd see you sitting here." I looked up to see Mr. Wilton with his hand extended my direction.

"Good morning," I replied hesitantly as I shook his hand. "How are you doing?"

"Fine, fine. And yourself?"

"Just drying off."

"I know this will sound odd, but I was out visiting garage sales yesterday and found this old jersey. I remembered how much you loved baseball back at Kickapoo and thought you might get a kick out of it."

Mr. Wilton handed me a brown pullover jersey, with a V-neck trimmed in gold and white stripes. It said "Chiefs" across the front with the number seven underneath the "s."

"This is marvelous. Thank you so much," I laughed.

"Those were good days, good memories," he said, and then walked off rather abruptly.

I sat in silence, again alone, and carefully folded the jersey. Thirty minutes later, Hogan found me.

"Where'd you get that?" he asked.

"From Mr. Wilton."

"Who?"

"An old... friend?" He was my vice principal from high school," I answered, slightly confused.

Together in that back pew, Hogan and I sang and prayed and wrote notes back and forth during Drew's sermon.

"Seek first God's Great Story," Drew said, "and God will take care of the rest of the details."

His words bounced around in my imagination as I wondered what kind of "Choose Your Own Adventure" I was currently living.

At Hogan's request, we spent Sunday afternoon hiking the long trail at The Nature Center. He spotted multiple snakes and threatened to pick them up and chase after me.

"Try it and you'll be walking home."

When we got home, Hogan practiced his cello for an hour. I sat and just listened, amazed at his talent and dedication to his craft.

It was after midnight when I finally crawled into bed, quite anxious at what Monday might bring.

That night, I had the baseball dream and I felt the massive a massive force on my chest again and the feeling being pulled backward.

35

October 19, 1992

I woke up to a pounding on my bedroom door. "Wake up! You're gonna be late! Nathan's going to be here anytime."

I jumped awake in a surge of pure adrenaline.

I got dressed and ready in a matter of minutes, then rushed to the kitchen and confirmed the day and date on the newspaper. Nathan honked, and I spotted my backpack propped up against my guitar case. Katy held the door open for me and I was climbing into the passenger's seat before I had a free moment to process anything.

"Hey Bryans! How was the weekend?"

"Well I was dancing in Branson," Katy sang to the tune of "Walking in Memphis."

"A real trip," I replied.

"Why have you been bringing a guitar to school so much?" Katy asked.

"You might wanna hang around the commons area before school," Nathan answered, winking at me.

"Why?"

"Just hoping to make Mondays a little more enjoyable," I answered.

Nathan and I were the last of the Losers Club to arrive; I couldn't believe it. The first Live Music Monday sponsored by the Losers Club had finally arrived. My brain was still in a fog, trying to process the weekend and the reality which was in front of me.

"How many songs until Wilton stops us?" I asked, setting down the guitar case near the base of the stairs by the concession stand.

Almost in unison, everyone said, "One."

"I think we'll be okay. He likes me," I said, getting awkward glances from everyone in return. Strapping on the guitar, I quickly added, "First song is 'The Lion Sleeps Tonight.' Junior and Henry, are you guys comfortable with the lead?"

They both nodded.

"Don't forget to smile, and sing loud!"

I spotted Katy on the opposite side of the commons with a couple of her classmates. She mouthed to me, "What are you doing?"

"Singing! It's my favorite!" It'd be years before she and I would quote Will Ferrell's *Elf* back and forth at any and every opportunity. As soon as I said it, I started loudly strumming the guitar.

We almost made it through two songs before Mr. Wilton appeared, determinedly walking in our direction.

"Singing, Mr. Bryan?" Mr. Wilton looked at me with a severe intensity.

It's hard not to look like the one in charge when you're the one wearing a guitar. I looked at him and, for a moment, thought he looked different. I had a quick flashback to yesterday morning's brief conversation and stared at him, wondering if he remembered as well, and then just as quickly pushed it to the back of my mind.

"Did you like it?"

"Were you guys practicing for choir?"

"No."

"Were you guys practicing for a different class?"

"No."

"Why then, do tell, were you guys singing?"

With each question, Mr. Wilton popped another knuckle and inched closer and closer to me. After that last question, he was significantly inside my personal bubble, actually bumping into the guitar.

"Nobody really wants to come to school on Monday. But it's scientifically proven that music helps people to feel better, and if people feel better then they'll do better scholastically, right? Like that guy, he was dancing while we were singing. And those girls over there were singing along, or at least lip-synching. We're just trying to start the week off on a good note — pun intended — and we'll stop when the bell rings so we can get to class on time."

"High fives last Friday and music today. Mr. Bryan, are you guys planning on doing something tomorrow?"

"Yep."

He stood there for a moment with his arms folded across his chest and waited for me to continue. I didn't. He then sighed a deep sigh, and shook his head.

"Very well, Mr. Bryan. I'll see you, most certainly, tomorrow."

To the tune of "Twist and Shout," Mr. Wilton walked away.

I excused myself from first hour French to go to the restroom, just for a moment of silence, a moment to myself. I thought about Hogan and the sizeable house and all the guitars. I thought about the stories I read on the tour blog and the videos I had seen of myself shredding across the strings.

Even though I had only the smallest of tastes of that life, it didn't feel true; it didn't resonate with my 40-whatever-year old brain. Hogan was a nice kid, but he didn't feel like my child. There was no Annie, no Elisabeth, no Sarah. I didn't want to change that much of my life. And I didn't want to be a rock star.

I determined to make the most of my time here, to try and make a tangible difference with my friends and in my school community. Maybe then I could go back to Annie and the girls a better man for all my experience.

36

October 20, 1992

Between the six members of the Losers Club, all four lunch shifts had a least one person performing voluntary tray duty; the cellophane-wrapped breath mints were a huge hit.

Tray duty was supposed to be the most humiliating and degrading of punishments for those who got in trouble during the thirteen-minute lunch break. Successfully performing tray duty required one to approach students who were finishing their meals and ask for their permission to stack plates, cups, napkins, trash, and anything else they wanted you to precariously pile on so you could return the tray to the dishwashing line after you had properly disposed of all trash.

Mr. Wilton was in charge of keeping the peace in the cafeteria and was known to take pleasure in doling out tray duty to anyone caught out of line. On one occasion during my junior year, he tried to give me tray duty for supposedly throwing trash across the room. I passionately proclaimed my innocence; he let me off with the strictest of warnings.

"I don't remember giving you tray duty, Mr. Bryan," Mr. Wilton said as I carefully threw away napkins and other trash items while balancing half a dozen plates and trays.

"Voluntary tray duty, sir, and a breath mint."

"You are truly an enigma, Mr. Bryan…" He trailed off before turning and walking away. Again, I remembered that quick back pew conversation. Was it possible he knew something?

I tried to shrug it off. If he and I were friends in an alternate future, then we had to better connect in my past? Maybe I needed to pay closer attention to my interactions with Mr. Wilton as well.

I couldn't keep the smile off my face as I walked back into English class. "Did you guys like tray duty?" I wrote then passed a note to Stacie.

I don't think anyone enjoyed the experience as much as I did, but both Junior and Nathan said they got some pretty good laughs. Neither Stacie nor Amelia were overly fond of tray duty, but at least they were able to work together.

"We took turns handing out the breath mints, that was the best part. Some of those football players really liked to pile on the dishes though."

"So, what are we going to do tomorrow?" Henry asked.

"What about 'Winning Wednesdays?' Sounds fun, especially since we're the Losers Club. Just not sure what 'Winning' means yet." I replied.

"Preferably nothing to do with sports," Henry responded.

Everyone agreed.

Nathan motioned to me for the piece of paper, "What if we choose someone and declare them the winner for the day, someone who's had a really rough day or week? We could decorate their locker and write 'Winner' on it, then attach a note that they need to find one of the members of the Losers Club to claim their prize."

"What's the prize?" Junior asked.

"A $5 gift certificate to Andy's?" I wrote.

Stacie added, "I love this idea and I know who should be first. Alex Kesinger's locker is three down from mine. Chris Henderson was his locker partner. They were such good friends. I think he's been having a tough time since Chris' death."

As the note got passed around, the countenance on the faces of the Losers Club changed. We had stumbled onto something sacred.

For the first Winning Wednesday, everyone agreed to pitch in five bucks. Alex was going to get a $30 gift certificate to Andy's.

"I can pick up the gift certificate tonight and meet you in the commons tomorrow morning," I wrote.

Amelia agreed to go to the store and get a card and some fun decorations.

The bell rang and the Losers Club stood up, almost in unison, ready to extend hope to Alex.

37

The first World Series game outside of the United States was played in the SkyDome in Toronto. The Braves and Blue Jays split the first two games in Atlanta. Dad and I were both in the mood for baseball. The overcast skies and cool breeze provided the perfect setting for a good session on the mound while we waited for the game to begin.

After dinner, as we watched the game, we trash talked and bantered possible bets.

"Bet we see a grand slam?" I said.

"No dice. Bet Atlanta wins the next three?"

"I'd take it. Bet we see a no hitter?"

"With these pitchers? It's possible. Bet someone streaks?"

"Always. Bet we see a triple play?"

Just as Dad started to say something in response, Toronto's centerfielder Devon White made an incredible catch of a deep fly ball off the bat of Darrell Justice. Immediately, White spun and threw the ball back toward the infield as there were two runners on base.

After Terry Pendleton was called out for passing Deion Sanders on the base paths, Sanders got caught in a pickle, and I thought he was tagged out as he tried to slide back into second base.

"Triple play!" I jumped up yelling.

"No, no, no. He's safe. Look, they called him safe."

The umpires did rule him safe, much to my disappointment.

The Blue Jays went on to win the first World Series game played in Canada and took a 2 – 1 overall lead.

It felt great to put the stress of school aside, to temporarily turn my brain off and just watch baseball with Dad. We laughed and cheered and told stories.

Thanks to the game, I was able to enjoy sharing this small blip of a moment without worrying about future ramifications. Thanks to baseball, I was able to fully live in this version of reality.

38

October 21, 1992

Stacie, Amelia, Nathan, and I met in the commons shortly after 7:30.

Amelia showed us the card she had picked out and we took a few minutes carefully composing a simple note:

Dear Alex,

You are the first Winning Wednesday winner. We are thankful you are part of our school. To claim your prize, head to the Journalism office (two doors down on the left) and ask for Nathan.

From your friends,

The Losers Club

We rushed upstairs as a group and quickly decorated his locker — construction paper, balloons, streamers, and the card all taped up nicely. Amelia took a few pictures after we finished then we scattered and waited for Alex to walk down the hall. I pulled the gift certificate out of my backpack and handed it to Nathan.

"Have fun," I said.

"He hugged me," Nathan wrote later that day in English class.

"He opened up the gift certificate and gave me a big hug. He told me he's felt so alone these last couple of weeks, he's even considered committing suicide. He feels horribly guilty and responsible for Chris's death because he was the one who brought all the beer. He told me to tell the Losers Club thanks for thinking of him, that Andy's is one of his favorite places. He and Chris used to go there all the time."

Nathan passed the note around. An Andy's gift certificate had turned high school hallways into a holy moment. *Thanks be to God*, I whispered to myself.

"I can't wait for next Wednesday," Henry replied, "I think I might know who our next winner will be."

"What's the game plan for tomorrow?" Junior asked.

"How about we pick a couple of hallways and go write on the teachers' chalkboards? Something like 'Thanks for all you do.' Sign it from the Class of '93," Amelia suggested.

"Sounds like fun to me," I wrote.

"No breath mints?" Nathan asked.

"Save 'em for another time." Henry commented.

I was particularly glad for the fun I'd had with Loser's Club that morning because Wednesday's offseason workout was a killer. It was all about the legs: squats and lunges and presses and raises.

Ever since my ACL surgery, I have been overly cautious when working out my legs, trying to find methods that are "knee-friendly." I settled on long-distance cycling as a way to strengthen my legs. But these legs are completely healthy, ready to be pushed and challenged.

I imagined myself pitching against Glendale, fighting for every out, wanting to throw a complete seven-inning game. By the time I had finished the suggested workout, my leg muscles were completely exhausted. I couldn't find Nathan afterwards, and slowly started the world's longest half-mile walk home.

As I reached the edge of the parking lot, I heard a honk and looked up — Mom was driving by in the big brown van.

"Need a lift?" she asked.

I gave her a thumbs-up and tried to jog across the street. Thankfully there was no traffic, because my legs simply refused to cooperate. I shuffled across the street and pulled myself into the van using the strength of my arms.

"How's my number one son doing today?"

It must have been the tone of her voice, for it sounded almost exactly like what she said two days ago. In the future. With me and Hogan. And it caught me completely off guard.

My scattered brain jumped to Hogan, thinking of what little I knew about him, and then made the leap to Elisabeth and Sarah and Annie. Tears welled up in my eyes. I sniffed a couple of times to keep snot from rolling down my face.

"Completely exhausted. And ridiculously grateful for the ride home," I said, swallowing my tears. "Is there anything I can do to pay you back?"

"Well, your sister needs to be picked up from dance class in an hour. If you could do that, it would make getting dinner ready a lot easier."

"Deal."

"You should take a short walk when we get home before you go, just so you don't get too stiff."

I nodded silently, knowing that she was right. A couple minutes later, we pulled into the driveway. I staggered inside, tossed my backpack in my bedroom, and put Dodger on a leash, hoping that he could go find help if I couldn't make it all the way around the block.

After a short walk, I took a speed shower, downed a couple of ibuprofen, then drove to Katy's dance studio and waited in the van for her to come outside.

"What are you doing here?" she greeted me as she climbed into the passenger's seat.

"Helping Mom with dinner."

"Gotcha. You cook well in a van."

"My thoughts exactly. How'd practice go, tiny dancer?"

"My legs feel like jelly."

"I'm right there with you. After school workout was ridiculous."

"Are you glad you're doing it?"

"Well, yeah. It gives me my best chance at playing ball. Are you glad you're whittling your toes away shaking your groove thing?"

She snorted. "Yes, I love to dance. Just wait until you see the performance in Branson. You'll be amazed."

"I bet I will. It's like what Dad told me about entrepreneurs. You gotta do the hard work to build your dreams."

"One of my favorite dance teachers always says, 'Keep dancing when no one's watching, and you'll be art when everyone's watching."

"Ooh, I like that. I wonder what the baseball corollary is? Just keep swinging?"

We drove the rest of the way home trying to think of a good baseball motto, with the windows rolled down, enjoying the whistling wind.

39

October 22, 1992

Mr. Wilton greeted me as Nathan and I walked into the commons Thursday morning, cracking his knuckles and raising his eyebrows.

"Mr. Bryan, took the day off yesterday?"

"Not exactly."

"Are you plotting any mischief today?"

"Always. But we gotta get moving if we're gonna keep it a surprise."

Mr. Wilton walked quickly behind me and Nathan, all the way to our locker, and stood behind us as we both unloaded our backpacks.

He gave a gruff cough, "Mr. Bryan, mind if I join you guys on your adventures this morning?"

"Mr. Wilton, I would be delighted, as long as you keep it a secret."

"I have a lot of experience secret keeping," he said.

"Me too," I laughed.

He gave me that pointed look again, "Yes. I believe you do, Mr. Bryan. We may have to talk about those secrets one of these days."

Once again, he left me wondering just what he knew.

The Losers Club gathered in the southwest corner of the school. Noting all the worried looks on their faces, I explained, "Hey guys, Mr. Wilton wanted to join us this morning. Let's hit every classroom on the southern hall, I counted eleven of them, and the five on the eastern hall and stop at the stairs. We can start there and hit the math hall next week."

We split up and quietly snuck into the all the classrooms on the two halls, writing notes of encouragement to the teachers, thanking them for their time, commitment, and generosity. I tried not to pay any attention whatsoever to Mr. Wilton.

The not-so-random acts of kindness really didn't take very long. We finished in less than fifteen minutes and met at the top of the stairs; everyone was smiling.

"I was not expecting that," Mr. Wilton stated. "Your secret is safe with me, I promise."

"Are you gonna help us with High Five Friday tomorrow?" I asked.

"I think I'll pass, but from now on, you have my permission to proceed with all of your whimsical shenanigans."

With his blessing, the Losers Club grew into a weekly rhythm, learning to approach the monotony of school through a new set of practices. We were constantly looking for people to choose as winners, choosing new songs to sing, and adding humor and variety to the selection of after dinner mints — orange Tic-Tacs being the runaway favorite.

On one occasion, the entire varsity cheerleading squad even joined us for High Five Friday. We were making new friends and having a blast in the process.

School was becoming more than a place for memorizing facts or acquiring information that would never be used once the test was over.

School was starting to feel like a real community.

40

October 25, 1992

It took six games, not seven, for the Toronto Blue Jays to win the World Series.

"How about that? Canadian champions of our national pastime," Dad said the next morning.

"Wouldn't surprise me to see them repeat next year," I replied.

We drove my mother crazy with our baseball talk all the way to church, where I grabbed my usual cup of coffee and a donut and sat down next to Drew.

"You gonna say it?" he asked.

I knew exactly what he was talking about. "American League reigns supreme."

"Next year, though, next year's gonna be the Cubs year."

"Doubt it. Pretty sure Back To the Future II said they'd win in 2015. So, you've got that to look forward to."

"Like you can predict the future," Drew quipped.

His choice of words caught me by surprise and I felt my heart skip a beat.

"Well, of course I can. Are you saying you can't?"

He smirked at my snide remark. "You're a dork. You know that don't you?"

"Hopefully we can settle this out on the baseball field next spring."

41

November 2, 1992

Mondays at school were made bearable because of the live music before classes and the offseason program afterwards. The schooling part of school was tolerable, at best.

Dad greeted me at the kitchen table with a cup of coffee, a stack of pancakes, and several slices of bacon. "Do you know who you're gonna vote for tomorrow? It's your first Presidential election. I voted for Nixon in my first Presidential election in 1968, crook that he turned out to be, but he was still better than Humphrey."

Of course, I had heard all the news about it being an election year, but I already knew the outcome. I was completely consumed with the new adventures of the Losers Club, with trying to get into baseball shape, with staying on top of my studies, and with fading memories of my future lives to give any prolonged thought to voting. It just wasn't high on my priority list in this iteration of 1992.

"Do you know who you're voting for?" I asked.

"Yes, but you should make this decision on your own."

"I think Clinton's gonna win hands down over Bush, but Perot will get a decent percentage of the popular vote," I answered.

"You don't think Bush will stay in office as the incumbent?"

"I would be incredibly surprised."

"How about we vote together after school tomorrow? Kickapoo's our polling station."

"Sounds like a plan to me."

Later that morning, I was sitting in Calculus, tracking along as best I could, when I suddenly realized what the date was. In 2015, it was Elisabeth's 13th birthday. I was now the father of a teenager.

My eyes immediately welled up with tears. Completely overcome by the weight of where I was and when I wasn't, I ran out into the hall without saying anything to Mr. Freeman. I didn't want to be in 1992 anymore.

I didn't care about the projects of the Losers Club or offseason workouts or playing baseball. I didn't want to try and fit into high school life and pretend to be 18-year-old me. I wanted to be grown up me, even with the banged-up knee and taxes and student loan debt and car problems.

I ran into a smoke-filled bathroom and almost gagged, then responded in a fit and flurry of anger. I screamed and kicked at the wall, the trash can, the doors to the stalls, letting go of everything I had been fighting to hold inside of me.

All of the buried frustrations of life in 1992 surfaced. I hated being dependent on others for transportation; I wanted the freedom of being able to drive myself wherever I wanted to go. I was pissed that, somehow, Life had sucked me back here without my permission.

Living this life wasn't fair. Some dreams are just supposed to remain dreams, beautiful and perfect and forever unattainable. And, in the next breath, the rage vanished. I crumpled to the ground and cried, not caring the least how disgustingly dirty the floor of a boys bathroom would be.

Soul-cleansing sobs.

I mourned for my 2015 life, convinced that I would never see it again.

The bathroom door creaked open. I didn't look. I didn't care.

"Ethan? Is that you?"

I glanced over the top of my glasses and immediately recognized Joshua, even with the almost-mullet and Looney Tunes tie.

In 2015, Joshua Leaders is one of my dearest friends. An honors history teacher at Kickapoo, he and I share a love of Royals baseball, good theology, and W. P. Kinsella books. His daughter and Elisabeth both play in the Springfield Junior Youth Symphony which practices for an hour and a half on Monday nights.

While they practiced, Joshua and I share stories about life and faith and baseball. Every Monday night during the 2014 MLB postseason was a cathartic celebration after 29 years of disappointing Royals baseball.

In 1992, I knew of Joshua from church. He and his parents attended University Heights, but Joshua was a few years older than me.

After Annie and I got married, we started attending the same newlyweds Sunday school class as Joshua and his wife. It was in that class where Joshua and I discovered our mutual obsession with Royals baseball and, oddly, that we both had the same wedding rings.

"Joshua? What are you doing here?" I asked, wiping my eyes and nose on my shirt sleeve.

"Umm… It's my practicum semester. I'm sitting in the back of Mrs. Bowen's class observing. I have to do observation hours for my education courses if I want to be a teacher. The next step after observation is assisting and then finally student teaching. I can't wait. Even the observations have been pretty fun. Your sister's in the class next hour."

"Huh," I grunted. "Good for her."

"Are you ok?" Joshua sat down on the gray tiled floor next to me.

Is it possible that he would believe my story?

I took a deep breath and replied, "Are you busy after school?"

"I've got a night class tonight, but that doesn't start until 6."

"Maybe we could go get something to eat? But you'd have to drive; I don't have a car yet."

"Taco Bell's about all I can afford, but I'm more than willing to drive."

"That works for me. I'll meet you near the office after school, then?"

"Sounds good."

I stood up and walked to the sink, splashed some water on my face to try and wash away any evidence of the tears, and dried myself with a cardboard-stiff brown paper towel.

"Better?" Joshua asked.

"Getting there."

I closed my eyes for a minute, thinking back to one Monday night, when my kid and Joshua's were practicing with the symphony. We hung out for a while, talking about W. P. Kinsella's fascination with baseball and time travel.

"Shoeless Joe is by far my favorite book of his. As someone fascinated by dreams and their meanings, that story resonates in the depths of my soul," I said.

"Yeah, but everyone is in Iowa Baseball Confederacy. Roosevelt shows up to make his 'Citizenship in a Republic' speech; Leonardo da Vinci arrives in a hot air balloon and makes it known that he actually invented baseball; Three Finger Brown pitches a gem for more than 2,200 innings; and Tinkers to Evers to Chance are turning double plays the whole time.

"That said," Joshua continued, "My favorite Kinsella quote is in Shoeless Joe. I memorized it years ago so I can recite it to my class every spring."

He closed his eyes and spoke as if he were reciting poetry.

Immediately I replied with my own quote from Shoeless Joe. We went on like that for almost an hour. I never thought in a million years I'd be sitting with him trying to convince him that our sci-fi dreams of time travel were indeed possible.

After ordering a half dozen tacos, we sat down in the same booth where I first tried to convince Nathan that I was from the future. This time, I decided to shoot straight.

"Joshua, I know you love the Royals and the writings of W. P. Kinsella," I started. "You have an incredible collection of Royals' memorabilia and an equally impressive collection of baseball books. You once submitted a story to Spitball Magazine and were thrilled that they not only accepted and printed it, they also sent you a free copy of that issue. You were a fantastic basketball player at Glendale, a point-guard, and just missed making a three-pointer at the buzzer to win what became the last game of your senior year."

I continued, rattling off every bit of information I could think of, "You thought about going to college on the east coast, but wanted to be able to make weekend trips to KC with your friends and family to watch the Royals play. You can't stand the taste of beer and are considering taking the assistant basketball coaching job at Jarrett Junior High next spring, even though the pay is horrible. You think that the Calvin and Hobbes and Peanuts comic strips are equal parts theology and humor. I know that your senior thesis at Drury University detailed the historic stories of downtown Springfield and that you had to get special permission from your advisor to pursue such a project. Most importantly, you are one of the best poets I have ever read. I carry two of your books with me any time I travel."

With each phrase, Joshua's eyes grew wider, and by the last statement, he had stopped eating and simply stared at me. Leaning in close, he whispered, "How do you know all that?"

"I'm from the future. You and I are really good friends in 2015. I know the results of for the first time in decades, thanks to the third-party influence of Perot. Clinton gets somewhere just north of 40%. Bush doubles Perot's votes, but neither one seriously contends."

"And how do you know that?"

"Because tomorrow's the first Presidential election I can vote in, and you just remember stuff like that from your first election."

"So...you were crying on the floor in the bathroom because..."

"Because today is my oldest daughter's 13th birthday. Your daughter will also turn 13 in just a couple of weeks. They both play violin in the same junior symphony and we visit while they are at practice."

"I have a daughter?"

"You have three. And a son. You waited a few years to get married; your wife is about my age. And you're a history teacher at Kickapoo, in a classroom just around the corner from Mrs. Bowen's room. You are a fantastic teacher and even won a national award once for some research and writing you did."

For the next ten minutes, neither one of us said much of anything, which was fine by both of us. Tacos needed to be eaten.

"So, how did you get here? Why are you here in 1992?"

"That, my friend, is the real question."

After I answered the majority of Joshua's questions, he graciously gave me a ride home. I knew he needed some space to think through everything I had said.

We agreed to visit again at church on Sunday. I felt a little better knowing there were now two people in my corner, helping me try to make some sense out of this quixotic journey.

42

November 3, 1992

For the second time in my life, Dad and I went to Kickapoo High School together so I could vote in my first Presidential election. And I voted for the same guy again, this time already knowing what the outcome would be. When I got home, I stuck the "I voted" sticker on my guitar case.

No sooner did I get home than Mom yelled, "Ethan! Phone!"

"Got it!" I hollered back, stretching the cord across the bed and pinning the earpiece against my shoulder so I could begin playing some RBI Baseball. After quickly blowing into the cartridge, I spoke, "Hello?"

"Ethan, this is Joshua. How are you doing today?"

"Hey Joshua! I'm better, honestly. Just pressing on after a really rough day the other day."

"Good call on the election results."

"Even blind squirrels find acorns."

"I guess so. Are you familiar with the butterfly effect?"

"Yep. It's a really bad movie with Ashton Kutcher. Let me save you some time and money, don't see it."

"What?"

"Seriously, bad movie."

"The butterfly effect…"

"I know, I know all about the butterfly effect and the murdering your grandfather conundrum and half a dozen other things that all time travel stories seem to have in common. And in almost every sci-fi story, nothing good comes from time travel. Well, except for *Harry Potter*, but you wouldn't know anything about that yet. So, I'm just trying to re-live my senior year."

"Except you wanna play baseball instead of golf?"

"Exactly."

"And the stuff you're doing with the Losers Club?"

"Yep."

"And you don't think that doing those things isn't going to completely change the rest of your life?"

I didn't know what to say. Should I tell him about my weekend with Hogan? I didn't even know how to explain what happened. I kept quiet and he resumed talking.

"You need to be really careful. Listen, I'm not a big fan of talking on the phone. Let's still plan on meeting after church on Sunday."

"I'll be there."

43

November 6, 1992

"A high five for you and a high five for you," I shouted, channeling my inner-Oprah. "Everybody gets high fives for coming to school! Woohoo! Thanksgiving break's getting closer too, so better load up on extra high fives to make it through!"

The Losers Club formed a gauntlet line right in the center of the commons area. With the assistance of a couple of cheerleaders, a couple of football players, and a couple of basketball players, we convinced almost everyone to run the high five gauntlet.

Just before the bell rang I caught a glimpse of Mr. Wilton watching us from the band hall; he was smiling.

That night, the first Friday night of November, it was cold enough to see your own breath. Cold enough a swing that didn't hit the club's sweet spot would reverberate all the way to your shoulder.

In my opinion, no one should have been at the driving range. For some odd reason, however, there was a steady stream of customers, the majority of whom told me they were preparing for a city-wide, two-day scramble tournament.

"It's always held the first weekend of November, no matter what the weather's like. That way, there's enough time to count the money and make a good donation to the Ozarks Food Harvest from the proceeds. We actually played in an early snow a couple of years ago. It was hilarious. The golf was horrible, but we still had a pretty good time," one regular customer told me.

Ken took the night off, figuring that I wouldn't have any trouble picking the range in between the few who might dare come out. Instead, I worked close to midnight trying to do two people's jobs.

When I finally got home, I crawled straight into bed, figuring that many of the same people would be back on Saturday night.

Early the next morning, after his daily jog, Dad made a quick trip to St. George's donut shop and brought home a dozen fresh donuts for the family including a couple of my favorites: chocolate cake with chocolate icing.

Unable to fall back asleep, I crawled out of bed shortly after 7:00 and headed straight for the kitchen to brew a pot of coffee.

"Surprised to see you up at this hour," Dad greeted me, "You seemed to be out pretty late last night. Good night at the range?"

"It was nuts," I answered with my morning-bass voice. "Whole bunch of golfers getting ready for some scramble tournament this weekend. Expecting the same tonight."

"You up for a small adventure? We can be back mid-afternoon even, in case you need to rest before work tonight."

"What about Mom and Katy?"

"Mom's taking Katy to Branson; she's got dress rehearsals all day for the December shows."

"How soon would we need to leave?"

"Thirty minutes would be perfect."

"Anything special I need to bring?"

"Wear layers."

Dad made a few trips from his office to the car, carrying bags and boxes and stuff. I didn't pay much attention to what he was doing as I was too busy figuring out what to wear and looking for a good sock hat and pair of gloves.

"Ready," Dad called out from the garage, "I'll be in the car!"

I grabbed a couple of donuts on the way to the garage and walked toward the passenger's side of the Taurus before I noticed Dad was already sitting there. "Driver's seat is all yours, Chief. I'll give you the directions as you need them."

Slowly backing out of the garage, careful not to hit the rearview mirror, I asked, "Where we headed?"

"North."

After about an hour of driving, Dad had me turn onto a dirt road in the middle of nowhere. "Just stay on the path and go slow. When you're surrounded by trees and don't see the trail any more, we're there.

"As you know, I grew up in Colorado with cousin Bruce. Most every weekend, we were out and about in the foothills of the mountains hunting whatever we could find — rabbits, rattlesnakes, rocks, you name it. And it occurred to me that you've never really had much experience around guns. A man needs to know how to safely and properly use a gun. You've never expressed much interest in serving in the military, so I thought that I could teach you the basics of gun safety, just in case you ever needed to fire one."

"I'm not gonna have to shoot anything living, am I?"

Dad laughed, "Just clay pigeons, soda cans, and bulls-eye targets."

We started with the revolver, a silver Ruger Vaquero six-shooter. Setting up the bulls-eye targets at a distance of ten paces, what Dad thought might be pretty easy, my first shots completely missed the paper.

Dad gave me a few basic tips — stance and gently squeezing the trigger — and I started hitting the target. When I closed my non-dominant eye, I was considerably more accurate still.

"Part of this is learning how to shoot a gun; part of it is learning about yourself. It takes courage to do something new, and even more courage to then do something new your way. Having the courage to take risks is an important part of growing up. So is having the wisdom to know when not to take the risk."

We shot the rifle second, an old .22 my uncle had given me. Of the three guns, the rifle came most naturally. I couldn't shoot it near as fast as Dad, but I was at least hitting all the soda cans I was aiming at.

It only took one shot to learn the importance of proper handling techniques with the shotgun. When I got the hang of securing the butt of the gun into my shoulder and getting my cheek on the stock, Dad started smiling.

"Ready for a moving target?"

Dad grabbed a couple of clay pigeons and a hand-held throwing device. "Be sure to lead it just a little bit and pull the trigger smoothly."

It took more than 30 clay pigeons before I finally hit two in a row. I was dripping in sweat and smiling from ear to ear.

"Getting hungry yet?" Dad asked.

"Starving."

"I know an awesome hole-in-the-wall pizza place about halfway back to town. Supreme minus the onions?"

"Perfect."

I had no memories of going shooting with Dad my first time in school.

"So, what gave you the idea to take me shooting?"

"My dad never did stuff like that with me. He was a loner," Dad said as I headed back south on the highway. "When you were born, I made up my mind to be different than my dad. The real reason I wanted to take you shooting is I wanted you to hear me say that I am very proud of you and always will be. Don't ever doubt that."

All of a sudden, I had an overwhelming urge to tell Dad all about his wreck that would take place the day I'd graduate from college. I wanted to warn him, to tell him to run just a little late or come extra early.

I tried to think of some way to say it, but I kept hearing Joshua's words of warning — *you need to be really careful.*

Instead I mumbled, "Thanks, Dad. That was a lot of fun. I really had a good time."

Twenty minutes later, we were sitting in the back of a dark restaurant, in a booth with torn red fake-leather cushions at a heavy oak table. The walls were covered with posters of a variety of sports teams and autographed pictures of Branson musicians who had graced this place at some point in time. In the corner stood two video game consoles, Frogger and Ms. Pac-Man.

After Dad ordered the pizza and a pitcher of Coke, I challenged him to a couple rounds while we waited, "Bet I can beat you at Frogger. Winner gets bragging rights."

"Not a chance!"

44

November 8, 1992

In Sunday school, I told Drew all about shooting guns with Dad.

"If you guys go again, I'd love to come along."

"I'll let Dad know, but no promises."

During the worship service, I couldn't sit still on the wooden pews. My legs were twitching and my feet were bouncing; my mind was already gearing up for my conversation with Joshua.

After the choir sang the offertory, an upbeat arrangement of "Soon and Very Soon" including an attempt at coordinated swaying, Pastor Gibson walked up to the large wooden pulpit, holding tight to the typed-out sermon in his hands, wearing his black preaching robe and gold and white stole.

Placing the papers on the pulpit, he adjusted his glasses, leaned forward ever so slightly, and grabbed both sides of the pulpit.

"God is not bound by our constraints," his bass voice resonated throughout the sanctuary and immediately stilled the jitters in my body. "The One who holds all things in the universe together, the Voice who sang all of creation into being, the Spirit who hears the prayers of the billions, the Word who is our salvation, is not limited by our understandings of time or space or the known laws of the universe.

"We label and define, systematize our theologies, grasping for ways to control or manipulate or even judge God, desperate to understand why certain things happen, why our world is so messed up. With fists tight, clinging to the smallest kernels of truth, we are braced to fight against anyone who attacks our faith or offends our preferences, as if God needs a bodyguard.

"Jesus, whose parents could barely afford a pair of pigeons to sacrifice at the temple, did not take advantage of his divinity and shove religion down our throats or entertain us like a street magician at our every whim and request. Jesus stepped into the world he created and experienced the same daily struggles we do — taxes and friends who don't understand and those who abuse their positions of power and take advantage of others at every opportunity possible.

"He knows the temptations we face and the frustrating limitations of an out-of-order creation and the pain of rejection. And he chose to love with reckless abandon, to trust that, despite how the circumstances looked, that God the Father was weaving together an epic story for the redemption of all of creation. After he was resurrected, Jesus sat down at the table of the feast of all ages, and pulled up a chair for everyone to join him.

"He got the attention of an obsessive-compulsive rule follower by knocking him off his…donkey…and sent him out across the Middle East and Europe. This guy was more like us than we dare to believe. He wrote letters to his friends, to these small gatherings of people throughout the Roman Empire, reminding them that the same Spirit who raised Jesus from the dead now resides in them, that they do not need to live by fear whatsoever, that God is pulling them to Him and doing new things in their midst, bringing heaven to earth.

"Too often, as Jesus followers, we are taught to shut down or ignore our imaginations, they can only lead us astray. But we need musicians and artists and those who challenge all of our conventional ways of approaching life to help loosen our fists and let go of the instinct to fight, daring to dream again of how we can conspire with God, partnering across racial and denominational lines so that those nearest to us can taste the goodness of the coming kingdom of God.

"God is not bound. No, we are the ones who time and time again attempt to bind God, refusing to step out of the boat and believe that maybe, just maybe, he's wanting to work a miracle through us."

And then Pastor Gibson sat down, without uttering a prayer or offering a formal invitation or doing anything that preachers usually do when they finish a sermon.

I looked at the clock hanging on the face of the balcony; the sermon was just a little longer than five minutes. It was so short and the ending so abrupt that the minister of music was completely caught off-guard and fumbled with a hymnal as the organist rushed to the organ to start the hymn of invitation.

"Yes, so, will you stand with me and sing, uhm, hymn number..."

But my mind was lost to the words of the music minister and whatever hymn was sung. I was busy replaying the last sentence of Pastor Gibson, "Maybe, just maybe, he's wanting to work a miracle through us."

I wrote the words down on the back of an offering envelope and stared at that last sentence. Is that why I'm here? To be part of some miracle? Hey God, I'm listening and I'm willing to step out of the boat, but a little direction would be nice. As the song concluded, I folded the envelope in half and stuffed it into my back pocket.

After the service, I found Joshua in the narthex, standing near his parents who were helping to serve the coffee and donuts.

"Nice tie," I said.

"Wile E. Coyote..."

"Pure genius. Lunch?"

"How about Fuddrucker's?"

"A man after my own heart."

We drove across town to Fuddrucker's, ordered a couple of half-pound bacon cheeseburgers, and settled into a booth.

"I hate to ask," Joshua said, "but what have you done this time through 1992 that you didn't do the first time?"

"There's the Losers Club stuff, playing guitar, offseason workouts, and I went to my wife's high school football game. Yesterday, Dad and I went shooting guns, and I really wanted to tell him about the horrible crash he's gonna have in a few years, but I didn't." Once again, I intentionally made no mention of Hogan.

Joshua ate a couple fries, carefully thinking through his response.

"Have you considered what would happen if you didn't make the baseball team?"

"Not really."

"And you're positive that's why you're here?"

"I don't think it was coincidence that I was dreaming it when whatever wormhole sucked me back here opened up. I think I'm supposed to play baseball. Then whatever cosmic tumblers sent me here can send me back," I shot at him, referencing *Shoeless Joe*.

Joshua smiled, "Cosmic tumblers, nice."

"I thought you'd like that," I smirked.

"You do know there's no way your 2015 life will be the same if and when you get back there. Your choices in the past can't help but affect your future and you are choosing to make an entirely different past."

"But I'm not going to gamble or buy stock and try to make my future-self rich," I protested, thinking of the room full of guitars and amps. "I'm not going to try and date my future wife. I'm not going to attend to a different college or drop out of high school or pretend to invent new technologies or make friends with people who'll become famous. It's just baseball. I'm just going to play baseball. I just *need* to play baseball."

"Ethan, you and I both know there's no such thing as 'just baseball,'" Joshua said with a wink.

I tried to smile, but my heart wasn't in it. I had suddenly lost my appetite afraid I had screwed up my future. No Annie. No Elisabeth. No Sarah.

"I didn't do this to myself, you know," my voice was louder than I intended. "If I could get back to 2015 now, I'd go. I'd leave all this. In a heartbeat. But there's no ruby red slippers or wardrobes or no magic words. So I'm just trying to make the most of the time I've been given here and..."

"Hey, hey, hey, hold on a second, just...stop. Take a breath," Joshua looked me straight in the eyes, "I know it's not your fault. I believe you. I'm on your side. I can't imagine how I'd feel if I were in your place."

I took a drink and unclenched my fists.

"Thanks. I needed to hear that. So...any wise words to live by until baseball season starts?"

Joshua took a couple of bites while he thought through the implications of my question.

"Trust your gut."

45

November 9, 1992

After the last bell rang, I rushed to the locker to drop off my books and asked Nathan to walk with me for a minute.

"Where're we headed?"

"I don't want to be late to offseason, but there's someone I want you to meet."

We quickly made the way through the uber-crowded halls toward Mrs. Bowen's room, where we found Joshua, still sitting in the back, working on filling out some paperwork.

"Having fun yet?" I called out.

"Living the dream."

"Joshua, this is Nathan. He's one of my best friends. Nathan, this is Joshua. He, too, is one of my best friends, back where I'm from."

Nathan raised his eyebrows and quietly asked, "He knows?"

"Yeah, he knows. I just thought you two should know each other, just in case something happens."

"Good idea," Joshua stood up and extended his hand toward Nathan, "Good to meet you."

"You too."

"Only 15 weeks until tryouts start."

"Always baseball." Joshua commented and shook his head, somewhat sarcastic, somewhat serious.

"That's why I'm here."

"Is he like this with you too?" Joshua asked.

"Yeah, when it's not Loser's Club stuff."

"But what if it's not all about baseball?"

I could feel the doubt and confusion already warring inside. Baseball had always been my dream; maybe this was my chance to live that dream out.

What if playing ball in high school prepared me for a bigger and better ministry? What if baseball became my ministry? Maybe I'd be one of those athletes that lived out their faith on and off the field?

"Guys, I still have to make the team first," I said. "One pitch at a time, right?"

46

November 10, 1992

Mr. O'Neal spotted me doing tray duty at lunch and motioned me to join him in the hall.

"I just got an envelope from the Kiwanis Club. Thought you might want to see what they have to say."

We walked quickly to his office; I was too nervous to say much of anything. Mr. O'Neal opened the envelope and scanned the letter before handing it to me, but his eyes and smile gave away the letter's contents.

"Congratulations! Job well done! Looks like they want you to come to a meeting next Tuesday night to read your essay and accept the prize."

I was positively beaming and couldn't wait to call Mom and Dad to tell them the good news. Mr. O'Neal let me borrow his phone so I wouldn't have to use the pay phone in the front hall.

Mom answered on the third ring, "Hello?"

"Mom remember that essay contest I told you about? I won!" I said like one ridiculously long word.

"Say again?"

"I won the essay contest!"

That night, Mom and Dad let me choose where to eat as a celebration. I voted for cashew chicken and Dr Pepper. Katy and I began the dinner festivities blowing our straw wrappers at one another.

I successfully reloaded my straw, only to accidentally shoot the wrapper into the gray-haired perm sitting in the booth behind Katy. We both collapsed in fits of laughter.

Once the food was served, the real conversation began, a quizzing of sorts in regards to the new scholarship.

"Will this scholarship affect where you go to school?" Katy asked.

"No, I'm still planning on SMSU."

"But it's good for any school in the state, right?" Mom followed up.

"It's good for any school in the country," I answered.

"Why are you so set on SMSU?" Dad asked.

The large bite of cashew chicken stuffed in my cheeks gave me extra time to think of an appropriate response. "I guess I'm just a homebody. I like it here. Maybe I'll use it to live on campus. I've actually thought about trying to walk on the baseball team, they've got a great program. Really, I'm just happy for the help."

Mom agreed, "We're proud of you, both of you."

Katy smirked, then busted a fortune cookie open on the table with a loud pop as the plastic wrapper contained most of the crumbled cookie pieces.

"That was awesome," I said and immediately followed suit.

The remainder of dinner was spend debating which aphorism was intended for whom.

Mine read, "Hope creates miracles."

I carefully folded it in half and placed it in my wallet.

47

November 15, 1992

I woke up to a strangely quiet house. Dodger was sitting by the back door, whining and wagging his tail, watching the snow and sleet fall — his first winter.

"Go on boy," I said, opening the sliding glass door, "Go chase a squirrel."

Walking into the kitchen, I found a note on the table.

"Mom and I left early to go to church. Drive carefully. Roads will be slick. Keys are on my dresser."

"Katy!" I yelled, "Wake up!"

A few minutes later, Katy stumbled out into the living room, the after-effects of another long and late Saturday of dance practice.

"Where's Mom and Dad?" she asked through a yawn.

"They've already gone to church. Dad left a note on the table. We should probably leave pretty soon if we wanna get there on time."

"And you're comfortable driving in this stuff?"

"No worries. I've got years of experience."

We arrived at Sunday school only a few minutes late to a class less than half of its normal size.

"Welcome, Bryans," Paula said with a smile. "Glad to see you guys made it. Looks like we'll have a pretty small group."

The planned Sunday school lesson was postponed; the eight of us who braved the elements talked about school and just about anything and everything else. I walked back downstairs with Drew to the sanctuary. Opening the large wooden doors, I grabbed a bulletin off the back pew and spotted Dad already seated on the left side, only a few rows back from the front.

"As soon as the service is over, you and Katy head straight home. Your mom and I will pick up lunch and meet you there."

The snow and sleet mix continued throughout the morning. Throughout the worship service, in the quiet, still moments, I could hear the soft percussive clicks as the sleet hit the stained-glass windows. Again, Pastor Gibson preached a short message. This time, I think, it was more in recognition of the weather outside and awareness of the average age of this congregation.

After the benediction, Katy and I made a beeline for the car. I got a kick out of running and sliding on the ice-covered asphalt. Katy's legs were still quite stiff and sore, especially after sitting the majority of the last two hours.

"If I try something like that, I'll wind up on my butt," she stated.

I started the car and scraped off the ice, waiting for the engine to warm up at least a little bit.

"You know I'm in Driver's Ed this semester, right?" Katy asked as I buckled in.

"Yeah...?"

"Well, we were talking about driving in these conditions on Friday and the teacher said that we're supposed to 'turn into the skid,' but I don't really know what that means."

And I remembered.

I remembered thinking that I'd be a good big brother and teach her how to maneuver a car through a skid on ice. I remembered accelerating through a turn and driving straight into the curb, significantly bending the frame of Dad's work car.

I remembered going car shopping with Dad the next week and watching him choose a powder blue Mercury Topaz. I always loved the color of that car. And I remembered seeing the Topaz flipped on its top, with the driver's side completely demolished, glass everywhere.

"You remember our house on Portland Street? There's a Presbyterian church across the street that has an open parking lot. Dad used to take me over there in the puke green Pontiac Catalina and let me practice driving donuts on the ice. I bet, if you asked him, he'd love to give you donut lessons, too."

"You sure you can't just give me a couple of pointers?"

Sounding just like my Dad I replied, "No need to take a risk in weather like this. Drive safe and smart."

I could feel my heart pounding. I had intentionally radically altered my past. I decided I wouldn't tell Joshua, there was nothing he could do about it anyway. I drove slowly and stayed on the main roads. Katy and I made it home without incident. Mom and Dad followed a few minutes later with spaghetti and meatballs and hot rolls from Pasta Express.

"Hey Dad, can you teach me how to drive on the ice?" Katy asked as soon as he stepped in the door.

"Sure. We can go to the back parking lot at Kickapoo. I think I had as much fun teaching your brother as he did spinning the car in circles."

After lunch, I spent the remainder of Sunday afternoon trying to teach Dodger how to play fetch and watching the Chiefs, 49ers, and Broncos all win.

48

November 17, 1992

I dressed my best, wearing the only sport coat I owned and tying a perfect Windsor knot in one of my favorite ties, excited for the presentation at the Kiwanis Club. I even took the time to carefully shave my peach-fuzz mustache.

"Lookin' sharp, Chief!" Dad commented as I swaggered into the living room.

Katy and Mom were again at a dance rehearsal; the Christmas show season in Branson would be in full swing the day after Thanksgiving, only ten days away.

"Nervous?"

"Nope. I'm proud of what I wrote. Reading it will be a breeze. Ready?"

Dad reached down and picked up the large bag containing the video camera. "Bought a new tape and made sure both batteries were charged. Figured your grandmas and aunts and uncles would like to see it at Christmas."

"You know, one of these days those things are gonna fit in the palm of our hands."

We climbed into the Taurus; Dad and Katy were incident-free in their Sunday afternoon ice driving escapades.

"I've never been to a Kiwanis meeting before," Dad said.

"Ditto."

The drive across town was quiet except for the radio. I stared out the window, imagining buildings and businesses from 2015 imposed over the current landscape. We pulled into a poorly lit parking lot and Dad shut off the engine.

"*Carpe diem*," he whispered, reaching for the camera in the back seat.

Carpe diem.

As soon as we walked in the building we were greeted by Santa Claus in a business suit.

"Evening, gentlemen! I'm Terry. I am assuming you're Ethan?"

"Yessir," I answered, shaking his hand. "Impressive beard."

"Almost Santa time. Best part of the year, even when a kid pees in your lap."

"That depends on whose lap."

"Mr. Lawson wanted me to keep my eye out for y'all. Said he needed to visit with you as soon as you arrived. If you'll just follow me…"

Dad and I followed Santa-Terry down the hall into some kind of office.

"Mr. Lawson, this here's Ethan and…"

"That's my dad, Dr. Doug Bryan," I said, putting extra emphasis on the "Dr." part of the introduction. I always liked being able to say that.

"Chad Lawson, pleasure to meet both of you. Please, have a seat. Terry, if you'll give us a minute."

Chad Lawson looked like he belonged on Wall Street, not at the Kiwanis Club. Dad and I sat down in a pair of folding chairs and Terry exited, slamming the door behind him. I almost jumped out of my seat.

"Oops, sorry about that," Terry said, re-opening the door, then slamming it shut again.

Mr. Lawson shook his head.

"Ethan, in the ten years we've held this essay contest, yours is, by far, one of the best we've ever read."

My head started turning a nice shade of red.

"But we made a mistake. Your essay should never have been accepted in the first place. One of the first rules listed," he paused, turning around to grab an entry sheet from the top of his desk and handing it to me, "states that the essay must not contain any information whatsoever about the author's high school.

"On the final page of your essay, you mentioned Kickapoo High School twice. Your essay should have been disqualified immediately."

I quickly skimmed over the rules sheet. "So, what's going to happen?" I asked quietly.

"The scholarship, I'm sorry to say, will be awarded to someone else. You are most welcome to stay for the program tonight, to read your essay and be acknowledged as the runner-up. I'm sorry, I really am. My deepest apologies on behalf of the entire Kiwanis organization for having to tell you in this manner."

I could tell by the way he stood up that Dad was furious, ready to unleash a verbal torrent in my defense.

"That's okay, Mr. Lawson. I broke the rules, I understand. It's my fault. If it's all the same to you, I think we'll just leave," I said quietly, standing up alongside Dad.

"I completely understand."

I turned around, my shoulders hung heavy as I reached for the door knob.

"Hey, Ethan? This really is one of the best essays I've ever read. You should look into writing as a career."

I nodded and mouthed the words, "Thank you," unable to get my vocal chords to cooperate. Neither Dad nor I said a word the entire drive home. Even though it was still early, I went straight to bed.

49

November 18, 1992

I really did look forward to the daily adventures of the Losers Club. Wednesdays were particularly fun, as word started to spread and people in the school wondered who would be chosen as the next "Winner."

Amelia and Stacie had a fantastic idea; they wanted to film and photograph the reactions of those selected.

"It could make a pretty cool scrapbook, maybe even a neat video montage like on *America's Funniest Home Videos.* Instead of people getting scared or hurt or embarrassing themselves, it would be a video of people being surprised to find that they were that week's Winner," Amelia explained.

Bethany was the first person they decided to try and record. A precocious young woman with Down's Syndrome, everyone in the school knew Bethany. Even though she was significantly smaller than everyone else her age, her big personality made up for it.

Bethany might have been the only person never to have a bad day. Stacie and Amelia did a phenomenal job of decorating her locker and as soon as Bethany saw it and read the word "Winner!" she started dancing. Bethany does not know how to dance alone, so after two or three minutes of inviting everyone she saw to join in her celebration, the hallway was packed with people clapping and cheering, forming a circle around Bethany, including the entire Losers Club.

"Sometimes, you just gotta dance," Junior shouted, as he hopped into the circle with Bethany.

When the bell rang, Amelia and Stacie presented her with a gift card to Andy's, and even said that one of them would follow up with Bethany's parents after school and explain about the weekly acts of encouragement.

As soon as I got to French class, I tore out a piece of paper and wrote down Junior's words, "Sometimes, you just gotta dance." Carefully folding the paper into eighths, I shoved it in my back pocket as a reminder for the remainder of the day.

The next day in English, we were all excited for the note passing to begin.

"I called Bethany's parents last night and Bethany picked up the phone toward the end of the conversation. She said, 'Thank you for being my friend,'" Stacie wrote.

Amelia pulled out Kleenex from her purse and dried her eyes. The "men" of the Losers Club just blinked quite rapidly.

50

November 20, 1992

"Madrigal Singers, if you could stay after class for just a few minutes, I'll write y'all passes for your next class," Mrs. Mullins said as we finished working on an arrangement of "Carol of the Bells."

Any excuse to be late for Calculus was fine by me.

The bell rang and the majority of the choir departed.

"Friends, I have some good news. As of 8:00 this morning, we have been invited to sing at Silver Dollar City in December."

My family has had season passes to Silver Dollar City for years. Silver Dollar City is an 1880's-themed park in Branson, Missouri that used to literally give change in silver dollars.

Back in the early 1980s, the workers in the park would stage humorous street shows using character names and cap guns. There were heroes to root for and villains to boot. There was even an undertaker who walked around the park measuring people named Digger Deeper.

Even in 2015, my family has season passes, as Elisabeth loves riding the roller coasters, Sarah loves going with friends, and we all love fresh taffy, frozen lemonade, and the fun shows.

"We'll be singing two shows at the gazebo, as well as some quartets at various places around the park. I'll have the date and times of our performances as well as a permission slip that your parents will need to sign ready on Monday. If you need a pass to get to your next class, stick around and I'll get you one."

I really didn't care if Mr. Freeman counted me tardy, so I started shuffling toward the exit.

Mrs. Mullins called out to me, "Ethan, plan on bringing your guitar for the group performances. I'm sure there's some place where we can keep it safe while you're wandering the park."

I gave her a thumbs up, privately thinking that doing the right thing and making the world a better place could be exhausting sometimes.

51

November 26, 1992

There were only two days of school leading into Thanksgiving break, allowing for a brief respite before running full steam into the chaos of December.

My family intentionally decided to stay at home and have a low-key Thanksgiving celebration, spending some time together before we went all over southern Missouri — dancing in Branson, singing at Silver Dollar City, and, eventually, celebrating Christmas at Grandmon's on the other side of the state.

Mom cooked her traditional Thanksgiving meal: lasagna, strawberry salad, green bean casserole, and raspberry brownies. We took time sharing things for which we were thankful as we ate.

Mom started, "I'm thankful to share all of life's adventures with the people around this table."

Dad continued, "I'm thankful for lasagna, for brownies, and for two kids who never cease to amaze me."

I was next. "I'm thankful for friends who drive me to school, for a Dad who lets me borrow his car whenever I want, and that I'm almost finished with high school."

Dad raised his eyebrows and smirked, "Whenever you want?"

Katy started before I could think of a response, "I'm thankful for the chance to dance in Branson. And I'll be even more thankful when it's January and I'm finished dancing in Branson."

"Yeah, except we've got finals as soon as we get back to school in January," I grumbled.

"Finals are just the big boss at the end of the level."

"Come again?" Mom asked.

"So much of school just feels like you're playing a game," Katy continued. "Everyone knows tests don't really measure learning. Tests don't inspire exploration or curiosity or questions. The only question students ask is, 'Will this stuff be on the test?' Schools have tests and attendance policies just so they can get more money from the government. It's a business more than anything, some place kids can go while their parents go to work."

Katy said it all in one breath. I tried not to stare at her. I had no idea she felt this way.

She glanced over at me for support and continued her speech, "I think a lot of my friends and classmates are brilliant people, but we've tried to cram them into a system where everyone has to perform the same way. Learning happens when we have the courage to think for ourselves, not when we all try to get the same answers. And the students who are losing the game are those who would probably make the most brilliant contributions to society if we could create space to let them learn in their own styles."

"Interesting thoughts," Dad said. "What are you going to do about it?"

"Mentoring and apprenticeships," Katy chimed in. "That's been around for centuries. You seek out a mentor who will teach you how to do what they do."

"Isn't that what school is, though? You have mentors, your teachers, who are trying to teach you what they know so you'll succeed," Mom said.

"Mom, teachers have so many students, so many different classes. Only a couple of teachers know anything about me more than I'm just the bald kid in the school," I retorted, sounding far more cynical than I intended.

"I don't really have any answers, but I know exactly what Katy's saying. It's frustrating to feel trapped inside the system, knowing deep down in my gut there's gotta be a better way, but at the same point I've only got a few more months until I graduate so why care so much, right? The only thing I know right now, is that I'd really like some more lasagna."

"Oh! Ethan! I completely forgot to tell you that Mr. Wilton called last week," Mom said.

As soon as she said his name, my heart skipped a beat. "And?"

"He asked if I knew anything about the stuff that you and your friends have been doing at school. He said that we should be really proud of what you're doing, that the staff and teachers have noticed and it's making a difference at the school."

"He said he could keep a secret."

Dad added, "Like I said, two kids who never cease to amaze me."

After our family feast, Dad and I watched some football and helped Mom and Katy get Christmas decorations down from the attic during halftime of the Detroit Lions and Houston Oilers game.

For the remainder of the day, Mom and Katy slowly transformed the interior of the house using lights and stockings and decorating the artificial tree with an abundance of picture-filled ornaments. My primary responsibility was to help Dad rearrange furniture. By the time the Dallas Cowboys game kicked off, everyone was finally settled down, together, enjoying multiple helpings of Mom's brownies topped with Andy's frozen custard.

52

November 27, 1992

"Opening night! Break a leg, Katy! If you can get extra tickets for tomorrow night, Nathan told me again that he'd like to come."

"Pretty sure I've got four tickets. If he wants to come, that's fine by me. Most of my friends are coming in December."

The bizarre snow and ice storm of mid-November had long since melted; a perfectly mild Friday night meant I'd be working at the range while Mom and Dad went to Katy's first performance in Branson. Thanks to the end of Daylight Saving Time, it was dark outside before 6:00. Unless there was another slew of customers prepping for some unknown tournament, I'd be able to leave by 7:00.

I called Joshua and left a message on his answering machine, seeing if he'd have any interest in going to a late movie or just meeting to hang out. He returned my call just as I emptied the cash register and flipped the sign from "open" to "closed."

Thirty minutes later, we met at the movie theater to watch Denzel Washington's portrayal of *Malcolm X*. After the movie, we stopped at McDonald's for a late-night snack and processed the movie for the next hour.

"I studied Malcolm for a couple of semesters," Joshua said. "He was a brilliant man and I don't think that Martin Luther King, Jr. would have been successful without him. He once said, 'The media's the most powerful entity on earth. They have the power to make the innocent guilty and to make the guilty innocent, and that's power. Because they control the minds of the masses.' I wonder how he'd feel about being featured in a commercial movie."

"I can't imagine what Malcolm would think about the media in 2015. It is nearly impossible to escape its never-ending noise and chatter. Everyone has a story, and everyone's story is spun to make them look good or someone else look worse. And *everyone's* story is for sale, for the right price. Print media struggle to stay financially viable, while electronic media feed into our addictions to always stay in the know or forever suffer the 'fear of missing out.' It's almost impossible to know who is telling the truth.

"Conspiracy theorists have a heyday while conservatives and liberals alike just call each other names and point fingers instead of working together. Those in power in Washington make so much more money they live in alternate universe; they have no idea what 'real life' is like for the majority of the US."

Joshua raised his eyebrows and opened wide his eyes. I could tell I caught him off guard and tried to explain myself.

"So many lobbyists, so many laws, so much meaningless debate and finger pointing across party lines while the average person is just trying to make ends meet and keep their kids healthy and out of the hospital. I bet they couldn't survive a month trying to live like a normal person on an average salary. It feels like they're just too rich to care. But I could be wrong. What do I know? Government's your thing."

"Money and power can be a very dangerous combination."

"The richer you are, the more tax breaks you get. We need a new revolution reminding us of the beauty of all persons being equal. We need another Malcolm or Martin who has the courage to speak truth to power."

"Power, ultimately, is a gift of God, entrusted to people so they can help those on the fringes of life. Too often, though, those in power use it for self-centered purposes, and we do need voices who help us remember power's place and purpose."

"Amen! Keep preaching!"

"You do know how weird all of this sounds coming from a 41-year-old guy trapped in an 18-year-old body, right?"

"Touché."

53

November 28, 1992

Katy was in the first dance number and had to be in costume an hour before the show started. We picked up Nathan on the way, heading to Branson via Nixa, and grabbed a late afternoon meal at Burger King.

Shoji Tabuchi is a Japanese-American country music fiddler who performs in a family variety show featuring multiple genres of arrangements of favorite songs of Americana. In 1990, he built an elaborate theater on the Shepherd of the Hills Expressway and is still going strong in 2015.

We were allowed into the theater before the doors technically opened because we were family of one of the performers. Nathan and Dad and I passed the time playing nine-ball and cutthroat on the pool table in the men's restroom while Mom tried to help Katy with costume and makeup backstage.

When the lights finally blinked off and on to signal the start of the show, we made our way to our seats, comfortably located just off-center stage in the middle of the theater. Mom met us there, "She looks gorgeous. There's just a buzz of excitement backstage. Everyone's ready for the show to start."

The lights dimmed and Shoji started playing an incredibly fast medley of multiple Christmas carols behind a closed curtain. The curtains opened and all the dancers were already in position. A small explosion of fireworks and the dancers sprang into action as Shoji progressed through multiple key changes.

I watched in fascination as Katy and her dancing friends interpreted the melodies with their feet and ever-present smiles on their faces. The audience rose for a standing ovation at the end of the first number. Shoji welcomed everyone as the audience sat down and the dancers exited the stage.

The first half of the show was filled with secular favorites of the Christmas season — songs about Santa and holiday traditions around the world. A brief intermission found Nathan and I settling a bet over another game of nine ball in the bathroom while snacking on foods from the concessions stand.

The second half of the show was an interpretation of the nativity story and started with an arrangement of *O Come, O Come Emmanuel* that seemed to linger in the air forever.

For several Advent seasons, I have played *O Come, O Come Emmanuel* as a duet with Elisabeth at multiple churches; it is simply one of my favorite songs of the Christmas season. We have worked hard at an arrangement that gives voice to the longing and yearning expressed in the lyrics. Hearing Shoji play stirred up memories of practices and performances with Elisabeth and reminded me just how far away I was from home.

O come, O come Emmanuel

And ransom captive Israel

That mourns in lonely exile here.

Lonely exile.

I was trapped in some alternate world, haunted by the melody line from the chorus as it was repeated throughout the second half. There was no joy in Branson.

The second half of the show ended with a live nativity scene, including camels and donkeys and sheep, under the spotlight on center stage.

Rejoice, rejoice, Emmanuel

Shall come to thee, O Israel.

We remained in our seats while the rest of the audience left. Twenty minutes later, when the dancers finally came back on stage having already changed into their street clothes, I took a small bouquet of flowers to Katy.

"I'm so proud to be your brother," I said.

"Thank you."

We posed while Dad took a couple of pictures of us with Shoji and then slowly walked out to the van, not overly anxious to face the Branson after-show traffic.

For the entire ride home, Nathan and Katy talked about the stuff that happens in behind-the-scenes dancing life. I was thankful for the chance to sit in silence in the back seat of the big brown van.

54

November 29, 1992

I caught up with Joshua after worship and asked if I could talk to him for just a minute. We stepped into a prayer room just off the sanctuary.

"Dude, everything is reminding me of 2015. We went to Shoji's show yesterday, and the cello music reminded me of Elisabeth. Any time I see a piece of art, I'm reminded of how Sarah carries colored pencils and paper with her wherever she goes, just in case she feels the need to draw. And I can't go anywhere in town without seeing some place where Annie and I've been together. Every day I'm becoming more depressed and I have no idea what to do about it. I honestly don't know how I'm going to survive another three months until the start of baseball season."

"Have you read any Einstein?" Joshua asked.

"Energy equals mass times the speed of light squared."

"Anything else?"

"He was a talented violinist."

"Really?"

"Yep. And he was once offered the opportunity to be the President of Israel."

"That's fascinating."

"He declined. Also, he hated onions."

"How about that. Did you know he thought time travel is theoretically possible?"

"Had no idea."

"But he thought it could only occur in one direction."

"Keep going."

"Basically, Einstein thought it was conceivable for people to 'travel' to the future if they were in objects — like spaceships — approaching the speed of light. He used that research to posit another theory, the Unified Field Theory, and he succeeded in combining his theory of relativity with electromagnetism. And everything that is taught these days completely ignores it, because almost all of the research was destroyed when a time travel experiment went wrong. Have you ever heard of The Philadelphia Experiment?"

I shook my head no.

"A Navy project in 1943, The Philadelphia Experiment used Einstein's research with the hopes of making a ship invisible to sonar and radar. Remember, this is in the middle of World War II. And the experiment worked. The ship became completely undetectable. It also became completely invisible. The entire crew, 181 sailors, and the ship disappeared. The ship reappeared 24 hours later some 250 miles north in Philadelphia. Out of the original crew, 120 never were seen again. Of the other 61, only 21 lived, and almost all of them went crazy. The survivors babbled incessantly about visiting the past.

"Einstein immediately destroyed all of his research in this field. Only a few notes survived, kept by a Master Chief Petty Officer who was present at the experiment. He quietly tucked away his copy in some military facility for years, until a researcher discovered them in the late 1970s and was able to use them to travel back in time. He tried to prevent the JFK assassination, but didn't have any success. He drove himself crazy trying to create a world where JFK lived."

"That's bizarre," I interrupted, "Stephen King just wrote a book a couple of years ago with a plot remarkably similar to that."

"A couple of years ago meaning..."

"Probably about 2011 or 2012 or so."

"Weird. Cutting to the chase, the reason why we are so fascinated with time travel as a culture is because it *is* a reality. There are people who travel both forward and backward, but at incredible risk."

"What kind of risk?"

"Well, it is much harder and significantly more dangerous to travel to the past than into the future. Based on the few stories I can find, the people who have travelled into the past almost always go crazy because their brains struggle with trying to keep up with multiple realities. Our brains were designed to live in the present tense, not in the past or in the future."

"How do you know all this?"

"I'm a historian. I read and write and research and think. Sometimes you just gotta follow where the rabbit trails lead."

"So, when I said something about being depressed…"

"I was worried you might be starting to go crazy."

"Have you read anything about how I can get back home?"

"I have found one other story quite similar to your experience. Every other story is about people intentionally experimenting with time travel. About thirty years ago, there is a story of a man who suddenly found himself in his own body but with a considerably older mindset."

"What happened to him?"

"He kept a journal and wrote about his future life, and his current reality, and having to make all these different decisions because of something that had radically changed in his new past, and…" Joshua paused.

"AND?"

"And then it just stops. It's just a handwritten journal. But, the weirdest part is," he spoke with almost a whisper, "the author was also from Springfield."

"Like, there's some kind of worm hole in Springfield?"

"'The right place *and* the right time' just like Kinsella wrote."

We sat in silence for a few moments as my brain tried to process the information Joshua had shared.

"So," I said, looking down and holding my head, "What do I do?"

"What I think has helped you the most is that you have focused on living in the present. Going to school and taking tests and doing homework, offseason workouts, playing catch with your Dad, all the stuff the Losers Club is doing, I think all those things have helped ground you in *this* version of reality. Those things have held your brain's attention *here*."

"So, what do I need to do to get back home?"

"It's only a gut instinct."

"You're the one who told me to 'trust my gut.'"

"The good news is I think you're gonna play baseball again."

"And the bad news?"

"This might be your new home."

I tried not to shudder. I heard Mom calling my name from the church's foyer and thanked Joshua for his time.

"I better go. It'd seriously suck to be grounded. See you tomorrow," I said with a half-hearted smile.

As soon as I got back to the house, I ran to the kitchen and grabbed a marker.

"Be here," I wrote on the meaty part of my left hand with the black Sharpie — a simple reminder of everything that Joshua had told me.

Be here.

Be here.

Be here.

The two-word mantra became my prayer, offering guidance and grounding when my brain felt drawn to future realities.

55

December 7, 1992

Having recommitted myself to fully living in whatever present time I was in, *carpe*-ing the heck out of every single *diem*, I poured my energies into the Losers Club adventures and preparing for the baseball season. Be here was my constant internal monologue.

On the first Monday in December there was a crowd of significant size waiting in the commons area to see what songs we would sing. We stepped up to the plate with our most over-the-top arrangements of some of the most ridiculous songs of the holiday season:

"I Want a Hippopotamus for Christmas" was first, followed by "I Saw Mommy Kissing Santa Claus," "All I Want For Christmas is My Two Front Teeth," and the grand finale, "Grandma Got Run Over By a Reindeer."

Nothing spreads Christmas cheer faster than planting an earworm in someone's head for the rest of the day!

It just didn't seem like enough, so later on I had another thought.

"Hey, Henry, you up for a challenge?"

We had survived Calculus and were on our way to lunch.

"Name it."

"I'll buy you lunch after school if you'll help me take back every single tray in the next fifteen minutes."

"Dude. That's gotta be, like, close to 200 trays."

"Yup."

"And you'll buy me lunch?"

"Wherever you wanna go."

"Cici's Pizza. All you can eat, plus an arcade in the back room."

"Deal."

For fifteen minutes, Henry and I hustled like waiters at a family restaurant, stacking and taking back trays and giving out breath mints, each keeping count of how many we had taken back — the 1992 high school version of Gimli versus Legolas.

Dripping with sweat, but absolutely beaming with pride at our efforts, I asked Henry how many trays he had returned as we headed to our next classes.

"109. You?"

"94. You win."

56

December 11, 1992

"Have fun stormin' the castle!" Dad yelled out to me as I climbed out of the van with guitar in tow, off to catch the school bus bound for Silver Dollar City with the rest of the Madrigal Singers.

"Thanks, Fezzik!" I shouted back.

Mrs. Mullins explained the order of events and how everything would happen once we got to SDC on the bus ride. She then walked to the back of the bus, since that's where the seniors sat, to fill me in on taking care of my guitar.

"They want to do a quick sound check when we arrive, and then I promise I'll take good care of it until we're finished and get back on the bus. You won't have to worry about anything except for playing during our two performances."

"Do I need it for the other performances in the park?"

"Just sing those *a cappella*. That way you don't have to carry it all night."

"Thanks, Mrs. Mullins."

Multiple meteorological studies have declared Springfield, Missouri as the premiere city in the United States for greatest variety in weather.

When people say, "Just wait ten minutes, the weather will change," they are really talking about Springfield, Missouri. In the hour that passed between loading the bus in Springfield and unloading the bus in Branson, a cold front passed through southwest Missouri, dropping temperatures by more than thirty degrees along with a biting north wind.

For years, I've joked that I'm a cold-blooded person. I wear a hat almost year-round, either to keep the sweat out of my eyes and sun off my head or to keep the heat in my body. While wearing a hat helps keep my head warm in the winter weather, it does nothing for my fingers, which feel like they are frozen solid. I sounded more than a little clunky trying to finger-pick the guitar at the sound check and worried about embarrassing myself.

"Hey Ethan," Mrs. Mullins said, "Don't worry about it. I've sang here on several occasions and have some pretty good connections. There'll be a space heater near you for the actual performances. You'll do just fine."

I tried to give her a thumbs up, but my thumb wouldn't cooperate.

Compared to the amount of mental energy expended trying to keep calm and focus and the hours upon hours of practicing at school, the first performance felt incredibly short. I picked up the guitar and stood stage left with my eyes glued to Mrs. Mullins, watching for her cue. She was right about not having to worry. There was a space heater right next to me; my fingers felt just fine. She counted off six beats and mouthed the word, "Go."

The guitar rang loud and clear on the cool winter's eve. After a four-measure introduction, the choir joined in. I snuck a quick peek to see how many people were actually listening. Hundreds of people gathered around the gazebo staring at us, at me. My heart pounded in response and I immediately looked back at Mrs. Mullins to regain my focus.

And then the song, and our show, was over.

A voice from the sound booth announced that we'd be performing again in two hours as a gracious applause sounded from those gathered.

"Nobody move," Mrs. Mullins said. "You'll be back here, ready to sing, bathroom business taken care of, twenty minutes before we go on. If you're late, I'll dock you a letter grade. No excuses."

I packed up my guitar, passed the case off to her, and gave her a real thumbs up.

Silver Dollar City is a beautiful place to be at Christmastime. The entire park is saturated in Christmas lights and holiday decorations; people are stopping everywhere to pose for what they hope will be the perfect picture for a Christmas card. As soon as Mrs. Mullins granted us our freedom, Junior, Henry, and I ran all the way across the park to ride the one and only roller coaster, Fire in the Hole.

In 2015, Silver Dollar City has evolved to more than just an 1880's theme park; it is also a growing roller coaster park. In fact, in 2013, their newest roller coaster, Outlaw Run, was voted the top new roller coaster in the world. In 1992, Fire in the Hole was *the only* roller coaster-type ride in the park. Even Thunderation was still a season away from opening.

Fire in the Hole is an indoor ride in the dark that recreates a story where vigilantes known as Baldknobbers destroyed a local mining city, burning it to the ground. The ride itself is very simple, with only a few short drops just long enough to make you feel like you're falling. The rumors of a fatality occurring on the ride are what really give it all of its excitement.

By the time we got there, there wasn't much of a line for the ride. The three of us rode it three times in succession before moving on.

"Where to next?" I asked.

"Well, we are supposed to do at least one small performance on our own. Should we do it now or after the next show?" Henry said.

"Let's just get it out of the way," Junior answered, "And I know a great place to sing."

We crossed the park, slowly winding our way through the crowds and the rolling terrain, deciding which two songs the three of us were going to sing, meeting the absolute minimum requirement set by Mrs. Mullins.

"We could always do one of the Losers Club songs, too," Henry said.

"Good idea. Hey Junior, where are we headed?"

"The swinging bridge."

Henry and I both laughed in complete agreement; the swinging bridge would be the perfect place to sing.

Had we known that the swinging bridge hovered above a natural amphitheater, we probably would not have chosen "Grandma Got Run Over By a Reindeer" as our first song. Or maybe we would have. Either way, we sang it loud and proud, then decided to play it safe with our second song and sang a solid three-verse rendition of "The First Noel."

Having fulfilled our extra-performance obligations and still with some time to kill, we bought some hot chocolate and toured Grandfather's

Mansion, where we listened to a fantastic performance by a group of altos and sopranos. They convinced us to sing an old French wassailing carol with them for their third song. We teased them relentlessly about being overachievers.

When we finished in Grandfather's Mansion, it was time to reconvene at the gazebo for our second main performance of the evening.

"You three, right here!" Mrs. Mullins greeted us as soon as she saw us. "I don't remember giving anyone permission to sing 'Grandma Got Run Over By a Reindeer.' Did you know that people all over the park heard it?"

We tried our best not to laugh as she scolded us. Thankfully, Mrs. Mullins also has a good sense of humor.

"No ma'am," Junior answered for all of us. "We were on the swinging bridge. I chose it because I didn't think anyone would be able to hear us."

"Well," she smirked, "*Everyone* heard you. You're lucky I like you guys. Solid job on 'The First Noel.'"

The crowd for our second performance was twice as large as the previous crowd. The temperature continued to drop throughout the early evening hours as snow started to fall — light, drifting, peaceful flakes.

When it came time for the last song, I moved into place and picked up my guitar. Staring down at my left hand, I saw the black Sharpie-tattoo — *Be here* — and realized that this would probably be the last chance I would have to play guitar at Silver Dollar City, a place where dozens upon dozens of music legends started their careers.

This will look fantastic on my résumé.

Thankful for the opportunity, I no longer felt nervous but truly enjoyed the experience of accompanying one of the best high school choirs in the state.

As soon as the song ended, Mrs. Mullins looked at me, winked, and gave me a thumbs up.

57

December 23, 1992

The entire last week before Christmas break was nothing but review and preparation for finals week in January. Students with borderline grades want to do well, knowing that the weight of a grade on a final exam can significantly help or hinder them. Teachers, of course, want all students to do well, and are allowing ample time for questions and in-class study sessions.

I remember well the anxious dread and weight of finals hanging over me every Christmas of my high school career. I always had good intentions of studying during the break, only to procrastinate and do absolutely nothing school related until the Sunday evening before classes resumed.

Not so this time. I have noticed that, not only do I possess greater self-discipline than I did as a teenager, but there is no internet to serve as a distraction. No dings, whistles, tweets, or buzzes to draw my attention away from the task at hand. No emails that need a reply; no constant updating of a Twitter-feed; no pictures taken that I'm convinced need to be seen by the world; and I'm actually *with* the majority of my Facebook friends.

There really are some advantages to living in a pre-internet world.

By the time school ended on Tuesday, I felt ready for all of my finals, even though they wouldn't start until the first week in January.

Time to have some fun.

The last day of school before Christmas break was near torture. Everyone was ready for some time off. For the last few weeks, the Losers Club has been brainstorming, trying to think of an epic way to end 1992, one everyone would remember. With the help of some co-conspirators, we were successfully able to pull it off.

Thanks to Henry's dad, who had connections to multiple copying machines at Kinko's; Amelia's mom, who willingly purchased boxes upon boxes upon boxes of candy canes from Wal-marts all over southwest Missouri; Nathan's mom, who donated a several rolls of Scotch tape; and a janitor who let us in the school late on a Tuesday night, on the last Wednesday of 1992, *everyone* was a winner.

On every single locker in the school, we taped up the small, copied sign, "Merry Christmas, Winner!" along with two jumbo, multi-flavored candy canes. The janitor agreed to let us into the main office, under his supervision, where we taped the sign and candy canes to the doors of the principal and vice principals and on the desks of all the secretaries. Candy canes on lockers — an incredibly small gesture compared to the larger scope of life, but I think God's pretty fond of a little whimsy here and there.

Finally, knowing that he took a huge risk in helping us, we gave the janitor a large copy of the "Merry Christmas, Winner" sign, the last box of candy canes, and a $20 gift certificate to the movies. Christmas is all about finding gifts in unexpected places and celebrating with those society overlooks.

"You kids are good in my book," he said with smile.

The next morning, we got to school early so we could walk around and enjoy everyone's reactions. Stacie and Amelia were prepared to photograph and videotape. Of course, there were a few students who smashed their candy canes to pieces on the floor and immediately shredded their sign. But, for the vast majority of the students, there were smiles and laughter and a contagious energy was created that lasted the entire day.

The bell rang, students headed to class. There were random lockers throughout the halls that still had their candy canes taped to them. The intercom buzzed as the principal addressed the student body.

"Good morning, students of Kickapoo! As you probably noticed, Santa Claus came early this year. On behalf of the entire staff, we would like to wish you a Merry Christmas, along with the happiest of New Year's. Please, be safe and smart in all of your celebrations, and don't forget, finals start on Tuesday, January 5, 1993!"

A collective groan was heard throughout the school.

Nothing remotely productive happened in any class. We watched movies and had parties and played games. When the final bell rang, as Nathan and I slowly meandered through the halls, I spotted Joshua visiting with Coach Engel.

"Be right back," I told Nathan.

I shook hands with Joshua and Coach, "Just wanted to tell both of you Merry Christmas. Baseball starts in less than ten weeks. I can't wait."

"Right back at ya," Coach said, blowing a big bubble and popping it.

58

December 25, 1992

I could hear the crackles and pops in the vinyl record long before the music started. The bright brass of Percy Faith and his orchestra sounded throughout the house. My sister and I have been classically conditioned; as soon as we hear the intro to "Joy to the World," we spring out of bed, ready to celebrate Christmas morning.

Dad does his best Clark Griswold impersonation, singing along with a ridiculous fake vibrato and exaggerated emphasis on every syllable. Mom chimes in simple harmonies as we all find a place to sit near the tree and the fireplace.

"Who wants to read the Christmas story?" Mom asked.

"Can I just tell it in my own words?" I replied.

"Sure, son. Go ahead."

"The Roman Empire was an impressive powerhouse of military might and seemingly endless wealth. Their motto was simple, 'Just do it our way.' The people of Israel waited as they suffered in an occupied land, their reminder of God's promise, and regularly heard the official proclamations that didn't reflect their daily prayer, 'Hear, O Israel, the Lord our God, the Lord is one. Love the Lord your God with all your heart, soul, mind, and strength.'

"They had waited for so long, for centuries, for a deliverer, a Messiah. 'Surely YHWH has forgotten us.' They clung to the thinnest threads of hope.

"And to an unmarried teenage mother, probably pretty close to Katy's age, in a city far from home, during the most stressful of circumstances — tax season! — in the smelliest and most mundane of places, a baby was born.

"The one whose Word shaped all creation was completely dependent on this girl for all of his nourishment and care. The one who would one day be lifted up as the King of the Jews wasn't born in a palace, but near piles of poop.

"The one who would heal the blind and make the lame to walk and proclaim the good news of the nearness of God's kingdom to the poorest of the poor, his coming into this world was only celebrated by a small group of local outcasts.

"The birth of Jesus wasn't celebrated in the tabloids or announced by the paparazzi; even the most religious people completely missed out on the event. The best gift, the reason we celebrate this season, is that love comes when we least expect it, in ways we could never predict, and is free for all people."

"Well, that was quite...different." Mom said, wearing a puzzled grin.

"I kinda liked it," Katy said.

"Thanks, sis! So...how about we open some presents now?" I asked.

The day after Christmas, my family prepared for another annual tradition, a pilgrimage to Grandmon's house. A minimum five-hour drive over some rivers and through the woods of the Mark Twain forest, and we'd be celebrating a day-after-Christmas dinner of hot tamale pie, coleslaw, and homemade apple pie in southeast Missouri with aunts, uncles, cousins, and Grandmon.

I volunteered to drive first and asked for permission to play the new-to-me Billy Joel tape I received as a gift. I drove until both sides had played and then pulled over at the nearest McDonald's to switch drivers. Mom took over the reins of the big brown van; I climbed to the back seat and slept a dreamless sleep until we pulled into Grandmon's driveway.

On my mother's side of the family, I am the oldest of the cousins and grandchildren. Every year, it was a game between the cousins to see where we measured compared to Grandmon who stood a perfect 5'0".

Naturally, I was the first to bypass Grandmon and for years I was the tallest cousin. But, sometime in the late 1990s, I went from being the oldest and tallest grandchild, to third tallest out of four, just barely a few inches taller than my sister.

I couldn't believe it when we walked into Grandmon's house and I saw my cousins still measuring themselves next to her.

They are so young, almost the ages of Elisabeth and Sarah...

Be here. Be here, no matter how much you might like to be with them.

We spent the afternoon doing puzzles, wrestling, and watching various sporting events on TV until Grandmon called everyone to the dinner table; it was time for the feast.

The problem with feasting at Grandmon's is that no one wants to move an inch after dinner, either to help with clean-up or to open presents. It usually takes at least an hour of after-dinner discussion before anyone is willing to relocate.

However, the constant prodding of younger cousins motivated everyone to gather around the Christmas tree.

"Dishes can wait," they implored.

When opening gifts at Grandmon's, there is one final tradition this side of the family enjoys. For Christmas the year my Uncle Mark turned 15, he was given a pink-ruffled, long-sleeve, dress shirt in a box with the face and name of Oleg Cassini on top.

For the last twenty-four years, every single Christmas, Uncle Mark has unwrapped the Oleg Cassini box and received a new dress shirt. This year is Uncle Mark's 40th birthday and everyone knows that Grandmon has something special up her sleeve.

Of course, by now, Uncle Mark knows the box by shape and feel and always tucks it under the couch to make certain that it's the final gift. The cousins opened packages of toys; Katy, being the only female cousin and granddaughter, unwrapped several packages of clothes; I got a new winter coat and a tool box full of tools from Uncle Mark's hardware store.

When every package but the Oleg Cassini box had been opened, Uncle Mark pulled the box out from underneath the couch. Dad grabbed his camera to forever catch the moment on film.

Grandmon had carefully wrapped the box in multiple layers of paper and one layer of tulle, which Uncle Mark absolutely hated. When he tore through the final layer, Uncle Mark held the box up and did his best serious-faced impression of Oleg Cassini.

Everyone laughed; Dad quickly took candid photos of everyone. Uncle Mark carefully peeled back the pieces of Scotch tape that kept the box closed, and opened it in such a manner that he was the only person who could see inside.

He reached in and pulled out the original pink ruffled shirt, covered in forty dollars' worth of $1 bills. He held up the shirt and posed for pictures while his sons tried to claim the attached money. He removed and pocketed the money, then called to me, "Think I've had too many years of hot tamale pie to fit in this one. Hey Ethan, come here a second. I bet this is about your size."

I smiled, stood up, and took off my sweater. Uncle Mark's 25-year-old pink-ruffled shirt fit perfectly. We posed for a few pictures before I took it off and handed it back, "I make pink look good."

59

December 31, 1992

We got back to Springfield late in the afternoon, at that awkward time when you need to think about what to do for dinner but food doesn't sound that good because you've been on the road for far too long.

I threw my duffel bag toward my closet and slumped on my bed, somewhat carsick. I thought about trying to sleep it off, but the phone rang as soon as I closed my eyes. I stretched for the phone and grabbed it by the endlessly tangled and looped cord.

"Hello?"

"Ethan? Hey, this is Drew. Missed you at church this week."

"Thanks, we were at my Grandmon's house for Christmas."

"Cool. I know it's last minute, but I'm having a movie marathon party for New Year's Eve. Just inviting some of the guys from youth group at church. First movie starts at 6 pm and we'll go to 6 am. Mom's taking care of all the food stuff."

"Count me in."

Six teenage guys — Drew, me, Aaron, Matt, Sam, and Brad — six movies, and a seemingly unlimited supply of Mexican cuisine, snacks, and caffeine. We stood around the kitchen table and munched on chips and queso waiting for everyone to show up. When Brad finally arrived, Drew quickly took charge.

"Get some food and something to drink and meet me downstairs. The first movie starts in ten minutes."

"What's playing?"

"Tonight's movies, in order, are: *Indiana Jones and the Raiders of the Lost Ark; Hoosiers; Star Wars: The Empire Strikes Back; Field of Dreams; Karate Kid;* and *The Goonies.*"

There was a fifteen-minute break in between each movie for food refills and bathroom runs. More than halfway through *Star Wars*, Drew paused the VHS player. We changed the channel to watch the ball drop on Dick Clark's New Year's Rockin' Eve, celebrated the arrival of 1993 with a midnight jog around the block, and then continued the movie.

At 7:30 am, everyone was still awake, barely, and the credits of *The Goonies* were scrolling.

"Happy new year, guys. Thanks for the movies, Drew. I'm outta here," I said while yawning and high-fiving my way toward the stairs.

While waiting on Dad to pick me up, I stood quietly at the door and considered the significance of the date — new beginnings, resolutions, do overs.

For some reason unknown to me I had been chosen, granted a do over. I have never really been a fan of New Year's resolutions, but in that moment, I quietly whispered a resolute prayer, "I resolve to trust You, even when I don't understand what's going on."

60

January 3, 1993

Baseball tryouts were less than two months away. I slowly savored and sipped my coffee while glancing over the sports headlines, waiting for the rest of the family to get ready for church. On page two, in the bottom left corner, was a list of today's broadcast games and their stations.

KY3TV (NBC) — Houston Oilers vs. Buffalo Bills.

The Comeback Game.

I remembered watching that game while trying to cram for finals the first time, the game that is still the largest comeback in NFL history. I'm more than ready for finals week and can't wait to watch this game again.

I found Joshua after church and whispered in passing, "Don't miss today's Bills and Oilers game. It's incredible." On the way home, I begged Dad to go through the drive-thru instead of eating inside.

"What's the rush, Chief?"

"Playoff game that I don't wanna miss."

"The Oilers and Bills? Since when do you care about either of those teams?"

"I've always been a fan of postseason games, regardless of the sport."

The Bills and Oilers played each other in Houston for their last game of the regular season, with Houston winning 27 – 3. In that game, Jim Kelly, the star quarterback for the Bills, strained ligaments in his knee, leaving backup quarterback Frank Reich to finish that game as well as get the start in this week's playoff game. With Kelly on the sideline, even though Buffalo had the home field advantage, many people expected Houston to easily win this game as well.

Just like I remembered, led by quarterback Warren Moon, Houston jumped out to an impressive 28 – 3 halftime lead. The third quarter had barely started, when one of Reich's passes was tipped, intercepted, and runback for a touchdown, increasing the lead to 35 – 3.

"This game is over, Chief," Dad commented.

Commence "The Comeback."

In the next ten football minutes, the Bills scored 21 points. On the very first play of the Oilers' next possession, Henry Jones intercepted Warren Moon's pass and returned the ball the to the Houston 23-yard line. Four plays later and the Bills were losing by a mere four points by the end of the third quarter, 35 – 31.

"Any given Sunday," I said during the commercial break.

With three minutes left in the game, Buffalo took the lead for the first time on Frank Reich's fourth touchdown pass. With time ticking away, Warren Moon then led a 60-yard drive that finished with an Al Del Greco field goal, tying the game at 38 and sending it into overtime.

"I bet whoever wins the coin toss will win the game," Dad said.

Houston won the toss and Moon successfully completed his first two passes in overtime before throwing his second interception of the game. After two running plays to center the ball, the Bills kicked a game-winning 32-yard field goal, to cap off the largest comeback in NFL history, 41 – 38.

"If I hadn't seen that with my own eyes!" Dad exclaimed.

We kept the TV on, waiting for the postgame interviews. When Reich stepped up to the podium, Dad turned up the volume.

"Before you ask me any questions, I want to share the lyrics to a song that have inspired me this week.

"In Christ alone will I glory,
though I could pride myself in battles won.
For I've been blessed beyond measure,
and by his strength alone I've overcome.
Oh, I could stop and count successes
like diamonds in my hand.

But those trophies could not equal
to the grace by which I stand.
In Christ alone, I place my trust,
and find my glory in the power of the cross.
In every victory, let it be said of me,
my source of strength,
my source of hope,
is Christ alone."

"Questions?"

As I considered the game and the interview, I was ever so gently reminded of the resolution I had whispered just a couple days prior. My source of strength, my source of hope, is Christ alone. Even though high school baseball has such a small impact compared to professional football, I determined to live these words on the diamond.

61

In honor of Finals week, the Losers Club suspended all of their extracurricular activities except for High Five Friday.

With genuine enthusiasm, the Losers Club members greeted and encouraged the test-weary students of Kickapoo.

"You can do it, only one more day!"

"The weekend is nigh!"

"This too shall pass, hopefully you will too!"

Even in 2015, my old high school still offered an amazing variety of creative innovative classes. I was thankful for my teachers' innovative curriculum, which still kept me interested, even the second time around.

With the start of the second semester, I had a small change in my schedule as *Literature of the Bible* was only a one semester class. For the rest of the year, after lunch, I would be taking *American Baseball History (1839 to Present)*. The first time around, when I played golf, I opted for a study period to catch up on naps. Since I'd been studying baseball history on my own for decades, this class could be exactly what I needed to keep school fun.

Coach Engel was listed as the teacher, which was both good and bad. On the positive side, I would be able to talk with him about all things baseball and be able to stay informed about baseball tryouts. On the negative side, Coach Engel taught my freshman honors history class — one of the hardest classes I had in my high school career.

"Good afternoon class and welcome to *American Baseball History*," Coach Engel greeted the twenty of us. "Ethan, come up here and pass out the text books."

"Yes sir," I replied, tipping my sweat-stained Royals cap to him.

He stared at the odd gesture, then blew a large bubble and sucked it in to pop it.

"We will be covering this book from cover to cover, a test every Friday, a paper every month, and extra credit will be offered for every varsity baseball game you attend, unless you're on the team. We've got no time to waste; let's get started. Who invented the great game of baseball?"

Abner Doubleday has long received credit for the invention of baseball, but I knew that that was *not* the answer Coach Engel was seeking. True to form, I said nothing.

From the front row, Zach raised his hand and spoke up, "Abner Doubleday in Cooperstown, New York in the summer of 1839."

"Good job, Zach, for saying exactly what you've been taught. It just so happens, it's wrong. Doubleday wasn't in Cooperstown in 1839, he was at West Point. At no point in his life did Doubleday ever say anything about helping develop the game we now call baseball. Fact is, he might never have seen the game played at all. So, for your first paper, which is due by the end of the month, I want you to research the origins of the game, more than what's written in the first chapter of this textbook, and submit no more than three pages double-spaced explaining your theory of the origin of baseball."

And that's exactly the Coach that I remembered.

After class ended, I lingered behind the crowd to ask Coach Engel a question.

"Hey Coach, uh, gotta second?"

"What's up, Ethan?"

"I was just wondering, do you really think I've got a chance of making the varsity team this year?"

"Well, you've been pretty consistent at offseason, and you've been throwing on your own, right?"

I nodded in the affirmative.

"I can't make any promises, you know that. But come tryouts, you give me your best, and it wouldn't surprise me to see you wearing a varsity uniform."

I heard him pop multiple bubbles as I exited his classroom.

As soon as the tardy bell rang in English class, I started the second and final semester of Losers Club note passing.

"Hey guys and gals, welcome to the last semester of your high school career! (Pause for rambunctious applause, hoots, and hollers.) Maybe we should change things up and do something different this semester? Thoughts? Ideas?"

The note was passed around and returned with only one comment written on it.

"Why not just keep doing what we've been doing?" Henry asked.

"Because it's too easy to grow into routines and forget why we're doing them. I can't help but think of Chris and wonder if there was something I could've done to prevent it."

"Keep High Five Fridays," Nathan wrote, "That one's my favorite."

"I think we could stop with the music and everyone's already been a winner," Amelia commented.

"And we're running out of affordable ways to thank the teachers and staff," Stacie added.

"High Five Friday only this week, and brainstorm on your own until next Monday?"

"No school next Monday, MLK day," Junior responded.

"Until Tuesday then, you bunch of losers."

62

January 15, 1993

I first realized it was report card day while giving high fives and hated that I'd have to wait until last period English to see how I did.

I tried to tell myself that I really didn't care about the grades, that grades really didn't matter at all, that grades wouldn't really affect my future, except I knew that wasn't completely true. I had studied and worked and tried my best to not only keep up, but to truly excel in all of my classes. I couldn't risk missing out on any other possible collegiate scholarships because of bad grades my senior year.

Mr. Clarke made us wait for almost the entire period before distributing the perforated edged, W-2 replica grade cards. I held my breath when Mr. Clarke called my name as I walked to the front to pick it up. Carefully folding back along the perforations, I tore along the dotted lines and peeled back the top sheet with the black carbon-copy underside.

"How'd you do, Slick?" Nathan asked as we walked to our locker. It seemed like everyone was looking at their grades in the hallway. The normal energy of a Friday afternoon was significantly dulled.

"All A's and a B in Calculus," I said with a sigh of relief. "A miracle if I've ever seen one. I was so nervous opening that stupid thing, too. You?"

"Straight A's, man. We should go do something to celebrate!"

"Yep."

"I've been wanting to go four-wheeling for a while. There's no snow and the ground's firm. No rain for a while, so we shouldn't get stuck in mud. And I think I know a pretty good place. Wanna come?"

"Yep, yep, yep."

In 2015, National Avenue southbound does not end at Republic road but continues for miles. There's a church and grocery store and hundreds of businesses and homes that now border the east side of Twin Oaks Country Club.

However, in 1993, National Avenue south of Republic is an enormous field. Instead of turning left or right onto Republic from National, Nathan went straight. "Been driving by here for weeks looking for a 'No Trespassing' sign or something, but I haven't found one. It's just an open field."

The weeds were easily seven feet tall; we couldn't see much of anything out the front window. We bounced and bumped along, occasionally making doughnuts and flat-out flooring it for brief stretches. It was a bone-jarring blast.

After ten minutes, Nathan asked if I'd like to take a turn driving; I couldn't help but say yes. As he slowed to a stop, we both smelled something burning. Looking out the rear window, we spotted a trail of fire slowly moving straight toward the Sidekick.

"FIRE!" Nathan shouted, "Fire! Get out! Get out! Grab your stuff and get out!"

I grabbed my backpack from the back seat and jumped out the door, sprinting fifty yards from the car, desperately wishing I had my cell phone to call for help. A large pillar of smoke rose toward the sky and I was oddly reminded of the phrase in Exodus, "The Lord went ahead of them in a pillar of clouds to guide them on their way."

"I'm going to run to one of those businesses and call 911," Nathan said handing me his backpack, "Stay here."

I nodded in silent agreement.

Seconds later, Nathan had disappeared into the weeds.

In the fall of 1992 throughout southwest Missouri, there was a rash of car robberies where the perpetrators stole vehicles and set them ablaze in fields all over Greene, Polk, and Christian Counties. Since I never watched the local news or read the front page of the newspaper, I wasn't aware that this was taking place in my community. I was, however, quickly informed of this fact several times over after multiple policemen and half a dozen firefighters showed up to the scene with lights flashing and sirens blaring. Apparently, one of the businesses on Republic Road had spotted the cloud of guiding fire and called 911 long before Nathan could get to them.

I started walking through the weeds toward the sirens when an officer grabbed me firmly on the bicep, "Just where do you think you're going?"

"To get help."

He forcefully escorted me back to his car and shoved me into the back seat. Leaving the door open, he started yelling at me, "You know what's wrong with this world? Skinheads like you! That's what's wrong!" He slammed the door closed; I felt a lump rise in my throat immediately and tried to blink back some tears. I turned my head so I didn't have to look at him and spotted Nathan sitting in the back seat of a different police car.

The officer climbed in the front seat and, still yelling, asked, "Anyone you want me to contact?"

"Could you call my mom?"

"What's her name and the phone number?"

After he had radioed dispatch to contact my mom, the officer asked, "What were you guys doing out here?"

"Celebrating our report cards," I answered quietly.

"What? Your report cards?" The officer got out of the front seat and opened the back door. "Hand it over. Let me see it."

I had carefully folded my grade card and put it in my back pocket so I could show Mom and Dad when I got home. I handed it to him without comment.

He grabbed it from me and again slammed the door closed. I looked out the back window and watched as a small fire truck drove slowly through the field and extinguished all the flames. They finished by thoroughly hosing down Nathan's car.

Ten minutes later, Mom drove up in the big brown van and was immediately approached by "my" officer. Another officer and a couple of firemen gathered around her as she climbed down out of the van.

They talked for quite some time while I sat in the back of the police car quietly developing multiple ulcers.

"My" officer came to get me and Nathan and walked us back to the circle of officers and firefighters.

"Five acres, boys," the fire chief started, "You nearly burned down five acres of city land and that car's gonna need some serious work to get running again. There's supposed to be a 'No Trespassing' sign posted at that intersection. Don't know what happened to it. Lucky for you, Mrs. Bryan here came to your defense. Said you're good kids who just made a dumb choice. And the report cards backed that up, too. You guys go home with her. We'll tow the car to the dealership. From now on, you guys stay on the pavement. Understand?"

"Yessir," Nathan and I said at the same time.

"Hey boys," the fire chief continued, "My senior year, I completely wrecked my family vehicle. Actually drove it into a police car. No one was hurt, just the cars. Had only had my license for two days. I was sure my father was gonna kill me. When he got to the scene, he gave me hug and said that cars can be fixed a lot easier than people. Good news is that city council's been talking about extending National south and some businesses are really interested in developing out this way. Guess they should thank you, huh?" he said with a wink.

The ride home was very quiet.

The big brown van rambled into the driveway; Nathan's dad arrived mere moments afterwards. Mom told me to wait in my room until Dad came home, adding that we'd talk more over dinner which I interpreted as time to develop more ulcers.

I told Dad the entire story as Mom and Katy ate and listened. No one interrupted; no one made a noise. After I finished, Dad took a deep breath...and then started laughing. Deep belly laughs with tears, might have even been a snort or two. Dad was laughing so hard he eventually had to stand up and walk away from the table just to catch his breath.

"Well," he said as he stifled a couple more chuckles and sat back down to the table, "I think you've learned your lesson. Don't do that again."

63

January 18, 1993

For the very first time, all 50 states officially observed Martin Luther King Day as a national holiday.

I spent the day cleaning — dusting, vacuuming, scrubbing bathtub and showers and sinks and toilets. It was the best way I could think of to tell Mom thank you for her help.

"Getting a call from the cops about your child is a mother's nightmare. I hope to never experience that again."

She hugged me hard and planted a red lipstick kiss on the top of my head. I didn't even care to wipe it off.

With the extra day off from school and the feeling that I still needed to stay close to home, I decided to get a head start on the essay for Coach Engel's class with the hopes of turning it in early.

I pulled multiple baseball reference books off of the shelf in my bedroom and started taking notes. Before dinner, the essay was finished.

Ethan Bryan

American Baseball History Essay #1

January 18, 1993

                    The Origins of the Game

The game of baseball is the result of a wide assortment of influences from different cultures across a significant span of time. After the Protestant Reformation of the 16th century, thousands of people sought religious refuge away from England and Scotland, taking their chances with the cheap land and freedoms found in the New England colonies. By the mid 1600's, tens of thousands of immigrants set sail from England, braving the treacherous and occasionally fatal journey across the Atlantic. Two distinctly British games also made the journey — cricket and rounders — which eventually evolved into "our" game of baseball.

Cricket is a game with an abundance of similarities to baseball. It uses a flat bat and ball, which is both harder and heavier than a baseball. Cricket is divided into innings, officiated by umpires, and each team tries to score runs. Compared to baseball, rounders use a significantly smaller bat which is typically swung with only one hand. But, rounders do have four bases around which players run in attempts to score.

There are stories of Revolutionary War soldiers who played a version of baseball at Valley Forge and reports that Meriwether Lewis and William Clark even enjoyed a quick game with the Nez Perce Indians as they slowly crossed the continent.

In the earliest versions of the game, there weren't any foul lines or even set positions on the field. There are some stories of games with as many as fifty guys on each team. What we now know as the pitcher was then called the "feeder," and his job was to throw the ball as the batter (the "striker") demanded it. No balls or strikes were called, and only one out was needed to retire the side. Much like dodge ball, in the earliest iterations a runner could be declared out if he was hit with the ball while running in between bases.

Most likely, the game we know of as "American Baseball" had its formal origin in New York City around the summer of 1842. A couple years later, under the vision and leadership of a devoted shipping clerk named Alexander Joy Cartwright, twenty-eight men officially started the New York Knickerbocker Base Ball Club in September of 1845. Cartwright, with the help of Doc Adams, established a set of rules that provided a solid foundation for the game's future.

The first official Knickerbockers match took place on June 19, 1846 on the Elysian Fields against the New York Base Ball Club. The Knickerbockers lost the game 23 – 1, although the scorebooks suggest they did not use their best players. The contest was never about winning and losing; it was about the pure joy of the being outside and being on the field.

A decade later, in 1857, the Knickerbockers joined together with fifteen other clubs to form the National Association of Base Ball Players; Doc Adams was the first president. With the advent of this association came some immediate improvements to the game. The distance between bases was established at 90 feet; umpires were given the authority to call strikes; catching a ball in one's hat was strictly forbidden; and most importantly, no player was ever to be paid.

Baseball has been played through all the major American wars, with some professional ballplayers serving their time in the military instead of on the playing field. Baseball paved the way for racial integration and found a place for women on the field, too.

While baseball historians know that Abner Doubleday wasn't the founder of the game, clinging to that mythology, much like several of the narratives of Founding Fathers, gives most people sufficient reason to claim the game as America's national pastime, even celebrating the game's best in the Hall of Fame, located, of course, in Cooperstown.

64

January 22, 1993

Following a week of wonderfully mild weather, Friday greeted Springfield with eight inches of heavy, wet snow. The school, of course, had a snow day. The gift of a free day felt exactly like a *Calvin & Hobbes* cartoon come to life. Days like this are much easier to focus on being here.

Dad agreed to take me and Katy to the driving range hill to sled after I shoveled the driveway. Sledders always make Ken incredibly nervous, so he posted "Sled At You're Own Risk" signs everywhere.

I couldn't help but notice the atrocious grammatical error on the sign.

"What's the risk?" Katy asked.

"Landing on a golf ball and bruising your butt? Actually, I think a couple of students got concussions last year here. Just going too fast over one of the ramps and landing wrong."

For a couple of hours, the three of us sledded, enjoying the bumps and ramps and well-packed runs. We were part of a ten-person sledding train and got involved in an incredible snowball fight.

"Guess that kinda counts as a throwing session, right?" Dad laughed.

Thanks to Dad's height, we were able to build an *S.O.U.S.* — snowman of unusual size, a family tribute to *The Princess Bride*.

When we finally decided to leave, Dad took us through the drive-thru at Steak 'N Shake for lunch on the way home. For the rest of the day, Dad kept the fireplace stoked and we all enjoyed watching movies, curled up under blankets.

In my exhausted state, I couldn't help but remember similar snow day adventures with Elisabeth and Sarah. There is something about the gift of a snow day that demands it be spent away from books, away from homework, with people and making memories. I knew in my heart that

Elisabeth and Sarah and Calvin and Hobbes would have thoroughly enjoyed today's adventure.

65

January 31, 1993

"Got plans for the game tonight?" Drew asked before the start of Sunday school.

"Not really. Might just stay at home and watch it with Dad."

"If you want, you can come over to watch it with me, you know, since Dallas is playing."

I do not know how Drew chose his favorite professional sports teams — the Chicago Cubs and the Dallas Cowboys. I can handle cheering for the Cubs because they have a rivalry with the St. Louis Cardinals. As a Royals fan, I'll cheer for any team that's playing St. Louis, unless it's the Yankees. I can't even begin to imagine a world in which I'd cheer for the Yankees. As far as the Cowboys are concerned, I've just never been able to cheer for them.

"You know I'm pulling for Buffalo, right?"

"Why?"

"I loved Frank Reich's postgame interview a few weeks ago. Thought that really put everything into perspective, upside-down kingdom kind of stuff, you know?"

"Upside down kingdom?"

"The way of Jesus is just backwards to the ways of the world. Love is the greatest force in the universe; power shouldn't be pursued at any cost; not obsessed with always winning, but cooperating and giving of one's self for the good of your neighbor, wherever your neighbor might be."

"Gotcha. So…you wanna bet on the game?"

"Only if it's an upside-down bet."

"Ok, I'll bite. What's an 'upside-down' bet?"

"Where the winner pays. If Dallas wins, you'd treat me to something. That way, losing doesn't hurt twice."

"Ha! For an Andy's custard?"

"You've got a deal." We shook hands on it; I was already looking forward to the free custard more than the game.

I rang the doorbell twenty minutes before kick-off. Drew opened the door wearing a Cowboys hoodie and hat. I wore my Royals hoodie, "Baseball is coming soon, right?"

"I don't know anyone that thinks about baseball as much as you do," Drew said, greeting me with our typical handshake and hug. "On the pre-game show, they said that commercials cost $850,000 for thirty seconds. Can you imagine someone spending that much for only thirty seconds on the air?"

"Crazy," I replied, remembering that the commercials in 2015 were somewhere north of four million dollars.

"Still on for the 'upside-down' bet?" Drew asked as we walked into the kitchen to load up on finger foods.

"Unless you're giving fifty points," I muttered quietly to myself.

"What's that?"

"Sure thing."

I filled a plate with chicken fingers, seven-layer nachos, and a handful of Oreos, grabbed a can of Dr Pepper, and headed downstairs to find a seat with a good view. Garth Brooks sang the national anthem and then O. J. Simpson walked to midfield for the coin toss.

"O. J. Simpson?" I exclaimed, more to myself that toward anyone directly, not quite believing what I was seeing.

"One of the best running backs the game has ever seen," Drew answered. "Played most of his career for the Bills. Funny actor, too."

I stared. O.J.'s earlier career was a blur, something my forty-year-old brain had nearly erased. In front of me was O. J. Simpson before the white Bronco chase and the trials and the "If the glove doesn't fit, you must acquit."

Seeing O. J. was by far the most incredible, unbelievable part of the first half. The Cowboys scored two touchdowns in the final three minutes of the half and went to the locker room with a 28 – 10 lead.

And then Michael Jackson came out for the halftime show.

I watched his performance in awe. For me, Jackson had been dead for over eight years. Seeing him alive again was more than surreal. I remembered that I was driving to a meeting in downtown Kansas City when I heard the news of his passing on the radio.

"Why so serious, E?" Drew asked, bringing me back here, to this version of reality.

"Oh, just looking forward to my Andy's. Pretty sure Dallas has all but got this one wrapped up."

"Buffalo's got a thing for comebacks."

"Just not feeling it."

The only memorable highlight in the second half of the game was Leon Lett's fumble of what appeared to be another Dallas touchdown from a turnover. Dallas won, 52 – 17. Drew was so happy we went out for Andy's custard immediately afterward to celebrate.

66

February 1, 1993

Coach Engel greeted the class with an enormous bubble, roughly the size of his head. "Quality work on the first essay, and good job on last Friday's test, too," he said as he passed out essays and tests in between a few more blown bubbles.

"Before we jump into baseball at the turn of the century, I figured I'd go ahead and give you your next essay topic. February is Black History Month.

"Baseball was played by slaves on farms and plantations in the deep south. Baseball also paved the way for the United States to begin to struggle through racial and civil rights. Your essay needs to cover some aspect Black American Baseball History. Maybe it's a player or one of the Negro Leagues teams. Again about three pages, double-spaced. I'm giving you a lot of freedom on this one, so if you need help coming up with a specific topic, see me after class."

As soon as Coach mentioned the assignment I knew exactly what I wanted to do and I hoped that Joshua would be willing to help me.

Now that the second semester had started, Joshua wasn't sitting in the back row of Mrs. Bowen's class anymore. It was too bad, but his observation hours were over and he was back on the campus of Drury University, taking classes to eventually finish his Master's degree. I had to wait until I got home to call him with my plan.

"Any interest in a day trip to Kansas City?"

"I can taste the barbecue already."

"I need to do some research for a project in Coach Engel's class and I think you're gonna love where I wanna go."

"Which is…?"

"To the soul of baseball."

"Not following you."

"To the Negro Leagues Baseball Museum."

"Never heard of it."

"You gotta trust me on this one."

"I trust you. How about Saturday?"

"Going to Kansas City, Kansas City here we come!"

67

February 4, 1993

Cincinnati Reds Owner Schott Suspended,
Fined $25K

Schott offended every ethnicity on the planet in her press conference. Thankfully, finally, she was not only suspended from baseball, but fined by her colleagues. If she wants to continue with a career in baseball, she will be required to complete multi-cultural training programs. 'Hitler had the right idea for them, but he went too far,' Schott said in simple admiration of the Nazi dictator.

Schott concluded her conference saying, 'I'd rather hire trained monkeys than a black person for my staff.' Known for taking her Saint Bernards to the ballpark, one of the former Reds' marketing directors, who refused to be identified by name, commented, 'This city would be a better place if she treated people half as well as she treats her dogs.' Schott has four weeks to get things in order before her official suspension begins.

I sighed after reading the story.

Kinsella is right: baseball really does reflect the times. Erase, rebuild, and erase again.

The remainder of the week crawled along; I was incredibly excited about the trip to KC. Joshua pulled into the driveway just a little after eight on Saturday morning, and we were northbound minutes afterward.

"I can't begin to count how many times I've made this trip over the years," I said. "But it's four-lane all the way now, with a couple of good-sized gas stations if you need to take a break."

I filled Joshua in on the details of the assignment and a little about the history of the Negro Leagues Baseball Museum. "It started in 1990 as a place where people could hear and remember the stories of those who played in the Negro Leagues, who were more than capable of playing in the majors. It's near 18th and Vine, the jazz district, in the heart of downtown KC."

"I know exactly where that is," Joshua added.

"In 2015, the NLBM is in a huge facility with all kinds of incredible memorabilia, a movie narrated by James Earl Jones, and the Field of Legends, where bronze sculptures of some of the best players are featured. I've been on multiple occasions, even once got invited to join a private tour with President Bob Kendrick. I really think you're gonna like this place."

"So, how have things been going for you this semester?"

"Coach Engel's class has definitely helped to keep me engaged. It's pretty fun going to school and talking about baseball. The Losers Club is backing off things, just to take a break. Overall, I'm better, I just can't allow myself to think about the future. Some days, that takes all my energy, just being *here*."

"I can't even begin to imagine," Joshua said, clicking on the radio and tuning into a classical music station.

"How's school for you?" I asked.

"I'm ready to get back in the classroom. I enjoyed being around you students, helping connect the importance of the past to today."

"'You students?'" I said in mock offense.

"You know what I mean."

Joshua and I were both hungry by the time we reached KC city limits and stopped at Gates Bar-B-Q to fill up on soul food.

As soon as we walked in the door a young woman greeted us loudly, "May I help you?!"

Even though there were a dozen people in front of us in line, it was quickly apparent she was talking to us, expecting us to order immediately.

I elbowed Joshua. "Guess it's our turn. Know what you want?"

We both ordered the daily special, which was far more food than we should've eaten, but we both cleaned our plates.

"Don't think I'll need to eat again until sometime next week," Joshua stated as we slowly sauntered back to the car.

"Kansas City barbecue and baseball in the same day. Must be heaven."

We slowly drove around downtown Kansas City, trying to find the location of the NLBM. Joshua parked the car relatively near 18th and Vine and we just started walking around. Ten minutes passed before I began stopping people on the street and asking if they knew where to look.

"Just follow me, young man," a slim, elderly gentleman said, wearing a long black dress coat and matching fedora. We headed toward the Lincoln Building on the corner of 18th and Vine, and walked inside the all-brick building with green awnings.

"Mind taking the stairs?" the elderly gentleman asked.

"Not at all," Joshua replied.

"Almost there," the man said as we reached the third floor. "Right here inside this door."

He opened the door for us and Joshua and I stepped into an unimpressive single-room office. A large conference table with ten chairs sat in the middle of the room; a few men were seated around it. Stacks of framed black-and-white photographs were carefully placed along the base of the walls, and a couple of gloves, bats, jerseys, and baseballs were scattered around the room. Our guide turned around and introduced himself in a baritone voice that seemed to sing in poetry.

"Good afternoon, gentlemen, and welcome to the Negro Leagues Baseball Museum. My name is Buck O'Neil. Who might you be?"

John Jordan "Buck" O'Neil, the son of a sawmill worker and grandson of a slave, the first black coach in major league baseball and tireless advocate on behalf of the Negro Leagues and the NLBM *was talking to me.*

When I lived in Kansas City, I once had an opportunity to meet Buck O'Neil while I was at a Royals game. My friend Kevin had given me his amazing ticket — mere rows behind home plate — as he was out of town. Close enough to the Royals dugout to actually hear the players talk and the hiss of tobacco spit. I spotted Buck sitting in his traditional seat and wanted to introduce myself and just talk baseball, maybe ask for an autograph on my program, but I was too nervous. By the time I worked up my courage, somewhere around the fourth inning, Buck had already left for the evening.

"Good afternoon, Mr. O'Neil," I reached to shake his hand and tried to act somewhat poised. "I'm Ethan and this is my friend Joshua. We drove up from Springfield to visit the NLBM for a project I'm working on at school."

"Lemme introduce you to the gang," Buck said, pointing to the men at the table. "These are just some of my friends from the Monarchs, from my ball playin' days: Connie Johnson, Herman 'Doc' Horn, Henry Mason, and that one's Bob Motley — he was an umpire. We like to spend Saturdays swapping stories and dreaming about the future of the NLBM together. Are you guys ballplayers?"

"I'm trying out for the varsity team in just a couple of weeks. Hoping I make the cut. And Joshua used to play ball. He's now studying to be a history teacher."

"You're here for a school project, you say? What kind of school project?"

"I'm researching stories about the Negro Leagues and their impact on modern-day Major League baseball."

"Son, I've got all kinds of stories for you, if you guys have got the time.

"All the fans wore their best to the games — the ladies in their fine-looking dresses, the men in coats and ties. Dressed to the nines, they were. Everybody wore hats, too. Every game, the stadium was filled with a contagious energy, the people knew they were watching something special, that the players on the field weren't just there for the sake of entertainment, but to attempt to do the impossible. Because baseball, well, it's like faith, like life. Baseball is a game for everyone.

"We played a game those in the major leagues didn't yet know — it was a fast game, quick like lightning. Never a dull moment, always keep the pitcher on his toes. Oh sure we had power, Babe Ruth was just a white Josh Gibson, but we had speed. Cool Papa Bell was so fast, I once saw him steal home from second base. Everybody was fast. Didn't dare blink, just might miss a triple and the whole field bursting into action.

"People are always telling me how sorry they feel for me, that I was too soon, ahead of the times. But there was jazz in the air, everywhere I went. I saw Bojangles dancing on the dugouts and Cab Calloway throwin' out first pitches. You name one of the great American jazz musicians, and they loved the Negro Leagues. Always comin' out to watch us play ball, called us ballplayers amazin'! Play ball by day and go dancing at night, man, that was the life!

"Satchel Paige, one of the greatest pitchers ever, he was one of my best of friends. We took care of each other out on the road. Always travelling, always on the go. But Satchel, yeah, he brought out the best in a guy, on the field and off. He had the guts to tell guys what he was gonna throw them, and would still strike them out. If Satchel had been in the major leagues during the prime of his career, man, he would've set records no one could touch. He was a comedian too, always crackin' jokes, always keepin' you in stitches. Sometimes he'd get bored on the mound and tell all the fielders to sit down, take a break, just to make things interesting.

"And Josh Gibson, flat out best hitter I've ever seen, and I'm pretty sure I've seen most of 'em. He would've rewritten the books as far as hitting goes. I'm convinced he died from a broken heart, because he never could play in the major leagues. Can you imagine knowing that you're the best, but never getting a chance to play in the majors because of the color of the skin God painted you in? He's playing in heaven now, and everybody wants him on their team, I guarantee it. They say he hit a ball out of Yankee Stadium, but you shoulda seen how far he'd hit 'em in batting practice.

"I have seen some of the worst things about people, about humanity. I have stood toe to toe with the Ku Klux Klan and had my life threatened. Hate is a powerful thing, and people filled with hate can be terrifying. Hate only lasts for a season, and sometimes that season seems like it will last forever, but love is stronger. Always. Well, love and having the commonsense to walk away from a fight.

"When Jackie got called up, I have never been so happy. Everyone was so happy for him. We knew it was gonna happen soon, the time was right, you could taste it in the air. And everybody knew that Jackie had a long hard road ahead of him there, lots of insults, lots of hate, lots of chances to fail. If he failed even one time, there probably wouldn't be any blacks in baseball today! Playing ball under that kind of stress really took its toll on him, on his wife, on his family. But we were all praying, all believing, we knew Jackie would open the doors for the world to see some of the best players ever.

"You see, there never shoulda been a Negro Leagues, no Negro Leagues Baseball Museum. There always shoulda been just one league where everybody plays together. No black, no white — all are created equal in God's eyes. Baseball is a game for everybody to play together. Why, there were even some women ballplayers too in the Negro Leagues. 'Peanut' Johnson and Toni Stone and Connie Morgan. 'Peanut,' she was a mighty fine pitcher, striking out guys all over the place. And I even saw Toni get a hit off of Satchel.

"Baseball will drive you to your knees to teach you humility, but then give you a pat on the back and tell you to keep your chin up and keep pressin' on, because there's always a-gonna be a tomorrow. Baseball is forever, for all the people, all of the time.

"Ethan, you say you're trying out for the varsity team? Here's a secret for you: play with heart! Play with passion! Play because there is no greater game on this planet and whether you win or lose, it is a joy to wear that uniform and toss that ball and step on the field in-between those lines. Play with a smile on your face and respect for the other team. Play hard and attempt the impossible. There are always gonna be people with more talent than you, but if you play with all of your heart, good things are gonna happen.

"And, Joshua, as a future history teacher, don't you forget these stories. Keep telling the stories of the Negro Leagues because they are an important part of who we are as a nation, when we couldn't recognize our brothers, when we forgot what it means to be human. All kinds of things baseball can teach us; we just gotta be willing to learn.

"You guys wanna see something really cool, or just hear me jabber on?"

"Whatever you want, Mr. O'Neil," I said.

With a sparkle in his eyes and a smile that never stopped he said, "Buck. My friends call me Buck."

And with that, he extended his hand and patted me on the back — my new friend Buck O'Neil.

"This here, this is one of Jackie Robinson's bats. He used it in a game and autographed it. His son's been holding on to it for years and as soon as he heard about the start of the NLBM a couple of years ago, he donated it to us for us to display. You wanna hold it?"

I couldn't believe what I was hearing. I carefully and cautiously gripped the well-loved piece of wood and lightly mimicked flexing my fingers and gently twisting my grip like Chadwick Boseman did in his portrayal of Jackie in the movie *42*.

"Now lookie here, everybody, just like Jackie. Where did you learn about that?" Buck asked.

"I, uh, remember reading about it in a book at school," I lied through my teeth.

I handed the bat to Joshua as Buck reached for another precious artifact.

"And this," Buck continued, "This, is one of Satchel's jerseys."

"Wow," Joshua quietly whispered.

"That is so cool," I said.

"Any questions for me or my friends?" Buck sang through a smile.

Joshua spoke up, "What do you think about Marge Schott and her suspension?"

"Now that's a good question. Hatred destroys a heart, but so does judging people. I never walked a mile in her shoes, and I ain't one to point fingers. This world is getting better all the time. Sometimes, it just takes us a lifetime to learn how to see it."

"I can't believe we just spent the last four hours with Buck O'Neil," Joshua stated as he started the car.

It was past time to head back to Springfield, we'd be significantly later than what I told my parents. Even so, I asked Joshua to make a slight detour through Lee's Summit, just so I could see how it looked.

Hope Church, where I would work for more than a decade, was literally just being built. The frame was in place and there were construction vehicles all over the property. So much of what I knew as Lee's Summit was years from becoming a reality — no coffee shops, no shopping centers, even my future house was not yet in existence.

"Like another world," I said smiling, shaking my head in disbelief.

As Joshua continued to head south, it didn't take long before the miles of rolling hills and open fields lulled me to sleep and I started dreaming.

Elisabeth and Sarah were running ahead, begging me and Annie to hurry up, so we could get wherever it was we were going. "Dad! Mom! Come on! We're gonna be late!" Annie was walking at my side, smiling, and wearing a skirt that showed off her long, tan legs. I could feel the concrete sidewalk beneath my feet but couldn't see anything past the girls or Annie. Music was playing somewhere and I turned around, trying to find the origin of the familiar melody, only to turn back and everyone was gone. I was by myself. I couldn't take another step; I was frozen in place unable to move as the sidewalk opened me up and swallowed me whole.

I jerked awake as Joshua tapped me on my shoulder. "Stopping for a bathroom break in just a few miles. You must've been dreaming; you were talking in your sleep."

"What'd I say?"

"Just a bunch of nonsense words and a bunch of names over and over. Annie. Sarah. Elisabeth. Whiffy. Who's Whiffy? That one made me laugh."

"Whiffy?" I almost started laughing myself. Had I been talking in my sleep about Wi-Fi?

Be here. I forced myself to think again.

"Need me to drive?" I asked. "Maybe you need a chance to talk in your sleep."

"I'll take you up on that."

We pulled over at a gas station near Collins, Missouri and filled up. I used the pay phone to make a collect call home, letting Mom and Dad know we were just running late, and that we had had an incredible day.

"I can't wait to tell you all about it."

Joshua did doze off and on while I drove, but he didn't talk in his sleep.

68

February 10, 1993

After multiple rounds of editing, my baseball paper was still ten pages in length. I had decided to turn it in early, anxious to hear Coach's feedback.

"Ethan, if you could stay after class for a few minutes, I'd like to talk with you," Coach Engel stated as the bell was getting ready to ring.

I absolutely hate that particular phrase, "I'd like to talk with you," and its cousin, "We need to talk." Nothing will raise my blood pressure faster than hearing those words. When it occurred to me that Coach probably wanted to talk about my essay, I was able to breathe a little easier.

The bell rang, the rest of the students left, and I stood near Coach's desk with my backpack slung over my shoulder.

"Am I supposed to believe that you actually got to spend time with Buck O'Neil last weekend?" Coach asked, raising an eyebrow.

"Yep. I didn't go alone, though. My friend Joshua went with me. I'm sure he'd be willing to serve as a witness. I can give you his phone number if you'd like to call him."

"No, thank you, that won't be necessary, I was just giving you a hard time. What an incredible experience, I'm pretty jealous. Buck O'Neil is a classy guy and the Negro Leagues are an incredibly important chapter in baseball and American history. I'm glad you got the experience."

"It really was an amazing day. Sorry the essay was so long. That's after I cut out a lot of stories, too."

"No need to apologize, it was fun to read. What I really wanted to ask is if I could have your permission to submit it to a journal for publication? No promises that they'll accept it, but I think they'd at least give it a good look, especially since it came from a high school student."

"Permission granted," I said with a smirk.

When I got home, I immediately went to see my father. With only nine days remaining until tryouts, I was both nervous and excited to see how my offseason workouts had paid off.

Dad agreed to take me to the workout facility at SMSU so I could get a good pitching session in and take a few swings off the tee. We were both surprised to run into Coach Goodwin on the way in.

"Hey, Doc! You guys coming to practice today? My team's getting ready for the kickoff tournament next weekend."

"I guess we hadn't really paid attention to the schedule; I didn't think you'd be here on a Saturday afternoon."

"No, no, that's fine. Maybe your boy would like to join us? Didn't you say he was a pitcher? Maybe Coach Evans could watch him throw a few."

"Now that would be awesome," I said.

"Follow me and I'll introduce you to a few guys."

After stretching and warming up with the team, Coach Evans took me and Dad to the indoor mound to watch me throw a few pitches. Dad was my catcher, sitting on an orange five-gallon bucket, and Coach Evans stood directly behind me, much like an umpire in little league baseball.

"What pitches do you throw?"

"Four-seam fastball, two-seam fastball, slider, and a circle change."

"Imagine you've got a right-handed hitter. Start with four fastballs, two inside then two outside."

I did as he said and was pleased with my effort.

"Now, let's see your slider. Two inside, two outside."

Again, I did as he said and was satisfied with the subtle movement on my slider.

"Make sure that when you throw those pitches, you start with your hands in the same position as you did with the fastball. You don't want to give anything away. And you don't have to rush your delivery, keep it smooth."

I nodded.

For twenty minutes, Coach Evans gave me pointers and simple suggestions and we talked about various pitching strategies.

Three pitchers and a catcher from SMSU made their way over to us, so I hopped off the mound. Dad and I watched their bullpen sessions, listening closely to the suggestions Coach Evans gave them.

As we got ready to leave, Coach Evans approached Dad, "While he's not gonna blow anyone away, he has really good control, throws all of his pitches for strikes and has enough movement to keep hitters off balance. Make sure he works quickly but stays smooth, and don't let him get into a habit of always throwing the same pitches in the same location in the same count. Mix 'em up. Keep 'em guessing. And most importantly, have fun."

69

February 14, 1993

Valentine's Day.

Knowing what day it was and missing Annie like crazy, I repeated my now time-worn phrase, "Be here."

It didn't seem to be working, but instead of thinking about the lump in my throat, I sighed deeply and rolled out of bed, not particularly looking forward to this over-commercialized holiday of sappy affections. Heading into the kitchen, I noticed that Mom had left cards and small boxes of chocolate on the kitchen table for me and Katy. Dad left the keys to his car along with a note, "Drove Mom to church for bell choir practice. See you guys there."

I was ready long before Katy was able to tame her mane of curls; one of the joys of being bald — efficient and minimal morning routines. I watched *SportsCenter*, flipped through the Sports page, ate a banana, and changed ties twice before she was ready to head to church.

After slowly trudging up the three flights of stairs to the youth room, I proceeded toward the counter with the donuts and juice; Darrell greeted me with a cup of coffee, creamer already added.

"Been waiting for you this morning. I'd like to hear what you have to say about today's topic."

I glanced at the white board. Written in red, surrounded by hearts, and underlined with an arrow for emphasis, was the simple question, "What is love?"

I could think of dozens of other places I'd rather be than talking about love with a bunch of teenagers on a Sunday morning on Valentine's Day.

"Not sure I've got much to say this morning," I quipped, then took a small and precious sip of my coffee.

"Sorry, that one's not gonna work with me. It's your senior year. Some of these younger guys really listen to you. Besides, the caffeine will kick in soon."

"Touché," I smiled, lifting my Styrofoam cup in a mock toast. "Well, maybe I can think of something."

As Paula walked around the inside of the pit distributing pencils and paper to each of us, Brett, one of the seventh-grade boys, plopped down immediately to my right and greeted me with a goofy grin that matched his equally goofy cowlick. I looked up at Darrell in a silent plea for help; he smiled and winked in return.

"For the next ten minutes," Paula started, "Darrell and I would like you to write down your own definition of love. If you want to use a Bible, there are some on the bookshelf in the corner. If you don't want to write sentences, then draw a picture of what love is."

I glanced to my right; Brett started drawing immediately. Putting pencil to paper, I started writing:

There is no greater power in the 'verse than love. Love is practicing patience when you are in the slowest lane at the grocery store. Love is choosing kindness instead of cursing the school bully. Love celebrates the success of another and is not envious, even if you finished in second place. Love does not always demand the spotlight, but delights in sharing, especially with siblings. Love does not give back-handed compliments or over-exaggerate the truth, although embellishment is necessary for every good story. Love forgives every single time. Love doesn't judge by comparison, but delights in the image of God in everyone. Love holds strong to hope, even when surrounded by evil. Love knows no bounds.

After about ten minutes, Darrell cleared his throat, "So, Ethan, would you like to read what you wrote?"

As soon as I finished reading mine, Brett raised his hand and volunteered to share his.

"I always have trouble thinking of love in words, so I drew a picture," Brett said, and he held up an incredible sketch of two hearts. One heart had an apparent crack running down the middle of it, but the crack was being mended by an over-sized band-aid.

The second heart was leaning into the first heart, holding an umbrella, shielding both of them from the rain. "Whenever I think of love, I think of the parable of the Good Samaritan," Brett added. "The guy didn't judge based on looks or circumstances, he just responded to the need he saw."

"Dude," I said, "that is awesome. I'll give you a dollar for that drawing."

"Really?" Brett asked.

"No, make that five bucks. This is incredible. I really love this drawing. Great job. This really is what love looks like."

I opened up my wallet and tossed a five-dollar bill to Brett. His goofy grin got bigger and then he leaped at me and gave me a hug.

"No one's ever paid me for my drawings before."

"You'll sign it for me, right?"

"You bet!"

Brett's hug was all the affection I got for Valentine's Day.

70

February 16, 1993

"Ethan, Mr. O'Neal would like to see you."

My heart skipped a beat as Mr. Clarke handed me a green slip for the counselors' office. It took my mind a moment to catch up and realize that it was Mr. O'Neal the school counselor that desired my presence, not Mr. Buck O'Neil, the baseball player.

"Good afternoon, Ethan, just wanted to check in with you and see how all the college stuff is going, if you needed any of my help or anything."

"As far as I know, everything's fine. I've already got an acceptance letter from SMSU and I'm supposed to do the scheduling thing for freshman sometime in July. Honestly, I'm just waiting for baseball season to start."

"And you've filled out all of your scholarship applications?"

"Everyone you've told me to."

"You should start hearing back from them by the mid-April or so. Wisdom comes in the waiting," he said.

"Lucky me."

After school, Nathan and I went to Taco Bell for our customary mid-afternoon meal. He had been grounded for the last month after our extra-curricular four-wheeling activity, including from use of the phone. Aside from trips to school and home again, we really had not had many opportunities to visit. Repairs on the Suzuki finally finished at the beginning of the week.

"Welcome back to the land of the free," I said as we sat down by the window and the soda fountain.

"Feels good to be able to go somewhere other than school and the grocery store."

"I bet," I said, taking a big bite of some super cheesy nachos.

"Are you ready for baseball tryouts?"

"Yep. 'Dreams are slow,' you know. Feels like I've been waiting forever for this chance."

"Nervous?"

"Yep. Gonna be hard to sit in Engel's class if I don't make the team."

"Hadn't thought about that one. How long do tryouts last?"

"Just until Friday. Not gonna need any rides home next week. The team will be posted first thing Saturday morning. What's new with you?"

"I got a good scholarship from KU, which helped ease some tension with the parentals. Also got a raise at the Y, so that was cool. Other than that, for the last month, life has been really boring."

"Sorry you had to go through that. Glad to be able to hang out with you again. Tell you what, after tryouts end on Friday, come pick me up and I'll take you to Andy's — I owe you one."

Nathan smiled, "Deal."

That night, Drew called. "Tryouts start next week," he said. "Ready?"

"Yep. You?"

"You know it. We've got a pretty good team this year. Looked at the schedule yet?"

"No, just thinking about surviving."

"Glendale plays Kickapoo three times."

"Well," I said in my best Saturday Night Live Church Lady impression, "Isn't that special?"

"You know I'd love the chance just to get a hit off you."

"You know I'd love the chance just to hit you," I laughed.

"What happens on the field…"

"…stays on the field, I know. It's just a game. And just so you know, I'd never intentionally throw at you. Never."

71

February 22, 1993

Coach Engel chomped his gum loud enough I thought I heard it echoing in the locker room.

"Twenty-one games and then the district playoffs start, gentlemen," Coach Engel informed us at the start of varsity tryouts. "Twenty-one games not to try and impress scouts or show off for your girlfriends, but to leave everything you've got on that field, to play for your teammates and for the joy of the game. For a lot of you, these will be the last twenty-one games of competitive baseball you'll play.

"Now, I can only keep twenty-two of you on the team, which means that more than half of you will be cut. Thanks to new rules of the Missouri State High School Activities Association, after tryouts, we've only got three weeks until our first games, which will take place in Kansas City on the last weekend of spring break.

"So, if you wanna play ball, you better cancel your fancy spring break senior trips now. Also, I expect everyone on the team to keep at least a B average. Every Friday, you need to get your grades from all of your teachers and have them to me before school is out. If you're worried about keeping up with school, gentlemen, might I suggest not playing ball. You need to be thinking first about your life after baseball.

"Ok, enough talk. Pitchers and catchers follow me, everyone else with Coach Bell. Let's get started."

The assembly of tight pants, tall socks, and brim-bent baseball hats split almost exactly in half. I followed Coach Engel closely, almost walking exactly in his steps, ready to get to work.

"Pitchers, I'm going to pair you up. You'll workout with your partner for the rest of the week, whether you're throwing a bullpen or doing fielding drills or running sprints or playing long toss or warming a bench.

"Branten and Bryan, you guys start on the bullpen mound with McHandley as your catcher. Thought it'd be easiest to keep all the Brians together. Warm-up, then take turns throwing ten pitches. Stop when you've thrown fifty."

On the field, Coach always addressed us by last name only. I was partnered with Brian Branten and Brian McHandley. Having a last name that could substitute as a first name has been a source of confusion my entire life.

I remember Brian Branten well; I followed his career into the minor leagues. As a senior in high school, Brian was already throwing in the low 90s and had a sharp curveball. He pitched at the University of Missouri in Columbia for three years before getting drafted by the San Francisco Giants in one of the late rounds the summer after his junior year. He steadily climbed through the minor league ranks until AA ball, when he pitched for the Shreveport Captains, and tore his bicep in the middle of a game. One year after surgery, almost to the day, he tried to make a comeback, but the bicep never fully healed and it tore a second time.

In 2015, Brian became a successful businessman in Chicago, faithfully cheering for the San Francisco Giants when they play at Wrigley Field.

Overcast skies made wearing sleeves necessary, but all in all, the weather was pretty kind to us for late February. Coach flipped me a ball and the Brians and I walked to the bullpen mound near the home team dugout on the third-base side of the field. McHandley stood near the plate, Branten stood on the mound, and I was five feet to the right of Branten. I flipped the ball to McHandley, who threw it to Branten, back to McHandley, then to me. This triangled game of catch lasted until we were both ready to get to work; Branten went first.

It is one thing to watch a 90 mph fastball on TV or from the stands. It is a completely different experience to be standing next to the pitcher as he releases it from his hands. You can actually hear the ball. Branten pumped fastball after fastball right down the middle, each one seemingly harder than the one before. After ten pitches, he turned to me and placed the ball in my glove. "You're turn, Big E."

I knew I couldn't throw like Branten and knew I didn't have to try to throw like Branten. I was supposed to pitch like me. So I did just what Coach Evans taught me — two fastballs inside, two fastballs outside, a couple change-ups, a couple sliders, and two more fastballs. I focused on location and movement and being smooth.

For the first time in months, I felt like I was in exactly the right place. I felt truly alive, like all of my senses were turned up to 11, that the God who exists beyond all time was near, that baseball mattered, that I was standing on holy ground.

"Nice work," McHandley yelled at me from behind his mask.

I tipped my hat and handed the ball back to Branten. We each threw four more times and then rejoined the rest of the pitchers and catchers with Coach Engel. I sidled up next to McHandley who was also a senior, who had no trouble growing a full beard; he was about my height, but definitely thicker, a perfect build for a catcher. "You make a great target back there. Thanks."

"No worries, Big E," McHandley smiled and thumped me on the butt with his catcher's mitt.

The rest of the first day of tryouts consisted of running sprints, pitchers fielding drills, and shagging fly balls during batting practice. I couldn't help but smile through all of it. The worry and anxiety of the last couple of weeks, of the last few months, completely fell away as I ran around that outdoor sanctuary.

After sliding to catch a line drive during batting practice, Coach Engel yelled at me, "Bryan, are you having fun out there?"

"I'm in heaven, Coach!"

I was still in heaven when I got home that night. "How were tryouts, Chief?" Dad asked as we sat down to dinner.

"Good. Half the people are gonna be cut, but I had a blast. Carpe diem, right?"

"Carpe diem, Chief."

Katy walked by and spotted my glove on the floor. She grabbed the baseball out of the web and tossed it to me.

"Think quick!" she said.

I dropped the ball.

Both she and Dad thought it was hilarious, laughing themselves silly. I shook my head somewhat frustrated at myself.

"Well, that won't get me on the team."

72

February 23, 1993

Almost all of my classes took a back seat to baseball, except for Coach Engel's class, which was really just another form of baseball. It was the last semester of my senior year and not only had I already been accepted to college, unlike my fellow classmates, my future was not uncertain.

Or so I hoped. I was basically on academic cruise control, not at all worried about maintaining a "B average" for the team. Time passed a little slower with each class; I just wanted to get back out on the field again.

Day two of tryouts was remarkably similar to day one. This time, however, Coach Engel watched Branten and I throw our sessions while the other pitchers and catchers ran and started the fielding drills with Coach Bell. Branten again pounded fastballs. The normal pops of ball hitting leather sounded like firecrackers in McHandley's mitt.

I toed the rubber for a couple moments, somewhat intimidated by Coach's presence, but more so determined to prove that I belonged on the team. Inside, outside, fastballs, off-speed — each pitch thrown with thoughtful purpose.

After our session, Coach complimented both of us and called over the next pair of pitchers. "Keep working hard, boys, and hustle!"

Pop. Pop. Pop.

I turned back to Coach and smiled, "The hard is what makes it great, right?"

Pop. Pop. Pop.

"Branten throws so hard, doesn't he?" I asked.

"He's got one of the strongest arms I've ever coached," he answered, without looking up from his clipboard. He was quickly reading through the names of those trying out for the varsity team, jotting down new drills for this afternoon's practice.

"I'd also like to try out at second base, take some ground balls, hit against live pitching. How do I do that?"

"Remind me after you throw today and I'll send you to work with Coach Bell. Johnson's been solid at second, and he and Hardwick can turn a double play pretty quick. You think you're better than Johnson?" Coach asked, looking up at me.

"No, I don't think I'm better than Johnson. I know he's better than I am. But if he got hurt or we had a double-header, then I want you and Coach Bell to know that I'm at least a possible back-up."

"A utility guy, huh?"

"Jack-of-all-trades, master of none."

By 2015, the baseball field at Kickapoo High School was one of the nicest public high school baseball fields in all of Missouri as the parents and boosters do a good job of keeping it in solid playing shape.

In 1993, however, field maintenance fell on the shoulders of the players, who were generally lazy and exhausted when the time came to picking rocks and raking the infield dirt.

Johnson must have known the secrets of this infield from experience, as he smoothly fielded all the ground balls Coach Bell hit at him, taking turns throwing to first, second, and home without any hiccups.

I stepped up and, while successfully keeping every ball in front of me, got bad hops and in-between hops and one ball that hit the edge of the grass and dirt, the ultimate bad luck hop.

"Stick with it," Coach Bell yelled.

"Tough luck," Johnson whispered to me. "Stay aggressive and you'll be okay."

We spent time working on turning double plays, bunt coverage drills, followed by base stealing practice, relay throws to the different bases, and bare-handing high bouncers. Pitchers were used as base runners to get sprinting practice in. Branten smacked the hat off my head as he walked back to first after sprinting to second, "Lucky." I shrugged my shoulders and smiled.

But infielders and outfielders had to do all of their running after pitchers were free to go home.

"Get outta here and go home!" Coach Engel yelled, and I fell to my knees on the field, trying to catch my breath. By the time the third day of tryouts was over, I was spent. My legs were screaming and I had several new bruises, courtesy of grounds balls and sliding practice.

"You doing okay, Ethan?"

I looked up and Coach Bell was standing in front of me.

I smiled at him, "Wouldn't trade it for the world, Coach."

Back at home, my bravado failed a bit. I limped past Mom and Katy, feeling the soreness in my muscles.

"Now you're walkin' like a dancer," Katy commented.

Her comment caught me by surprise and made me laugh.

"Ice and ibuprofen, Chief," Dad said, handing me a couple of pills and a bag of frozen peas. "You know you don't get bruises like that playing golf. Sure you don't want to switch?"

"Never, never, never give up."

Dad gently patted my back, "Atta boy!"

73

February 25, 1993

"Today, each pitcher will throw to three hitters," Coach Engel said, looking down at his trusty clipboard. "Two from the wind-up, one from the stretch. We'll be rotating infielders and outfielders in and out behind you. You only need to worry about the guy on the mound and the guy at the plate. Gentleman, this is no time to dawdle. Work fast. We've still got a lot to do. We'll go alphabetically: Branten, you're first, then Bryan, Cantrell, Clark, and Davis. Pitchers to the visitors' dugout; hitters have the home dugout."

I gave Branten a thump on the back with my mitt, "Show 'em what you've got, dude." He laughed and promptly struck out all three hitters, barely working up a sweat. One guy did manage to foul a couple pitches off, but Branten threw a fastball at eye-level, and there was nothing the guy could do but swing and miss.

I played catch in the visitor's bullpen with Davis and tried to peek into the opposite dugout to see who might be facing me. The fourth hitter was a friend from my JV days, Chad, and he had been watching Branten pitch, taking dry swings in the on-deck circle, focusing on his timing. He didn't know that he would be facing me, not Branten, so I decided to have some fun.

Coach Engel called for the switch, and Hardwick and Johnson also ran out, taking their places behind me at shortstop and second. Chad smiled at me and nodded his head as he walked to the plate.

I started him off with a slow slider, and Chad swung way too early and over the top for strike one. My second pitch was an even slower change-up. Chad tried to stay back on it, but was still considerably out in front and hit a weak pop-up to Johnson.

Luke stepped up to the plate, a tall, lanky junior, with a long swing. I threw fastballs inside and got him to ground out to the first baseman.

I didn't know who the third hitter was, but he tightened his batting gloves and popped his neck as he strode toward the plate.

"From the stretch!" Coach Engel yelled.

I threw a slider that didn't slide but just spun like a merry-go-round. The hitter made solid contact with it, driving it to left-center, but Alex was playing centerfield and got a great jump on it, running it down and catching it one-handed.

Jogging off the mound, I exhaled loudly. Coach Engel heard me and chuckled, "Not too bad, not too bad. Cantrell! Get out there, hustle!"

The next couple of hours were a whirlwind. I played second base off and on, but the only action I saw was a relay throw to second on a ball hit to deep right field. I ran sprints with Branten and took my turn at the plate against Casey, one of the southpaw pitchers, successfully dropping a bunt down the third base line for an infield single.

Coach Engel called everyone in to close practice.

"Gentleman, it's been a good week so far and we've had great weather, considering it's still February. Tomorrow, all pitchers will work with me in the upstairs gym and everyone else will be out here with Coach Bell. Cuts will be posted by 10 AM Saturday morning. I really wish I could keep all of you, you are all skilled, talented young men. Thanks for playing hard and having the courage to try out. That's all, guys. Get some rest tonight. Only one day left."

74

February 26, 1993

Coach Engel was drafted twice. The first time he was drafted, it was straight out of high school, by the St. Louis Cardinals in the 21st round of the 1965 MLB June Amateur Draft.

Two years later, the New York Yankees drafted him in the 5th round from the University of Missouri. Both times, he was drafted because of his dominating performances as a pitcher.

"When you've got good pitching, everything else just falls in place," he claimed.

"In a game, I call every single pitch," Coach Engel said. "If you strike someone out, I get the credit. If someone hits a home run, it's your fault for not executing the pitch. There won't be any shaking off of the signs, unless I give you the sign to shake off a pitch. Today, you'll pitch side-by-side with your partner, whatever pitch I tell you, where I tell you to throw it.

"McHandley, Snyder, Batemann, and Rangle will be rotating in as catchers. When you're not throwing in here, I expect you to be doing long toss and your sprints outside, just like every other day. Any questions?"

"What if we don't have the pitch you say?" someone standing behind me asked.

"If you'd rather throw a slider than a curve or a curve instead of a slider, that's fine by me. Anyone else?"

I raised my hand, "What about if you've got another position, too?"

"Good news for you, you and Branten are up first. You'll get the best of both worlds now, won't you? All right, gentlemen, get to work."

I intentionally stepped to the mound opposite of McHandley as I was most comfortable throwing to him. Branten was paired with Rangle, who cussed and started massaging his hand in preparation for Branten's fastballs.

"This is your final exam, gentlemen, twenty-five pitches, pass or fail."

"Grades are posted tomorrow?" I asked.

"Grades are posted tomorrow. Fastball, inside," Coach announced the pitch and the location and the catchers set up correspondingly.

I took a deep breath, smiled, and whispered to myself, "*Carpe diem.*"

Nathan picked me up after tryouts. I was starving, sweat-coated, and ready for a substantial intake of protein and caffeine.

"Wanna get a pizza first, and then I'll treat you to Andy's?"

"How'd it go?"

"Hard, but fair. I bloodied my knee taking grounders at second today, landed on a stupid rock when I tried to slide. Did good work from the mound, I think, and didn't embarrass myself taking swings. Now, the waiting game begins, and I'm looking for as many distractions as possible until 10 AM tomorrow."

"We could catch a movie tonight?"

"What's playing?"

"There's that new one with Bill Murray, *Groundhog Day.*"

"I could definitely see that one again. It might give me nightmares, but my mind could use the break."

75

February 27, 1993 — 6:00 AM

I was awake and had been awake for most of the night. Questions always seem to hit between sunset and sunrise, when everything else has gone silent.

What if I don't make the team?

What if I do make the team?

Who else made the team?

Who else didn't make the team?

How will I get back to 2015?

Fighting back the pressing dread, I whispered a short prayer, rolled out of bed, and walked to the kitchen. No one else in my family was awake, so I didn't turn on the TV. Dodger greeted me with a cold nose and I let him out the back door, smiling while watching him chase squirrels and run around. I quietly opened the front door and gingerly walked barefoot out to get the newspaper. Pulling it out of the orange plastic sleeve, the headline on the front page stunned me.

World Trade Center Attacked; Bomb Suspected:

At Least 6 Killed, Thousands Injured

Immediately, I remembered sitting in my office at Hope Church watching the coverage of the attacks on September 11, 2001 and was reminded of the world in which I really lived. I walked back inside and sat down at the kitchen table, slowly reading through the entire article while I ate a banana.

Somehow, I had completely forgotten this incident. My self-centered baseball worries seemed ridiculously petty in comparison to those who had suffered at the hands of terrorists. I thought about Chris and I thought about the Losers Club. Questions came with a vengeance, each one heavier than its predecessor.

Was I caught up in my own selfish ambitions, or was I living the life I was supposed to live the first time?

What good is baseball in a world of fear and terror and pain and death?

Who cares about baseball when there is war and famine and disease and rampant poverty?

Who cares about a game when millions are just trying to live?

God, why am I even here?

And as soon as the questions surfaced, an answer also came to mind.

Because when the world forgets how to play, they forget what it means to be made in the creative image of God.

A couple hours later, Drew called, "Did you make the team?"

"Won't know until 10. Did you?" I asked, already knowing the answer.

"Yeah. Want me to go with you?"

"That'd be great. Wanna pick me up and drive me to the school?"

"Sure thing, I'm on my way."

I thought there'd be a swarm of people waiting for the cut list to be posted at 10 AM. When Drew and I pulled up into the parking lot, there was only one other car there, and I recognized it immediately as Coach Engel's.

There was a simple piece of paper taped up to the window from the inside right next to the door. I walked up the sidewalk, taking deep breaths, while my heart thumped inside me. Drew walked silently a couple of steps behind me. I skimmed the list as quickly as possible.

1993 Varsity —

1. B. Dellen
2. J. Lunding
3. J. Jackson
4. P. Snyder
5. R. Davis
6. **E. Bryan**

There it was in the center of the page. I stared in stunned silence and struggled to believe that what I was seeing was real.

I made the team.

All those off-season workouts and throwing sessions with Dad had paid off.

I did it.

76

March 1, 1993

"All right guys — new month, new essay," Coach Engel started the class on the first Monday of the month. "Choose one person who is currently not in the Hall of Fame and write three to five pages explaining why they should be in the Hall."

"What if it's someone you know will eventually be in the Hall of Fame, but the required time hasn't passed between their retirement and induction?" Jeff asked.

"Like who?"

"Well, I was thinking specifically of Ozzie Smith. He hasn't retired yet, but I just know he's Hall of Fame material."

"Ah, good question. Current players can be included in this essay."

In last period, I was buzzing with excitement from making the team, and ready to celebrate the good news with the Loser's Club. "Way to go, Loser! I knew you could do it!" Nathan started the English class note-passing session. The rest of the Losers Club all added words of encouragement, celebrating my achievement. Junior even composed a poem on my behalf:

To the only bald guy on this year's team

I tip my hat to you

Please keep yours on and cover that gleam

You now play for the 'Poo!

I folded up the paper and stuck it my back pocket, relishing it as one would a trophy.

My celebratory mood continued throughout practice that afternoon. "Gentlemen, first of all, congratulations," Coach Engel greeted us in the locker room as we changed into our practice clothes.

"You've made it this far, now get ready to work. In less than three weeks, we'll be heading to KC for our first two games and the season doesn't slow down until May. Turn in your grades to me every Friday, always give me your best effort, and everything else will turn out all right. After practice tomorrow, you'll pick up your uniforms. I'll see you on the field in five."

I was assigned #2, because the #1 jersey was lost and there was no one on the team smaller than me.

Immediately, I thought of Derek Jeter, the 20-year shortstop for the Yankees and famed #2 wearer. He retired in 2014 and every team gave him gifts in a season-long retirement party. Toward the end of the season, when it was apparent that the Yankees wouldn't make the play-offs, Jeter was asked how he chose his number.

"They just assigned it to me. I was unaware of the significance of the single-digit number in Yankees' history. I always assumed it was the smallest jersey."

77

March 5, 1993

With baseball practice every day after school, my life's routine became very simple.

Wake up.

Go to school.

Go to practice.

Go home.

Eat.

Study.

Sleep.

Repeat.

The routine greatly helped me focus on living in the present tense, on *being here*, and not worrying about all the unknowns regarding the future and getting back home.

As Friday's practice ended, I saw Joshua sitting in the bleachers and ran over to say hi.

"Looking good out there," Joshua said.

"Coach Engel is definitely working us hard. What are you doing here?"

"Had to drop off some paperwork stuff for school and saw you guys practicing. Doing ok?"

"No idle time is a good thing."

"I'd love to catch a few of your games."

"I can bring a schedule on Sunday. Wanna lunch?"

"How about Casper's?"

"See you Sunday," I said, jogging off toward the locker room.

I woke the next morning determined to stay on Coach Engel's good side. I knew that a solid five-page essay would only take me a couple of hours to prepare and, since I had nothing else planned on this Saturday, I asked Dad if he could drop me off at the SMSU library to research for Coach's paper while he went on a few of his veterinary house calls.

"It'll probably take me two to three hours to come back and get you. You okay with that?"

"I'll have the paper finished and printed before you return."

Ethan Bryan

American Baseball History Essay #2

March 6, 1993

In Defense of Charlie Hustle

The first time I saw Pete Rose play, he *sprinted* to first base on a walk. It wasn't a casual trot or a simple jog down the first base line, but an all-out sprint, as if he had to get to first base in a certain amount of time or risk being called out. Over the course of his career, Rose sprinted to first base after a walk more times than any other switch hitter — 1,566 times to be precise. Compared to the few athletes who dominate the sport by their athletic giftedness and possession of the "five tools" of baseball, Pete Rose only has two gifts: he always hustles and he can hit *anything*. He holds more than twenty Major League records, including:

- Most career hits — 4,256

- Most career outs — 10,328

- Most career games played — 3,562

- Most career singles — 3,215

- Most career runs by a switch hitter — 2,165

- Most career doubles by a switch hitter — 746

- Most career walks by a switch hitter — 1,566

- Most seasons with 600 at bats — 17

- Record for playing in the most winning games — 1,972

Only player in MLB history to play more than 500 games at five different positions

But Pete Rose committed the only unforgiveable sin of baseball.

And then he lied about it.

In every clubhouse of every Major League team, one rule — Rule 21(d) — is clearly posted:

Any player, umpire, or club or league official or employee, who shall bet any sum whatsoever upon any baseball game in connection with which the bettor has a duty to perform shall be declared permanently ineligible.

On August 24, 1989, Major League Baseball Commissioner Bart Giamatti declared that Pete Rose was banned from baseball for life because of his gambling actions. "One of the game's greatest players has engaged in a variety of acts which have stained the game," Giamatti said, "and he must now live with the consequences of those acts." Giamatti's declaration was based on The Dowd Report. John

M. Dowd, a lawyer, discovered that Rose bet on several games daily in all sports, and was regularly in debt to bookies. Dowd's report totaled 225 pages and was turned in to Giamatti in May of 1989. Giamatti's job was relatively simple — enforce Rule 21(d). The ban means Rose cannot appear at any official MLB function — not a game, or any festivities before or after a game.

Last month I asked my friend, Buck O'Neil, if Pete Rose should be in the Hall of Fame. Buck replied, emphasizing the redemptive power of forgiveness, "As far as his playing ability is concerned, Pete Rose should be in the Hall of Fame." But then Buck continued. He spoke of Rose's mistake and rule violation. He spoke of Rose's arrogance and pride. He spoke of Rose's disregard for everyone else in the game.

"Always Pete wanted to be bigger than the game, always all about Pete. But when you play ball, you play for your team, you play for your friends who step on that sacred dirt with you.

"I pray for Pete," Buck continued. "I pray he gets a chance to know what the word 'forgiveness' means. I know a thing or two about forgiveness. It's a choice one has to make every single day. Forgiveness leads to freedom, leads to life, to joy! Yes, I pray for Pete that he might know forgiveness and again be an ambassador of this amazing game."

Baseball is the greatest game because of the lessons it teaches us for life. In order to be your best, you need the help of others; it is impossible to succeed on your own. Baseball teaches us perseverance and hope in the face of failure. Baseball teaches that talent can only carry a person so far; hard work, hustle, and heart can make a player better. Those who play the game professionally are honored culturally, and have both the responsibility and privilege to serve as role models for those who dream of following in their footsteps.

I do believe that Pete Rose belongs in the Hall of Fame. The "Hit King" survived 24 grueling Major League seasons, setting several records that will be near impossible to surpass. His poor decision to gamble on baseball should not be the end of his story, but a chance to demonstrate that baseball can teach us about forgiveness, too.

78

March 7, 1993

Joshua drove us to the Quonset hut with the simple hand-painted sign hanging out front, "Casper's." Stepping inside, the bohemian decorations made me smile — a bright orange ceiling, small booths with seats covered in blue, and colorful stools near the countertop bar. Posters of bands, old celebrities, and optical illusions covered every square foot of wall space.

The quirky atmosphere was the perfect setting for the best cup of chili, smothered in cheese, no onions. A young family was already occupying the stools at the countertop; Joshua and I sat at a small booth toward the back of the hut.

"How's life treating you these days?" Joshua asked softly as the waitress brought us a couple of Dr Peppers.

"Did you know that there are stories about Lincoln playing ball on the White House lawn? One reporter said that his strides were so long the tails of his town coat flew out behind him. And did you know that there's a reference to George Washington playing catch with one of his aides in a soldier's letter? And that Drew Johnson regularly gave government employees time off to watch Washington Nationals games?"

"Studying about the presidents and their relationship to baseball in Engel's class, I see. And the first president to throw out a first pitch was...?"

"William Taft in 1910; Opening Day for the Washington Senators. But he threw it from his seat, not from the mound. Do you know about Truman?"

Josh smiled, "That he was ambidextrous, and threw out Opening Day pitches with both hands? He went to a lot of games because he thought it was a good display of peace after WWII. He thought that baseball could help restore the morale of the country."

"I don't think he was much of a player, though," I said. "There's a funny story about his vision, that since he couldn't see well enough to play, they made him an umpire. How about this...the most impressive first pitch I've ever seen is one that you couldn't possibly know about."

I looked around Casper's; no one was particularly close to us, and no one was paying any attention to us anyway. "It doesn't happen until 2001. Wanna hear the story?"

I could tell that Joshua was truly interested in the story, but honestly wrestling with knowing about future events. "Sure," he shrugged his shoulders, "Why not?"

"Remember when the World Trade Center was attacked last month? Well, in 2001, on 9/11, there's another terrorist attack on the twin towers. Both of them are completely destroyed. Thousands die and it's one of those events where you remember where you were and what you were doing when you heard the news.

"Fear dominated the air waves and all interactions with people. I remember hearing reports on the radio about what to do if you thought a terrorist lived near you. No one felt safe, really, and life in America changed dramatically. Flights were grounded, and then new procedures put in place which made trying to fly a hassle. Everyone was afraid that Al-Qaeda would attack again. So, the Yankees and Diamondbacks were in the World Series and it was the end of October."

"The Diamondbacks?"

"Yeah, Arizona Diamondbacks. National League expansion team in 1998. Because MLB games were cancelled for a few days after 9/11, the World Series was played much later, actually a couple games were played in November. For game three, at old Yankee Stadium — there's a new Yankee Stadium now — President Bush was set to throw out the first pitch."

"A new Yankee Stadium? And did President Bush have a split-term then?"

"Yes, a new Yankee Stadium and this President Bush is the son of Bush number 41, also named George. President Bush, number 43, walked onto the field from the Yankee's dugout wearing a bullet proof vest under a FDNY jacket, and waved at the crowd from the top of the mound. There were chants of 'USA! USA! USA!' echoing in the stands and he responded by giving them a thumbs up. And then he threw a perfect strike. Baseball was again a healing agent when our country was completely gripped by fear. Man, I'd love to tell that story or, better yet, show the video in Engel's class. It's just really powerful."

"Wow, that's pretty scary to think about, hard to imagine that something like that's in our nation's future. To be honest, part of me really does want to hear more stories about the future, but I just don't think that's in either of our best interest. Focusing on the here and now, however, you never answered my initial question."

"Yeah, I know. Coach Engel's class is really about the only thing keeping me from going crazy this last semester."

Joshua raised his eyebrows and looked at me straight-faced at the mention of the word "crazy."

"Not really crazy, it's just, well, being a teenager is exhausting. School is boring, it's barely more than glorified babysitting at this point. And I feel trapped, fake, like who I am is some kind of game. As long as I'm on the field, I'm so focused on what I'm doing there that everything's okay, it's just managing the rest of life. And the rest of life…"

Joshua interrupted, "Do you remember that guy from Springfield I was telling you about? The one who disappeared?"

"The journal writer?"

Joshua reached into his back pocket and placed a carefully folded up copy of a magazine article on the table. "It's by Mr. Wilton."

I choked on my Dr Pepper.

"A couple of years ago, I was researching Einstein and The Philadelphia Experiment and other time travel stuff. It totally consumed me. I was spending almost all of my free time in the library at Drury. One of the books I needed was located in the historical documents section and right next to the book I was looking for was this leather-bound journal.

"One of my researching habits is to skim and read other books from the same section, so I picked it up and started thumbing through it. When I noticed that it wasn't a library book, I stuck it in my coat pocket and took it home.

"I read it from cover to cover that first night. The date was written, centered, at the top of each page and then the author started writing, almost in a secret code of sorts. I could tell from some of the references that it was written by someone local, but all of the names were abbreviated. And that's when it struck me — this was actually someone's journal."

My heart started pounding as Josh continued, "The author was probably a student at Drury researching something in the same section and had set it down on a shelf or dropped it and someone just picked it up and placed it on the shelf.

"When you first started telling me your story, the similarities were too much to just be coincidence. I had hidden the journal in a safety deposit box and started re-reading it after our initial visit at Taco Bell, looking for clues, connections. So, last week, I was thumbing through the newest issue of Sci-Fi Monthly and saw this," Joshua said as he pointed to the biography of the torn-out story.

Thomas Wilton's time-travelling thriller, *Here to Stay*, will be re-printed by Galaxies Press, a vintage publishing company, at the end of the month in honor of the 30th anniversary of its first print.

Wilton, who is now a Vice Principal at Kickapoo High School in Springfield, Missouri, was a student at then Drury College when the book first published.

"I never imagined anyone would want to read it," Wilton said at our interview, "I just wrote for myself, for the fun of writing, to help keep myself sane." The sci-fi community would like to thank Wilton's roommate for submitting the original manuscript! The first two chapters are reprinted on the pages that follow by permission.

Joshua continued, "As soon as I started reading it, I knew that this was somehow connected to the journal I had. If you check out the dates, you'll see there's some overlap, but with significant gaps. I bet he looked for that first one for a couple of weeks and then gave up on it, so he started a second journal.

"In the second journal, it starts like he's trying to write down all the critical stuff he's done and the things that have changed so he doesn't forget. I have no idea how or why Wilton stayed in the past, though."

My mind reeled. How was this possible? Had the same thing happened to him that happened to me? Or was the journal perhaps nothing but a rough draft for his science fiction work? If it was real, it would certainly explain why Wilton always seemed to know that there was more to my life recently than what was on the surface.

I nodded, coming to a decision, "Can you meet me at school sometime to visit with him?"

"This week is Drury's spring break. I could come at lunch time tomorrow?"

79

March 8, 1993

Joshua was waiting for me in the lunch room, "Ready?"

"Didn't sleep at all last night."

Mr. Wilton was watching the lunchroom closely, waiting in seemingly eager anticipation to bust any student who might do something remotely inappropriate.

"Mr. Wilton, if you've got a few minutes, we were hoping to visit with you."

"Mr. Bryan? I wasn't aware that you two were friends."

"Yep. We've gone to church together for a long time. Any chance we can talk in your office?"

"I'm pretty busy gentlemen. Is it important?"

"Life changing."

Mr. Wilton walked with us to the office and asked one of the other vice principals to take his place in the lunch room.

"How can I help you two?" Mr. Wilton asked as he cracked his knuckles and sat down in his leather office chair.

Even after mentally rehearsing what I wanted to say into the wee hours of the night, I had a hard time getting started.

"Well, uh," I cleared my throat and started pacing, not knowing how to start. Joshua interrupted me.

"Do you recognize this?" he asked, handing the journal to Mr. Wilton.

Mr. Wilton carefully thumbed through the journal. Without changing the expression on his face, he replied, "Where did you found this?"

"I found it in the library at Drury a couple of years ago."

Mr. Wilton barely nodded his head without taking his eyes off the journal. He raised his hand and pointed at us, his finger shook, but he didn't say anything. He tried to pop his knuckles again; they made no sound.

"I thought that it might belong to you after I saw this," Joshua handed him the torn out story.

"Mr. Wilton," I blurted out, "you're from the future, aren't you?"

He stood up, walked over to the door of his office, and locked it.

"I knew this day would come. Who else knows about this?" His voice was cracking and beads of sweat began to form on his forehead. He tried his best to maintain his composure.

"No one."

Mr. Wilton opened a desk drawer, and, for a brief instant, I imagined he was going to pull out a gun and shoot us. Instead, he pulled out a second journal, identical to the one Joshua had handed him.

"This one's the original manuscript for the book," he said. "They gave it back to me after the book was formatted and published." He sat down again in his leather chair, and collapsed into himself, softly sighing into his hands. All pretense of authority had vanished.

"Sir?" I said after a couple of awkward moments, "Sir, we're not going to tell anyone. We came to you because we need your help."

He wiped his eyes with his hands, took a deep breath, and looked at me. For the first time, I wasn't intimidated by Mr. Wilton. I saw him as he truly was — a man whose life was based on a secret no one would ever believe. That kind of stress rips you apart from the inside.

"Mr. Wilton, sir, I'm from the future, too."

After a lengthy pause, Mr. Wilton gestured for us to sit. "Well, that certainly explains a few things, doesn't it Mr. Bryan?"

I nodded my head and smiled, waiting for him to continue.

"In 1984, I was married and had three children," Mr. Wilton said, staring at his desk. "My family was truly the joy of my life. The oldest two were identical twins, Katrina and Anna-Marie, born the day before my birthday. The youngest was also a girl, Rosa, she had just turned one. We lived in South Carolina. I met my wife when I was in college at USC in Columbia and we made our life together there. My dad had just died of a heart attack and we were driving back to Springfield, where my parents lived and I grew up, for his funeral.

"My entire adult life, I had lived in fear of my dad. He was physically bigger than me, abusive at times. A mean man. Racist to the core. As a cop, he was well-connected in Springfield and no one messed with him. In 1961, my senior year in high school, Springfield was a mess when it came to racial issues and civil rights. The vast majority of Springfield was white and most minorities were barely treated as second-class citizens.

"You are familiar, I assume, with the Supreme Court case *Brown v. Board of Education*? *Plessy v. Ferguson* made it legal to have separate public schools for black and white children; *Brown v. Board of Education* overturned the rulings of *Plessy*. Mr. Oliver Brown was born in Springfield but lived in Topeka, Kansas during the 1950s. His daughter, Linda, was one of the first children to attempt to desegregate a school in Kansas, Sumner Elementary. Since Oliver was the only male parent, the case bore his name as the lead plaintiff.

"After the case was settled in the Supreme Court, Oliver and his family moved back to Springfield to try and escape all the attention. The summer after I graduated was unbearably hot, and in that heat, tempers flared daily. That June, my dad was on a rampage against all blacks, doing everything he could to make life miserable for them — tickets, jail time, beatings, whatever — justice was not a word in dad's vocabulary. Dad held Oliver Brown personally responsible for everything he thought was wrong with the country. He cussed him out regularly at our family dinners. So, one night, while dad was walking on patrol near the square downtown, he spotted Oliver Brown on the north side of the square."

He sighed deeply and continued, "I was driving back to our house from an event at Drury. I still hadn't decided where I was going to college and Drury was a possibility as it was affordable because of some of my dad's connections. I knew he was working near the square that night, and, for some reason or another, decided to try and find him on the way home.

"Because of the one-way streets, I had passed the square and had to turn around, approaching it from the south. And then I saw my dad kill

Oliver Brown. He choked him to death from behind; Oliver never saw dad coming, never had a fighting chance.

"When I pulled up next to dad and the dead body, I thought dad was gonna kill me too. He growled at me, 'Don't you ever say a word to no one.' I left town the next day for South Carolina.

"The official report said that Oliver Brown died from heat stroke, and for years I carried the guilt and deep shame of not saying anything to anyone. Not a week went by that I didn't have nightmares about that horrible night. I even visited a therapist on a couple of occasions to deal with the nightmares.

"So, after dad's death, we got to Springfield on a Tuesday, a couple of days before the funeral, and stayed in a hotel near my parents' house. It took my daughters forever to fall asleep, they were so excited about the hotel and the road trip. That night, the dream was more vivid than ever. I could feel the humidity in the air and I saw Oliver wearing his favorite black fedora as he walked on the north side of the square. As dad started to run up to him from behind, I tried to yell, to do anything to warn Oliver. And then it felt like I was having a heart-attack, I couldn't breathe, I couldn't do anything, and the next thing I knew I was back in my old Buick and had just witnessed the murder again. Again, I was powerless to stop it.

"Still, I tried. I pulled up next to dad and jumped out of the car. I started screaming at him, hitting him, threatening that I was going to tell one of his superiors. Years of pent-up regret and anger and hate surged through me. My aggression completely caught my dad by surprise. Dad pulled his gun out of his holster, and I just knew he was gonna shoot me, and then he turned it on himself, pulled the trigger and killed himself, falling dead right on top of Oliver Brown.

"After my father's death, I knew I couldn't move to South Carolina. I needed to stay home and take care of mom. Everything changed."

Mr. Wilton told us about choosing Drury, about writing the journals and researching time travel. "I never really got along with my college roommate. I was intentionally quiet, keeping to myself most of the time except for classes. I wrote to keep everything straight, to help process the multiple realities that I knew. After I lost the first journal, I started the second one and my roommate had seen me writing in it and tried to take it from me to read it. He came in late one night, and I had carelessly fallen asleep while writing. He read the whole thing and thought it was a story, not a journal. He bribed me into submitting the journal to a campus-wide contest they were having for writers and it ended up winning. And the rest, as they say, is history.

"I never made it to South Carolina, never met my future wife, no kids. Mom died a few years ago, so I'm pretty much alone now except for the time here at school. They gave me a pretty good bonus to re-release the book, and I could always use a little extra cash."

Mr. Wilton stopped talking and just sat, staring at his desk. Joshua and I said nothing.

After a few moments, Mr. Wilton looked up, "So, that's my story. You said you needed my help. What's your story?"

I missed two class periods and Coach Engel's class talking with Mr. Wilton.

"Playing hooky today, Ethan?" Coach asked me in the locker room.

"No sir, I was talking with Mr. Wilton. I needed his help with some life after high school stuff."

"Gotcha. You're throwing batting practice today. See you on the field."

After practice, Coach Engel pulled aside all of the pitchers for a quick meeting.

"Gentlemen, our baseball season is seven weeks long. Each week, I'll be making the pitching assignments based on our opponents and previous outings. Starters for the first six games are as follows:

Branten against North Kansas City;

Masterly against Winnetonka;

Steale against Hillcrest;

Bryan against Parkview;

Mahoney against Mountain Home;

Wilson against Glendale.

"If you're not starting, you'll be worked in relief or used in the field. Everyone plays on my team. Any questions?"

After changing in the locker room, I looked at the schedule to   write down my start on the calendar. My first start would take place on March 23.

Sarah's birthday.

Be here. I repeated to myself. Then I wondered if being *here* was truly what I wanted.

80

March 12, 1993

"Our first game is in one week, gentlemen," Coach Engel started practice with a short motivational speech in the locker room.

"We'll be heading up to Kansas City for two games, then have an off-day, followed by games on Monday and Tuesday then another off-day, and then another pair of games. Six games in eight days and I expect us to get off to a good start. We've got the talent; we just need to play smart.

"Next week, all practices will be game scenarios. When you're in between those lines, you gotta be thinking, gentlemen, you gotta be focused and ready. If you're on the field, you want the ball to come to you because you know you're gonna make the play. If our team's hitting, you want to be at the plate because no pitcher can get anything by you. Don't be afraid to be a little bit cocky, gentlemen. I chose you for a reason — I believe you have the talent.

"Now, don't let me down."

Nothing makes me work harder than hearing Coach say he believes in me. By the time practice is over, there is not a square inch on my body that isn't covered in dirt from sliding or diving. When practice is over, I slowly gather my stuff and head to the locker room. Stopping by the water fountain on the way, I felt someone pat me on the back and choked. Jerking around, I spot Mr. Wilton wearing a Kickapoo baseball hat.

"Hat looks good," I said between coughs.

"Watched you at practice, Mr. Bryan. That was quite an impressive display of hustle."

"That's my only real talent."

"That's an important one in my book. I was just asked to go with the team on their trip to KC, thought you might like to know. Also, I know this will sound weird, but it was so good to talk with you this week. I haven't told anyone the truth for longer than I care to count, so, thank you. Have a good spring break. I'll see you next week."

81

March 13, 1993

For Spring Break, almost all of the Losers Club fled Springfield. Stacie and Alison drove south to some beach in Texas to work on tan lines; Nathan, Henry, and Junior went west on a church ski trip to Winter Park, Colorado. It didn't bother me at all that I wasn't traveling to a beach or a ski resort or any other kind of "special" trip for my senior year Spring Break. I knew that, if I made the team, my Spring Break would be cut short regardless.

Dad let me sleep until close to 11 before opening the door to my bedroom and unleashing the hound. Dodger jumped on my bed and licked my face, my ears, my head, any small portion of skin he could find. Overwhelmed by dog-breath, I wrestled with Dodger until he finally had enough and jumped down from my bed then proceeded to run circles throughout the house.

"Got any plans for the day, Chief?"

"Nope."

"Your mom and I are heading out of town for the weekend, just a last-minute trip for our anniversary. You and Katy will have to take care of each other. We left the numbers of where we're going on the table in case you need to reach us and we plan on being back Monday afternoon. There's plenty of money on the table to cover your meals and for gas, too."

After Mom and Dad left, Katy and I went to Pasta Express for lunch and then stopped by Blockbuster to rent a few movies for the rest of the day. Katy chose a couple of classic dancing and singing movies; I picked up 2001: A Space Odyssey and 2010 and laughed at the irony of both the titles.

A coin flip determined that Singin' in the Rain would be the first movie of the afternoon. As Katy loaded the tape into the VHS player, I grabbed the laundry basket from my room and started making a pile of all my grass-stained-sweat-saturated practice clothes in the middle of the living room.

"Sorry about the smell, but I gotta pre-treat some of these before I throw them in the laundry."

Katy cocked her head and furrowed her brow, "Since when do you know how to do laundry?"

"College is coming. Had to learn sometime."

My answer seemed sufficient as she pushed play and settled into Dad's recliner with a heavy red blanket to enjoy her movie.

I started the laundry and slothed on the couch, wondering what Moses supposes and being made to laugh by Princess Leia's mom. The movie finished and we were about to start the second feature of the day when the sirens sounded.

With the front door closed and dead-bolted and the shades drawn on the back door, neither one of us had noticed the change in the weather outside. Dark, heavy clouds swirled overhead as Dodger paced around the living room. I quickly switched the TV over to one of the local stations and listened to the weatherman tell of multiple tornados that were threatening to touch down in southwest Missouri. Out of curiosity, I opened the front door and stepped out on the porch. I couldn't see anything that looked like a tornado, but figured it was best to take appropriate precautions.

"Let's head to the hall bathroom. I'll grab the radio out of the kitchen and we can listen to it."

"What about Dodger?"

"Just bring him in there with us."

I walked into the kitchen as Katy wrangled with the dog. As I stepped back into the living room, I saw Katy cover her mouth with her hand. She rushed into the bathroom and promptly threw up. A few moments later, Dodger and I joined Katy in the bathroom.

"These storms always make me so nervous."

"We're in a safe spot. All we can do is wait it out."

I turned on the radio and ran back to the kitchen, grabbing snacks and drinks and a deck of cards.

"Wanna play war?" I asked, setting the cans of soda, chips, and pretzels on the counter.

"I guess, sure."

One more time, I left the bathroom in search of a couple of blankets to cover the tile floor. Dodger fell asleep on the bathmat as Katy and I flipped card after card after card, listening to the sirens drone in the background and radio reports details of tornado sightings.

After close to two hours, the sirens finally stopped. I went to the front door to see if there was any damage in our yard and neighborhood. Other than a few tree limbs down in a neighbor's yard, our street was clean. "Official reports" continued to stream in on the radio; no tornados hit within Springfield city limits. Three different tornados actually touched down; one was in the middle of a field some twenty miles south of town, the other two were near small towns east of Springfield. The radio reported no one was injured, although there was significant damage done to multiple farms and a couple of businesses in Marshfield.

Katy joined me on the porch and we decided to go ahead and grab an early dinner when she heard the phone ringing. Katy ran into the kitchen and answered the phone, twirling the cord around her finger while she talked.

"Hey Mom…Yes…yes…we're fine, the power didn't even go out…the sirens just stopped a few minutes ago…Are you guys okay? We were just going out to get something to eat. Love you, too. See you Monday. Bye."

82

March 16, 1993

I walked to school; the "voluntary" field clean-up day was for anyone not out of town on Spring Break. By the time I got there, Coach Engel was already on the field raking as others were picking rocks out of the infield dirt and pulling weeds from the infield grass.

Another small crew was walking around the stadium on trash detail and a couple more were in the bleachers, scraping gum to their heart's delight. I walked into the home dugout and saw the "to do" list posted above the bench. I grabbed a can of paint and a paintbrush and headed to the visitor's dugout.

After an hour and a half of thinking through Mr. Miyagi's "Up, down, not side to side, Daniel-san," the back and sides of the dugout were painted and my shoulders were stiff. I slowly walked to the water spigot behind the concessions stand to wash out the brush; Coach Engel met me there.

"Ready for the weekend?" he asked.

"Yep. You?"

"Ethan, the start of the baseball season is one of my favorite times of the year. Spring's here and new things are blooming, even if we have to pick a few extra weeds and rocks. I love all of the smells, the fresh cut grass and ballpark foods; the sounds of the game and the intensity of the competition. God, it's just beautiful, isn't it?"

I looked at Coach and he was smiling, not looking at me, but gazing out at the field, seemingly lost in memories from seasons past. I could tell from his expression that his last sentence was not uttered in vain, but more as a prayer.

"When was the last time you played baseball, Coach?"

"Competitively?"

"Yeah."

"After the Yankees drafted me, I had a decision to make. I decided to stay at MU and posted a 6 – 1 record in the Big Eight. And then I became a new father and everything changed. I visited with a lot of my friends who had gone pro and viewed the travel and time away from my family as an issue to be weighed carefully. I was the only returning starter that spring, and thought that I had earned more financial help to stay in school and support my family.

"My Coach didn't see it that way, so I started interviewing for coaching positions. I was the only pitcher who didn't get to pitch in our last series of the season. That's why it's so important to me that everyone plays."

He gave a heavy sigh, "You just never know when your last game is gonna be. Once I made the decision to pursue coaching, I never really looked back on playing. I took my education as a gift from the sport and went into coaching with the same passion I had had for baseball from boyhood. And, honestly, I have no regrets."

I considered his words. Was I making the decision he didn't? Would playing baseball prevent me from being a father?

Coach broke through my thoughts, "How you feelin' about the season?"

"It's like a dream come true," I answered, hoping to believe what I said.

Coach blew a large bubble, reached into his mouth and grabbed it with the tips of his fingers, and then stuck it to the top of my hat.

83

March 19, 1993

Dad took me to the school for the 9:00 AM sharp departure. The bag containing my baseball gear was considerably bigger than the small duffel bag with my change of clothes and toiletries. Parents and siblings waved good-byes as the team and coaches loaded up on the charter bus which had been generously paid for by the booster club. Mr. Wilton sat in the seat right behind the driver and winked at me as I boarded the bus.

"Good morning, Mr. Bryan," he said flatly, with a small smirk on his face. It was the first time I had seen him not wearing a coat and tie.

"Morning, Mr. Wilton."

"Did you have a good Spring Break?"

"Yep. Heading to KC *is* my senior trip."

"I have some news you might be interested in. Maybe we can visit later on."

"Sounds great, sir."

Branten nudged me in the butt with his duffle bag, "Keep moving, man. I need a nap before I throw today."

There was plenty of room on the bus. Everyone got a seat to himself. I picked a seat in the middle of the bus, fell asleep shortly after we left city limits, and dreamed I was on a trip to a Royals game with Annie and our daughters.

Brian McHandley nudged me awake. "Hey, Snoring Beauty. We're in KC. Lunch stop." We stopped at a strip mall with a couple of choices for lunch: McDonald's, Subway, or some local barbecue joint. I chose Subway, figuring I'd better eat light on a nervous and somewhat carsick stomach; the majority of the team went for barbecue.

Walking into Subway, Coaches Engel and Bell were already sitting in one corner, filling out a scorer's book and talking about starters and strategy for the first two games. The only other person from the bus in Subway was Mr. Wilton.

"Mind if I join you?" I asked.

"This is my last year working at Kickapoo," Mr. Wilton said quietly as I sat down.

"Really?"

"I was born in 1943. It was only a few weeks before my 41st birthday when I got pulled back into the drama of 1961. By the end of this school year, I'll be celebrating my 73rd birthday. It's tough when your mind is so much older than your body. I'm so tired all the time; I need a break. I just want some rest and quiet. I submitted my notice of resignation just before we left."

"What are you gonna do?"

"With the money from the re-release and money I'll get after selling my house in Springfield, I'll rent a cabin near Table Rock Lake and just stay there. I should be pretty well set for quite some time."

"Ever thought about trying to track down your wife?"

"Yes, but I don't think that's a good idea. That life is long gone."

"Does anyone else know that you're, uh…"

"No."

"Don't you think you'll be lonely by yourself at the lake?"

"All I've known is lonely, Mr. Bryan. Loneliness is not dependent on being around people. Loneliness is when no one knows the real you."

"Maybe I could come visit you over the summer?"

"I would like that."

I left the table, needing to get my mind back to the present for the game.

That afternoon, Branten pitched well, especially so with the biting spring wind, allowing only three runs on a couple of bloop hits and one horrible error. As a team, however, we couldn't do anything offensively, taking horrible hacks at the plate, never getting more than one hit in any inning. I kept the bench warm while keeping track of the books and blamed our sluggish, uninspiring play on a barbecue overdose.

"Well, gentlemen," Coach addressed us after the game, "a shutout is definitely one way to start a season. We'll grab a bite to eat on the way to the hotel. If anyone is caught out of their room after 10 pm, you'll be kicked off the team. Don't test me on this one, gentlemen. Masterly, you've got the mound tomorrow. Get some rest tonight. Let's get a win tomorrow and even things out."

84

March 20, 1993

When I worked at Hope Church, I was once asked to help umpire a baseball game when one of the real umpires showed up drunk. Even though it was just 12 and 13-year-olds on the field, I quickly learned how hard it is to be a good umpire, making the right call quickly and decisively.

As I walked toward my car that day, I got more than a few sarcastic and cynical comments from parents of the losing team. I never umpired another game.

Against Winnetonka, we scored two runs in the top of the first inning before any and every "bad break" possible happened to us in the field. I swear the home plate umpire was being paid handsomely by Winnetonka. Masterly walked six in three innings and we ended up walking an abysmal *sixteen hitters* as a team. Even after Coach Engel told us not to swing until we had two strikes, Winnetonka only walked one.

Calls that seemed blatantly obvious from the bench all went in favor of the home team.

Coach was furious at the horrible umpiring and actually got kicked out of the game arguing a play at the plate.

In the top of the seventh inning, I got the chance to pinch hit, my first at bat of the season, and grounded out to the shortstop on an 0 – 2 count.

We lost the game 9 – 2 and boarded the bus having lost the first two games of the season.

It was a quiet ride until, just south of Kansas City, Coach Engel addressed the team.

"Gentlemen, that was one of the worst games I have ever seen through no fault of your own. I apologize for losing my temper, but wanted you guys to know that I did it supporting you and your efforts on the field. I will be giving the Missouri State High School Activities Association and the coaches and principal at Winnetonka a piece of my mind this week."

A roar went up from the bus as several of my teammates offered suggestions, most of them ridiculously inappropriate, as to what Coach should say. Coach wisely let them vent. After a few minutes, he raised his hand.

"That game was fixed and you didn't stand a chance of winning it, even if Nolan Ryan was pitching. I'm proud of you guys for staying focused and playing hard. You represented the name on the front of your jerseys well. In my books, you guys won that game. The good news is that game doesn't count against us in conference. We've got two conference games to start the week, and I know you're all ready to get some wins under your belt. Gentlemen, enjoy the ride home."

It was hard to enjoy anything after such a loss. I was quite for the ride back to Springfield and listened to the banter of teammates.

After picking me up from the school, on the way home, Mom wanted a play-by-play. I did my best to oblige, knowing what it was like to be a parent who just wanted to connect with their kid for a few minutes.

"Coach Engel really got thrown out of the game?" she asked.

"Yep. Like I said, it was an awful game. Probably would've been smarter just to forfeit and walk off the field."

"Did you get to play any?"

"I pinch hit in the second game, but it wasn't any fun. Tough way to start to the season, though, losing both games."

Mom pulled the big brown van into the driveway. I went inside and threw all of my stuff in the laundry room, then headed straight for the shower. I was still pretty frustrated after the first two games of my second chance at baseball and needed a break from people for a bit.

85

March 21, 1993

"We play you guys on Friday," Drew said as I sat down with my coffee and chocolate donuts. "You gonna be pitching?"

"Doubt it. I'm starting Tuesday against Parkview. Might be a chance I'll play second or possibly in the bullpen. Most likely I'll be the book keeper," I said, nudging Drew with my elbow.

"Heard about your game against Winnetonka."

"Who told you?"

"Masterly's grandma lives next door. His family comes over a couple of times a month for dinner with her and we've talked some. Saw them pull into the driveway last night and asked him how the trip went and he told me the whole story."

"I feel bad for him. I think there were actually a couple of scouts at the game, and with him being a southpaw, he's got a real chance of at least getting a scholarship somewhere, if not a late round draft. That ump, though, that was ridiculous."

I was thinking about my start on Tuesday and only half-heartedly listening to the message when Pastor Gibson said something that caught my attention.

"The Lord All-Powerful is with us. The God of Jacob is our shelter. The God who wrestled and struggled with Jacob is the same God who wrestles and struggles with us today, refusing to give up on us when we've long since given up on ourselves.

"By re-naming Jacob as Israel, God shows that he understands and honors the struggle still. No one ever said that faith was supposed to be easy. Faith, my friends, is the willingness to believe that God will bring good while you're neck deep in the struggle."

I grabbed a new pew envelope, jotted down the essence of Pastor's faith definition, and folded it up and stuck it in my back pocket.

86

March 22, 1993

Mr. O'Neal pulled me out of class personally to tell me the good news. "I just got word from SMSU — you've got a full-ride! Four years of hard work has finally paid off. You should get a letter of confirmation later this week, and it'll also tell you about scheduling stuff and the other things you'll need to know for your freshman year. A few of your classmates also got the scholarship. Gotta go tell them, too. Good job!"

I didn't have much time to process what he'd said before he walked away. In my first life, I only received a small scholarship and had to work throughout college to graduate debt free. A full-ride meant freedom! The bell rang, the school day was over, and I didn't have time to wonder.

I had to run. I had volunteered to keep the scorebook for the Hillcrest game, knowing that, since I was pitching tomorrow, I'd only get a chance to play in a blow-out. As I quickly looked over the line-up card of the Hillcrest team, one name jumped out immediately.

Adam Dean. My future brother-in-law.

The line-up card had him hitting clean-up and playing third base. I looked toward the visitors' dugout and spotted him immediately; he already had his helmet on and was swinging two bats on the far side of the dugout.

He has absolutely no idea who I am.

Everything went right in our first home game of the season. Steale took the mound against Hillcrest and struck out the side in the top of the first inning. In the bottom half, we hit through the line-up and scored five runs, three coming on a bases-loaded double by Buckett. With a ten-run lead in the top of the fifth, Coach put me in to play second base. With two outs and no one on, the batter lined a sharp grounder to my right. I dove and knocked the ball down, then scrambled to my feet and picked it up, throwing the runner out at first by a couple of steps. Game over.

We had our first win of the season. Walking through the high five line, I said something to Adam other than the usual, "Good game."

"Hey third, way to hustle out there."

"Nice play there to end the game."

"Never hurts to be lucky."

After a quick speech from Coach, I met Dad behind the dugout. "Just had to get your uniform dirty before tomorrow's game, huh?"

"Yep."

87

March 23, 1993

I woke up fifteen minutes before my alarm went off, incredibly stoked about pitching later that afternoon. As soon as I had had that as my first thought, I immediately remembered that today, 22 years in the future, was also Sarah's ninth birthday. And it felt like my soul was being torn in two.

For as long as I can remember, all I've wished for was one more chance to play ball — to step on the mound, toe the rubber, and pour my heart out; to flip *Field of Dreams* on its head and wink at the hitter just before I got him out.

Now that the day was finally here, after months of pretending and playing the high school game, after studying and re-learning and all the tests and all the trying to be a teenager again, my heart was two decades in the future, missing a curly tow-head and her loose teeth and her heart for animals and nature.

There is nothing I can do to see her, nowhere I could catch a glimpse of her or wish her a happy birthday. A growing part of me wanted to melt back into the sheets and not get out of bed. Ever. I whisper the only prayer that comes to mind, *Jesus, have mercy on me.*

Though I heard no audible voice, I was positive I felt a response, "I AM here."

Those three simple words reminded me of the mantra from Joshua, the one still Sharpie-tattooed on my left hand — *be here.* I got up and started getting dressed for school.

As soon as Nathan pulled into the school parking lot and shut off the engine, I hopped out and made a beeline for the office.

"I gotta go visit with Mr. Wilton about one of my scholarships."

"See you in English, loser."

I knocked on Mr. Wilton's door and waited anxiously for a response.

"Come in."

"Hey, Mr. Wilton, gotta moment to talk?" I asked.

"What's on your mind, Mr. Bryan?"

I double-checked to make sure that the door was closed. "Well, it's just that…today is my youngest daughter's birthday. In 2015. And I remembered you said you had kids and just wondered if you still thought of their birthdays and how you dealt with all of that kind of…stuff."

"I know exactly how you feel. It took me a long time to work through those powerful emotions, to find a way that I could honor my memories of my kids and still focus on living in this reality. What I do these days is buy a gift for them, something I imagine they'd really like, then donate it some place in their honor. Sometimes, I'll even bake a cake and blow at candles at my house. It's impossible for me to forget them. I only hope that, somehow, a God who can resurrect a man from the dead can also find a way for me to be with my children from another life."

I daydreamed in most all of my classes thinking about Mr. Wilton's advice. Baking cakes really isn't my specialty and if I did that at home my family would know that something was up. But buying and donating a gift, what a brilliant idea.

I checked the baseball schedule. With no weekend games, I committed to doing something to honor Sarah's birthday.

The Losers Club was obnoxiously loud as I walked into English class; I loved every moment of it.

"Thought you'd want to know, we're all coming to the game today," Henry told me.

"No pressure, man," Junior winked.

"Even if you suck and lose the game, you'll always have a home with us," Stacie said.

I was thankful for her words. I didn't know why Coach Engel chose me to start against Parkview. The guys on the Parkview team were my friends from elementary and junior high school. Had my family not moved while I was in eighth grade, I probably would be playing ball with them instead of against them.

"You and me, Big E, all day long. Just you and me," McHandley thumped my butt with the catcher's mitt as we ran onto the field.

Eight warm-up pitches, a toss down to second base, and the umpire pointed at me and shouted, "Play ball!"

A quick glance in the bleachers and I saw my parents, my sister, and the entire Losers Club. I spotted parents of friends on the Parkview team as well as other friends from Kickapoo. My longtime friend and future neighbor Kevin stepped up to the plate and politely tapped McHandley's shin guard as a greeting. I took a deep breath and focused on McHandley's fingers.

Fastball inside.

I had waited more than two decades for this chance — to be in uniform, in between the lines, on the mound.

Teammates on the bench cheered and Coach Engel chewed and popped his bubble gum with piercing intensity.

Be here.

I chose four seams over two and threw the pitch right where I wanted. Kevin swung and looped a duck snort that landed on the foul line in right field. He made it to second base standing up.

Johnson lobbed the ball back to me and I snapped at it as I caught it. I could feel adrenaline surging through my body as I bit the inside of my lip.

Shawne then walked up to the batter's box as he watched the signs of Parkview's third base coach. Shawne, a future firefighter and local celebrity for his actions in rescuing a family trapped on the top floor of an apartment complex.

McHandley pounded his mitt and gave the sign. I shook it off which prompted an extra-loud bubble-popping from the dugout. Again, McHandley gave the sign for an inside fastball and I nodded in agreement. I threw it as hard as I could, but there was no "inside" to this pitch whatsoever. Shawne lined it over my head and back up the middle for a single. Kevin scored easily.

Two pitches and we're losing 1 – 0.

I simultaneously wanted to scream and cry.

I tried to ignore the jeers and comments coming from the Parkview dugout and walked off the back of the mound, kneeling down to untie and retie my cleats. McHandley asked for time and jogged out to talk to me. "Well, they've had their fun. Shut 'em down and shut 'em up. Just you and me, Big E."

Something in my brain clicked. I tuned out everyone else and saw only McHandley behind the plate. I no longer paid any attention to who was hitting or the friends and family in the bleachers. I was just playing catch with McHandley. With the help of my defense, I got the next three hitters out — ground out, fly out, ground out. I walked toward the dugout, jumped over the third baseline, and slammed my mitt on the ground as I sat on the very end of the bench.

"Hey!" Coach Engel shouted at me as he blew a large bubble and walked out of the dugout, "Remember rule number one? No thinking!"

I took off my hat and inhaled deeply, focusing on the mantra while my teammates took their swings.

Be here.

After giving up two hits and a run in the first inning, aside from a walk in the fourth inning — who McHandley promptly threw out when he tried to steal second — no one else reached base. My team continued its offensive prowess from the day before and scored seven runs in the first three innings.

I pitched five innings in all, striking out three, walking one, allowing two hits and one run. Snyder pitched the last two innings and retired everyone he faced. We won 7 – 1; our record was now evened up.

After walking through the high-five line, saying the mandatory "Good game" to everyone on the opposing team (as well as getting a few more comments from Parkview friends), Coach Engel gave me a pat on the back and placed a ball in my glove.

"Game ball, Bryan. Way to pitch!"

I softly spun the game ball in my right hand while Dad drove us home.

"Heckuva game, Chief."

"Yep."

"Don't forget to ice your arm after your shower. At least twenty minutes. Maybe two or three times."

"Will do."

"Proud of you, man. Your grandmas and uncles will wanna hear about this."

"Maybe I can call them tomorrow? I'm spent."

"Sure thing, Chief."

I was already lost in thought, knowing exactly what I wanted to do with the game ball.

After I showered and changed, I went out to the garage and started rummaging around, digging through Dad's veterinary stuff, and found an empty Styrofoam square box originally used for mailing medicine.

Perfect.

I took the box back to my bedroom and sat down on my bed. Using a blue ballpoint pen, I carefully wrote on the game ball:

To Sarah —
Happy birthday!
KHS 7
PHS 1
5 IP, 1 run, 2 hits, 3 Ks, 1 BB
3 – 23 – 1993

I wrapped the ball in an old t-shirt, placed the ball in the box, and sealed it completely with packing tape. I put the entire thing in a plastic garbage sack and slid it under my bed where it would stay hidden until a time when I could bury it in the back yard.

88

March 24, 1993

The Losers Club spent Wednesday afternoon composing ballads and poetry *to* me in honor of my "outstanding performance on the field."

Everyone's words were brilliant and hilarious and encouraging, but Junior's five stanza poem was truly a work of art.

He took center stage, the smallest of Chiefs,
His coming of age to be tested.
His heart on his jersey, with steadfast belief
As savage Vikings jeered and protested

His weapon of choice, 108 double-stitches
Of cow-hide and cork and string
He rocks, he fires, he executes pitches
Vikings miss with most ev'ry swing.

His gaze is fierce, his stare is cold
A smile never crosses his face
He looks for the sign and throws what is told
Having a catch of effortless grace.

His fastball, on corners, it lives and it hides
His change-up makes hitters think twice
With B-Mac his partner, his trustworthy guide
Even Coach Engel can't help but say, "Nice!"

He walks off the mound, his journey complete
He delights in the work he has done
He takes off his glove, grabs a handful of seeds
And pure joy at Kickapoo! For the mighty Chiefs have won!

I didn't fold this one up, but carefully placed it inside a folder instead, hoping to frame it and keep it for years to come.

With two more games on the schedule for this week and a steady rain falling, Coach Engel cancelled practice.

Katy and I decided to spend our Wednesday evening with the youth group at church. I sat out the four square games to avoid any potential injury and visited with Drew and Melissa, sharing the story of yesterday's game.

"Only two hits? That's impressive, man," Drew commented.

"And a walk. It was just one of those times where all my stuff was working. I mean, I was hitting *all* of my spots. And the defense behind me was stellar, truly lights out. Are you gonna be at Friday's game?" I asked Melissa.

"Actually, I'm working the concession stand as a fundraiser for NHS, so I'll be there, but I'm not sure how much of the game I'll get to see."

Curtis, the youth minister, called us all together in the pit. We spent time worshipping through song, praying for one another, and imagining what the story of the feeding of the 5,000 might have looked like today.

"A couple of peanut butter and jelly sandwiches might not look like much to you, but Jesus does amazing things with the most humble offerings. Every act of kindness resonates throughout eternity."

89

March 26, 1993

I joined the Losers Club in the commons area to celebrate High Five Friday and encouraged as many people as possible to make the trip to the east side of town and watch the game.

"Gimme five! Game's at five! Gonna need your help to beat Glendale!"

There was nothing remotely fast or particularly furious about Friday at school. We watched an episode of *The Simpsons* in French class, the one where Bart learns to speak French. We were then tested on our comprehension of what he said.

In Choir, soloists and ensembles were preparing for contest and state performances. I had opted out of both, knowing that the schedule conflicted with baseball games.

Thanks to some tutoring sessions with Dad, Calculus actually made a little bit of sense. I was able to complete one problem on the board in front of the class without any assistance from Mr. Freeman.

For personal entertainment, I assisted with tray duty at lunch, but didn't have any mints on me to distribute.

Not even Coach Engel's baseball class held my attention for long. The weekly quiz was easy; I finished it in fifteen minutes and knew I had aced it.

Earth Science put me to sleep, literally. I woke up when the dismissal bell rang.

Thanks be to God for the Losers Club and English. In an effort to support me and get me prepared for the game against our rivals, we spent our time composing "trash-talk" poetry using Shakespearian slang.

Dad drove me to Glendale, still driving the tan Taurus. Conversation was brief; I was too nervous to want to talk.

"Anxious?"

"Yep."

"Think you'll play today?"

"Doubt it."

"Think Drew will play today?"

"Yep, he's their starting centerfielder."

"Think you'll win?"

"Hope so. But they are really, really good."

I grabbed a bag of sunflower seeds out of my baseball bag and stuck a handful in my cheek.

Pastor Gibson spotted me jogging across the parking lot toward the field. He walked over and greeted me before I got inside the fence.

"I'll be cheering for you, too, you know. You're just like a son to me, too."

"Thanks, Pastor, we need all the help we can get today."

"Just remember, regardless of the outcome of the game, I am proud of you," he said.

Both teams scored a run in the first and in the third. With two outs and two on in the fourth, O'Malley lined a ball to deep centerfield that carried over Drew's head and landed at the base of the fence. Both runners scored easily and O'Malley wound up with a stand-up triple, scoring moments later on a single by Lunding. We were up 5 – 2 and our dugout was getting rowdy. Standing in the coach's box at third base, Coach Engel gave us a look; we toned it down immediately.

Wilson gave up a run in the bottom of the fourth and the bottom of the fifth. We tacked on an insurance run in the top of the sixth on our first over-the-fence home run of the season, a blast to left field by Buckett.

In the bottom of the sixth inning, Coach Engel started substituting players to make sure most everyone got in the game. Leaders came in to pitch for us, and Glendale started hitting him hard. By inning's end, the game was tied, 6 – 6.

Mackler flew out and Leaders was scheduled to hit second in the top of the seventh inning; Coach put me in as a pinch hitter. On an 0 – 1 count, Coach gave me the sign and I rolled a bunt up the third base line, barely beating the throw to first on a bang-bang play. As the Glendale coach called time and came out to talk strategy with his battery and infielders, Coach Bell pulled me aside at first base.

"Pitcher doesn't have that good of a move to first, still, don't take too big of a lead. Try and get a feel for his timing on the first pitch and then we're sending you on the second."

 I nodded as I listened.

My heart pounded as I took a decent lead off of first. I was able to get back standing up on the first pick-off attempt and increased the size of my lead accordingly.

The pitcher delivered; ball one, high. I stood on first and confirmed the steal sign from Coach Engel, reaching up to touch the bill of my helmet. As soon as the pitcher lifted his left leg, I broke toward second, not daring to glance at home.

When I heard the ball hit the bat, I knew it had been drilled; aluminum bats make such beautifully distinctive sounds. What I didn't see is that Jackson had lined it straight to the first baseman, who promptly stepped on first base as I was sliding into second. I was doubled-off; inning over.

Drew passed me at second as he ran toward the Glendale dugout, "Tough luck there, E."

Davis came out to pitch the bottom of the seventh inning. A walk, a stolen base, a bunt, and a sacrifice fly and the game was over; we lost 7 – 6. The Glendale fans and team were going crazy.

We muttered our "Good games" as we passed through the mandatory high five line, crossing in front of the umpires at home plate. We slowly and thoroughly cleaned out the visitors' dugout as Coaches Engel and Bell tried to encourage us on a game well-played.

"Tough one to lose, gentlemen, tough way to end the first week of the season. Hold your heads high; you did yourselves and the school proud. Have a good weekend and we'll be back at it again on Monday."

Dad, Pastor, and Drew were visiting behind the visitors' dugout, all waiting on me. Dad talked me and Drew into posing for a post-game picture, dirty uniforms and all.

"Only two weeks and we get to do this again," Drew smiled.

"I'll be ready."

90

March 27, 1993

Mom and Dad were at the grocery store and Katy was still at a friend's house having spent the previous night. I decided it was as good a time as any to try and bury the baseball.

After remembering Dodger's penchant for digging holes, I found a place on the side of the house that would be easily covered over and well-hidden by the gravel landscaping.

Using one of Dad's shovels, I carefully dug a hole about two feet deep and buried the ball. The whole process felt exactly like a funeral service — somber, quiet, a deep sense of loss — like I was saying good-bye. I was mourning, grieving the future I might not ever see again.

I carefully arranged the gravel to hide the spot then stood back to make the best mental note I could about the position of the ball. I had already showered and was watching *SportsCenter* when Mom and Dad returned home from the store.

91

March 28, 1993

Drew and Melissa were already talking when I got to Sunday school. Darrell greeted me with coffee and donuts and a pat on the back; he didn't say anything. Paula was busy writing the question of the week on the white board as I walked over to sit between my friends.

"It really was a good game," Melissa said, hoping to encourage me.

"What's your guys' record now?" Drew asked.

"We're 2 – 4. What's yours?"

"We're 5 – 1. We lost to Columbia Hickman last weekend. When do you pitch next?"

"Tuesday's game against Hillcrest. Coach is really doing a good job of making sure everyone plays in most every game and almost half of my team can pitch."

"I'm pretty sure we're off that day, maybe I can come watch. Where's it at?"

"Playing there."

"Ooh, I'd like to come, too," Melissa added. "Can you give me a ride?"

"Sure," Drew said.

Paula cleared her throat and got everyone's attention. She opened the class in a time of prayer and then pointed at the question on the white board. I sat in silence for the remainder of Sunday school, quietly sipping my coffee and being thankful for good friends.

"There is always, always a reason to hold on to hope." Pastor Gibson was preaching the story of Ezekiel's vision of the valley of dry bones. I remembered that I had once preached on the same story and even wrote a song to go along with my sermon. I tried to write down the lyrics on the bulletin, but it had been far too long since I'd played it to remember the majority of them.

"The circumstances may seem impossible, but God is greater than our presumptions. Out of place and seemingly out of options, Ezekiel walked among bones that surely stretched his comfort zone as a trained priest. The same wind that danced on the waters and first breathed life into creation, dances and breathes again, bringing dead bones to life. We are to live, always, as a people of ridiculous hope."

I wrote down the last sentence to add to the growing stack of quotes on pew envelopes on top of my dresser.

92

March 29, 1993

Branten was the first pitcher for the second week of season, this time against Joplin, yet another southwest Missouri baseball powerhouse. We had the lead for the majority of the game, a scary one-run lead, and every time Joplin tied it we were able to respond the next inning. But, for the second consecutive game, we lost the game in the bottom half of the last inning.

"Gentlemen, sometimes you lose, it's just the nature of the game. Don't get down on yourselves because you're playing good ball, you're playing smart ball, and there's still a lotta games to play in this season. Tomorrow's a new day and we get the joy of playing ball together."

I asked Coach if I could bring the scorebook home to study our previous game against Hillcrest. I remembered watching Steale pitch and that Adam played for them. I also remembered that everyone on my team was hitting the ball hard in that game. I slowly worked through the scorebook inning by inning then player by player determined to have a plan, desperate for another Kickapoo victory.

93

March 30, 1993

"I know you call all the pitches, Coach, but thought you might like to see these notes I made." I handed Coach Engel a player by player summary of our first game against Hillcrest. "I'll throw whatever you call as best as I can against these guys, but I know that Steale's a better pitcher than I am."

"Steale's a different pitcher than you are; you both have your strengths and weaknesses. And since you're now exploring the coaching side of the game," Coach said clearing his throat and pausing for dramatic effect, "it's never a good idea to throw the same pitcher against the same team in back-to-back games. I'll definitely look this over, but your biggest focus today will be to keep them off-balance."

"Sounds like a good plan."

Dad picked me up at the school to take me across town to Hillcrest. The game didn't start until 5, but from Kickapoo, factoring in Springfield traffic and drivers, it was close to a thirty minute drive to get there. Considering Coach wanted us there about an hour early, we didn't have a lot of time after school to waste.

Dad stopped at Sonic on the way and bought me a cheeseburger, some tater tots, and a large Dr Pepper.

"Fuel for your fastballs," he said.

I finished the mid-afternoon meal just as we pulled into the parking lot. We were still a little early, so Dad read John Grisham's new novel, The Client, and I tried to scribble away on some Calculus homework to pass the time.

I spotted Adam walking to the field from the school with a couple of his teammates, laughing about something or another. While I watched him walk, an uninvited thought crossed my mind, How will the outcome of this game affect our future relationship, if we're still family? I started flexing my fingers, getting lost chasing the what if's of all things future when Dad spoke up.

"Know one of them?"

"Sorta."

In 2002, just before Elisabeth was born, Adam married Annie's sister; I was one of the groomsmen in the wedding. The four of us regularly spent time together through the years, most often playing games. And Adam and I are quite the competitive brothers-in-law.

Whether it's spades or Settlers of Catan or just taking swings in the batting cages, Adam and I are constantly trying to one-up the other. To this day, I simply refuse to play in any fantasy league with him. There are times both of us have wanted to win so badly that we've had to excuse ourselves just to calm down.

Sometimes it's not so bad being the visiting team, especially when your team absolutely blisters the ball in the top of the first inning. Coach chose a DH for me, so all I could do was cheer and wait until it was my turn to head to the mound, which I eventually did with a four-run lead.

While working through my warm-up tosses I spotted Drew and Melissa sitting near Dad in the sparsely populated visitors cheering section. Before the first pitch, McHandley ran out to the mound, "Just you and me, Big E. Just you and me."

The first two hitters both grounded out, to Johnson and Hardwick, respectively. I caught too much of the plate with a fastball, though, and their third hitter roped a double up the left field line. And then Adam sauntered up to the plate.

In 2015, I am inches taller than Adam. In 1993, Adam's got me by a few inches.

I could pick out his mom's voice from the crowd, cheering him on, willing him to at least put Hillcrest on the board. I started over-thinking the situation and immediately my emotions followed suit, bouncing all over the place. Taking off my hat to wipe some of the sweat off my head, I saw the two-word mantra written on the inside of the bill of the cap: Be here.

Glancing toward the dugout, I saw Coach Engel looking down at the paper I had given him as McHandley gave the sign for a slider, low and away. I took a deep breath and focused intensely on McHandley's glove, finding the grip I wanted, and threw a beautiful slider. Adam swung and missed for strike one.

McHandley called for a slider, this time inside, and again Adam swung over the top of it and missed.

Fastball high.

I couldn't throw it hard enough to blow it by Adam, even though his timing was a little off. He hit a high pop-up to short right field. Johnson drifted back and caught the ball for the third out. I took a quick look in the stands and saw Drew give me a thumbs up.

Coach pulled me aside as I walked into the dugout. "You okay out there?"

"Probably just ate too much on a nervous stomach. I'm good. I'm where I wanna be."

In the top of the second, Buckett hit his second home run of the season, this time with two runners on. The next time I walked out to the mound, we were winning 7 – 0.

Focusing on McHandley's mitt, I settled into a rhythm, though my pitches weren't quite as sharp as they were in my first outing. At the end of four innings, I had given up a couple of runs and was really having to work hard for every single out. Hillcrest hitters were getting good swings and fouling off a lot of pitches.

"Hey Snyder, go warm up. You're going in next inning," Coach called out as I sat down and toweled off my head and hat.

"Come on Coach. Gimme just one more inning. I can do it," I protested.

Coach stared hard at me, "You've done exactly what we needed you to do today and we're in a good position to win this one. Why should I send you back out there?"

Because I want to pitch to Adam one more time.

Adam was due up second in the bottom of the fifth inning. After popping out in the first inning, he singled in the third and scored one of the three Hillcrest runs.

"I just feel like I've got more to give."

For a second, I actually thought Coach was going to give in to my selfish plea.

"There's still another month of ball to be played, you'll get plenty more opportunities. You've thrown a lot of pitches already. Play much more today, you could get injured and miss the rest of the month. Go get some ice from the concessions stand, your day's done."

McHandley, Branten, and several other teammates patted me on the back as I exited the dugout and headed for the concessions stand. I visited with Dad and Drew and Melissa for a couple of minutes while we tacked on a couple more runs. Several parents of my teammates also said encouraging words about my efforts.

We won the game 10 – 4. Walking through the high five line, Adam called me out, "Hey pitch, good job out there. You had me guessing."

"Thanks."

"I was kinda hoping for one more chance, I was finally starting to see your pitches."

"Maybe there will be a next time."

94

April 5, 1993

Out of our next three games, we only won one. We lost to Marshfield, another heartbreaking one run defeat; barely survived a last inning rally to beat Parkview; and Branson beat us by two. Going into Palm Sunday and Holy Week, our record stood at a paltry 4 – 7. Our dry bones were desperate for a breath of new life.

Still, Coach wasn't letting up on us on the field or in the classroom. "For your next essay, I want to you take from what we've talked about and what you've learned so far this semester and apply it to life. Three to five pages detailing your philosophy of baseball," Coach Engel said right after the bell rang.

"Philosophy of baseball? What's that?" Zach asked.

"Philosophy, from the Greek, meaning 'love of wisdom.' Think about what you have learned about baseball and the history of this country and use it as a lens for developing a way to live, an approach to life.

School is supposed to be more than just memorizing dates and names and formulas and spitting them back out on tests. I'm here to teach you how to think, to draw from the experiences of others so that you can go and make this world a better place. That, Zach, is the point of philosophy. That's real wisdom."

"You're joking, right? What can baseball teach us about life?" Zach replied.

"Exactly. Due by the end of the month."

Just after the bell rang in Coach Engel's class, an office worker knocked on the door and walked in with a green pass.

"Ethan? It says to bring all your stuff," Coach said, handing me the pass.

Slightly confused, I grabbed my books and backpack and slowly walked to the office where I was greeted by Dad.

"Come on, Chief. Gotta get you to your doctor's appointment," Dad said, with a subtle wink.

He signed me out without saying anything until we got to the car.

"I don't need to go to the doctor."

"It's Opening Day for the Royals. Wish I could've taken you to the game, but the timing just didn't work out. Besides, it's your senior year, you've already got college paid for; you're allowed to have some fun."

Dad drove by Andy's on the way home, where we each got a large chocolate concrete. On the back deck, Dad had set up a radio so we could listen to Denny Matthews call the game.

"There's some Cokes in the fridge when you want, and in a little while I'll grill some hot dogs for dinner."

The Royals hosted the Red Sox, Kevin Appier pitching against Roger Clemens. In what would be his last Opening Day as a player, George Brett doubled in the only run for the Royals as they lost 3 – 1.

The game was fast, ending just after 4 pm. I decided to hustle and try and catch the second half of practice. Dad dropped me off at the field where Coach Bell greeted me.

"Everything ok?"

"Yep. Picture of perfect health. Coach announced this week's pitchers yet?"

"The list is in the dugout."

Tuesday vs. Central — Branten

Wednesday vs. Columbia Hickman — Steale

Thursday vs. Francis Howell — Bryan

Friday vs. Glendale — Masterly

"Hey Bryan!" Coach Engel yelled at me from across the diamond, "You're late! You owe me some laps!"

"Yessir, Coach!" And I spent the remainder of the second half of practice running.

95

April 6, 1993

On March 4, 1990, Hank Gathers, a phenomenal collegiate basketball star at Loyola Marymount University, collapsed on the court seconds after scoring on an alley-oop tomahawk dunk. Moments later, at the age of 23, Hank Gathers died from an untreated heart disorder, hypertrophic cardiomyopathy.

Central was the home team, which meant that the game would be played at Nichols Park on the west side of town. Dad had a few afternoon house calls to make and would eventually meet me at the game. Thankfully, Coach Engel volunteered to give me a ride.

"How do you feel about starting at second today?" Coach asked.

"Sounds great; I'd love to get some more at-bats, something other than a bunt, you know?"

I took extra infield practice with Johnson hitting me fungos, trying to get used to the bounces of the well-packed all-dirt infield. Coach Bell hit fly balls to the outfielders and we slowly worked through our pre-game warm-up routine while waiting on the umpires to show up. Coach Bell dropped a ball in front of home plate, simulating a bunt, and McHandley pounced on it and threw it to first. Walking back toward home plate, McHandley appeared to bend over to fix a strap on his shin guards, then collapsed and started seizing.

Time froze.

Coach Bell got on the ground next to McHandley and yelled for help, for someone to call 911.

Even though it had been several months since I'd used it, I immediately thought of my cell phone, and then realized the gut-wrenching truth, there were no cell phones.

The whole team gathered near home plate as someone from the stands rushed to the corner gas station to make the call. An eternity passed before we heard ambulance sirens. Someone's mom or aunt was attending to McHandley in the meantime; she was a nurse and kept yelling at us, pushing us back, wanting space as she administered CPR.

The ambulance drove as close to the field as possible. As the medics finally rushed toward McHandley, Coach Engel gathered the team near first base. There we stood in a tight circle, crying, hugging, scared for our friend and teammate. After a few moments, Coach spoke up, "Gentlemen, I'm gonna say a prayer. You can pray with me, if you'd like."

Every person in that circle bowed our heads and took off our hats as Coach spit out his gum into the grass and then started, "God, I don't know what to say. Brian really needs your help right now. Sometimes we get so caught up in this game that we forget about the incredible gift you gave us, this gift of life. Please, breathe life into Brian. Amen."

We opened our eyes to see McHandley being carried on a stretcher to the ambulance. The nurse walked over to us, "He's being taken to Cox North."

Coach Engel walked over to the home dugout and visited with the Central coach. The game was cancelled. Dad pulled into the parking lot as the ambulance was leaving. I grabbed my stuff and ran out to him, "Take me to Cox North."

The whole Kickapoo varsity baseball team, plus parents and grandparents and some siblings, packed into one of the waiting rooms at Cox North Hospital. The room smelled like a locker room and no one really said much of anything.

There were occasional whispers, people retelling the story of what happened from their perspective. I overheard Coaches Engel and Bell talking about postponing the games against Columbia Hickman and Francis Howell.

An hour passed before McHandley's mom walked into the waiting room. "I know many of you remember the story of Hank Gathers. Brian has the same kind of heart problem as Hank did, but he's been on medication to treat it.

He did have some kind of stroke on the field, but he's also young and the body can do amazing things. He's stable now, sleeping, and can't have any visitors until tomorrow."

Then, pointing her finger at Coach Engel, she continued, "Now I know you boys have games all week, and I know that you might be thinking about forfeiting or cancelling them and I don't want to hear any such nonsense. Brian loves this game and loves playing on this team. You boys go out and play for Brian."

I glanced at Coach Engel and saw tears rolling down his face.

96

April 8, 1993

Coach didn't have to call off the games. It started raining late Tuesday night and didn't stop for two days. It seemed like all of southwest Missouri was under a flash flood warning.

I went to the hospital yesterday after school to try and see McHandley, but he wasn't taking any visitors.

Today I was allowed into the room, but only for a short time.

"Hey, Big E. Man, you're ugly," McHandley greeted me with a smile.

"Dude," I said, taking a deep breath, "how are you?"

"Dammit," he stuttered after a few moments of silence. "Words are hard. Helluva way to end the year. No games, huh?"

"Yeah, rained out yesterday and today. Still hoping to play Glendale tomorrow, though. When do you get to go home?"

McHandley shrugged his shoulders and rolled his eyes. Though his speech was somewhat slow, he was easy to understand. "Doc says I gotta lotta work to do. Had to shock me in the ambulance. My heart was just barely beating. Hurt like hell. Don't let them shock you. One of my legs isn't working so well, just kinda dragging it. Have to do therapy. No more baseball this year."

"I am sure gonna miss throwin' to you. You're my favorite catcher, you know that, don't you?"

"Just you and me, Big E," McHandley smiled.

"Is there any chance that McHandley gets to play ball again?" I asked Dad when I got home.

"Hard to say, Chief. His body's been through a lot. Good chance his days of ball are over."

97

April 9, 1993

Blue skies and a strong south wind helped dry the field, making it possible to get at least one game in this week. Coach kept the same line-up against Glendale that we were supposed to have against Central, with the exception being that Rangle was catching instead of McHandley.

Coach called a team meeting in the locker room before heading out to the field.

"It's gonna take us pulling together as a team to win today, and I'd love nothing more than to take the game ball to McHandley tonight and tell him the story of beating Glendale. Gentlemen, today's game is for McHandley. Have fun out there and play hard."

I played catch with Buckett while watching Branten warm-up with Rangle in the bullpen. Every few pitches, Rangle took off his mitt and massaged his hand. There was an intensity in Branten's every move and I started laughing, thankful that I didn't have to face him.

We ran out onto the field and took our positions while Branten tossed his warm-up pitches. Twelve pitches later, we ran off the field; Branten struck out the side.

"I've never seen him throw this hard," Rangle said. "It's like he's pissed off at the world."

Since I was hitting seventh, I grabbed a handful of sunflower seeds and sat down next to Branten on the bench.

"Well, that was easy. Think you can do it again next inning?"

"Yep."

With two outs, Buckett singled, but Lunding flew out to Drew in centerfield. No score at the end of one.

Branten almost made good on his plans in the second inning, striking out the first two hitters and getting the third to ground out on a dribbler back to the mound.

I grabbed a helmet and stood near the dugout door, ready to step in the box. Rangle singled to start the inning and took second on a hit-and-run when McKenney grounded out to third. I started walking to the plate as Coach Engel called time and motioned me toward him.

"Keep an eye on the third baseman. I have a hunch they're expecting you to bunt. If he moves toward the plate at all, swing away, let's get on the board here."

I felt the effects of the adrenaline surging through my body. I stepped into the batter's box and shot a glance down the third baseline; the third baseman was already moving in on the edge of the grass. Fastball on the inner half of the plate and I swung from my heels, pulling my hands inside and dropping the barrel of the bat, just like I had practiced for months in the batting cages. The ball screamed over the head of the third baseman and down the left field line. Coach Engel waved Rangle home as I rounded first, thinking double all the way.

And then, almost halfway to second, I felt it. My right knee popped and buckled.

I fell straight to the ground, tumbling and sliding in the dirt.

I pushed myself up and tried to stand but the pain was far too intense. I started to try and crawl back to first when I saw the second baseman running toward me with the ball and, mercifully, tagged me out.

I lay on my back as the field ump called time. Coach Bell reached me first and Engel joined him moments later. I could see Drew standing just past the coaches in my peripheral vision.

"Can you stand up?" Coach Bell asked.

"Maybe?"

Coach Bell squatted down and wrapped his arm under my right shoulder. I leaned into him and stood up on my left leg, not bearing any weight at all on my right. Drew jogged over and gave me five and a quick bro-hug. As he pulled himself close, he whispered, "I'll be praying for you."

By the time we made it back to the dugout, Dad was there with a bag of ice from the concessions stand.

"What happened?" he asked.

"Something's wrong with my knee."

I already knew the extent of the damage.

I sat on the bench with an ice pack on my knee for the remainder of the game. Branten threw an incredible six innings, striking out eleven. He did give up one run, and Steale gave up one run in relief in the seventh, but we held on to win, 3 – 2.

I used my bat as a cane and made it through the high five line where several Glendale players wished me luck and a speedy recovery.

"Maybe you'll be okay for our third game," Drew said.

"Maybe."

98

April 10, 1993

The next morning, I couldn't completely straighten my leg. I was able to walk without the assistance of a cane or anyone else, kind of an old-man-shuffle step, and spent most of the day watching TV from Dad's recliner.

After several hours of sitting still, I really had to go to the bathroom and instinctively tried to push the foot of the recliner down with my right foot. This time, I *heard* my knee make a popping sound and passed out from the excruciating pain. I woke up in a puddle of urine.

Embarrassed, I took a long bath to clean myself up as well as have some time to think. Intensely melancholic and introspective, I thought about the highs and lows of the past several months.

Perhaps the best news really was the second chance to play baseball, but I still wasn't satisfied. I still wanted back on that field. I still wanted to compete. I still wanted the chance to out think a hitter and come through with the big hit. As the hot water soothed my tensions and anxieties, my mind drifted toward my resolution.

"I'm trying to trust, God, I'm trying."

99

April 11, 1993

After one day of sitting around and feeling sorry for myself, I was grateful for the opportunity to get out of the house and go to church. It took a long time to hobble up the three flights of stairs for Sunday school. Drew told everyone the story of the incident and the game while I munched on donuts and savored my coffee.

As usual, Paula started Sunday school with prayer, but asked everyone to gather around me and lay hands on me, "Just don't touch his knee!"

After the prayer, Melissa leaned over and kissed the top of my head; I turned a million shades of red.

"Heaven has broken into earth!" Pastor Gibson belted into the microphone after the choir's offertory special of *Christ the Lord has Ris'n Today.*

"In the midst of a broken world, where death and suffering seem to haunt our waking lives, where hate and radical inequality create artificial divisions between brothers and sisters, where war and power and greed seem to rule — in a dark, borrowed tomb now empty, a new world has been born into the midst of this one.

"Death does not get the last say. The resurrection of Jesus is a new beginning, where we are now sent to be bearers of heaven's joy to the ends of the earth.

"All things are made new, a new creation, and everything — every single thing we set our hearts and minds and hands to — can be part of instituting the kingdom of God, the reign of God, here on earth.

"Heaven has broken into earth. Do you have eyes to see?"

Joshua and I visited quietly in the fellowship hall after the service.

"Well, barring any 'resurrection-miracle-all-things-being-made-new' in the middle of my knee, I'm pretty sure my season's done. And without baseball occupying my brain space, I've been thinking about 2015 all weekend, and I don't have any answers. I'm thinking about talking to Mr. Wilton to see if he has any advice. And I can't help but wonder why? Why all that time getting ready to play and then this happens?"

Joshua nodded and listened and said nothing.

Sometimes, saying nothing is the best thing a friend can do.

100

April 12, 1993

After I left, I headed over to see Dr. Hailey, my doctor since I was in second grade. I rarely get sick, a fantastic benefit of my genetic anomaly, and I had never broken any bones, so my trips to the doctor were just the annual check-ups and physicals I needed to play sports.

"I don't like what I'm feeling here. I'd like to refer you to Dr. Talley for a second opinion, to confirm what I think has happened," Dr. Hailey said.

"What do you think happened?" Dad asked.

"I'm 90% certain that's a torn ACL, but it's been a while since I've seen one. I hate to say it, but it would mean your baseball season is finished. If it is a torn ACL, then there's basically two options. One, we could get you a brace and wait until summer to do surgery. Or, we could try and push you through the system in hopes that you'd be off crutches by the time you graduate. Dr. Talley's a good friend of mine and an excellent knee surgeon. I think, given the circumstances, he'd be willing to help you out."

"So, when can I see Dr. Talley?" I asked.

"I bet we could get you in first thing tomorrow morning. Means you wouldn't have to miss too much school."

I thought about this possibility while I sat on the bench and kept score for the game against Joplin. The team looked as flat as I felt. I tried to encourage the guys to play hard and not give up, but Joplin simply out hustled us. We lost 6 – 10; our official record now stood at 5 – 8.

101

April 13, 1993

"So, Lachman test or pivot-shift test or drawer test?" I asked as I climbed onto the exam room table, remembering the names of the tests from the first time I tore my ACL.

Dad looked at me, "How do you know about those tests?"

Thankfully, Dr. Talley answered my question, "I use all three while you tell me the story of how it happened and what you felt."

While Dr. Talley pulled and pushed, I told him about the game and the hit and he seemed to listen with great interest. "My son used to play ball for Glendale, but he never made it to varsity. I hate to say it, but I agree with Dr. Hailey. We're looking at a torn ACL here."

Dad patted my back, "How soon do you think he should have surgery?"

"Good news! I have an opening in my schedule on Thursday. With some hard work, you should be able to walk without crutches at graduation."

I took a note from Dr. Talley to all of my classes, letting my teachers know about the surgery and that I'd probably miss at least a week of school. Most were sympathetic and said they weren't worried about me or the homework. Mr. Freeman assured me that the stuff I'd miss would definitely be on the final, so while he wasn't going to assign me official homework to be graded, I'd be responsible for knowing how to do the work.

"Out for a week, huh?" Coach Engel asked.

"Surgery, crutches, and therapy, oh my."

"I still expect an essay from you."

"I figured."

Thankfully, I had friends willing to support me no matter what I was going through. The Losers Club tried to make me laugh through poems of random absurdity, but the melancholy side of my personality was showing.

I was lost in thought, trapped between the unanswerable whys and the future I wondered if I'd ever see again.

102

April 15, 1993

Even though it was 5 AM, I was starving. After several months of living the teenage life, I was still amazed by my body's remarkable metabolism. Some days I ate four or five meals and never seemed to gain a pound.

"I'll get you whatever you want for lunch, after the surgery," Dad said.

I checked into the surgical ward of Cox South Hospital and was given "surgery-appropriate" clothing, which is another way of saying I was naked under a piece of paper. The nurse entered the room and asked me a few questions.

"Do you know why you're here this morning?"

"For ACL surgery."

"Do you know which knee needs to be fixed?"

"My right."

"You passed the test!"

With a red Sharpie, the nurse drew a large "X" on top of my left-knee, "Just a little nurse humor, so the doctor doesn't mess up and fix the wrong knee."

I smiled weakly.

Before long, I was rolled back to the surgery room and a mask was placed over my nose.

"Good morning Ethan," Dr. Talley greeted me. "Think you can count backwards from ten for me?"

"10...9...8..."

I heard a voice talking to me, saying my name and asking me questions, but I couldn't get my eyes to open. Thanks to the after-effects of the anesthesia, I couldn't really control my responses, either.

"So, Ethan, do you have a girlfriend?"

"Been married for eighteen years."

"Really? A young guy like you is already married? For your whole life?"

"Got kids, too. Two girls."

"And what are your daughters' names?"

"Elisabeth and Sarah."

"How old are they?"

It took a few moments for my drug-addled brain to process this question.

"Uh, thirteen and nine, I think." I heard myself answer this question and forced my eyes to open. Sitting to my right was a beautiful young nurse, maybe in her late 20s, smiling at my answers.

"Pretty strong drugs in your system, honey. Must've been giving you quite the dreams."

"I don't feel so good," I replied, then promptly leaned over the bed and threw up all over her shoes.

"Bet you feel better now. Don't you worry, honey, I've got a spare pair of shoes that I keep in my locker just in case I get a patient like you."

After another thirty minutes in the recovery room and another round of throwing up, Mom and Dad came back to get me and wheeled me out to the van in a wheelchair borrowed from the hospital. Dad already had my crutches stashed behind the middle seats and encouraged me to slide myself into the floor of the van using the strength of my arms.

"We've gotta come back tomorrow to get that drain tube removed," Dad said.

I knew he was speaking to me, but the words really didn't make any sense. By the time he started the van, I was already back asleep.

I woke up in my bed and squinted, trying to focus on the numbers on the AM / FM clock radio.

3:13.

Judging by the light in my room, it was 3:13 in the afternoon. I started to try and move and then realized that I was *completely naked.*

"Hey! Hey! Where are my clothes?" I shouted. I scrambled to pull on shorts and a shirt.

Mom must have heard me because I could hear her laughing outside my bedroom door.

"You can come in. What happened?" I asked.

"You don't remember?" she laughed again

I shook my head.

"When we got home, you kept telling us that you could do it yourself, that you didn't want any help. So, you used your crutches and as soon as you stepped in the front door, you stripped off all of your clothes and then put yourself to bed. It was hilarious.

"Your dad's been monitoring your drain tube, making sure you didn't do something stupid. To answer your question, then, your clothes are still in the front hall, right where you left them."

Glad no one caught that on their cell phone.

"Can I have something to eat?"

"I'm making you Mexican cornbread, should be almost done. How does that sound?"

"Just what the doctor ordered."

With Dad's help, I relocated to the living room, where I spread out on the hide-a-bed couch and watched movies to my heart's delight. Mom and Katy steered completely clear of the drain tube, insisting it remain covered by a towel. Dad was amazed at the amount of fluid such a skinny body could produce as the bag needed to be emptied almost hourly.

"It's like all the blood in your system is coming out your leg." Dad pushed play on *Field of Dreams* as Mom brought me my fourth helping of Mexican cornbread.

"Now this," I said with a bite of piping hot cornbread in my mouth, "this is heaven."

Later that evening, Nathan, Henry and Junior, came over to visit bearing gifts. Nathan brought a bag of chocolate-frosted mini donuts. Henry brought a bag of caramel Crunch'N'Munch. Junior carried two cases of Dr Pepper.

"Wow, guys." Over the course of the next couple of hours, we talked about school and the surgery. Nathan and Junior were fascinated by the drain tube and CPM machine; Henry wasn't all that impressed with either. The four of us finished both bags of snacks and one case of the sodas while watching sit-coms on TV.

Nathan let loose a belch that actually echoed in the hall. From her room Katy yelled, "You guys are so gross!"

"And on that note, we bid you farewell," Nathan said, taking a deep bow as I clapped.

103

April 16, 1993

"Now, this might hurt a little bit," were the exact last words I heard Dr. Talley say just before I passed out for the second time in a week.

A couple moments later I woke back up, both Dad and Dr. Talley were quietly laughing at me. "It happens to a lot of people. Good news is the worst part is all over. I gotta tell you, Ethan, that was one of the worst tears I've ever seen — ACL, MCL, meniscus, cartilage — you really ripped it up good."

"I had a feeling you'd say that."

Dr. Talley gave me a handout with information about the suggested timeline for healing. Due to the extent of the damage, he made notes informing me that my timelines would be a little slower than what was printed.

"By the end of week two, full extension of leg and at least 90 degrees when bending (with the help of the CPM). Between weeks three and six, we'll get you off your crutches and start physical therapy. By late summer, most likely, you'll be jogging again."

I read it quickly. It was confirmed — my baseball career was finished. All I could do was silently repeat: *Be here.*

104

April 19, 1993

"Want to get outta the house today, or just stay here?" Dad asked.

The weekend had been a blur of sleeping and stretching and eating and sleeping.

"Got anything in particular in mind?"

"Well, there's a new movie showing I think you might like."

I tried to think through the logistics of navigating the seats at a movie theater with crutches and a wrapped knee. "What's the movie?"

"*The Sandlot.* Heard of it?"

"Heard that movie's got a lot of heart."

"I've got to run a few errands. I'll be back shortly and we'll see if you're up for it."

I started to go back to sleep, but mere moments later, Dad bolted back in the front door with such force it startled me.

"Turn on the TV! Turn on the TV!"

"Heard something on the radio," he explained, switching the channel on the TV to the local NBC affiliate.

On the TV, thick black pillars of smoke rolled into the air as a three-story building was engulfed in flames. The commentators were silent as the live footage streamed.

"The stand-off with those religious nuts in Texas is over," Dad said. I sat mesmerized, staring at the screen, and immediately remembered the stories of Mr. Whaley.

Mr. James Whaley was a deacon at the first church I worked at, First Baptist Church of Elm Mott, Texas. He was truly one of the most compassionate, generous, and wisest people I have ever met.

He was also a Texas State Highway Patrolman and actively involved in the 51-day siege and stand-off at the Mount Carmel Center a few miles east of Waco. During my three years at seminary, he told me numerous stories of what it was like going to work in that siege, always knowing that there was a very real chance you could die.

"David Koresh was one scary guy," Mr. Whaley said. "He abused children and was very manipulative. He convinced almost everyone in that building that he really was the second coming of Jesus. Kinda odd for a guy that had to file a petition to get his name changed. These people just gave him their wives to sleep with, all the time while he was buying stockpiles of guns and ammo.

"In the end, a lot of people died that didn't have to die. There are reports and videos and interviews of who did what, fingers point every which direction. Religion, in the wrong hands, can be quite the weapon."

I remembered asking Mr. Whaley, "So, given everything you've seen, does it ever make you doubt your faith? Ever make you wonder about Jesus and church and everything?"

"Of course it does. It makes me think and doubt and ask question after question."

"Do you ever get any answers?" I wondered.

"The answer, Ethan, is children. Children know how to love and they are almost always quick to help a hurting friend. They don't let the differences they see stop them from inviting someone new to play. When I spend time with the kiddos at church, I hold tight to the words of Jesus about becoming like a child, and those parts of me that are bitter and dark are healed, just ever so slightly, broken bit by broken bit.

"Children help me get out of my head and in touch with the real me that God whispered into being. So many kids died out there at Mount Carmel, kids who never really had a chance to be a kid, it made me physically sick."

Every Sunday, in that small country church north of Waco, Mr. Whaley was surrounded by children. They called him "Papa W." and he gave them bubblegum and they all packed tightly into his pew, all stacked side by side, some even sitting on laps, like a can of human sardines.

I sat propped up against the back of the couch with my right leg strapped to a stupid machine that was doing my exercises for me. My body was broken, my dream was broken, and now my heart was breaking re-living the horrors of David Koresh and the Branch Davidians in Texas. Nothing, *nothing*, not one single thing, felt right about my life.

I wanted to tell him. I was ready to give up. I was exhausted. So, so tired of pretending, of trying to keep it all together.

And in that moment, I opened my mouth, ready to tell Dad *everything*, the whole truth, wanting to experience that soul-cleansing freedom of bringing everything out into the light.

Dad turned to me and could read my heart on my face, "Everything okay, Chief?"

But, for some reason, words wouldn't come. I couldn't say anything. With tears in my eyes, I clinched my fists and nodded slowly. And then I remembered the words of Alfred Pennyworth, Batman's closest confident and only true friend, and quietly whispered back, "Some men just want to watch the world burn."

105

April 20, 1993

For the first time since surgery, I grabbed my Kickapoo baseball hat and was going to wear it when I saw the now-familiar two-word mantra written on the underneath side of the bill: Be here.

Here I am God…where are you?

I took a deep, cleansing breath and slowly let it go, re-committing myself to living fully and intentionally in this iteration of 1993.

Since there really weren't any other movies I wanted to watch and I was beyond tired of being unproductive, I decided to start working on the essay for Coach Engel's class. I crutched into my bedroom and pulled a few books off the shelf, then crutched back to my living-room-hide-a-bed office to read and start organizing my thoughts.

Ethan Bryan

American Baseball History Essay #3

April 20, 1993

The Way of Baseball

Three Hall of Famers were asked to detail their philosophies of baseball. Babe Ruth said, "Baseball was, is, and always will be, to me, the best game in the world."

Rogers Hornsby echoed that sentiment, "People ask me what I do in winter when there's no baseball. I'll tell you what I do. I stare out the window and wait for spring." And Willie Stargell approached the heart of the question, "To me, baseball has always been a reflection of life. Like life, it adjusts. It survives everything." No other sport resembles the beautiful, quixotic, and heart-breaking journey of life here in America quite like baseball.

The primary action of baseball centers on the individual. The pitcher stands isolated on the mound with ball in hand while the hitter waits in the batter's box wielding his weapon. They both carry on internal conversations, battling the demons of failures past and bearing down to better focus on the present moment and the task at hand, doing what each can with the talents he has worked so hard to refine. Success for one is failure for the other. At every game, kids wear t-shirts and seek autographs bearing the names of these individual heroes past and present, dreaming that the talent might rub off.

America is a nation whose dream and government strives to honor and encourage the individual, as stated in our foundational documents. In the

Declaration of Independence we read, "We hold these truths to be self-evident, that all men are created equal, that they are endowed by their Creator with certain unalienable Rights, that among these are Life, Liberty, and the pursuit of Happiness." And the Bill of Rights, the first ten amendments to the Constitution, is written to protect the individual from his or her government, to safeguard the freedoms of the individual. Even the slogan of the United States Army stresses the power and importance of the individual, "Be All That You Can Be."

But no matter the extraordinary talent one individual might possess, baseball requires a team to win, to succeed, to survive. Before one can begin to think about competition, one must learn the power of cooperation, starting with a simple game of playing catch. Trust is developed through the tossing of the ball with a friend, and slowly we learn that we need one another to be good at this game. Being part of a team does not mean that everyone thinks alike or looks alike or acts alike. Being part of a team means everyone is using their gifts toward the same goal. And winning teams embody the wonder of synergy, where the effort of working together is greater than any individual could produce by himself.

For the majority of my life, I have attended University Heights Baptist Church where Pastor Gibson has repeated one phrase year in and year out, "We follow Jesus together." Life is meant to be shared for it is only in a community that dreams can be realized and the voices of fear suppressed. In a healthy community, sorrows are halved and joys are shared. I might be able to get things done faster by myself, but if I want to be part of something that lasts, I have to do it with others, with credit to the African proverb of origin.

"Baseball is a game of failure." It's the expected answer from journalists and former players and current players and coaches. Baseball is supposed to show who you are at your core when you fail time and time again.

When your team doesn't win.

When you strike out multiple times in a game and strand runners on every base.

When your pitch or error costs your team the lead.

The grind of baseball breaks down the strongest of bodies, minds, and hearts with one consistent beat: failure is inevitable.

Fans remember these failures for life, clinging to them and bringing them up in theoretical discussions ad nauseam.

The ground ball that went through Bill Buckner's legs in the 1986 World Series.

The missed call at first base in Game 6 of the 1985 World Series.

Fred Snodgrass's dropped ball in Game 8 of the 1912 World Series.

Merkle's base running mistake against the Cubs in 1908.

But I believe that baseball is more than a game of failure.

It's a beautiful game managed and played by human beings that helps us catch a glimpse of everything good about life.

I am beyond tired of the "baseball is a game of failure" narrative. People become immobilized, unable to do anything because they are afraid of failing. Schools try and motivate students through rigorous tests and essays and threaten them with failure giving students nightmares for years after they graduate, feeling like they've forgotten something, that they aren't good enough, that they won't measure up and will fail.

In baseball, if you strike out, make an error, get picked off first, lose the last game of the year, you haven't failed. You are in the arena, daring greatly, contributing your chapter as part of the greater story of the game. Failures are those who point fingers and critique and assign blame. Failures expect perfection out of human beings, something human beings were never designed to achieve. Failures forget that winning really isn't everything.

Baseball isn't a game of failure.

Baseball is a game of hope.

Hope is not an ethereal emotion, fragile and frail and changing with every passing wind. Hope is the deepest conviction of the heart that, echoing the words of J. R. R. Tolkien from The Hobbit, "There is some good in this world, and it's worth fighting for." Hope is why a baseball game is composed of nine innings and twenty-seven outs. Hope is daring to step into the batter's box one more time. Hope is having the gracious humility to applaud your opponent for a game well played and gives your teammate a hug. Hope simply refuses to give in, no matter how large the obstacle appears.

Ultimately, for me, baseball is a game all about the journey home.

As long as there have been philosophers, they have tried to capture the essence of home. In the first century AD Pliny the Elder wrote,

"Home is where the heart is." Poets ponder its power, as Maya Angelou did, "The ache for home lives in all of us, the safe place where we can go and not be questioned" and Emily Dickinson, "Where thou art, that is home." Movie lovers can't help but remember Dorothy and her now-famous heel-clicking mantra, "There's no place like home." Home is much more than the place of our permanent residence or where we sleep at the day's end. Home gives us the courage to go out into the world and face life's challenges head on knowing full well that, should we return, we will not be the same person as when we stepped out the door.

Just a few weeks ago, I dug into the batter's box, adrenaline surging in my system, bat resting on my shoulder. I hoped to touch all the bases, to return safely and touch home plate, and contribute to my team's victory. I remember swinging and feeling nothing as the ball hit the sweet spot on my favorite Easton bat. I rounded first, collapsed, and was tagged out. I never made it home. But because of my efforts, one of my teammates did. And because we are on the same team, I can share in his joy as if it were my own.

I believe with all of my being that there is a coming day when all of heaven will break into earth and all things will be made new. Heaven will be in the middle of cornfields of Iowa and heaven will be in Missouri and baseball will be played. There will be no more sorrow, no more pain, no more torn ACLs. And there will be no need to keep score because there is an art, a beauty, and a joy that transcends the numbers.

This game was meant to be played for all time.

106

April 22, 1993

I knew going back to school on crutches would be hard and that I'd have to spend hours at home after school on my stupid CPM machine, but I was so ready for a change of scenery. Besides, getting out of classes early to use the elevator is cool in its own way.

Dad decided to drive me and Katy to school in the van so he could drop me off close to the door. He offered to help carry in my backpack, but I wanted to do it on my own.

Mr. Wilton greeted the two of us, "Mr. Bryan, Ms. Bryan, good morning to you both."

"Good morning, Mr. Wilton," we replied in unison.

When Katy couldn't see me, I quietly mouthed, "I need to talk with you."

Mr. Wilton winked in acknowledgement.

I handed Coach Engel my essay and he promptly started filling me in on the latest adventures of the baseball team. Without any help whatsoever from me, the team went on a winning streak. After losing to Joplin and our record falling to three games below .500, the team beat Branson, Parkview, Central, Hillcrest, and Columbia Hickman and Francis Howell in rescheduled games.

We were now three games above .500 and scheduled to play Glendale for the third and final time tomorrow. The rubber match would be played at Meador Park, the current home field of the Southwest Missouri State Baseball Bears.

"And then district play starts next week. If we could somehow beat Glendale again, that'd put us in a really good position, give us terrific momentum," Coach said. "Are you gonna be able to make it to the game tomorrow?"

"Wouldn't miss it for the world, Coach."

As soon as the bell rang, the Losers Club started a "roast" of sorts, teasing me and mocking my injury with poetry that would've made Elizabeth Barrett Browning and Robert Frost proud. It was apparent they had been working on these poems for the last week.

Halfway through the class, there was a knock at the door; it was Mr. Wilton.

"Excuse me, but I need to see Mr. Bryan for a few minutes," he said.

I reached down, grabbed my crutches, and slowly stepped out into the hall.

We quietly walked the length of the hall toward an upstairs supply room and went inside.

"You wanted to see me?"

"It's just, I've had a lot of time to think this last week, too much time really, and, well, I didn't know if you had any ideas how I could get back my real life."

"It's the place and the time, Ethan," Mr. Wilton referenced Shoeless Joe. "Have the cosmic tumblers clicked into place? Is the universe opening?"

"W. P. Kinsella was a wise man," I replied, not knowing how to answer his questions.

"When I was a senior at Drury, I remember having a dream about my wife, and it was so real, so vivid. It was like I could almost touch her. The dream felt like an invitation, and I knew I was being given a choice, that if I wanted to go back, I could. But I couldn't do it, I couldn't chase the dream. Too much time had passed in this new reality. I was afraid of what future I'd be returning to. I think, when the time is right, when the cosmic tumblers click, you'll be given a chance to go back."

"I mean, I can't imagine that I would, but what would happen if I chose to stay here?"

"Since that night, I have never had another dream about my wife. Some dreams never leave you alone, which is exactly how I got here, how we got here. But some dreams, you only have one sacred chance to choose."

107

April 23, 1993

My uniform was so clean, too clean. Mom had worked quite hard to get all the grass and dirt stains out of it, never once saying anything to me. It took me a little while to get the socks and stirrups to cooperate with the bandages around my knee, to stay pulled tight without touching the new and numb scar from the incision. The whole family was waiting on me to get dressed so we could head to the game together. If I had been in my right mind, I would have suspected something was up.

Dad dropped me off at the front gates to Meador Field then parked the van a considerable distance away in hopes of avoiding all foul balls. I crutched to the dugout full of brown and gold and was greeted by high fives and several shouts of "Big E!" Coach Engel walked over to me.

"Hey Ethan, I was visiting with Coach Shelton from Glendale. We'd like you to throw out a first pitch for today's game."

This was the first time I'd ever heard about a first pitch for a high school game.

"I'm not sure how good it'll be."

"You could airmail it to the backstop and it'd still be perfect," Coach said.

"Can I pick who my catcher is?"

"Absolutely."

"I choose Glendale's centerfielder."

Coach laughed and reached to shake my hand, "That's an excellent idea."

I shoved a baseball into my back pocket and carefully crutched my way to the mound as a local DJ addressed the impressive crowd using the PA system.

"Throwing out today's first pitch is Kickapoo senior, Ethan Bryan. Ethan was injured the last time these two teams met, driving in the game's first run. Catching for Ethan is Glendale senior and centerfielder, Drew Gibson, who just today signed on to play collegiate ball with our very own SMSU Bears. Fire away, Ethan!"

I stood at the foot of the mound, knowing that it would be stupid to try and throw from the rubber and keep my balance. Drew crouched behind home plate in his white uniform with red pinstripes and pounded his mitt. I dropped the crutch in my right hand, propped up the other one under my left armpit and leaned hard into it, trusting that it would hold me. Pulling the ball out of my pocket, I tried to figure out how to actually throw the ball. I couldn't wind up. I couldn't stride. I couldn't even rotate without risk of falling over. I lifted the ball high and threw it like a dart. It did make it all the way to Drew in the air, but it was far from a strike, as he had to take a large step to his right to catch it.

Drew ran the ball back to me at the mound and picked up my other crutch off the ground. We posed for a couple of pictures for the Springfield News-Leader and for Dad.

"Did you really get a scholarship to play here?" I asked Drew.

"A small one. Just thankful that I get to keep playing. I was gonna tell you at church Wednesday night, but you didn't come."

"Congratulations, dude!"

I volunteered to keep the scorebook, knowing that I couldn't chase down foul balls or warm up outfielders in between innings or do anything else that pitchers normally do on their off-days. I took a moment to study the lineup and noticed minimal change over the past six games.

We were the home team and Steale was our starting pitcher. Drew was hitting third for Glendale when Coach Bell tapped me on the shoulder and pointed out multiple scouts in the stands. "They're hoping we'll throw Branten today."

Steale started off the game by striking out the lead-off hitter, but then gave up a blistering double down the right field line. Drew worked a full-count, fouling off at least six pitches, before earning a walk, which put two on base with only one out. On the first pitch, the clean-up hitter tried to check his swing and hit a slow roller to third base. Buckett was able to throw him out at first, but now two runners were in scoring position. Thankfully, Steale ended the inning with a soft ground ball back to him, getting the final out at first.

In the bottom of the first, with two outs and Mackler standing on first, Rangle hit a deep line-drive, perfectly splitting the gap in left-center field. Drew cut the ball off before it got to the fence as Coach Engel waved Mackler home. Drew's throw hit the cutoff man perfectly, who turned and relayed home. The ball and Mackler seemed to arrive at the same time, but the catcher had blocked the plate, catching the ball and tagging Mackler in a bang-bang play.

"He's out!" yelled the umpire and the Glendale side of the stands erupted. No score at the end of the first inning.

Glendale got on the board first. With two outs in the top of the fourth inning, their shortstop hit a ball that barely stayed fair inside the left-field foul pole for a home run. Steale struck out the next hitter, but shook his head as he walked toward the dugout.

"Branten," Coach Engel yelled, "go warm up. You're going in next inning. Steale, great job out there. Keep your chin up. It was a lucky hit."

After a lead-off walk to Johnson, Hardwick grounded into a double play and Lunding popped out. We were down 1 – 0 at the end of four.

The fifth and sixth innings were uneventful; three up and three down for both sides in both innings. No one reached base. As a team, we were staying hopeful, refusing to give up, determined not to lose this game by one run.

Drew led off the top of the seventh inning, and was ready, turning on Branten's fastball and cruising into second with a stand-up double. Branten promptly uncorked a wild pitch and only two pitches into the inning, Glendale had a runner on third. The third pitch wasn't really hit all that hard, but it was deep enough for Drew to score on a sacrifice fly. Branten was so pissed off at giving up a run he struck out the next two hitters, throwing the angriest fast balls I'd ever seen. Going into the bottom of the last inning, we were down two.

"Rally hats!" Wilson shouted. "This is when the magic happens!"

Glendale brought in a new pitcher to try and close out the game.

Johnson dropped a bunt and almost succeeded in reaching first, barely thrown out on a terrific barehanded play by Glendale's third basemen.

"Still got time, guys, we've still got time!" And Wilson's words proved prophetic.

On a 2 – 2 fastball, Hardwick singled to Drew, and then stole second on the first pitch to Lunding. Lunding doubled on a bloop to right field and Hardwick scored standing up. Our dugout exploded; we were only down by one run with the tying run on second. White quickly fell behind 0 – 2, and actually smiled when he stepped out of the batter's box to look down to Coach.

Coach Engel clapped his hands in encouragement, "You're ready, now, you're ready."

White blistered the next pitch, right back up the middle, almost knocking the hat off the pitcher. Drew was playing deep and the throw home was up the first base line. Lunding never hesitated rounding third and scored standing up — the game was tied.

Glendale called time and Coach Shelton went and visited with the entire infield at the mound.

McKenney swung at the first pitch he saw, a high fastball, and stroked a single to short right field; White slid into third safely. The winning run was only 90 feet away. Even I couldn't stay seated.

Every person in our dugout was on their feet, screaming, cheering, willing White home. Coach whispered to White; he was headed home on contact. Mackler didn't disappoint, and with the infield pulled in, he hit a sharp ground ball toward right field. The Glendale second baseman picked the ball cleanly on one hop and made a perfect throw home. White was out by a mile. When Buckett struck out, *everyone* in the stands was on their feet cheering. After seven innings, the game was tied, 2 – 2. For the first time all season, we'd be heading to extra innings.

Masterly was sent out to pitch the eighth and promptly got a ground out to Buckett and a pop up to Johnson for two quick outs. The Glendale catcher singled on a line drive to Mackler and had Masterly's attention, as he threw five pickoff attempts in a row. At Coach's loud insistence, Masterly paid no more attention to the runner on first and got a strike out for the final out of the inning. The game was still tied.

"Rangle, Dellen, Johnson — let's end it here!" Coach Bell shouted as he ran to the first base coach's box. Glendale also brought in a new pitcher, and Rangle greeted him with a soft single to left field. The new pitcher wasn't fazed and struck out both Dellen and Johnson before hitting Hardwick with a wild pitch.

"There is no *way* that was a strike!" Lunding yelled as he threw his helmet against the back wall of the dugout. From our perspective, everyone agreed. It was low. It was outside. It was practically unhittable.

"It doesn't matter, gentlemen," Coach Engel loudly interrupted, "Ump called it strike three. Hustle back out there."

I flipped the scorebook over. Drew was due up second. Mahoney was sent out as our new pitcher; Coach wasn't going to risk them getting comfortable at all. Mahoney is a southpaw who can't throw anything straight to save his life. His curveball is incredible and regularly buckles knees. When Mahoney pitches, those in the dugout spend most of the time praying his fastball is somewhere around the plate.

On a full count, Glendale's leadoff hitter lined out to Mackler. Drew dug into the batter's box, his back foot past where the back chalk line was hours ago. Four pitches later, Drew jogged down to first base and easily advanced to second as, on the first pitch to their clean-up hitter, Butler, Mahoney bounced a fastball in the dirt. Butler laced a 2 – 2 fastball for a single to left, but Lunding had him played perfectly. Glendale's coach waved Drew home as Lunding unleashed a perfect throw on one-hop to Rangle, who easily tagged Drew out. Mahoney again issued an unintentional four-pitch walk, putting runners on first and second. Coach Engel called time and slowly walked to the mound. He visited with Mahoney and Rangle and, three beautiful curveballs later, the game remained tied going into the bottom of the ninth.

I was thrilled that we had won, but felt incredibly awkward about *how* we had won.

White lined out to the shortstop to start the inning. McKenney followed with a single, stole second, and took third on Mackler's sacrifice fly to center. With two outs, Buckett walked, putting runners on the corners. Buckett took an enormous lead off of first and faked a move toward second, at which point the pitcher lost his balance and stumbled off the rubber.

Balk.

Both runners advanced; McKenney scored and we won.

I stayed in the dugout while the teams exchanged high fives.

Seven wins in a row.

I crutched out to the stands and visited with Mom and Dad while waiting for Drew to leave the Glendale dugout.

His baseball bag slung over his shoulder, Drew received congratulatory handshakes and high fives from several other parents and people regarding his SMSU signing.

"Kinda glad that one ended. Coach told me that I might have to pitch the tenth inning," Drew said, greeting me with a handshake and pat on the back.

"That was an intense game with one of the weirdest endings I've seen."

"Baseball happens."

108

April 28, 1993

I wrestled with the decision whether or not to make the bus ride for the first round of district play against Waynesville. Thanks to time on the CPM, I was getting more flexible, but I still wasn't supposed to put any significant weight on my leg until after my first therapy session on Friday.

"You're still on the team," Coach Engel told me, "and you are more than welcome to go with us. But I understand how hard it can be to sit on the bench and know you don't have a chance of getting in the game. I'll respect your decision either way."

I decided to go to the game rather than stay at home and feel sorry for myself. The team played lights out, run-ruling Waynesville in five innings 13 – 3, extending the winning streak to eight games.

Coach Bell bought me dinner on the way home.

"I'm just a little superstitious. Don't you even think about skipping tomorrow's game," he said.

Which was how I ended up sitting in the dugout getting my bald head rubbed every few minutes. I was pretty sure Johnson started it, though it might have been Branten. Every half inning, teammates were patting me on the head for "good luck." Baseball players are such a superstitious lot.

The result was the same, even against the Zizzers of West Plains, one of the best power-hitting teams in the district. We shut them out for six innings, allowing only two runs on a small rally in the bottom of the seventh and won 7 – 2. Our record now stood at 14 – 8.

I didn't have the heart to tell anyone I couldn't make Friday's game.

109

April 30, 1993

"Hey! Big E!"

I crutched into the therapy center and looked up; McHandley was yelling at me.

"What are you doing here?" he asked.

"Time to learn how to walk again."

"Ha! Me too!"

We talked baseball while our therapists prompted us through a multitude of tedious and repetitive exercises.

"Stick your heel out as far as you can before you reach for the ground," my therapist Nancy said at least a hundred times in the hour I was there. At the end of the hour, she handed me some copies of exercises I needed to do on my own at home, then sat me down on a bench next to McHandley. "Stay still for twenty minutes," Nancy said as she filled a compression wrap with ice and tightened it around my knee. "You also might want to take some ibuprofen when you get home. You're probably gonna be sore tomorrow."

"Team's doing really good," McHandley said.

"Yeah, sucks not being part of the ride."

"There's always next year, though, right?"

I nodded in silence.

Next year? Which next year? Would I have to go through all of college the way I'd gone through high school? Maybe I should I try out for the college team? If I was still going to be here and if I didn't have to work, I'd have time.

There was little time to think about the repercussions. After our icing, we walked out to the waiting room together, me using crutches, McHandley leaning hard on a cane, and had our parents schedule our next therapy appointments at the same time.

"It's a date," I laughed.

"You and me Big E!"

Kickapoo was the underdog, the visiting team, playing against top-ranked Lebanon in the district finals at their home field. Lebanon, Missouri is only an hour away from Springfield, and a pretty easy drive at that. With the game scheduled to start at 7 pm, if Dad and I hurried, we could probably get to the game by the end of the first inning.

But therapy had sucked so much energy out of me. I was physically exhausted and had trouble staying awake on the fifteen-minute drive home. I knew Coach and the team would understand if I didn't make it out to the ballpark.

I forced myself to stay awake until 10, to watch the news and see if there was any report of the game during the sports.

The Royals lost to the Orioles; the Cardinals lost to the Braves; the SMSU Bears lost to Creighton. But no word about Kickapoo and Lebanon.

Since I no longer needed the CPM machine, I had returned to using my bedroom. I collapsed onto the covers, the weight of the last several months pulling me deep into the bed. I fell asleep almost immediately. It was a heavy, dreamless sleep.

1 10

An incessant buzzing noise stirred me from my dreamless slumber. I opened my eyes just in time to see my cell phone dance off the wooden nightstand and fall to the floor.

"I'm back," I practically shouted.

I grabbed the phone and started to flip it open — *flip it open?*

September 19, 2015

I glanced around the room. Where in the world was I?

Nothing in the room looked remotely familiar. A velvet Elvis hung on one brick wall, baseball posters on its opposite. Movie posters and girls in bikinis decorated the ceiling. The actual living space of the room was sparsely decorated: a green recliner, a large flat-screen TV, a card table with one folding chair, and a small bookshelf. I didn't recognize one thing in the room, but when I flipped open the phone, I confirmed what I already knew. I was back in 2015.

I swung my feet off the side of the twin-size bed and grabbed my glasses. I stood up and started to walk across the room only to stumble significantly, barely catching myself against the wall. It was then that I noticed a baseball-bat cane with the word "Wonderboy" burned into it propped against the back side of the nightstand. I grabbed the cane and rushed to the window near the kitchenette area. From the skyline I could tell that I was somewhere in downtown Springfield. I clicked through the contacts on the cell phone when I noticed that I wasn't wearing a wedding ring.

What happened?

I found Joshua's name and sent him a message.

"Knock knock."

"Who's there?" he replied moments later.

"Coffee?"

"Mudhouse in 30."

I sat in the back corner of Mudhouse Coffee close to the kitchen, listening to the '80's music filling the store, smelling the freshly baked muffins and scones, and slowly sipped a mocha.

My cane Wonderboy was carefully propped in the corner behind me. Joshua walked in a few minutes after me, ordered a coffee and chocolate chip scone, and greeted me with a smile and a nod of the head.

"Morning Ethan! How are you doing?"

"Yesterday was 1993."

Joshua choked on his coffee and looked me square in the eyes.

"Welcome home."

"What home? This isn't home at all."

"How much do you remember?"

"I remember a ton from my senior year, but none of this. What happened? Why do I need a cane?"

"I knew from the moment I saw you. It was the first Sunday in May and we were talking about the district game after church. You still had your crutches."

"Against Lebanon? How'd we do?"

Joshua shook his head, "This has been the problem, Ethan. You're still obsessed. Who would care about one high school baseball game 22 years later? You lost, okay? And the only reason I know that is that every time we get together, you relive every game. Is any of that really important now?"

I stared at him, not knowing what to say.

He continued, "Anyway. After visiting with you at church…"

"Wait, Joshua. What happened to my family?" I interrupted as I showed him my ring-less finger. "What happened to Annie? The girls?"

Joshua avoided eye contact and stared at his coffee.

"Nathan started dating Annie the summer after you graduated."

I opened my mouth to say something, but nothing came out.

"He went to SMSU instead of KU to be with her. They got married right after college and moved soon after. He's a real estate developer somewhere on the west coast and she takes care of their three kids."

I thought my heart was going to explode.

"How could he do that to me? How could she?"

Several customers at Mudhouse turned and looked our direction. Wisely, Joshua said nothing.

"I'm sorry. Please, continue."

"Like I was saying, after visiting with you at church, I could tell you were different, really different. Things you were saying weren't the same as what you had been telling me all year. So, for the last twenty-two years, about once or twice a month, I've been checking up on you, hoping and waiting for this moment. Your first semester in college, we'd go grab a bite to eat or talk after church…when you bothered to show up for church, anyway. Then you switched colleges to play ball…"

"Switched colleges?"

"After knee rehab, you became obsessed with the idea of getting back on the field again. You couldn't stand the thought of ending your career on a freak play. Three Rivers Community College said they'd give you a chance to walk on, so you transferred after your first semester.

"You were un-officially practicing with the team over Christmas break when another guy who was also trying to walk on to the team slid hard into you at second base with high spikes and broke your ankle — a horrible, horrible break. Multiple surgeries were needed to fix it. You got hooked on painkillers, dropped out of college, and moved back to Springfield."

I couldn't believe what Joshua was telling me. Pushing down my sock, I noticed several scars around my left ankle.

"I'm a broken, druggie drop out?"

"Well, yes. You never got your degree."

"No seminary?"

Joshua shook his head. "You still come to church once in a while, but the drugs changed you, and…" he trailed off.

"Why didn't you do something?" Anger was building up in my chest.

"I tried, Ethan. But honestly, I didn't know what to do. You were obsessed and your whole personality changed."

"What do I do now?"

"You manage a gas station."

"I don't write?"

"You despise technology. You don't have a single social media account or even a computer."

Joshua did his best to catch me up on 22 years of my life in a short, though painful, period of time. I tried to keep my interruptions and interjections to a minimum. Mom and Dad had to sell the house, trying to get enough money to put me through rehab. I'd apparently gone three times, but nothing stuck. My sister had moved to South Carolina to get further away from me. Katy and I were no longer on speaking terms, and a few years after selling the house, Mom and Dad moved down South to be closer to her.

It seemed like they'd abandoned me, but Joshua assured me, I'd been the one to reject their help or advice years ago. The situation was less them giving up on me and more me pushing away everyone I'd ever loved or cared about.

I felt physically sick. "What about Mr. Wilton?"

"He retired at the end of that school year…."

"…and moved to the lake?"

"Not exactly. He kept writing. He's now regarded as one of the best sci-fi writers in the country. A new bestseller every year. Several of his books have been made into movies."

"No way."

"With all that money, he built a castle. Just a little way south of Springfield. One of the largest homes in America, even bigger than the White House."

"A castle?"

"He hosts readings and fundraisers there almost every weekend."

"I've got to find him."

With the help of Wonderboy, I had walked the three blocks to Mudhouse from my loft. Joshua gave me basic directions to Wilton's castle — "It's impossible to miss, trust me." — and helped me find my car, a blue 1988 Mazda 323 hatchback with 324,000 miles. The back of the car was covered in obnoxious bumper stickers and rust.

"This is my car?"

Joshua laughed, "You always say it gets good gas mileage and has great air conditioning. And most importantly, it's paid for."

"Hard to argue with that."

The keys in my pocket did, in fact, open and start the car.

"Wish me luck."

"On what?"

"Never coming back here again."

111

Following Joshua's instructions, I drove north through the downtown square and turned right onto Chestnut Expressway. As soon as I turned, my cell phone erupted into a series of chirps and buzzes. I pulled it out of my pocket, flipped it open, and tried to decipher the text shorthand.

I never saw the light turn red.

At forty-plus miles per hour, I t-boned a southbound car. Metal crunched. Tires squealed. Glass exploded. I hit my head square on my steering wheel and was knocked out.

I came to in an ambulance with a horrendous headache, a bruised chest, and a chipped tooth. My thinking felt fuzzy, at best, and I had trouble answering the paramedic's questions. I asked about the other driver.

"We think one of her legs is broken, and her car's totaled. You both got lucky. Seatbelt's helped, but you could have killed her."

My head felt fuzzy. I could barely breath, let alone think. "I need to call someone," I said, which caught the attention of a nearby police officer.

"Good luck with that," he said, handing me my cell phone in two pieces, along with a severely scratched-up Wonderboy. "Where were you going in such a hurry?"

Holding a piece of the phone in each hand, my brain was drawing a blank.

"I don't know."

I didn't have many answers for all of the officer's questions, just a nagging feeling that I was forgetting something important. After getting a sizeable ticket and a good lecture about texting and driving, I made my way to the other driver to apologize, but she was screaming in pain as the paramedics lifted her into the ambulance. As the ambulance doors closed, I collapsed to the road and vomited.

"We should take him to jail," one officer said as he passed.

Mercifully, another officer interceded, "It was an accident, Will. You know we can't hold him for that. This guy's going to have enough trouble for a long time. He should be thankful he didn't murder her or himself."

I felt a hand on my back, "Do you a ride home, sir?"

I teared up, realizing I didn't know my own address. When I started to say something, I saw he was holding my license and was already reading my address.

"Anyone going to check on you?" he asked.

"Not that I know of."

"Do you need to call your wife, family, or boss or someone?"

I shrugged my shoulders.

The officer wrote down his number on the back of his card and handed it to me. "Don't hesitate to call if you need anything, okay?"

I nodded and stepped out of the vehicle in front of my building. As the cop pulled away, I nearly collapsed against the door of my building. I was all alone. Painfully, completely, horrifyingly alone.

I spent the remainder of the afternoon trudging around downtown, sitting on benches, resting at parks, people watching with the hope of seeing a familiar face. The only comment tossed my direction was from a homeless man panhandling on the corner. I gave him my last five dollars.

I followed him at a distance and eventually stumbled into a homeless camp, finding a crowd who cast no stones.

I sat near an open fire pit, slightly overwhelmed by the pungent odors of those sitting near me, and was swallowed by my thoughts.

How did I get here? Did God do this to me? I thought He had tried to take care of me, tried to give me a second chance, a better life. I was trusting...What did I do to deserve this?

I had ruined my life, and I couldn't even remember how.

I had no answers.

I had no hope.

I felt completely numb.

As the sun set, I eventually wandered back to the place I now called home. Looking around the room, I began to weep until, exhausted, I finally fell asleep in my battered green recliner.

112

September 20, 2015

I didn't sleep well, however. My dreams were jumbled and nonsensical. I woke up, stumbled across the room, and stared out the window. And then I heard the unmistakable sound of church bells.

It must be Sunday.

I showered, shaved, and put on the nicest clothes I could find, given they were all in piles around the floor of my cramped room. I started walking toward University Heights Baptist Church, thankful it was only a couple miles away.

An hour later, I sat in the very back of the balcony as the blue-robed choir sang just before the sermon. A bearded and bald pastor I didn't recognize climbed into the pulpit and preached from Hebrews 11.

"Faith is living in between stories, where we cling to the promise of God with every ounce of strength within us," he said. "These heroes of faith, as we call them, they had no inklings about how their stories were going to end. They leaned into faith. Which story are you living?"

I didn't even recognize the story I was in.

I listened to the remainder of the sermon while my brain tried to connect the dots from the previous day. After the benediction, I stood up to leave and slowly made my way down the stairs. Knowing my cupboards at home were bare, I grabbed a handful of donut holes and a cup of coffee, jumping when I felt a tap on my shoulder.

I turned around carefully and was absolutely thrilled to see Joshua standing there.

"How was your Saturday?"

"I got in a wreck, totaled my car, and busted my cell phone," I looked down. I didn't have the heart to tell him the rest.

"So you never made it to see Wilton?"

And in that instant, everything came back at once: Annie and 1993 and baseball and my daughters and the tears just started pouring.

"Come on. I'll drive," Joshua said.

Joshua generously treated me to lunch along the way. The drive south through the edges of the Ozark Mountains only took about 20 minutes. I sat in the passenger's seat in stunned silence as Joshua did his best to answer all of my questions. When we pulled up to the front gate of Wilton's castle, I couldn't believe my eyes. It looked like something straight out of Harry Potter. Or Narnia.

"Welcome to Weathertop" the stone sign read next to a small stop sign.

Or *Lord of the Rings*.

We were stopped in front of a wrought iron gate at least twenty feet tall. I just stared at the massive concrete structure.

"Impressive, isn't it?" Joshua asked.

"Incredible."

The ground opened up and a speaker rose to the height of Joshua's window. I was counting windows as was at 21 with more than half the castle remaining to count when a voice boomed through the speaker.

"May I help you?"

"We'd like to see Mr. Wilton, please."

"And you are?"

"Ethan from Kickapoo High School and Joshua Leaders," I shouted loudly.

A beat later and the gate swung open, ever so slowly, without a sound. As Joshua pulled forward, I saw Mr. Wilton running out the double front doors, silver beard and ponytail flying behind him. He directed us to a parking spot and beamed like a 6-year old on Christmas morning.

"Mr. Bryan! Mr. Leaders!" he yelled so loud it echoed in the hills behind us.

No sooner had I stepped out and grabbed Wonderboy than he greeted me with a full body hug.

"I know the secret!" he whispered into my ear.

I pushed him away and stepped back.

"Come, come! Follow me!"

"I can't," Joshua protested. "I have to get back to my family, we're headed to Silver Dollar City for the day. I think Ethan can handle it from here."

I started to say something when Joshua shook my hand, "I'll keep my eye on you, I promise. Good luck."

As soon as Joshua left, Mr. Wilton practically danced through his enormous residence, pointing out paintings by famous artists hanging on almost every wall, telling me the name and theme of each room.

The Red Room.

The Great Hall.

Picasso's Paradise.

The Marvel Universe.

I had to skip and power walk just to keep up with him.

"I tell people that I built this place to survive most any disaster — earthquakes, fires, bullets, bombs, bugs, even tornados. But I really built it because this is the perfect location for time travel."

"In the middle of nowhere?"

"There's magic in the air…"

"What are you talkin' about?"

"Springfield is the number one location of weather variety in the United States. Eighty degrees one day, stormy and thirty the next. Happens all the time. No one knows why. It's because Springfield, and most of southwest Missouri for that matter, is sitting on top of a…of a thin place… a wormhole of sorts."

"A wormhole?"

"Do you know your Einstein?"

"Somewhat…"

"Long story short, Einstein theorized a bridge of sorts between two places. Springfield is the place and harnessing the power of dreams makes it possible to transverse that bridge."

"Come again?"

"Our dreams contain the essence of who we are and travel fast enough to get from point A to point B without compromising who we are."

"And how does that happen exactly?"

"With this."

"This" looked like nothing more than a New York Yankees baseball hat.

"The Yankees?"

"Always thought those pinstripes were classy."

"Why does it have to be the Yankees? I hate the Yankees."

"When I was a kid, I wanted to be Yogi Berra."

"Really? I met him once…" I raised the hat up to put it on.

"Stop! Don't!"

I froze.

"Let's talk."

Mr. Wilton motioned for me to sit down in his lavishly decorated and appropriately named Dream Room — plush black carpet, a massive chandelier with electric candles, huge black leather recliners, a replica statue of The Thinker, and a wall-to-wall screen.

"It's great for watching ball games and movies."

"I bet."

Mr. Wilton didn't hesitate in asking about the discrepancies in my experiences, about the dreams that took me back and forward in time.

"And you honestly don't remember how you got back to 2015?"

I shook my head.

"That's completely fascinating and probably the problem. My bet is you are experiencing what your future would look like if you let fear govern all of your choices."

His words resonated deep in my soul.

"Can you send me back to 1993?"

"Without a doubt."

"Can you tell me how to get back to my 2015?"

"That's a solid maybe. Now. What's your strongest memory from 1993?"

"The first game I pitched. Same day as Sarah's birthday."

"I remember that day, too! You asked for birthday gift advice."

"That's the day."

"When you put on that hat, that game is all I want you to think about."

"But how do I get back to my 2015?"

"Find me after the game."

"Wait. If I go back, what happens to all of this?"

"Mr. Bryan, you can't begin to imagine how many lives I've lived. Don't you concern yourself with me and 'all of this.' Now, are you hungry?"

"Hungry?" The question caught me off guard.

"It's always best to jump on a full stomach. Prevents time sickness."

"Oh, I see," I said. "Not really."

"Then close your eyes and trust me."

I took a deep breath, closed my eyes, and felt Mr. Wilton place the hat on my head.

113

March 23, 1993

When I opened my eyes, what felt like only a few moments later, I was standing on the mound at Kickapoo High School, ball in hand, with my back to the plate. I slowly rubbed down the baseball and tried to catch my breath.

I took off my hat and sweat immediately streamed down my bald head, pooling on the inside of my glasses. As I wiped off my head and then my glasses with my sleeves, I stared at the mantra Sharpied on the underside of the bill:

Be here.

Incredible. I turned around and kicked twice at the dirt in front of the rubber. Dad's voice carried above the other parents seated on the rusty bleachers at Kickapoo High School, "Show 'em what you've got, Chief!"

I looked at the stands and saw friends and family. Sitting off by himself was Mr. Wilton wearing a Yankees hat. I'm pretty sure I saw him wink at me.

Teammates on the bench cheered and Coach Engel chewed his bubble gum and blew massive bubbles.

Settling into position, I looked up and wasn't surprised at all to see Kevin digging into the batter's box. McHandley called for a fastball inside and I shook him off.

Pop. Pop.

This time, McHandley signaled a slider and I threw a perfect one. Kevin swung and hit a dribbler back to me. I fielded it cleanly and easily threw him out at first.

Shawne stepped up to the plate and I struck him out looking on three pitches: slider, fastball, change up. The next hitter, Derrick, fouled out to McHandley on a weak pop-up. I walked toward the dugout, jumped over the third baseline, and sat at the very end of the bench. McHandley thumped me on the shoulder as he passed by, "Just you and me, Big E. All day long."

"Hey!" Coach Engel shouted at me as he blew a large bubble and walked out of the dugout, "Remember rule number one? No thinking!"

"Understood, Coach."

I pitched an absolute gem, scattering a couple of hits over five innings and held Parkview scoreless. My team knocked the cover off the ball and scored 14 runs. The game was called by run rule after the fifth.

Once again, Coach Engel gave me the game ball.

After gathering my stuff, I walked out of the dugout and Mr. Wilton was making a beeline in my direction.

"Excellent game, Mr. Bryan! Might I visit with you for a moment?"

I followed Mr. Wilton a safe distance away from the crowd and he handed me a small brown paper sack.

"In this sack is the Yankees hat. Wear it the night of the game against Lebanon and think as hard as you can about your former future life. In the meantime, don't change anything else. And be sure to look me up when you get back."

When I got home, I hid the sack under my bed and showered. I looked at a calendar and the baseball schedule and, again, tried to write down everything I remembered from what was the previous month of my life.

McHandley's stroke. A torn ACL and surgery. Rainouts and losses.

I took out the game ball and wrote on it:

To Sarah —

Happy birthday!

KHS 14

PHS 0

5 IP, 0 runs, 2 hits, 5 Ks, 0 BB

3 – 23 – 1993

114

March 24, 1993

Nathan honked and I ran out the front door. As soon as I saw him, I felt enraged. I couldn't believe he dared to date and marry Annie. I climbed in the front seat and punched him quite hard in the shoulder.

"Hey! What was that for!?"

"Just...don't get any wise ideas about dating Annie."

"Are you on drugs?"

"Well, I might be."

Overall, I was proud of myself for living quietly for five weeks, trying my best to do what I remembered doing. I didn't tell Nathan or Joshua anything about my future excursion. Mr. Wilton seemed to know, but I couldn't tell for sure.

Watching McHandley collapse again was heartbreaking.

Tearing my ACL was horrendous.

And watching David Koresh destroy lives was horrific.

After therapy with McHandley and heading home to watch TV, I got ready for bed. I gave Mom a hug and kiss goodnight and gave Dad a high five and pat on the back. I closed the door to my bedroom, sat on my bed, and whispered the simplest and truest prayer I could.

"Lead me home, please."

Pulling the brown paper sack out from underneath my bed, I found a note stuffed in the hat from Mr. Wilton.

"Tip of the hat to you, Mr. Bryan."

I clutched the Yankees hat, took a deep breath, closed my eyes, and put it on.

115

"Mom, Dad, wake up! I'm gonna be late! Practice is in half an hour!"

I woke up in a fog and immediately noticed how stiff and sore my body was.

Therapist was right. Gotta grab some ibuprofen.

The muscles in my lower back were knotted. My shoulders were tense. My knee had a throbbing, dull ache. The fingers on my right hand were tingling, still trying to get adequate circulation.

I rolled over and opened my eyes and the first thing I saw was my cell phone. My beautiful-piece-of-crap-dropped-a-million-times cell phone.

Pressing the lock key, I squinted to read the screen:

September 19, 2015.

It worked!

I grabbed my glasses off the nightstand, unintentionally knocking a stack of theology books to the floor. I looked for Wonderboy, but couldn't find it. Adrenaline flooded my system as there was another pounding at the bedroom door.

"Mom, Dad! Wake up!"

Jumping out of bed, I threw on a pair of jeans, and opened the door. Elisabeth was knocking and yelling and greeted me with a perfect teenage frustrated glare, "I can't be late for this practice, the concert is tonight."

I wrapped her up in a tight hug, "Don't worry, kiddo. Everything's gonna be fine. Go eat some breakfast and I'll get ready to take you."

She rolled her eyes and huffed at me.

"Are you going to your parents' house after you drop her off?"

As I closed the bedroom door, I turned around and saw Annie still trying to sleep.

I cleared my throat, "Good morning, beautiful."

She smiled, "You said you were going to mow their lawn since they're on their annual hiking vacation."

Dad's hiking?

"Yeah, that's right. I'll go mow after I drop off Elisabeth."

"Sarah and I will be gone when you get back; we'll meet you tonight at the concert. I think Katy and the kids might come too. She and Joseph have been busy lately, but she texted me she'd love some quality family time this weekend."

I leaned over and gave her a kiss on the forehead.

"See you at the concert."

While I brushed my teeth, I tried so hard to remember, to see if, somehow, my mind would connect the dots across the years.

I looked down and saw the faded scar on my knee and gently massaged it.

I nervously looked at my ankle; it was scar-free.

Walking into the hall, I was greeted by a black lab, ferociously wagging its tail while carrying a blue and orange rubber ball in its mouth.

It's not Dodger.

"Hey girl, how are you doing?" I squatted and petted the dog, but was temporarily lost on the name.

"Dad? Ready?" Elisabeth called again.

I looked up and spotted a Royals backpack with a laptop cord lying across it.

"Just let me grab my laptop really fast."

Ask Elisabeth the right question and she can talk for an hour without taking a break. As I started the van, a vehicle I did not recognize, I asked, "Where to?"

"Dad!" she said, rolling her eyes. "Tonight's the symphony concert. You know that."

"Just testing you. Nervous?"

"Yes! Tonight we're playing…"

As Elisabeth talked, I listened half-heartedly. I wanted to hear what she was saying, but also had to find out about life after my leap.

I pulled into the parking lot at the Juanita K. Hammons Center for Performing Arts on the campus of Missouri State University, "What time do I need to be here?"

"They are feeding us lunch and dinner. The concert starts at 7, but if you want a good seat, I'd be here by 6."

"See you then. Have fun! Love you, kiddo!"

Elisabeth grabbed her cello and concert dress out of the back seat, "Love you too!"

I drove around downtown Springfield until I found a secluded parking spot, and, completely overwhelmed by raw emotion, laughed, and shed happy tears.

I reached for my back pocket; there was already a folded-up piece of paper in it. I unfolded it and quickly skimmed it, but was disappointed to discover it was just a crossed off grocery list. Grabbing a pen out of my backpack, I started writing a new list of key word questions.

Joshua?

Mr. Wilton?

Nathan?

I decided to head to my parents' house to mow when I remembered the buried game ball.

I pushed the speed limit driving south on Campbell Avenue, until I spotted the large Krispy Kreme logo.

Without hesitation, I stopped for coffee and couple of donuts.

I sat in Dad's recliner, sweat dripping down my bald head, laptop humming nearby, carefully re-reading the inscription on the ball. I was impressed with how well it had survived the last twenty-two years.

After successfully resetting my password, I logged on to Facebook and messaged Nathan. Hoping he was also online, I started typing.

"Knock, knock?"

Five minutes passed before he responded.

"What's up, Slick?"

"How much do you remember about our senior year?"

He posted a thumbs-up icon.

"Yesterday was 1993."

"Can you talk?"

The phone rang almost immediately, "I knew something was different when I picked you and Katy up on that Monday. It was like the teenage you had just been watching everything happen. I waited until after Katy had gone inside and asked you a question about the future. You just shrugged your shoulders and looked at me like I was crazy. We never talked about it again. We've stayed in pretty touch pretty well, though, for two guys who haven't see each other in person in about fifteen years. How are you doing?"

"I think things are pretty good, no thanks to you!"

"What are you talking about?"

"Long story. I don't know if you'd believe me."

We talked for almost an hour and Nathan filled me in on west coast living. I was grateful our friendship had survived all of the adventures. Even though I was home, where I wanted to be, I was still worried about being sent back again. I couldn't afford to lose my family a second time. I got into the van, my van, hoping a drive would clear my head, when I passed Kickapoo.

Once again, I was impressed: Kickapoo in 2015 was so different than Kickapoo in 1993. Even on a Saturday, the parking lot was packed. There was a soccer game, a softball game, and judging by the signs posted, some kind of debate tournament inside.

Trusting my gut, I carefully tucked the game ball in my pocket and walked inside. And there, where the outdoor courtyard used to be, just behind the double-door main entrance in the brand new atrium, sat Joshua at the registration table.

"Morning Ethan! How are you doing?" he stood to shake my hand.

There were far too many people around to say anything.

"When you've got time for a break, I'd love to visit with you. Catch up on the last year, ya know? Feels like more than twenty years since we last talked."

He caught my not-so-subtle hint.

"Hey Chrissy," Joshua called out, "can you come help at registration for a few minutes, please?"

When we were a sufficient distance from anyone else, I quietly whispered, "Yesterday was 1993."

Joshua turned and looked me square in the eyes. "I gathered. How much do you remember?" he asked.

"I remember a ton from my senior year. I don't remember much of anything other than my previous life."

"Follow me."

Joshua walked me upstairs to his classroom, welcomed me inside, then closed and locked the door behind us.

"I knew from the first moment I saw you," he said as he walked to a closet in the corner. "It was the first Sunday in May and we were talking about the district game after church. You still had your crutches."

"We lost, right? Against Lebanon?"

"I think so. To be honest, it's been a long time. The old noodle, you know?" He knocked on his head, grinning. "Anyway, after visiting with you at church, I started thinking. While you were in college, about once or twice a month, I made sure to check up on you."

Standing in front of me, Joshua handed me a stack of a dozen or so journals. "These are for you. Each one covers about two years' worth of our conversations. Hope you don't mind, but some of our conversations really clicked with me, and I wrote some poetry in there, too."

"This is incredible. Do you know anything about Mr. Wilton?" I asked while thumbing through the first journal.

"He passed away in 2001. He retired at the end of your senior year…"

"…and…?"

"Got married by the end of that summer and wrote another book. I've got a copy of it over here."

Joshua scanned one of the numerous bookshelves in his classroom.

"Here you go, you'll get a kick out of it. It didn't smash any sales' records or land him on the best-seller's list or anything, but it's really pretty funny."

I looked at the title and grinned — *Confessions of a Time Traveler.*

"Do you know if I visited him? Did I stay in touch with him?"

"You'll have to read the journals and the book, but you might want to check out the dedication."

To Ethan –

High fives, my friend.

I reached my hand into my pocket and found the baseball. "I've got something for you too," I said as I flipped him the ball.

He laughed, "Welcome home, old friend."

116

October 3, 2015

Every day, while Annie and the girls were at school, I voraciously read through the journals. Joshua was right; a lot of my life really was the same. There was one question, however, that still haunted me.

What real difference did playing baseball make?

I found a satisfactory answer in a journal entry dated October 20, 1996. In Joshua's own handwriting:

Tonight, I invited you and Annie to join me and Madison for dinner and to watch the first game of the World Series together. Neither one of us were excited that it was Yankees verses the Braves, but at least it was baseball.

It was the first time the four of us had been together since the Sunday school party at the beginning of the school year. You two are busy planning wedding things and Madison and I are trying to figure out life as newlyweds and junior high school teachers.

Just before the game started, I asked you, "Are you glad you played baseball instead of golf your senior year in high school?"

I had been waiting to ask you this question for a couple of years, and this finally felt like the right time. As soon as I asked it, however, the National Anthem started and you seemed to ignore the question, so I didn't press the issue. In the third inning, you finally responded.

"Yeah, I'm glad I played baseball. I knew in my mind that I didn't have the skills necessary to play professionally, even at the college level, and I was okay with that.

"My biggest talent was I played with heart, Coach Engel told me that all the time. I think that, whenever you do something simply because you love it, even if it's just a game like baseball, and especially if you have to work hard for it, love is extended out into the world.

Baseball has always been my first and truest love. Sometimes love means having the guts to chase your dreams and trust God with the results. And sometimes, love so deep, love so true, leaves scars so you'll remember it forever. And I am so proud to have that scar."

117

March 4, 2016

Although it felt like a dream, it wasn't. The Royals really did win the 2015 World Series. Joshua and I kept each other company through the nerve-wracking extra innings of Game 5.

Before the Series started, I made a bet with Dad that, if the Royals did win, I'd get a tattoo. It took me quite a while to decide on a tattoo parlor and what exactly I wanted a tattoo of. I thought about those few days in the other 2015, and that incredibly brief weekend with my son.

And I realized that since my return, I had not once had the old recurring dream of playing ball, for which I was deeply grateful.

Life finally slowed down and I was no longer worried about trying to get "back to the future. I started writing again. A quirky narrative came quickly — a magical, mystical account of Henry, a boy who lived in a musical theater.

I sent an early draft to the Losers Club who helped me better shape the story. Henry, in particular, loved the tale, convinced that I wrote it in honor of his legendary musical career after high school.

But Henry wasn't the only one who loved it. I just opened a contract from a publisher who agreed to publish *The House of Music* in 2017.

I haven't told anyone that it's really a tribute to Hogan.

When I signed the book contract, I decided to honor my agreement with Josh about the tattoo. I had pondered it for months, not wanting to make the wrong decision. Finally, realizing what I needed, I went alone to our local parlor Body Creations and braced myself.

In a simple hand-written font on the inside of my left forearm, the artist penned the words.

Be Here

THANKS FOR READING!

If you think other readers would enjoy Ethan's journey through time and baseball, we would be honored it if you would visit Amazon or Goodreads to leave a review!

ABOUT THE AUTHOR

Ethan D. Bryan is the author of Dreamfield. His other books include *Superheroes are for Real*, *Run Home and Take a Bow*, *Catch and Release*, *The Cowboy Year*, *Striking Out ALS: A Hero's Tale*, and *Tales of the Taylor*.

Ethan is convinced baseball helps tell some of the best stories. His baseball stories have landed him ever so briefly in an ESPN 30-for-30 (#BringBackSungWoo), as a background ballplayer in an Emmy-award winning documentary (First Boys of Spring), an invitation to the White House for the Royals World Series celebration, and a chance to go to Cooperstown and read his baseball poetry.

Ethan lives in Springfield with his wife and two daughters. He still dreams of playing baseball for his beloved KC Royals.

Connect with him on Twitter @Ethan_Bryan

If you want to read about Ethan's latest baseball adventures, check out his writings at www.americaattheseams.com

Music Theory by Brian McCann

Basie Wenger, a twenty-four-year-old trained percussionist from Philadelphia, impulsively takes on a sudden posting as choir director for a church in Kansas City. Trying to adjust to small town life is difficult enough. But as she begins her new job, Basie has make peace with angry church board members, single-handedly save a children's dance recital, manage a growing list of potential boyfriends, and complete three bizarre and humiliating challenges commanded in the will of a recently deceased church member. Oh, and lead the choir... all while keeping the secret that she can't actually sing.

The Christmas Letter by Steven Berman

Mary is a naïve twenty-year-old in 1945 when her high school sweetheart, Jack, returns to their small Indiana steel town wounded from World War II and makes her his bride. While Jack struggles to find his place in the world, Mary begins her own journey of self-discovery.

As the years and letters unfold, Mary and Jack have five children, including their first-born son, Junior who is not "right," an issue that contributes to the turmoil in their marriage and impacts their lives in unforeseen ways.

Mary's Christmas letters track her children from toddling to adulthood, while also commenting on her marriage, her friendships, and the world around her-- advances in technology, the dawn of the nuclear age, the Cuban Missile Crisis, The Cold War, Vietnam, Woodstock, and more. Through disappointments, triumphs, dark moments of doubt and suspicion, loss of loved ones, and the lessons learned from hard experience, Mary's Christmas letters are a constant in an uncertain world. A part of the ritual of Christmas, these letters are a touchstone from which Mary takes strength and comfort.

Hidden Thorns

Recently divorced after thirty years of marriage, Lil is on her own for the first time. The last thing she anticipates is an exciting new relationship... or a stalker. After Lil gets a series of disturbing hang-up calls, roses and cryptic notes start showing up in her home.

Lil never expected to have feelings for someone so soon after her divorce, particularly someone with such a sordid reputation. But the mutual attraction between Lil and Michael is obvious, a complication that will transform both of their lives. Unfortunately, their growing relationship emboldens Lil's stalker. His threats increase, testing Lil's faith and friendships, while endangering both her second chance at love and her life.

Baggage Claim by Aaron Davis

Aaron Davis hid the fact that he struggled with a rare genetic disorder and severe depression for most of his life. For 15 years, he served in churches as a pastor and missionary. Eventually, depression got the better of him and Aaron was admitted into a psychiatric hospital for 4 days of observation. This gripping memoir details the factors that led to his depression and pastoral burnout and the plans and choices he made to finally become whole.

Made in the USA
Lexington, KY
19 June 2017